DARK MINDS

For aspiring writers all over the world

All profits from the sale of this book will be passed to the Sophie Barringer Trust (charity number **1111154)** and Help the Hospices Trading. Help the Hospices Trading is a subsidiary of Hospice UK, (charity number 2751549) and passes all its profits on to Hospice UK.

Copyright

Published by Bloodhound Books

ISBN 978-0-9956212-7-5

Printed and bound in Great Britain by Clays Ltd, St Ives plc.
www.bloodhoundbooks.com

Table of Contents

Foreword by Fred Freeman

Co-Founder of Bloodhound Books

"Fiction is the lie through which we tell the truth."
— **Albert Camus**

It's not surprising that in uncertain times readers turn more then ever to crime fiction. A form of escapism is the oft pedalled reasoning for the renaissance and continued rise of the genre. Of course this may be partly true, but the inquiry ought to dig a little a deeper.

The masters of the art so often use their stories to tackle wider issues from gender and race inequality, to the corruption of authority and the challenges and unknowns of treating mental illness. These real world problems are presented to us in a thrilling and entertaining way. Our deepest fears may be thrust into the spotlight and this can linger with us for days; it's a quirk of human nature that this experience ultimately proves to be life-affirming and helps us to recalibrate what is most important in our own lives.

Bringing together some of the most talented authors in the business, *Dark Minds* is a celebration of crime fiction. A collection of short stories that are thrilling, spine-tingling and thought-provoking, it brilliantly showcases the diversity of the genre, from the domestic chills of Anita Waller's *I've Gone*, the dystopian horror of Emma Pullar's *London Calling* and the captivating mystery of L.J. Ross', *The Shepherd's Bothy*.

As a publisher of crime fiction I am privileged to work closely with so many talented authors on a daily basis. However, introducing *this* book to you is an even greater privilege. The authors showcased are from all over the UK and beyond. They include authors at different stages in their journeys, from those published by the giants of the industry to some phenomenally successful self-published authors. What is truly extraordinary is that every one of these authors has poured their heart and soul into their stories for no gain of their own. Every penny, cent and dollar from the proceeds of this book will be donated to Hospice UK and Sophie's Appeal, two remarkable charities that are fitting beneficiaries of this very special book.

Bloodhound Books is hugely grateful to each and every person who has donated their time to this book.

I hope you enjoy reading it every bit as much I did.

TEN GREEN BOTTLES

B A Morton

They came with the spring and were gone by autumn's end. Malevolent crows, black as the devil himself. By the end of that first day I sensed my life would never be the same again. I wasn't wrong. By the time the last leaf had fallen, those inane things I'd held so dear had ceased to matter. Death does that. So they tell me. I don't agree. Life does that. Death is God's reward for the good. The bad have to live with their guilt forever.

***

There's blood on my shoulder, sticky and brown. On my arm, in the creases of my palm and between my fingers, I splay them wide and stare.

There's blood all over me and I don't dare think about why.

Around me, doctors, nurses, white coats and green scrubs are frozen mid-buzz like angry bees and they're shouting and yelling urgently, at each other – at me. I don't hear a thing, except a count in my head. Ten – nine – eight… I close my eyes when I get to one. I can't go there again. On zero everything switches back on and it's loud – so loud. Machines beep, alarms whine and off stage somewhere in the distance, the rhythmic scream of sirens punctuates the chaotic soundtrack.

Deep in my stomach I feel the beat of a million frantic butterfly wings.

Oh God.

I open my eyes. I'm still covered in blood.

I don't think it's mine.

'You're safe now, miss,' someone declares, all matter of fact.

That's okay then – isn't it?

I turn toward the voice but they're already gone, in a blur of blood-splattered disposable apron, on to the next victim, survivor – whatever. The room is filled with bits and pieces – bits of people, pieces of meat. I struggle to breathe. The air is heavy with the weight of all those souls caught against the ceiling looking down. I'm beyond shock. I count my fingers, wriggle my toes, why me? Why not me? And then I see him slouched against the doorframe, watching.

He's not a doctor.

He's a great hoodie crow come to peck out my eyes.

Detective Sergeant Neil Fuller. Right now I hate him with a passion, not least because his sudden appearance has ripped a gaping hole in my trauma blanket, but because now I realise that he was right and I was wrong. Again.

'You took your time,' I mutter accusingly, as I slide from the trolley, bare feet slapping on the tile floor, legs unsteady, hands flailing for balance. I'm the only carcass left standing. The only chicken left in the coop, and my neck is about to be wrung.

'Sorry. Thought you must be dead. Turns out you're not.'

Ha fucking ha. 'Wishful thinking?'

'That's harsh, Zoe. City's in lockdown. Fucker blew up a knocking-shop with bottles of piss. I mean, who could have predicted that?'

Who indeed.

'Come on, speak to me. What in God's name happened? Comms goes down and all hell breaks loose. The Super's going ballistic. Willard's taking a beating on our behalf and I've been wasting precious time checking body bags looking for you.'

I reach a sticky hand inside my top and begin to extract the remnant of wire that's caught beneath my left breast. I get a sudden, blinding flashback – sweaty fat fingers poking and grabbing, insane snotty laughter up close in my ear. A bloke who giggles like that, well, I should have known.

'He clocked the wire. You warned me he might. I didn't listen. I'm a fool, but Bale's not. A nutter yes, but not a fool.'

Fuller's eyes track my progress as the wire is extruded inch by inch from my cleavage. I feel his frustration as he tries to balance his own actions with the disastrous outcome, but I have no sympathy for him, not yet. I'm raw inside, still in denial. Still hoping I'll wake up. I coil the offending article into the palm of his hand and force his fingers to close around it until the sharp ends bite.

'You were meant to call in,' he scolds as he bags the wire. 'A double-check, a safety net, that's what we agreed. You and me, Zoe, we're a team, aren't we?'

I shrug. It doesn't matter now. People are dead. Our team lost.

'You didn't call, Zoe. You didn't fucking call.'

He feels bad. I feel worse.

'How many?' I ask.

He looks away.

'How many, Neil?'

'Six so far.'

'So far..?'

'There's a girl in ICU.'

'Which girl?'

'Roxy. I think it's Roxy.'

'You think?'

I turn on the spot and skim the emergency room in a macabre slow-motion game of snap, where I try to match body parts and hope to locate a piece out of place among the loved and lost. He's not in the room. I'd know if he was. I feel anger that he escaped and relief that his blood has not anointed me.

'And Bale?'

'Still at large.'

***

I strip down to my underwear in the car and scrub myself with best-buy baby wipes until my skin tingles. I don't wonder why Fuller keeps wet-wipes in his glove-box. I do wonder about the pistol taped under the seat, but I'm not paid to wonder about Fuller. He has history. Who doesn't? I'm just grateful that he keeps his eyes on the road as I try to comb rat's tails and blood from my hair. I'm supposed to look enticing to a certain clientele, a pot full of lip-smacking honey. Now I just look knackered, every one of my twenty-seven years hanging like a lead weight across my shoulders. I'm relieved to be rid of the tart-in-a-box outfit I wear to work these days, just wish circumstances didn't mean it was now bagged for evidence. I scrub a palm across my face, feel the crust of day old mascara and wish for a rewind button, some magical shit that would allow me to replay my life from then until now, without the crap in the middle.

***

It was too early to take him. Far too early. I knew it. I bloody knew it. The evidence wasn't watertight. Sure, Bale knew the first girl, might have crossed paths with the second, and of course there were the bottles, but who doesn't have empties under the sink. Bottom line, the CPS weren't happy. Another few hours crunching data and the team would have found that elusive thread linking the monster to all three victims, Alice Bond, Rita Spinetti and Mary Shea. Three lost souls who lived on the edge of humanity and died in that Godless time between dark and dawn when evil stalks.

Bale is evil. Bale is the devil in human form. Bale arrived with the crows.

***

And then Roxy called and common sense deserted me. *Come to a party, hun,* she said. I knew it was him, behind her words.

Felt it inside, all twisted up like barbed wire, like someone jumped on my grave and yanked my corpse right up out of the ground.

So I pressed the green for *Go* button.

And here we are.

Fucked.

Sometimes you go with your gut, make a snap decision and the world applauds you. Tonight isn't one of those times.

***

We're headed back to The Palace now, a rundown dive that sits like a festering boil amid row upon row of derelict East End terraces. The North East's go-to night spot if you're a man of a certain age with certain predilections. Fuller's ignoring protocol as usual, jumping red-lights and burning rubber in the hope that our number one suspect, Leslie Vincent Bale, might have returned to the scene to gloat. Six dead women in one fell swoop is an undisputable coup for any serial killer worth his salt. He'll need to bask in his infamy somewhere and he can't go home. Not now. I've made sure of that.

I wriggle into my trackies and toss my gym bag onto the back seat. My vest top barely covers the bits that matter but that doesn't account for the shivers that are currently rippling up and down my spine. Turns out, six weeks playing a fifty quid prozzy delivered unexpected consequences. I made new friends, despite Fuller's advice not to get too close. Friends who thought I was one of them, women whose pitiful no-hope lives made mine seem almost bearable. Girls who now rest in a jumbled heap on a mortuary slab because I thought I'd caught a break, thought I knew better than the whole of serious crimes unit put together – and DS Neil Fuller believed me. Like I said, God takes the good ones and leaves the rest of us to fight among ourselves.

The team are waiting when we arrive. Fire crews are damping down, stringing safety cordons around the teetering shell. Arc lights flood the area in post mortem clarity. Blue lights flash in my periphery. I shield my eyes from the glare, from the reality of my mistake.

'Hey, kidda, put this on,' Fuller sighs, as he throws a hoodie at me. 'You look like shit. If you play the loser card, people will believe it. We didn't lose. Not yet.'

I force a smile and take the hoodie.

It's been in his boot along with his stab vest and crime-scene kit. It smells of car freshener, disinfectant and corpses. It's too big. The sleeves are too long. I hug it around me and wish I could disappear forever beneath the giant iron-on *Police* lettering.

'DS Fuller. DC Harte – Zoe – luv, should you be here?'

My boss, DCI Charlie Willard, the size of a mountain and the wrong side of fifty, risks his life with a forty-a-day habit. Tonight he looks like he's one step closer to the grave, and I helped put him there.

'Yes, sir, I'm fine.' I jut out my chin and dare him to contradict me.

Instead he hooks a meaty paw around my shoulder, draws me to one side and cheese-grates my ear accusingly.

'So tell me, detective, was there a good reason why you didn't wait for back-up?'

He's staring at the blackened building, at the melee of emergency personnel, at the huddle of stunned gawkers and coffin-chasing paparazzi held fast behind crime scene tape. I'm staring too, but I know we're not seeing the same thing. In my head I prowl The Palace, the dingy flock papered corridors, the bar with sticky carpet, the private rooms that stink of sweat and sex. The crows are storming overhead, I hear them cackle and caw, but I'm too hyped to understand what they're telling me.

'There wasn't time, sir. I got a call, made a bad decision...'

'Aye, you're not wrong there, lass.' He squeezes my shoulder, hard, practically severing a nerve. 'But don't beat yourself up too much,' he adds. 'Neil told me what happened.'

He did? I seek him out, catch the shrug. Nod my thanks, such as they are.

Willard spots him too, showers him with an acid bath of *see you later* promise, and I flinch on Fuller's behalf. This isn't going away. We have to catch Bale or I'll be wet-wiping blood off my hands forever.

'If I had a quid for every time I jumped the gun as an eager DC I'd be a rich man,' laments Willard, sticking a cigarette between his lips and lighting up. I watch the tip flare. 'It's hard, getting it wrong when you think you're right, but it's how we learn.' He exhales a lung full of smoke in my face. 'So what have you learned tonight, DC Harte?'

'That I'm crap at this game, sir.'

'No rules to this one, luv. Never is with his kind. That ruddy shite is out there somewhere laughing at us. All we can do is roll the dice again and get on with it. You've seen the man close up, dipped a toe in his world...'

The Godawful scent of Bale suddenly catches me somewhere between reality and nightmare. Petrol, piss and blood. The more I try, the harder it is to shake off the stench. I sniff loudly and scrub my nose with my sleeve.

'Any thoughts?' he continues. 'Where he might run, where he might hide? I've got officers combing the area, but you're the expert here, luv.'

He's asking *my* advice?

My assignment to the investigation, just after Rita

Spinetti's mutilated body was found and Willard realised he had a serial killer on the loose, was by recommendation. He needed someone to infiltrate the seedy world that weirdos inhabit – a honey trap.

Send Zoe, he'd said, *nice tits, potty mouth, she'll do.*

Yeah. Right.

'He won't run anywhere, sir, and he won't hide. He'll wait and he'll watch.'

I scan the darkness beyond the halo of security and imagine him watching me. The Palace is ringed by uniforms. Crime scene officers are suiting up. Armed response await the command to go in for a final sweep. I feel reassured by their presence, but as I told Fuller, Bale is no fool, and he's on the kind of high you get when you believe you're winning. The deaths tonight have brought his count up to nine. I've a feeling he's going for double figures.

'Time to stand down now and let the rest of the team nab the bastard,' says Willard. 'You're in shock, understandable, nowt to be ashamed of. You might want him dead. Neil Fuller definitely does, but me? I just want the bugger in custody so I can get the Super off my back and we can all sleep safe in our beds.'

There's a buzz of static from the Airwaves as the officers prepare to re-enter the building. Fuller is with them. He turns to me and motions with a raised hand for me to stay put.

Red rag to a bull – usually. Not tonight.

'I think Bale's been playing with us since Mary Shea, sir. The party was a trap.'

'That you walked straight into.'

'Yes.'

'Why?'

'Why did I walk in? Or why the set-up?'

'Both.'

'Because I believed I could catch him – and he believed he could catch me.'

'So why aren't you caught?'

I stare at Fuller's retreating figure and shrug. I don't know the answer.

***

Roxy was already there when I arrived, sweating vodka. The party, in a private room, had already started. I was late. I'd wasted time chewing Fuller's ear to set me up with the wire, convincing him to get Willard on side. I was so sure of myself. Fuller was pissed at me, I was mad at him. The wire wasn't right. He'd wanted to call it off. I wouldn't let him. Told me to wait, I wouldn't listen.

You up for this, hun, Roxy had trilled in my ear. She was smiling, tottering on her six-inch heels, rubbing coke on her gums and I smiled back at her. *Sure,* I said.

***

'Roxy and me were last to arrive,' I say to Willard, 'Something in that, maybe?'

'Did you see, Bale?'

'Briefly. He was at the door, meet and greet, drooling at the mouth, hands all over me like he'd paid up front. I slapped him away. Told him to fuck off and play nice.'

Willard's lips twitch. In anyone else it would be a smile.

'And did he… play nice?' he asks.

I close my eyes, picture the scene. It's hard. It hurts. I don't want to go there again. The last time I saw the girls – with all their limbs intact.

'He was mad, in a manic, giggling weird-shit way. He'd been doing lines. They all had. He left the room, said he had a surprise for me. I was thinking meat cleaver or Stanley blade. I wanted to catch him with his tool in his hand… so to speak.'

'And then?'

'Dunno, boss. Next thing, I was sitting in A&E covered in blood and Fuller was giving me earache.'

Willard shakes his head. He's heard enough. But it's not enough. Not really. 'Go home, Zoe. Get some sleep. I'll get a uniform to drive you.'

***

It's 6am, and dawn is dragging itself out of the dark like a drunk from the gutter. I haven't slept. I've showered, twice, drank enough coffee to drown all of my butterflies, but I haven't slept. The leaves are falling and the crows are in my head, cawing nonstop.

There's something wrong with the story I told Willard. It's just out of reach… and if I could only think straight I might just remember.

I go through each step again and again…

I'm on step nine, Bale slobbering over my cleavage, when the sound of breaking glass intrudes and the avian mob fall silent. On the sofa arm my phone vibrates. I watch as it wriggles its way to the edge and drops like a lemming to the rug.

Shit.

There's someone at the door, tapping. Hesitant at first then more confident, more belligerent, as if they're braying at the wood with both fists, banging so hard the door rattles in the frame. The buzzing phone is in my right ear, the banging door in my left, and suddenly I'm back in A&E with the noise and the flashing lights and the confusion.

I jam my hands over my ears.

And then – clarity.

I freeze-frame on step ten, the image of what I *actually* saw back there at The Palace.

Jesus.

I make a grab for the phone.

It's a text from Fuller: *Open the fucking door!*

'They were already dead...'

Fuller falls in through the open door. He looks like he hasn't slept either.

'What?'

'At the party, the others, they were already dead, mutilated just like Alice, Rita and Mary. Bottles of petrol hanging above their heads and blood everywhere. That's what I saw when I stepped in the room. And him, Leslie *fucking* Bale, grinning like a Cheshire cat.'

'You just remembered this?'

'Yes. No. My head...' I'm a crap detective and an even crappier witness. But it's there now in wide-screen Technicolour detail. Bale grabbing at my top, yanking the wire – and dropping me like a stone.

'I was late. You made me bloody late, with all of your fucking about.'

'I saved your bloody life then – with all my *fucking about.*'

'No. Well yes, but you saved Roxy's and that's what's important here. You see, we interrupted him, spoilt the game and he threw the ball back in our face. He wasn't done, Neil. He still isn't. The explosion was just his calling card – times six. Smoke and mirrors to cover his escape, to give him time to think.'

I don't realise that I'm screaming in his face until Fuller grabs my upper arms and shakes me – hard. 'Slow down. Take a breath. Wipe your nose for fucks sake. It's not over yet. That's why I'm here. Bale's been sighted in The Haymarket.'

I pull away, take that breath and realise that Fuller's donned body armour and signed out a firearm.

Shit.

'I told you, the game's not lost. Not yet. Grab your vest. We're meeting the team there.'

'Does Willard know you're here?'

'Willard sent me.'

***

We're on the Great North Road, approaching the Hancock Museum when a ruddy black crow plants his beak at my throat.

Of course!

Bale hasn't finished playing the game. Bale needs his number ten.

I shoot out my hand and force the wheel hard right.

'What the fuck!'

'Go right, go right,' I yell. 'Bale isn't waiting for a bus. He's going after Roxy at the hospital.'

***

We're running now, following the blue line in a giant maze of antiseptic arteries. Fuller's on the radio doing the right thing, trying to get back-up, trying to get all Willard's horses and all Willard's men to move their arses up St Thomas Street to prevent another nasty fall. It's slowing him down, talking and running. I storm ahead, the crows are with me, a massive black cloud of determination, swooping and diving, clearing a path for me. I follow the signs, left, right, straight ahead for ICU.

***

The doors are swinging when I get there. My momentum carries me straight through and lands me in a heap against the nurse's station. I catch a breath and wait for Fuller. The white coats have fled. The green scrubs are nowhere to be seen. The room is deathly silent except for one solitary, repetitive metallic tap.

There are ten beds. All are vacant except two. The covers are drawn up over one unfortunate. In the other, the patient is heavily bandaged. I see peroxide hair. Roxy, beautiful, crazy Roxy with her vodka breath and six inch heels. I can't see her face. But I do see him.

***

Bale is seated alongside Roxy's bed, cigarette lighter in one hand. He's tapping the edge of a serrated hunting knife against the bed rail – and he's singing. Badly.

If that one green bottle…

A wine bottle hangs from an IV stand directly above Roxy's head. It sways in time to the metallic beat. It doesn't contain Prosecco. The glass is beaded with moisture. The excess drips on to the bed as Bale taps.

Should accidently fall…

His lips are wet, the corners of his mouth white with spittle. My stomach heaves. I plead silently for Fuller to hurry. But I can't wait any longer.

'Put the knife down, Mr Bale.'

He points the tip directly at me before swinging the blade back to rest on Roxy's chest. His knuckles are clenched. His eyes are chemical bright. Madness leaches from his pores.

There'll be no green bottles…

I try again.

'Leslie Bale, you're surrounded by armed officers. You can't escape. Please put down the knife and move away from the bed.'

Hanging on the wall.

I take a step closer.

Bale applies more pressure to the blade.

Roxy doesn't flinch. Sedated. Oblivious. Thank God.

I take another step and Bale flicks the lighter.

Shit.

He's actually going to do it.

The bed ignites with a phosphorescent whoosh. It sucks up all the air, the oxygen from my lungs and suddenly the crows alight as one. They're in my head, they're in the room, but it's not black feathers whipping up a storm. Directly behind Bale, a great white corpse the size of a mountain rises from its bed.

Willard.

He drops his shroud with a bellow and launches his colossal bulk at the monster. At the door, Fuller skids to a halt, raises his weapon, and squeezes the trigger just as Bale flings the knife.

I dive for the bed, grab Roxy's wrist and yank her to the floor. She lands with a deathly thud and I throw myself across her, smother the flames with my body, too desperate, too wired to feel the searing pain as Bale's knife glances my shoulder.

***

The medics are swarming, they're pumping Bale's chest. It's all in vain. The devil is waiting – black wings, sharp beak. Foulness pools the floor like raw sewage. Willard steps around it and pulls out a cigarette.

'Nice work, Zoe. Good shot, Neil. Bugger me. I'm getting too old for this malarkey.'

***

I cradle Roxy in my arms, hold her close, stroke her hair, rock her gently. She's covered in blood. Mine. She's cold. Ice cold. Her skin is marbled.

The tag on her toe says *number ten…*

Fuller drops to his knees at my side and untangles me from Willard's macabre, mortuary bait.

Bastard. *He lied to me.* He knew. He knew Roxy was already dead.

I scream silently.

He wraps an arm around me and sighs. His expression says, *'It's over. We won, kidda. We bloody won'.*

He's wrong. We didn't win. God did.

Like I said, God takes all the good ones and the devil gets to play with what's left.

LONDON'S CRAWLING

Emma Pullar

Crisp autumn leaves loop and tumble across the ground beside my boots. The rushing wind is the only indicator that time is flowing, for the streets of London are dark and silent. The sharp edges of tall buildings are diluted by the lingering fog. An amber weather warning was issued by the Met Office earlier today and most of my co-workers chose to get out of the city early to avoid train delays. I get a ride home and my manager knows this: she asked me to stay with her and finish up. I couldn't refuse, really. I need the money, and besides, I'm meeting my friends for a drink, as we always do on a Friday.

A bitter breeze slithers down the back of my neck. I shiver and pull up my coat collar. I didn't expect to be hurrying through central London after work, alone, literally alone. It's just a bit of fog. Where is everyone? Did the whole of London decide to go home early? Surely the bars and restaurants are open? I glance to my left; every building I pass is asleep. I look up to make sure I'm not about to bump into someone and the wind slaps my face with its icy hand. The place is deserted; the emptiness makes it feel eerie, like a graveyard nobody visits. Fingers numb with cold, I reach into my coat pocket for my gloves – they're not in that side.

Clack.

I stop, crouch down and feel around in the dry leaves for whatever has dropped out of my pocket. The brown leaves part under my hands and all the while the wind sends more rolling onto the pile. I scatter the browns and reds with the tips of my fingers and a white edge peeks through.

I curl my fingers around my ID card and lift it. 'JODY WINTERS' is written in capital letters across the top of the card. I wipe debris from the miserable greyscale photo of me, my hair dull. In reality, it's the colour of the rusty leaves.

A small spider crawling out from under the plastic

card and onto my hand makes me hop around and shriek. Its spindly, fast-moving legs cause my skin to itch. I shake it from my hand then brush down the arms of my coat, worried there might be more. I look down paranoid that hundreds of bugs are crawling up my legs. To my relief there's nothing but leaves. Phew! I pocket my card and, head down, I hurry on my way.

Across the ground, streetlamps cast the silhouette of a tall, elegant lady wearing a flared dress. The reality is a short, twenty-year-old office clerk wearing a lapelled coat over a pleated skirt and thick socks up to the knees, and I'm glad of them. It's freezing, colder than it should be in early November.

I walk briskly, my boots cutting through white wisps which sneak out of the storm drains like tentacles. The child inside me takes control of my rational adult mind and I imagine a monster is lurking underground. He sits down there in the dark, embers glowing from a pipe between his gruesome lips, all the while he quietly puffs toxic smoke into the city above.

I try to tread lightly but my footsteps insist on clopping loudly against the empty streets. I fold my arms tight around my body and shrink back into the protection of my winter coat and I think about the phone call I took a few hours ago. It was Nick. He said we were all to meet outside my office block. I'm sure that's what he said. So why wasn't he there?

Although I haven't seen another living soul for the last fifteen minutes, a prickling ripples over my skull, and I get the feeling I'm being watched. I quicken my pace but resist the urge to run. Instead, I remove my mobile from deep inside my pocket and my shadow copies. The numbers glow five past seven, yet it seems much later. The lack of bustle makes it feel more like midnight.

I tap out a message to Amber. *'I thought you were meeting me. Sorry, I'm on my way to Nick's work now.'*

Ping!

The words: *Can't send message. Try again,* pop up on my screen. Damn it! Why haven't I got any signal?

I shove the phone back into the warmth, keeping my hand wrapped around it for safety. In case I need to punch an attacker with it because what else can I do with no signal? I can't call emergency services. I suddenly feel vulnerable without the connected feeling my phone usually brings.

I turn onto the twisted metal of the Millennium Bridge and glance sideways at the white blanket rolling across the river Thames, silently whispering over the water, swallowing everything in its path. Ghostly fingers curl around buildings and over bobbing boats, surrounding everything but never touching; unlike the intrusive wind, mist never ruffles hair or lifts up skirts.

'I should have listened to the weather warning,' I whisper to myself, dread prickling my skin.

My teeth start to chatter and plumes of hot breath sneak out from between my frozen lips. Beyond the cotton-covered water I can just make out the lights of Tower Bridge and in front of me, I should be able to see St Paul's cathedral. There's nothing but unusual darkness. The dark isn't scary, I tell myself, but a deserted and dark London is never good.

I glance back at the nothingness behind me and the furthermost bridge lights flicker out. It's as if the darkness is following me. Lump in my throat, I start to run and the wind's cold fingers rush through my auburn hair, before throwing my scarf around behind me like a kite tail. My boots thud against the metal. Clonk, clonk, clonk, clonk. I'm almost to the other side.

'Jody?'

I stop dead. I don't recognise the male voice. Slowly and calmly I turn around. A scrawny man wearing a tatty leather jacket and ripped jeans stands before me. He looks as if he hasn't eaten for days.

'I'm sorry, do I know you?'

The words leave my lips in jitters.

'No,' he replies, breathing vapour into the air.

He takes a step forward. I take a step back. The fluorescent lamps either side of the bridge throw light up onto the stranger's sunken face; bearded and framed with a windswept mess of black hair. No, I don't know him. Why does he know my name?

'Did my friends send you to find me?' I ask nervously.

'No,' he replies.

The wind suddenly leaves, as if someone switched off the fan. Everything is still. The only sound I can hear is the quiet ripple of the water beneath us. The moon is a wheel of cheese, bottom half glowing through the haze as if it has sunk into the river. The man doesn't move.

I casually look over my shoulder. I'm not far from St Paul's cathedral. Not far from where Nick works.

I turn back to the man on the bridge. He's the only person I've seen all night. He grins at me and I feel the colour drain from my face. Green fangs stretch out over his black beard. I step nervously backwards. Back away. Back away. Prepare to run. The man remains still, he blinks, and then his temples blink. Two pairs of eyes! That's enough. Whatever prank this idiot is pulling has worked. I'm scared.

I turn on my heel and my leg is yanked backwards. I fall and the side of my face slams painfully into the illuminated metal below the mist. I look back at my leg. A hand grips my ankle. My eyes follow on from the hand, up a thin arm, to a smiling mouth with protruding green fangs and blood stained lips. A scream rushes from my throat, echoes over the bridge and gets lost. My muscles become petrified as a little girl with pigtails crawls out from under the bridge and up my body.

'What the hell?'

I thrash and squirm, unable to tear my legs from her grip or my two eyes from her four, which blink separately back at me from within her delicate face. An angry hiss rushes past her green fangs and my heart hammers against my chest. I kick away and scramble to my feet, stumbling backwards; arms like a windmill.

I gain my balance and my ears prick up. A scuttling sound grows louder, closer. Beyond the crouching, fanged child and the lone man, the bridge surges. Eyes wide, I watch on as a mass spills onto the metal structure from beneath like spiders trying to escape a smoke billowing cauldron, mist disguising their number – more than fifty? Hundreds, maybe.

'Get away!' I scream at them – but the words are for me.

I break into a sprint. I move faster than I've ever moved before. Lungs on fire, my cheeks blistering, I swing my arms and breathe out puffs of fright. Get to St. Paul's! Get to St. Paul's!

I leap across the dead street. No traffic. Double decker bus, lights out, abandoned in the middle of the road. My heart pulls my body along, beating hard, urging me to move faster. I look over my shoulder. They aren't following me. Why aren't they? What are they? The mist thickens and the only light I can see is a traffic light, flashing orange behind a misty veil. I charge up the steps of the great towering cathedral and lean up against a wide column and catch my breath. I reach into my pocket. *Please let me have signal.*

The phone lights up my face. I look to the bars. All dark. Not one bar of hope. I sigh. What do I do now?

'Jody...'

I look up towards the direction of the faint female voice and my heart crawls into my mouth.

'Amber?'

I tilt my phone from left to right and the light shines on several sleeping faces embedded in the architecture – cocooned in giant webs above me.

'Chris! Neil!' I scream at them but they don't open their eyes. Oh my God! Are they dead?

'Jody... Spians... run!' Amber croaks at me.

The others remain motionless. I pocket my phone.

'It's okay, I'll get you down. Hold on...'

I pull at the bottom of the sticky web but soon my arm is stuck fast.

'Run!' My friend closes her bloodshot eyes.

'Amber! Amber!'

I yank my arm free and sleeve cold sweat from my brow. The mist draws in around me. Too close. Too thick. Suffocating. I run back out onto the street to find help. Where are the police? The army? Anyone!? And where's Nick?

It's then I hear it. That terrible scuttling. I peer round the column and in the distance I see them. Clambering over one another in a mess of bodies – some of them clothed, some of them not, skin covered with black fuzz – all of them undulating like a sea of death. I dash across the road and duck down behind a hedge. Through the rolling mist the army advances. An army of human spiders. *Spians!* That's what Amber said. *Oh, I've left her to die.* Tears spill from the corners of my eyes and run towards my jaw. I tremble in the darkness.

'You can't stay here, Jody.' I whisper to myself. I close my eyes and grit my teeth, 'You have to do something!'

'You can do nothing...' a whimsical voice stretches around me, 'nothing... nothing.'

'Who's there?' I whisper into the hedge. No reply. I lift my head just high enough that I can see St Paul's from my hiding place. The steps are shrouded in white, its crown crawling with parasites.

I notice one clinging to the top of the nearest column; head bent over my friend Neil, limbs curled around his cocooned body. It lifts its head, green fangs with red tips, tongue darting out to lick the wet from its chin. I stare at Neil's ghostly face and silk covered body, which drips with blood. My bottom lip quivers. The creature leaps across to the next column. To Amber! I hear Amber's screams. I can't cope!

I run in the opposite direction. I have to get away. The wind whips up. I force my body against it. It pushes back, aggressively rustling leaves on nearby trees and throwing my hair around my face. It's pushing me back towards the infestation, pushing me to my death. I can't see my hand in front of my face. How far have I been swept?

'Is there anybody out there?'

'We are out here... here... here.'

The echo whispers from all directions.

'Who said that?'

The mist is so thick I could reach out and touch it. It's touching me! Get it off!

'GET OFF!'

I feverishly flick the fog from the arms of my coat but it evaporates and returns in one swift motion.

'Someone help me!'

'We're coming for you... you... you.'

I back up into something solid. I pull forward. I can't

move. I'm stuck, stuck in sinister cotton wool.

'Help! Someone please!'

My throat constricts. My body is squeezed, floss wrapping around my legs, arms and torso. Arms pinned to my sides I manage to push my hand into my coat pocket. I drum the screen with my fingertips, hoping I've dialled 999. Nothing. I close my eyes and slow my breathing. Don't panic, Jody. Think calmly and you can get out of this. When I reopen my eyes my mouth springs wide to let out a blood curdling scream! Fangs sink into my neck. The pain! I vomit a red river. Pain is replaced with numb and the sound of slurping and swallowing. My eyelids droop. I hear a muffled voice in my pocket.

Jody! it's Nick. Can you hear me?'

I finally have signal. The voices are quieter now. I blink. The mist fades to black. My eyes are jarred open as quickly as they closed, startled by a buzzing sound, which is followed by the sound of shrieks and hissing. Warm liquid splatters across my face. Something clatters to the ground, quick breaths near my face. Cracking and ripping noises float up to my ears but I can't see, the mist is too thick and my brain too fogged. Maybe the clouds have fallen to earth bringing with them these Spians. Perhaps the clouds are webs? I can't think straight. I feel as if the fallen sky webs have infiltrated my mind and clouded my thoughts.

My body is yanked forwards, I do nothing to stop it, I can't feel my limbs. Are they still attached to me? I'm thrown over a shoulder like the carcass of a hunter's first kill. My neck throbs. Am I dead? My eyelids flicker. I can just make out something on the ground, hedge trimmer splattered with blue paint? Hurried strides jolt my body along. The pain! I feel as if my neck might tear leaving my partially severed head lolling.

'It hurts,' I croak.

'Hold on, Jody,' a male voice pants. He moves faster, 'we're almost there.'

Nick? I think it's Nick! He's okay! My brain fizzes. No, no, he's dead like the rest of my friends, like me. We're all dead. No one can escape those monsters. Below my dangling hair, the chewing gum speckled pavement wobbles all over the place. I watch Nick's dress shoes clomp along at speed and my eyes roll around in their sockets while my stomach feels like lava is erupting inside it. Nausea burns up my throat and I close my eyes, to lessen the chance of vomiting down Nick's jeans. I will myself not to spew and not to pass out.

The next thing I hear is Nick's voice shouting and a rattling of metal. I tilt my face upwards. London's crawling; covered in mist and cobwebs and death. My head swims as I'm lowered onto my feet, boots hitting the ground with a thud. My legs buckle, bones gone soft. My arm is quickly lifted around a slim neck and draped over slender shoulders.

'Have you got her, Nadine?'

'Yeah, I got her,' A cockney voice yells beside me.

My eyes open as far as slits and I let the blurry stranger help me down a flight of solid steps. I look over my shoulder at Nick's pixelated form. He drags metal shutters across and secures them with a chain or wire, I don't know, too dizzy.

'Where am I?' I ask the stranger who Nick called Nadine. My voice comes out raspy.

'Safe,' she hushes into my ear.

A nasty metallic taste coats my tongue. I spit blood onto the grey steps as I stumble down them, slumped against the stranger. I'm too heavy for her; she staggers trying to hold me up.

'She's been bitten, badly,' Nick says as he takes up

29

my other arm and helps me down the last few steps.

Our footsteps echo loud against the desertedness. A faraway light shines through an archway to our left. We turn left, into the dim light.

'How long?' Nadine asks, talking through me.

'Only about thirty seconds.' Nick says to the floor.

'She isn't 'arf lucky,' Nadine says They talk as if I'm not here or unconscious. 'Two minutes is all it takes to drain the body completely.'

I think of my dead friends, of Neil's ashen face, of Amber's terrified screams.

I'm lowered onto a cold plastic seat and get a whiff of Nadine's perfume mixed with stale sweat. It's hot down here; water beads on my top lip, I wipe the moisture from my lip with the back of my hand and push back my hair, pulling plastered strands off my face. Some are stuck to my neck and painfully rip away from my skin.

'Ouch!' I suck air in through my teeth at the sudden sting and bring my hand up to the pain. The tips of my fingers brush over two gaping holes in my neck, wet running down around the parts already starting to congeal. Bile hits the back of my throat, I swallow it down and my lip trembles. *What the fuck is happening?*

'We don't know.' Nadine says, as if reading my mind.

I must have spat my thoughts out of my mouth without realising. I look down. Nick sits crossed-legged on the floor in front of me. The one ceiling light working at the far end illuminates the left side of his face. I blink and his rugged features come into focus but now I can see him clearly I wish his face had remained a blur.

He's as grey as a tombstone and covered in cuts and bruises and his bottom lip is a swollen blood blister. He's wearing his lucky shirt, the one he wears when he's on the pull. It's stained light blue. What is that? I look down at my hand, smears of blue on the back of it. I touch my cheek with my fingertips. More blue stuff.

'What is this?' I ask Nick.

'It's their blood,' he says darkly. 'The one that fed on you has one less arm.'

My mind conjures an image of the blue splattered hedge trimmer.

'Thanks Nick,' I say, swallowing hard.

'My pleasure,' he says, smiling for the first time.

I wipe my hands down the front of my coat, undo the buttons, struggle out of the sleeves and throw it on the seat next to me. Nick seems despondent, yet unfazed by the blue blood which has ruined his favourite shirt. Behind him, beyond the yellow safety line, set back on the dim curved wall is the blue and red underground sign for St Paul's tube station. It looks fuzzy and at first I think it's my eyesight but then I realise it's the mist. It's seeped into everything. How did this happen? Did the government know about this? Did they seal off the city once most people were out, and to hell with the rest of us? Oh, why didn't I just leave early like everyone else?

I turn my attention to the girl sitting in silence beside me. Her scraggly two tone ponytail is a mess on top of her head. The blonde curls are stained pink and a chunk of her hair and skin is missing, replaced with a blister. One side of her face is dipped in shadow, the other dipped in red. She wears running gear, green and black lycra. As her stare meets mine I'm almost chilled by her dark brown eyes. They look dead, as if the Spians sucked out her soul instead of her blood. She hands me a bottle of water, which also looks to have been bleeding, smears of red all around it. When it leaves her hands I notice her palms are also bloody. I don't even want to ask what happened to her.

'Drink,' she says.

I spin off the bottle lid and chug down the lukewarm water.

'Sip it, girl, you don't wanna—'

I splutter, water burning in my nose.

She tuts. '—choke.'

Nick hands me a chocolate bar, I reach out and just as my hand closes around the crushed packet, a sound like a cage being rattled travels down the station steps.

CRASH, CRASH, CRASH

'They're trying to get in.' Nick says, eyes wide.

I grip the arms of the station seat, fear driving my heart into high-speed like a train charging down the tracks.

'Those shutters won't hold for—' Nadine falls silent.

CRASH, CRASH, CRASH

Panic prickles over my skin and I leap to my feet, legs trembling. My body feels as if it's made of jelly.

'We should go,' I croak. My mouth is still dry but the water's gone.

The remaining tube light flickers. Nick shines the torchlight from his phone down the dark tunnel. I feel around in my coat pocket, pull out my phone and flick on the torch app. Nadine gets to her feet.

'Lost mine,' she says, annoyance in her voice, 'I smacked one of them Spian fuckers in the boat with it.'

She tilts her head to the side and three cracks rip out. I wince. The last working tunnel light flickers out. I widen my eyes in an attempt to force them to adjust to the darkness. I jump down onto the tracks, which feels weird because even though I know a train won't come, I still feel stupid for walking on the tracks.

Our two phone lights do little to light the path ahead, I can just about sshoeee to put one foot in front of the other.

I'm not sure if it's the humidity or hunger but I'm starting to feel queasy. I lost a lot of blood: perhaps the chocolate will help – sugar boost. I tear off the wrapper with my teeth and bite off a large chunk; it's sticky in my mouth, like chocolate sick. I force it down. The awful crashing noise of Spians trying to break in becomes fainter as we tread deeper into the dark tunnel.

The tunnel snakes around and a pungent smell wafts into my face. I drop the half-eaten chocolate bar and hold my arm over my nose and mouth.

'What's that stench?' Nadine asks. I can't see her but I can feel her walking beside me.

I walk into something wispy, and feverishly wipe it from my face and hair. Nose exposed again, the disgusting musky odour has thickened; it pushes up my nostrils and down my throat. I dry retch and wonder if the tunnel walls have been insulated with hundreds of shoe inners donated by past London Marathon runners.

'Wait,' Nick whispers. We stop advancing and wait. The crashing of shutters has stopped. 'Hear that?'

Nick shines his torch light towards a faint sound coming from above. A clicking sound, like a class of students simultaneously clicking their pen tops. I reluctantly raise my light up too; fearful about what might be up there. I have to repress a scream and Nadine gasps beside me when the light reveals hundreds of webspun sacks hanging from the tunnel ceiling. The clicking noise is coming from inside them.

'Nick,' I whisper.

'We're in trouble,' he whispers back.

'We have to go back,' Nadine hisses.

Scuttling echoes off the walls behind us. They're in the tunnel. No way back. My spine twinges as if a poisonous spider is crawling up it.

'We've disturbed a nest!' I say, panicky, mind racing.

'All the little spiders are going to rain down on us and eat out our eyeballs or something or there'll be some giant queen spider, hell-bent on protecting her babies …!'

'Calm down, Jody!' Nick says voice low and shaky, 'Spiders don't have queens.'

'No, but Spians do,' Nadine says.

We turn our phone lights on her. Her eyes shine like emeralds, 'and she needs to feed.'

Nadine rips the blister from the side of her head revealing a third eye and on the other side a fourth eye opens. They all blink. Nick and I shrink back when hairy spider legs unfold from Nadine's waist, two on each side. I can feel Nick's frustration leaching into the humid air. She sure fooled us! Is this how it started? Millions of mutant spider people hiding among us, waiting for the right moment to strike?

Queen Nadine bares her green fangs. Her Spian subjects arrive behind her and Nick's torch app shines over several emerald eyes, in sets of four. My heart sinks into my boots. We're screwed.

I hear a door whine open to my left. I don't wait to find out who's behind it. I run, Nick hot on my heels. Nadine sends out a high-pitched scream and the scuttling starts up again. I stumble between the tracks, torch light all over the place. I head towards the bright yellow rectangle cut out of the dark wall; the doorway spills light down the emergency exit steps and I sigh with relief.

'Thank God,' I whisper to myself, 'a light at the end of the tunnel.'

The figure leans forwards, hand stretched out, beckoning me. I dash for the strange man, better him than what's behind us. He steps into the light spillage, fangs bared.

'Shit!' I yell and skid to a stop.

Nick bumps into me. I topple, sending us both sprawling across the metal tracks. My shoulder slams down hard, as does my head. The impact judders my bones and I drop my phone. The pain in my shoulder is overridden by my throbbing temples. I hold my face in my hands, trying to stop the pain hammering all over my skull.

Nick grabs my arm and drags me to my feet. He shines his phone light back on Nadine.

'Where did you come from?' he yells out in frustration.

Spians close in around us – close in to protect their queen. Nadine smiles, green fangs protruding over her thick bottom lip.

'Our origin is not important,' she says, and takes a graceful step towards me. 'They're calling it an infection and I suppose it is.' All four of her eyes stare at me and I touch the puncture marks on my neck. 'Infections have a tendency to spread.'

'Nick?' I say, fretful.

Nick's tired eyes water; he looks at the floor, defeated. Burning shoots through my abdomen and I double over, holding my stomach, oh the pain! They took too much blood, I'm dying! I squeeze my eyes shut and the pain stops. I straighten up, and when I open my eyes the tunnel has changed. I can see almost three-hundred and sixty degrees around me and in high definition night vision. I blink, my eyes passing over ultraviolet cobwebs, suddenly visible in the darkness. My stomach lurches again, this time in hunger. I'm starving!

'Jody?'

I look up at Nick and slide my tongue down my right fang. The colour drains from his face. I look to my queen. She nods.

Adrenaline rushes through my new body and I jump

35

towards my friend, arms and legs wrapping around him.

'Jody, no!' Nick screams.

I bite down hard into the soft flesh of his neck; my fangs break the skin with ease and sink in, blood spilling from the sides of my mouth. Nick struggles and yells out, I hold him still and suck. Frenzied I rip flesh from his jugular and gulp… gulp… gulp. Warmth runs down my throat and rejuvenates my body. The rush is intense, like nothing I've ever felt. It's thrilling – euphoric. As I drain the life out of him, life fills up inside me.

Nick falls silent. His body shrivels beneath my grip, no need to wrap him, easy prey; he was never going to get away, not with my brothers and sisters here to support me.

I lift my head from the neck gash. I've made a bit of a mess, not as neat as whoever bit me. Nick's face is withered, skin sunk to the skull. I drop the sack of bones and the bloodless body hits the tunnel floor, folding into a crumpled mess. I step over it and lick Nick's blood from my lips.

'Very good, Jody,' Nadine coos, and then inside my head I hear, *Welcome to the family.*

THE SHOES MAKETH THE MAN

Louise Jensen

B ill shivers and pulls the itchy grey blanket up to his chin. It smells of stale smoke and cabbage. Laundry was always Maureen's domain, and it's another one of the many things he hasn't got to grips with. He really should put the gas fire on – his hands are tinged blue – but he can't afford to. One pension doesn't go far at all.

In the corner, the TV glows and flickers. The news reader has a solemn expression as he reports on last night's brutal murder of a local girl, comparing it to a spate of crimes years before. But it's the following story that makes Bill's insides turn to liquid, just like they did the first time he tried to cook a roast after Maureen passed. How was he to know how long to leave a chicken in for?

It has happened again.

Another pensioner has been terrorised in their own home. Beaten and robbed. The third one this month – and just around the corner this time. Bill shudders. What's the world coming to when you're not safe inside your own home? When he hears things like this, a tiny part of Bill is relieved Maureen isn't here to witness society plummeting to new lows.   Anxiety wraps itself around Bill like a second skin, just like it did during Maureen's first brush with cancer, but Bill can't seem to calm himself down as easily nowadays.

There's a thud. Did that come from inside his flat, or outside? Bill's heart beats a little faster, his breath comes a little quicker. He hoists himself out of his armchair. His knees creak and he winces in pain as he hobbles to the lounge door and peers out into the hallway.

There's a bang. Bill's blood pounds in his ears. Did he remember to lock the door when he came home? His memory is full of dark spaces lately. He screws his eyes up and recalls coming home after his evening visit to the supermarket, where his habit is to hover around the reduced shelf, waiting for them to mark down the perishables. The handles of the carrier bags were slicing grooves into his hands and he banged the door shut with his hip; but did he come back to lock it?

Edging down the darkened passageway, wishing he hadn't had to choose between a new light bulb or a loaf of bread, he reaches the door and presses his ear against it. Footsteps. The sound of a throat clearing. Slowly the handle begins to move. Fear turns Bill to stone and he can only watch in horror... But the door doesn't open, and Bill lets out the breath he'd been holding as he realises he must have locked it. With a shaking hand he draws the chain across and leans his forehead against the door, imagining someone doing the same on the other side, their hot breath against his neck. There's a stillness. A heavy silence.

Retreating to the lounge Bill huddles in his armchair once more. The air is thick with the scent of his own fear and to distract himself he aims the remote with a hand that trembles, and scans the channels. Television – such a wonder when he was a boy – now there are a hundred choices of nothing. Girls and boys locked in a house, on a beach, in a jungle. He jumps as music blasts and the thump-thump-thump of bass seeps through the paper-thin walls, causing his collection of cat ornaments to shiver and shake on the shelf. Another party next door. Perhaps this one won't go on too late. Bill's eyes are gritty with tiredness but he daren't complain. People can be so aggressive nowadays.

Bill's stomach growls, loud and fierce, and he places a hand over it as if to reassure it food will come. There's some liver in the fridge he could fry with an onion. That might get rid of the stench in the flat. The lift was out of order again last Thursday and he couldn't take his rubbish down into the communal area. 'The Courtyard' they call it, but it's always littered with needles and condoms and chills creep up Bill's spine whenever he has to go there.

He is thankful he doesn't generate much rubbish. He was a war baby – waste not, want not. Each tea bag is meticulously squeezed, dried and used again, and he always cleans his plate.

In the tiny kitchen Bill scoops the trash spewing from the overflowing pedal bin into a plastic bag, but his arthritic fingers can't tie a knot, and as the bag slumps onto its side a cracked eggshell tumbles out. It would be nice if that pretty social worker would call again this week. It's been a long time since he's seen her. He can't remember her name and he screws up his face as he tries. He's getting more and more forgetful. There are half-started lists everywhere but the words, written in spidery handwriting he barely recognises, don't mean anything to him when he reads them back.

From his friend Ethel's flat upstairs, there's a crash... a scream? Bill's hearing isn't what it used to be and he stands still, ears straining. A chair scrapes across the floor. Another scream, muffled this time, and the sound of something being dragged. Images of Ethel being beaten flit across Bill's mind and he presses the heels of his hands against his eyes as though he can force them away. It's them. He knows it is, but he can't ring the police, he just can't. He doesn't want to be next and he swallows hard, tasting shame as there's a smash. The sound of pleading.

Outside the window there's a shriek and Bill shuffles across the room. His bony fingers are like hooks as he scoops back the curtain and peers down into the inky blackness. There's a girl, a slip of a thing, glossy blonde hair shimmering under the streetlight. Her beauty almost makes him weep. If he and Maureen had been blessed with a daughter this is what he thinks she'd have looked like.

The girl shouts into one of those mobile thingys all the youngsters seem to be glued to, and waves her hand around as if making a point. She stops talking and slumps on the bench at the bus stop. Her breath billows out in icy clouds as she jabs at her phone, frowning at the screen. There isn't a bus due for forty-five minutes and Bill worries she'll get cold. She looks like an angel in her silver sparkly dress but she should have worn a jacket. Some tights at least. Bill has a vision of himself covering the girl with his blanket, warming her. She shouldn't be alone. It's not safe out there, you only have to watch the news to know that.

He has time, if she waits for the bus. He could go down if he wanted to. He can't help Ethel, but this? This he can do. But what if whoever is in Ethel's flat comes down and grabs him? It doesn't bear thinking about – but the girl turns and her profile in the orange street light, is so much like Maureen's. It's an effort to wrench himself away from the window but he must hurry if he wants to reach her in time, and he does.

Bill moves as fast as he can towards the bedroom but his slipper catches on the faded Chinese rug and he almost falls. He freezes for a moment. He can't imagine what would happen if he broke something. Who would find him? He steps forward, carefully this time, splaying out his fingers for balance.

The doors to the mahogany wardrobe creak open and a fusty smell hits his nostrils. He pulls out his suit. He is grateful it is black so you can't see the stains. He sniffs it. There's a foul smell but he thinks that's probably him. It always seems so pointless showering every day. He hesitates. A quick rinse? But he doesn't have time and he struggles out of his pyjamas and into his shirt. The buttons are tricky and by the time he's finished sweat beads on his top lip. His black dress shoes are packed in tissue in their original box, but Bill blanches as he pulls them out. There's something sticky on the soles. He didn't notice when he put them away. It's tempting to put the shoes on as they are but he knows he can't. What would his Dad think if he could see him? '*The shoes maketh the man*' he used to say.

In the kitchen he tries to ignore the wailing upstairs. Bill's knees protest as he crouches, thrusting his hand into the cleaning cupboard and fumbling around until he clasps the cool metal tin. One brush to put the polish on, one to rub it in and he shines the shoes with a piece of old vest until he can see his reflection in the toes. Lacing them is tricky, he grits his teeth as he tries again and again to make a loop, but at last he is nearly ready. The kitchen clock shows eight. He only has ten minutes and cold panic bolts through him as he thinks he may not make it. But will he make it anyway, with those thugs in the flat above him doing God knows what to Ethel? Is this worth the risk? He thinks of them getting hold of this girl who looks so much like his darling Maureen and he knows he has to try and reach her at least.

He pulls his bag out of the cupboard and clips it around his waist before dropping his door key inside along with his heart pills: you can't be too careful.

The drawer of the dresser is stiff. Bill yanks the handles as hard as he can. He pulls out a roll of gaffer tape, checks it's still sticky and pops it into his bag. His hunting knife is next. He holds it to the light and his heart quickens as he studies the serrated blade, shiny and sharp. He zips up his bag and snaps on leather gloves. It's time.

He hopes the young girl is still there. He'll tell her he needs to get to his daughter's house on Green Street but he's feeling wobbly. She'll help him, he's sure of it. She looks kind. They'll cut down the alley off Gilmore Way. It will be quiet and if he surprises her she shouldn't struggle too much.

Bill thought he'd put all this business behind him, he really did, but that was before all the attacks on the elderly. He wishes something else could calm his anxiety but he's found nothing like the utter terror in someone else's eyes to alleviate his own fear.

It's harder than it was all those years ago – he's not as strong – but last night's victim was smaller, weaker and he hadn't had such a good night's sleep in ages. But when he woke, the calmness didn't last. It never does.

The lift judders towards the ground floor. Bill closes his eyes. He can almost hear the knife slicing through the air. Feel the resistance as it strains against flesh before popping open the skin. Can almost taste the blood.

The doors ping open and, as he steps out into the cool night air, he wonders if she'll scream. He does hope so.

NEVER TELL A LIE

Tara Lyons

It was during the winter of 2015 I became a real man.

The frost welcomed me every morning and I hid behind a large oak tree in Roundwood Park. The grass crunched under my feet as I hopped from side to side, waiting from 5am. Fiona wouldn't jog by for another hour, but I never wanted to miss her. The black, tight leggings showcased her beautifully long legs and toned arse. I wanted to rip the jumper from her chest, fully expose the bouncing cleavage it masked. I'd waited so long. My tense body was like a mountain of frustration until she ran by. I'd grow hard as I yearned to touch her. She was my release and I needed to see her every day. Except on a Sunday; Fiona didn't run on Sundays and I went to church.

I had met Fiona a month earlier at the coffee shop, and instantly wanted her. Her hair shone like the sun and her blue eyes enticed me, pulling me in like the waves of the ocean. I served her a large latte to-go every day for a week before I summoned the courage to ask her out. She swiftly held up her hand and pointed to the gleaming diamond.

'I'm married, sweetie. Thanks for the compliment.' She laughed and left the café.

I'd never been turned down before. My teeth clenched together in anger. I was used to getting what I wanted – as a handsome man with a great sense of humour, it was what I expected. Her rejection was like a punch to the gut. But, the more I thought about her, the more I wanted her. She was playing hard to get and that was new. That was exciting.

For another week I watched Fiona's every move. I followed her on Monday morning, after she'd collected her usual beverage; disappointment hit me when she didn't notice I wasn't serving. She seemed to breeze through life with such dignity. My respect for her grew; Fiona was the type of woman I could see myself starting a family with. I had waited so long to find the right woman – the kind of woman my father had spoken about when I was a boy.

The week turned into a month and soon I knew everything there was to know about Fiona. Her daily exercise routine, where she lived and worked, which shops she frequented and the journey she took home. She was so busy with her daily tasks, or always with her nose stuck in a book while travelling, she barely took notice of anyone around her. Never once did she notice me watching her.

Her home was nestled in a quiet cul-de-sac. A semi-detached cottage with a quaint thatched roof that had become so difficult to find in London. It was another way she was showing me her uniqueness and style. Its location was an ideal spot – far enough away from the noise and city yobs that you weren't involved in its tourism and fast-living, but still close enough to actually work there if you so desired. It was important to earn a good wage, and I knew Fiona did. It was also perfect for my evening viewing. I was protected by the foliage; trees everywhere hid me from sight. Sadly, for Fiona, this was her undoing.

One night, while watching from the safety of the shrubbery, I spied her through the living room window. She sat in front of the TV with a large glass of white wine, relaxed onto the sofa and pulled her feet up. As she slipped the diamond ring off her finger and placed it on the coffee table it suddenly dawned on me... I had never seen a man enter or leave her home. In fact, I'd never seen anyone there but her. She had completely played me. I had become the fool my father feared I might. That was the evening I waited... waited and really paid attention... but no one ever came. Fiona was alone. And every morning she placed the ring back on her wedding finger before leaving the house.

My excitement for her was soon replaced with anger when I fully realised Fiona had lied to me. She had discarded my advances with an imagery husband. Why couldn't she have given me a chance? I would have brought such joy to her world. Instead she chose to work and exercise and sleep; her days were meaningless. Boring. Empty, even. In that moment, I decided to give her one more chance.

So, that Saturday after she jogged by, I waited a few seconds before running out from behind the tree. I pounded the pavement behind her in a ridiculous pair of shorts I'd purchased the day before. Just as she reached the side entrance of the park, a young boy on a bike whizzed past us and clipped Fiona with such force she stumbled and landed in a heap on the ground. As I ran to her aid, the boy looked over this shoulder and winked at me. It's amazing what people will do for a tenner.

'Are you okay?' I asked, kneeling down beside her.

Fiona's hands were grazed and bleeding, her leggings had ripped slightly between her thighs, revealing a glimpse of her milky white flesh. The blood rushed down through my body. I quickly readjusted myself and helped her up.

'I'm fine, thank you. Arsehole on that bike – and they're always mouthing off about cars not looking out for them… but do they care? Do they look out for anyone? No! It's not the first time I've been hit by a cyclist. They have their own bloody lanes in this park.'

Her wrath resonated from every pore of her skin; I'd never seen her like this before. It was enthralling. Sheer rage produced a red glow in her cheeks that had nothing to do with exercise. I'd never felt this way before – the overpowering desire to grab her, throw her onto the ground and please myself. For a moment, I thought about her rejecting me again and, if she did, the control it would bring me. I would show her what kind of powerful man I was. I would teach her a lesson. Fiona had created something new and exciting inside of me, and it needed feeding.

'My house is just around the corner, actually,' I explained. 'Would you like to come and clean yourself up?'

Fiona's eyes trailed the length of my body and she smiled, unable to disguise the craving she now possessed for me. My heart beat like a drum inside my chest. So beautiful. How could one person be so breath-taking? I'd never known feelings of passion like the ones that ran through my veins in the instant she looked at me with fire in her eyes.

She squinted. 'Do I know you from somewhere?'

I could have lied, but that's not the kind of person I am. And it's certainly not who my father would want me to be. He was a strong, Irish man who travelled to London in the sixties and made a good life in this city for his family. Above all else, he prided himself on always being truthful; dishonesty is an unforgiveable trait. So, I smiled back at Fiona.

'Well... I have served you a few times in Lizzie's café – my café – on the high street. Large latte, no sugar, every morning at about eight-twenty, give or take if you miss the bus.'

Her expression changed – the stunning smile faded, replaced by a taut, ugly expression. She fidgeted, fingers twined around each other and her eyes darted around the park. It was empty. The winter daylight was making its morning climb through dark, brooding clouds. Rain was promised, thunder a possibility. We were alone. Fiona's skin was so close to mine, I could see the goose bumps prickling her neck. She shivered and I took another step towards her.

'My husband will be wondering where I am,' she snapped, and moved away from me. 'Thanks for the offer.'

Without waiting for my reply, Fiona spun and raced

off back through the gardens. I stared at the back of her head until the distance between us became too vast. I sucked in the cold air and pulled up my chest. My hands balled into fists.

I want to share something with you: I wasn't abused as a child and no one bullied me at school, but I had become accustomed to getting what I wanted in life; it's the way my father had raised me. And that day I wanted Fiona Summers more than I wanted to breathe.

I sped off in the opposite direction to her, out of one of the many park entrances and jumped into my car, which I'd parked nearby. With no rush-hour traffic, I drove the normal twenty minutes to her home in just ten. She hadn't returned yet. I used my time wisely, parking my car at the end of the road. I then strolled down to Fiona's house and hid behind the large grey bin outside her front door. It's amazing how people rush through life, never stopping to think about their safety, to observe an area and really see what's around them. Tell me, would you notice a strange car at the end of your street? Do you check behind the bins before entering your home? Fiona didn't.

When she finally arrived, Fiona ran up the drive with her keys in hand and stopped, jogging on the spot while she opened the door. Before she had a chance to close it behind her, I pounced from my hiding place and shoved her into the hallway. With a swift kick I slammed the front door shut and prepared to live out my fantasy. I forced Fiona down onto the beige carpeted floor. She opened her mouth to scream and I smacked my fist into her jaw. She'd be sorry for treating me with such disrespect.

***

Two weeks later, a news article launched an appeal for witnesses to come forward after Fiona Summers had been found raped and murdered in her home. The journalist called her 'a lonely woman who was unknown to her neighbours'. Undisclosed sources had confirmed the woman's attacker had left a message on the hallway mirror. Written in Fiona's blood were the words 'never tell a lie.' Metropolitan Police had spoken to her colleagues and were now looking for anyone who may have had a romantic connection with the victim, or anyone who could shed light on her whereabouts the morning of her murder. At present they had no suspects.

I dropped the newspaper into the bin before I entered the café.

'What time do you call this?' my mother yelled from behind the counter. 'You're always late these days, working whatever hours suit you.'

I rolled my eyes and pulled the apron over my head. Since my father passed away six months ago the woman was always mad at me. Nothing I did was ever good enough for her.

'Your father would turn in his grave if he knew you weren't helping me. I was the love of his life, and he mine.' The fake tears were summoned and my mother ran upstairs.

Another woman who thought I was stupid; she didn't really love my father. On his deathbed that man truly became my hero when he imparted his wisdom to me. Gripping my hand, he exposed my mother for the bitch she is, revealing that during his dying months she had sneaked out of our home to meet other men. But he had simply laughed it off. You see, I now understand that women are weak and unable to survive without the strong hand of a man. My father built his empire in Lizzie's chain of cafés, slept with many young women and had the fun he wanted and deserved. But he chose to always come home to the woman who had a duty to look after him. And that's the reason he said I must protect her. I agreed to my father's dying wish… but I've hated my mother since that day.

As the weeks dragged on, I was filled with deep misery. My father promised I would find someone who I could mould into the woman I wanted. But after Fiona… I felt nothing. I began to wonder what it was I needed to do to make myself feel better. To feel whole. And that was when she walked in…

Her red hair blew behind in the wind as she stood in the doorway of the café. The snow crept in with her. She was a true vision of what a woman should be – an angel sent from my father. She was here to rescue me. She wouldn't lie or cheat.

My angel ordered our Christmas special – a pumpkin latte – and that's when I knew she was the one. Who else could have chosen my café to wander into and then order my favourite winter beverage? It was fate. I smiled and added extra whipped cream and pumpkin spice topping. Fiona was yanked from my thoughts; I'd never seen a sight more stunning than the one standing in front of me now.

I wonder what her name is…

A CHRISTMAS KILLING

Richard T. Burke

Christmas Eve

An out-of-tune rendition of the Big Ben chime rang from the doorbell. I peered through the glass panel beside the heavy wooden door before unlatching it and pulling it open. In front of me slouched a man in filthy grey overalls and brown working boots. He was one of those disconcerting people whose eyes don't focus at the same point.

'Your delivery, sir,' he muttered, straining under the weight of the plastic-wrapped package he held between his arms.

I resisted the temptation to glance behind me to see what he was staring at and, after a second of indecision, identified which eye to follow. Once I had gained my bearings, I focussed on a face with beetling eyebrows and a ruddy complexion topped by a mop of unruly brown hair. He had the look of somebody who spent most of his life outdoors. His bored expression remained unchanged throughout my moment of inspection. A blast of frigid air washed over him bringing with it the odour of something unpleasant, the scent of decay – not surprising, I supposed, considering his line of work.

'Where do you want her?'

'In the kitchen, please.' I nodded towards the door on the right at the end of the hall. 'Do you need a hand?'

The man gave an almost imperceptible shake of the head and fixed me with a stare from his dominant eye. I led the way along the oak floor, the man's boots clumping a short distance behind.

A scraping sound made me glance backwards. One of her legs had touched the cream-coloured wall leaving a pale red streak. The deliveryman appeared not to have noticed. I would have to remember to wipe it off afterwards.

I passed through the doorway and gestured at the large, wooden farmhouse table. 'On there, please.'

With a grunt, he leant forwards and deposited her on the pockmarked surface. Yes, she would do nicely. I tried not to think about how she might have died; perhaps at the hands of the man who stood before me. He didn't look like a killer but how could you tell? I wondered if she knew it was coming, whether she made any attempt to escape before the fatal blow, if she suffered any pain.

The man stared down at her, making no indication that he was about to leave. Did he want a tip? This was all a little outside my realm of experience.

Just as I was reaching into my back pocket to extract my wallet, he turned and, without another word, retraced his steps.

I followed him down the hall. He opened the door for himself and crunched across the gravel to his grimy white delivery van. 'Thanks!' I called to his back but he didn't acknowledge me. He got into the vehicle and started the engine with a cloud of noxious black smoke. The tyres threw up several small stones as he dropped the clutch and accelerated away.

After closing the front door, I returned to the kitchen. I studied the package and pulled back a section of the clear plastic material. All the colour had leached out of her skin, leaving it pale and bloodless. I reckoned she had probably been dead for a day or two. When I touched a finger against her, she felt cold and clammy. Through the plastic, I could see her head had been severed, exposing a dark, gaping hole in her neck where it had once connected. Her limbs were bound together with twine. A watery puddle of crimson was forming beneath her but it was clear that most of her blood had already been drained before I took possession of her.

Grabbing a cloth from beside the sink, I mopped away the fluid. I didn't want to stain the table's surface, battered though it was. Flinging the cloth into the bowl, I turned back to her and folded my arms, deep in contemplation.

I felt I ought to name her. I was going to be doing some pretty personal things to her so it was the least she deserved. After all, even storms had names. Each one began with the next sequential letter of the alphabet. When they got to Z they restarted at A.

I walked around the table a couple of times, stroking my chin. *Angela. That's it. I'll call her Angela.*

'Hello, Angela,' I said. 'Pleased to make your acquaintance. Man, I love roast turkey. There'll be more than enough for Christmas Day and you'll keep me going for weeks.' I reached out a hand and patted her. 'We'll have to make space for you in the fridge though. We want to keep you at your best.'

Needless to say, she didn't respond.

I crossed to the white-fronted appliance and yanked the handle towards me. I crouched down and peered inside. The interior was so crowded with food for the Christmas period that the automatic light had no effect.

'No room in there. Looks like we're going to have to put you in the big fridge.'

I glanced at Angela once again, trying to memorise her size, then pulled open the door to the utility room. I flipped the switch and waited for the flickering of the fluorescent light to stop. I moved across to the tall fridge-freezer standing in the corner. The seal gave way with a slight pop, almost as if it was inhaling. *Not as cramped as the other fridge.* I would need to do some reorganisation including the repositioning of one shelf but I was sure there was enough room.

I removed the items on the bottom two levels, some wrapped in cling film, others in silver foil, and placed them on the ground.

When the area was clear, I slid out the plastic-coated grid and positioned it vertically on the floor in the gap down one side. Angela would fit perfectly in the space I had created.

I returned to the kitchen and wrapped my arms around the bird.

'God, you're a heavy one.'

I lurched back into the utility room and staggered towards the open fridge door. A green light on the top edge was flashing, accompanied by a persistent beeping sound.

'I know, I know,' I said, levering Angela inside. I was careful to avoid stepping on any of the sealed items I had removed. I nudged the door to confirm that it would close. Perfect.

'Right. Let's sort this lot out.'

I picked up the first foil-wrapped package, peeled back the edge, and took in the garishly painted fingernails.

'Ah yes, Xenia. How are you holding up? How are you feeling?'

Next, I grasped the jam jar. I held it to the light and peered in at the severed ear still wearing the pearl earring.

'Good evening, Yvonne. How are you? I haven't heard much from you recently.'

Finally, I grabbed a package wrapped in cling-film. Through the transparent layers, I could just about make out the red-painted toenails.

'Hello, Zoe. I hope I haven't kept you sitting around too long.'

'All of you, I want you to meet Angela. She'll be

staying with us for a few days.'

***

Christmas Day

I drove the blade down hard, the edge trembling in the bright lights. A tear rolled slowly down my cheek and paused, quivering at my chin. I was reaching up my sleeve to brush it away when the doorbell played its discordant version of the Big Ben chimes. I really would have to replace the damned thing.

Sniffing loudly, I headed towards the front door. Halfway down the hall, the sequence of notes began once again.

'Okay, okay, I'm coming!' I called, although whoever was waiting would more than likely be unable to hear me. I reached up with my left hand and unlatched the door.

A policewoman wearing black trousers and a yellow high-vis jacket stood before me. On her head, she wore a black flat-topped hat. Her hair was tied back in a short ponytail. She was not unattractive and smiled as she greeted me.

Despite the unflattering uniform, I could see that she had promise. My gaze was drawn to a strand of hair that had worked loose and dangled alongside the delicate features of her neck. She – or at least part of her – would make a fine addition to my collection. I pushed the thought from my mind and gave her my happy expression.

'Good morning sir–' She stopped speaking and the smile dropped from her face. She took a step backwards, staring at my right hand. I glanced down and realised I was still holding the knife.

'Oh, I'm sorry,' I said. 'I was just chopping onions.'

Hastily, I deposited the kitchen knife on the small wooden cabinet in the hall. When I turned back, she seemed less on edge but still wary.

'So, what can I do for an officer of the *leu* on this fine Christmas morning?' I asked.

She shot me a puzzled look. 'The *leu*?'

'You know, an officer of the law. Inspector Clouseau, Peter Sellers, The Pink Panther.'

She stared at me blankly. 'I'm sorry, sir, I don't know what you're talking about.'

I guess it's true what they say; the police are getting younger. 'Never mind,' I said. 'It's an old film about this incompetent police inspector, not that I'm suggesting for a moment... You should watch it sometime. Anyway, what can I do for you?'

The woman shook her head. 'We've had reports of screaming on this road the past couple of nights. The person who called it in was sure the cries were human. We sent a patrol car but they didn't see anything.'

'Screaming, you say?'

'Yes, sir. I was wondering if you might know anything about it.'

'Me? Why would I know anything?'

The woman frowned. 'I was thinking you might've been at home the last two nights. One of your neighbours rang the emergency services sometime between one and one thirty this morning and about the same time two nights ago. I thought maybe you'd have heard something.'

'Oh, I see. No, I'm sorry, I can't really help. I'm a heavy sleeper. There are a lot of foxes around here, though. They have a cry that can sometimes sound like a woman screaming.'

'That was our first thought but the caller was adamant that it sounded human.'

'Maybe kids, then.' I jerked a thumb behind me.

'They always seem to be having parties in that house backing onto my garden. There's normally loads of shouting and screaming. I don't remember there being one last night, though.'

The policewoman shrugged. 'That's a possibility. I'm planning to talk to all the residents in the vicinity.'

'So has anybody been reported missing?'

'No, that's why they sent me.'

'Okay. Good luck. I hope you find a *cleu*.'

This time, she got it. 'Let me guess, the incompetent inspector.'

'That's right. I'd offer you a glass of Christmas cheer but I suppose you're not allowed to drink on the job.'

'Thank you, I'd love to but I can't until I knock off this evening. Have a good day, sir.'

'You too. Merry Christmas,' I replied as I closed the door.

***

The smell of roast turkey permeated my small bungalow. I glanced at my watch. They would be here any minute. My sister, brother-in-law and their two boys were making the short trek from the other side of town. Despite my successful career, I had remained in the house where I was born just over forty years earlier. My sister, who is three years younger than me, had also stayed in the area to help look after our ailing parents. Now they were both gone and it had become a tradition for the remainder of the family to get together on Christmas Day.

The doorbell signalled their arrival. I opened the front door and the whirlwind comprising my two nephews swept into the house.

'Uncle Dave, look what I got for Christmas!' the first boy shouted as he rushed past holding up a blue model aeroplane. 'It flies too.' Jake was ten years old and a bundle of nervous energy.

His twin brother, Ben, was more restrained. 'I got one too,' he said, proudly displaying a red plane. It was a never-ending conundrum for my sister and her husband to treat their twins equally yet make them feel like individuals. 'Can we fly them later?' Ben asked eagerly. 'Dad said you'd help us.'

I smiled. 'Of course, once we've had Christmas dinner. We'll need the fresh air after all that turkey.'

My sister appeared in the doorway and enveloped me in a hug. 'Merry Christmas, David. I hope you've got lots of energy because the boys are even more excited than usual this year.'

'Hi, Helen. I'm sure I'll survive. I only get them in short bursts. You have this all the time.'

She laughed. 'They do sleep occasionally.'

She was followed in by her husband, Steve, a bottle of wine grasped in each hand. Condensation had already begun to form on the glass in the warm atmosphere of the hallway. 'I'd shake your hand, Dave, but I'd have to let go of one of these first.'

'Thanks, Steve. I'll take them off you and put them in the fridge if I can find any room. Make yourselves at home in the lounge. We'll be eating in about twenty minutes. Can I get you a drink?'

Both my sister and brother-in-law requested wine.

In the kitchen, I rummaged in the drawer for the corkscrew. I filled three glasses then replaced the cork in the opened bottle. Knowing there was no space in the small fridge but plenty in the fridge-freezer now that Angela had been removed, I carried the two bottles into the utility room.

I placed the bottles in the fridge door. 'They're not for you, ladies, so leave them alone please.'

'Who are you talking to?' a voice asked from behind me.

I turned to face Helen. 'Oh, you know, just talking to myself, making sure I've got everything ready.'

'I'm sure you have it all under control. Is there anything I can do to help?'

'No, everything's fine. Let's go through to the lounge.'

***

The meal went smoothly and Angela was every bit as succulent as I'd hoped she would be. My stomach was so full it wouldn't take another mouthful and we hadn't yet started on the mince pies.

'When can we fly the planes, Uncle David?' Jake asked, once we were back in the lounge.

'Let's give it a few minutes for the food to settle,' I replied.

'Have you got any batteries?' Ben said.

'Um... what type?'

'It's okay,' Helen said. 'They recharge from the mains. I've got the chargers in my bag. Let's get the washing up done before we think about flying any planes.'

'How long does it take to charge them up?' I asked.

'Twenty minutes or so. If we plug them in now they'll be ready by the time we've washed the dishes.'

The two boys groaned. They had reached an age where they had to help with household chores to earn their pocket money.

'It won't take long if we all do it,' Steve said.

Jake perked up as another thought occurred to him. 'Hey, Uncle David, can we see the ladies?'

I glanced across to my sister who gave a slight frown of displeasure.

'If your mother says it's alright,' I replied, turning

back to my nephew.

'Go on, Mum,' the boys chorused in unison.

'I suppose so,' she said. 'Let's just hope they don't give you too many nightmares, though.'

'Please, Uncle David, can we see them?' Ben asked eagerly.

'Come on then,' I said.

The two brothers leapt to their feet.

'I'll make a start on the washing up,' Helen said as all five of us trooped into the kitchen. She made a beeline to the sink as I drew out chairs for the rest of us.

'No touching, though,' I said, wagging a finger at the twins.

'We won't, we won't,' Jake replied.

'Wait here.' I headed into the utility room and pulled open the fridge-freezer door. 'Hello ladies, my nephews want to say hi.' I carefully removed the three packages and transported them back to the table. I gently placed them on the surface. The boys immediately crowded round.

'I call this one Xenia,' I said, unwrapping the silver foil to expose a severed hand with brightly painted fingernails.

'Ew, gross,' Ben said.

Steve leant forwards and studied the limb. 'You can see all the tendons and everything.'

My sister turned round from the sink and shook her head in disapproval.

'This is Yvonne,' I said, holding up the jam jar containing the severed ear.

'Can I hold her?' Jake asked.

'Um, okay, but be careful. Don't drop her.'

'Is that a real pearl?' Steve asked.

'Yes. Nothing but the best for my ladies.'

'I can see some earwax," Ben exclaimed.

'And finally, Zoe.' I peeled back the layers of cling-film to reveal the foot with the red toenails.

Steve leant in again. 'Incredible, so lifelike.'

'Surely you mean death-like.'

Steve laughed nervously. 'I guess.'

'Can I touch her, Uncle David?' Jake asked.

I hesitated for a second. 'Okay, but gently, and just one finger.'

He reached forward and tentatively placed a forefinger on the big toe. No sooner had he made contact than he whipped his hand away. 'Ugh. She feels all cold.'

'She has been in the fridge for a few days,' I said. 'So what do you think of them?'

'They're certainly gruesome,' Steve said. 'Which film are they for?'

'*Night of the Zombie Apocalypse*. They start filming the week after next.'

'So why do you keep them in the fridge?'

'If I didn't, they'd decompose.'

An uneasy smile flashed across Steve's face.

'I'm joking. They're made of a special rubber that has to be cooled down to cure properly. They need to spend two or three days in a cool environment before they're strong enough to be handled.'

'Do you know what scenes they're going to be used in?'

'Ones where the victims lose bits of their bodies I should imagine. The special effects people just tell me what they're after and I make what they ask for.'

"He's always had a fascination with gruesome things,' Helen said over her shoulder. 'As a boy he used to stuff dead animals.'

'Why do you bring them home, though?'

'I can work on them at night. I prefer it here to the office.'

'Can we see the film when it's made, Uncle David?' Ben asked.

'I think you'll have to wait until you're a bit older," I replied. 'I'm fairly sure it's going to be an eighteen.'

'They're amazing,' Steve said. 'How do you do it?'

'You don't expect me to tell you all my secrets, do you? Basically, they're made from a mould and then painted.'

I explained some more of the process. Of course, I didn't reveal to him how I managed to make my moulds look quite so realistic.

BY THE WATER

Betsy Reavley

I stood in the river letting the freezing cold-water trickle over my feet. My toes were like ice cubes in a drink. They felt as if they were melting into the water. The blood ran slowly down my face, collecting with the dribble that hung from my mouth in a red stream, dangling from my chin.

This was not where I was supposed to be.

I don't know why I came to the river. Perhaps I wanted to be clean again. The noise from the water was deafening, as it tumbled over rocks and made its way back to the sea. Here everything felt so simple. It wasn't real. None of it was real. It hadn't happened.

I almost don't remember stabbing her. Or any of them. What led to that is still a blur. I just remember holding on to the knife and seeing it in her stomach as the blood turned her white jumper a beautiful crimson.

The others just stood watching. No one said anything. It was nearly normal but then when I looked her in eye and saw the hurt and the shock I realised what I'd done. But she is me. And as I stand, blood dripping from my face and the wound in my stomach, I wonder which one of us I am.

I hate the silence but here the rushing water plays like music and I feel the need to dance. But that would be odd, wouldn't it? Dancing in the river covered in blood.

That wasn't how the day begun, although I knew, when I looked in the mirror at the familiar face staring back at me, something was different.

I wondered, at that moment, if I ever really existed. Maybe I was a fabrication of my own mind. A character that never was, but one that came to life after a storm – Biblical, almost, but lacking god.

Standing, tremoring in front of the mirror, I got

dressed, because that's what people do. Then, wearing the strange clothes that I knew belonged to me but that I'd never seen before, I made my way downstairs towards the smell of brown toast and bacon.

I wouldn't eat that day. I couldn't.

When I stepped into the kitchen, absorbing the feel of the large cold flagstones on my feet, the panic set in. Every sentence in my head was there already like a script and before each question came, the answer was ready and waiting.

If you'd shaken me at the time and said this isn't real, I would have understood. Like a strange screenplay I took on a character – the one who spoke too much, who swore too much, who said things to shock. The mask was there to hide behind. But the more I embraced it, the more I lost sight of where it all began.

In years to come I would look back at press cuttings and wonder if I was really there. The House of Blood, they called it. Like something gothic and fantastical.

***

When we met she was so unlike what I was used to. She was tiny, blonde, curvaceous and friendly. The role she adopted was to please, even though I got the impression that, underneath it all, she knew her own mind better than most.

She reminded me of a can of Coke. Full of fizz and promise but if treated badly, might explode in your face.

No one was issue-free, but she seemed to own her past, whatever it was, and wore it like a badge of honour. I admired that. Butter wouldn't melt, or would it?

Then there were the others. The strange experiment was only just beginning. The star was maybe my favourite. She was glamorous and intelligent and had just enough about her that was fucked up to make her endearing. I always felt like a patient on her couch, but I think that said more about me than it did her. She had an air of authority that worked both for and against her. I wanted to dislike her but I couldn't.

Then there were the other two. The girl who was about to marry a feeder and the woman who would never be really happy. The way that some fat people sweat, she had this sheen on her skin which sat there, almost invisible, and warned you not to press her too hard. She wasn't dangerous, or even close to it, but she was delicate in a way that made you want to cry. Her clear rules about personal space left me all off kilter. In this place I didn't know anything.

I don't want to skim over these other characters because they are as important as the rest, I just didn't realise that quickly enough. In my head, time and time again, I'd tell myself to stop talking, to breathe, to listen. And I really wanted to, but my nerves got the better of me and that led to a spiral of verbal nonsense. I'd always figured that in order to make friends you had to share. It turns out that sometimes, keeping your mouth shut works better.

So it went on like that until lunchtime. Then everything changed.

When I entered the kitchen I looked at the walls and questioned if they had always been that deep moss green. Had I not noticed before or had something changed?

In a pan on the hob a cheese omelette bubbled away.

'Want a cuppa?' She stirred her milky tea trying to disguise the fact she was disappointed I'd entered the room.

'No thank you.' I'm more a coffee kind of girl and the answer was formulated long before the question was asked.

Sitting down at the kitchen table, wishing I were brave enough to rearrange the fruit bowl like I wanted to, we sat in silence while she slurped and chewed. My stomach rumbled and food envy kicked in but I didn't feel comfortable eating. Still my hands tremored and the journey the egg would have taken on the fork, from the plate to my mouth, would have been problematic. It still seemed like a disjoined dream and I wondered how we all ended up here.

As I tried not to stare at her plate of food, music filled the room. Bill Withers' rich voice bounced off the old walls echoing in the large square sink before disappearing down the plughole. She didn't bat an eye as I undertook a visual search of the room.

Just the two of us… I could still hear the chorus ringing in my ears.

Trying not to fixate on the coffee ring on the table I started to hum the tune. When I sang it, then it became real.

Through a mouthful of egg and yellowing teeth she glared at me.

'You don't like me, do you?'

She put her fork down and sat back.

'Do you want me to be honest?'

'I doubt it, but please go ahead.'

'You are strange.' She dabbed her mouth with a crumpled napkin. 'People like us, pet, we aren't meant to co-exist. One of us will always be on top, one on the bottom and a lucky few sit in the middle. I don't suppose you like me much either but I interest you, don't I?'

It was true, she did. Skimming over the fact she hadn't denied her dislike for me, I wondered whether it mattered.

'You're a bit needy. I mean, best will in the world, you're sitting here, with a virtual stranger, asking me if I like you.'

'No, I don't like that. Not one little bit, pet.'

'Fine,' I wriggled in my seat realising how quickly the situation was moving away from my comfort zone. 'How's work then?'

'Why do you ask me that?' I noticed a small piece of grated cheese remained stuck to the corner of her mouth. It put me at ease, making me feel more confident again.

My grip on what was happening then melted away and I couldn't remember my line. I'd been so certain, up to this point, that I knew my words but suddenly I didn't and I was lost, wishing I was somewhere else. Anywhere but here.

The others came into the kitchen at various stages in the day, like chess pieces positioning themselves, until at last all the main players were there.

Between then and getting to the point where I was holding the knife, I don't know what happened. A pressure had been building all day and the next thing I know, I'm holding onto the handle of a large serrated blade wedged deep into human flesh.

They all lay on the floor in a puddle of blood that stretched from wall to wall. I killed them one at a time, the knife cutting through their skin like butter. None of them fought me. They accepted their deaths with a quiet welcome.

Standing over the bodies slumped in different positions, their wounds open and bleeding, I watch the sunlight pour in through the window making the blood shimmer like liquid silver.

Then time shifts, again, and I am standing in the river watching the stream of blood trickle from my sagging stomach into the rumbling water. I start to panic just before I hear a soothing voice travel over the hills.

'Now, Christine, you are back in your safe place. Feel the cool water around your feet. Look up at the blue sky and start to count back from ten.'

Ten.

'Your body starts to feel light.'

Nine.

'The bird song is more distant now.'
Eight.
'You can feel the sun on your skin.'
Seven.
'The rhythm of each breath is calming.'
Six.
'Nothing can hurt you now.'
Five.
'This is a safe place.'
Four.
'Your eyes are getting ready to open.'
Three.
'You can feel yourself floating away from that place.'
Two.
'And on the count of one, you will open your eyes.'
One.

'Christine. It's fine, just breathe, it went really well.' The woman sitting opposite me, with her crisp white Marks and Spencer shirt and her boring little glasses perched on the end of her nose, gives me a caffeine-induced smile.

'I don't understand,' my fat hands start flapping. They look like sausages in hot pan. 'Where have they all gone? Where am I?'

'Do you remember, Christine, we came here so that you could say goodbye.'

What the fuck is this woman talking about?

A man, who I didn't notice, leans against the magnolia wall and shakes his head before leaving the room.

Last time I checked I was standing in a river; now I am sitting on a chair in a small, bland room. None of it makes sense.

'I can see you are beginning to look distressed.' Her coffee breath and M&S demeanour start to frighten me, 'but it's fine. Just remember what we talked about.'

'What about the river of blood?' The sound of my voice rings in my ears, the bass deafening.

'Do you want to go back to the beginning and start again?' Her attempt to contain her displeasure fails.

'What beginning?'

'OK. So please explain to me, again, what is wrong with the place you are in?'

'I don't know. Too many windows, light and air all around but it feels more as if I am trapped inside a bubble.'

'And which one of the ladies is keeping you there?'

'All of them, except I know that they don't want me there. Not really.'

Her aging lips, which remind me of dead slugs, suck the plastic lid of the pen leaving a trail of white, sticky saliva.

It reminds me of the cuckoo spit I would look for on plants when I was little.

Wiping my own mouth, I am conscious that paranoia is setting in.

She removes the glasses, folds them and put them back into their case.

'It hasn't worked. Don't worry. We'll try again tomorrow.'

Two men, wearing pale green uniforms, step into the room, as she disappears through the door.

'Time to go back now, love.' The width of his shoulders is inhuman and the longer I look at him the more I am convinced he is actually a bull. 'When you get there,' he continues in his droll northern accent, 'you'll be much better for it. 'Might take some time, but it'll all be worth it.'

As I begin to inspect the beefcake, thick, black hairy legs, appear on his shoulder, tapping their way into existence. I watch one stray leg stroke his earlobe.

'What's she looking at?' The Silent One has found a

voice.

'Buggered if I know.' The Bull wipes his nose with the back of his hand. 'Tomorrow she's got more therapy so we'll have our fun with her then.'

'Don't you think they have a smell about them, after they've been fried?' says The Silent One.

I really have lost the thread of conversation but I am more scared now than ever before.

'Yeah. She's gonna be fried for sure. The regression shit don't work. Don't know why the doc continues with it.'

As we arrive at a door at the end of a long corridor The Silent One opens it and The Bull ushers me in. There is a bed in the room and a desk with a chair. The room has one small window, which has bars, preventing my escape, on the outside.

'I don't understand. Please, can you just tell me what is going on.'

The Bull chuckles.

'Mad as a box of frogs, this one.' He nudges The Silent One who looks at me with pity.

'I'm not going in there. Please, just tell me where I am.' My hands start to quiver again, like they did in that place; the house by the river.

'Just get in there.' The Bull flares his nostrils.

'No. I want to speak to someone.'

'I'll get the doctor to come and have a word, okay?' The Silent One seems kinder. 'But you have to go back into your room.'

Looking down the long corridor I make the instant decision to run and before either of the men know what has happened I am tearing along the corridor, my white nightdress flapping against my legs.

I hear the sound of their footsteps closing in and seeing an open door charge into the room looking for an exit.

'Christine?' The man, who shook his head when I came to, in the room with that woman, stands up from behind a desk.

Panting and sweating, I slam the door, shutting us in the room alone together and prop a chair against the handle.

'Christine, it's okay. It's me. Dr Law, remember?' I can see the concern written on his face. 'What's the matter?'

'They wanted to lock me in a room.' My voice sounds foreign to my ears.

'You need some rest. No one is here to cause you any harm. We are trying to help you get better.'

I hear the sound of fists banging on the other side of the door and start to move backwards feeling trapped between The Bull on one side and the terrifying doctor on the other.

'Don't come any closer!' My back against the wall, I wave my hands about.

'Todd, Rick, it's fine. I've got this under control,' the doctor calls out as a sickening smile spreads across his face.

I start to wonder if I was safer before I entered this room.

'Yes, boss,' the Bull calls out, his voice fading into the distance.

'Sit down, Christine, please.' The doctor returns to his seat behind his desk and beckons with his hand at the chair I propped against the door. 'You are quite safe. Let's have a talk.'

I don't know if I can trust this lunatic. I decide I don't have a choice so pull the chair away from the door and sit tentatively on it.

'Are you aware of the other four women?' He picks up a glass of water and takes a small sip.

'The women at the house?'

'Yes. Those women.' He removes a pen from the pocket in his shirt and clicks the biro before jotting down something on a notepad. 'You are here as my guest. You are a very special guest.' That maniacal smile returns to his lips. 'You are suffering from Dissociative Personality Disorder. Your case is the most extreme I have ever come across in my career. After discussing the severity of your illness with fellows in my profession it was decided that I would conduct an experiment by which you would be put into a deep state of hypnosis, so that we could then eradicate the other personalities.' He sits back in his chair still holding the pen. 'The idea behind this new therapy was that through hypnosis you would be introduced to the other personalities living inside you. Then, at our suggestion, you would kill each one in turn. Upon coming out of the hypnotic state we hoped that this would cure you of the disorder. For the last three weeks we have been taking you through this process on a daily basis. Each time, you arrive at the house, meet the other personalities and in turn, kill each one. However, so far, this has not translated into results after you have been returned from your hypnotic state.'

'You are mad.' The word comes out of me in a whisper.

'No, Christine. I'm afraid you are the one suffering from delusions. What we did not anticipate was that you would lose the ability to tell the difference between the real world and the world that we created in order for you to face the other personalities. It seems,' he sighs, 'we have failed. That leaves us with only one option.'

Sweat gathers around my hairline and begins its slow journey down my forehead.

'Electroconvulsive therapy will begin tomorrow.'

Before I have a moment to react The Bull and The Quiet One come bursting through the door.

I fall off my chair and, edging away from them on the floor, both men stand over me like giants casting their shadows over the world.

'Bedtime,' the Bull says brandishing a syringe while The Quiet One pins me to the floor, the burden of his body on my chest.

***

I'm sitting in a large armchair watching the particles of dust dance in the low autumn light. Unable to move, my arms and legs feel heavy and my head lolls to one side, cocked slightly unable to bear its own weight.

From a distant corner of the room a television set blares, making my ears ache.

What is this place?

An elderly man, with urine-soaked pyjamas, stumbles past pulling at the white hair on his head repeating the same word over and over: 'Rubble, rubble, rubble.'

When he has shuffled off out of the room I am able to focus on what the newsreader is saying.

'An experiment on a woman suffering from mental health problems, known as Patient C, was conducted by Dr Karl Law in the confines of his home earlier this year. The inquiry carried out by the local authority concluded that Patient C was the victim of cruel and systematic abuse at the hands of the renegade consultant. After weeks of unauthorised psychological experiments were conducted the woman, referred to by authorities as Patient C, turned on the four members of the facility and killed them. The crime scene, now referred to as The House of Blood, was discovered a week later when a postman arrived at Dr Law's remote country house with a delivery of what is now known to be psychedelic narcotics, which the doctor had been using on Patient C. After discovering Patient C standing in the river, at the bottom of the grounds of Dr Law's property, the postman called the emergency services. Police made the grim discovery of the four bodies in the house and health professionals confirmed that Patient C also had injuries.'

I crane my neck round to try and get a better look at the TV.

Are they talking about me?

'As the inquiry into one of the most bizarre and tragic cases in recent years comes to an end, one question remains unanswered – whatever happened to Patient C?'

As drool rolls from the corner of my mouth and down my chin she appears in front of me again. Full of fizz, just as I remember her.

'Hello, pet. I've come to keep you company.' She sits down heavily, pulling her chair closer to mine, pulling up her sagging beige tights and adjusting her nurse's uniform.

'That's better.' She smoothes the creases on the blue cotton and the smell of bleach that seeps from her skin, begins to tickle my nose.

I want to get up and run again but I can't and when I try to scream no sound comes out.

'Why, you're as white as a sheet.' She reaches out a fat hand and rests her clammy palm on my forehead. 'What's the matter?' Her dead eyes seem to look right through me.

I try to wriggle away from her in my seat but a static haze hangs over my body keeping me locked in one position.

'Now, now pet.' She smiles through her yellow teeth, 'You didn't think you were going to get away from me that easily…'

A CUP OF COLD COFFEE AND A SLICE OF LIFE

Tony R. Cox

Ash was not stupid; he knew that a degree, any degree, would help him get a decent job and stop his parents, especially his dad, constantly whinging about how hard he worked at the factory and how little his son seemed to be doing. That was why Ash was now sitting in a coffee shop in the centre of the West Midlands city where he'd been a student at the university for nearly a year and a half.

He looked down at the bright, colourful face of the phone in his hand and decided that, while he wasn't that bothered about the tall, milky concoction in front of him, he'd use the time for a bit of research: that essay on eighteenth century canal building was not going to write itself.

He stared at the ceiling. It was always like this when he wanted to concentrate: his mind drifted away. This time it was his twin sisters, both of whom were the apple of their dad's eye. They were destined for far brighter futures than Ash was as a prospective civil engineer. The money would be OK if he got a job with one of the contractors, but Paramita and Sadhika were different. They weren't just bright, they were stunningly beautiful and brilliant, or maybe that was just a doting brother's infatuation. They were in their last year of school before going to Durham University, one of the top law schools in the country. Sadhika would probably end up as a Labour politician, she vehemently believed in a fairer society and she'd probably become prime minister. Paramita was a top judge in the making; her measured, thoughtful approach was only thrown out of kilter when the pair of them hit the dance floor.

The phone bounced in his hand. Thankfully he'd put it on silent. It was a five-a-side mate reminding him about that evening. It meant nothing, but it shocked him out of his reverie. Ash shook himself. The iPad didn't rule his life, but right now he needed to delve into the history of James

Brindley.

Sitting just down from him were two old women. They looked a bit like the two on that Les Dawson programme his mum had watched, but they were better dressed and, considering their ages, more attractive. They weren't fat, but then they weren't thin like so many of the girls his age, and they had pronounced, heavy breasts. *Chunky*, he thought: that'd be about the right word, but perhaps they wouldn't like that.

The one closest to him was wearing a blue top with white collar and cuffs at the end of the long sleeves, and the other wore a rustic, reddish-brown jacket over a cream blouse. With their legs under the table, Ash couldn't see if they were wearing trousers or skirts, but he thought it would more likely be skirts. They didn't look like the trousers type: that would be too modern or not stylish enough for a trip to town. Posh might be a better description.

Ash smiled. Like so many people, the women had commandeered the table and placed their coats and bags on the chairs opposite. Nobody was going to sit there and intrude on their space.

He blushed. It was the size of their chests that had made him think of the TV comedy duo, and he shouldn't have thoughts like that. He shook his head and turned away. He tapped at the small screen, comfortable in a technological world that now included the biography of one of the UK's greatest canal builders.

***

Gladys and Brenda were also smiling, oblivious to the scruffy young man. Gladys took a glossy white card from a little stack she had in her other hand and held it up. The women giggled. Their heads, bearing recently coiffed, bouffant styles that made their hair look like rounded, painted wigs, touched.

Brenda took the small photograph, held it away from her then brought it towards her face, lifting her glasses to allow her eyes a natural focus. She giggled, whispered something, then placed it on top of a much smaller stack. Gladys passed her another.

'Ooh. I remember that day. It was ever so hot in Colwyn Bay, wasn't it?' Brenda said, and her shoulders shook in a silent laugh: silent, because you never laughed out loud in a café like this; you never knew who might be listening.

Gladys nodded and looked at the photograph in Brenda's fingers. It was a beach scene with two young girls in ill-fitting one-piece swimming costumes. They were sitting on a dark, old wooden groyne that loomed out of the sand at a low angle, like the ribs of a long-sunken galleon. To their left, about three yards away, was a skinny young boy in swimming shorts. He was sitting on the sand between the long legs of a tall, well-built man who was posing like a circus strongman, his biceps forming distinct camel-like humps either side of a round, handsome face with a broad smile and sparkling eyes. In the distance there was a brown-creamy horizon of muddy sand and the flecks of white-topped shallow waves.

'That was before we had proper bodies, wasn't it?' Gladys said and pointed at one of the two girls.

'Yes. We had flat chests then, but not for long.'

Brenda looked at her friend. Their eyes met. Their smiles broadened and their expressions showed a deep affection; the sort of love that comes of being comfortable in each other's presence. Gladys and Brenda had been like this for nearly fifty years: theirs was an indefinable love, a friendship way past anything sexual or affectionate. It was a love based on sharing of thoughts, memories, expressions. It was a love that blended them together and had manifested itself by making both physically more attractive together than they were as individuals.

'It was good of your dad to take me with you on your holidays,' Brenda said.

'Don't be daft. That was only a day out. The proper holidays came later.'

'Yes, but that's where it all began, isn't it?' Brenda replied and took hold of Gladys's arm and stroked it. 'We've been best friends for a long time now, haven't we?' she added, rhetorically.

The cafe was filling up, but Gladys and Brenda were in their own world, oblivious to their surroundings. They'd been going there at precisely ten o'clock every Tuesday for the last two years, ever since the big department store with the waitress service café had closed.

If they'd looked up, they'd have seen in the café, in microcosm, almost the entire life of a modern city that had once had a proud engineering and manufacturing heritage and was now dominated by students and office workers. The customers ranged from scruffy young men and women, probably just teenagers or in their early twenties, to a few men in suits, and pinched-faced women in groups – young mothers, obviously, whose kids were at school. The lights in the ceiling were bright and their rays joined the murky daylight from the floor to ceiling windows, but almost everybody seemed to have their own extra and personal little square of electric light pressed almost to their noses, even those chatting with apparent friends. Some were tapping away like human woodpeckers on the bright screen in their hands.

Gladys glanced up briefly. She'd seen all this technology; it meant nothing to her. It was just transient, pointless ephemera that lasted for a split second and then disappeared forever, to be replaced with another fleeting image or perhaps a tuneless two notes and then blankness. Nobody used them for anything worthwhile in her opinion – people just didn't talk to each other like they used to. The world wasn't a friendly place anymore.

'They use those to look at porn, you know,' she said, and her nose turned up. She nodded solemnly to Brenda, a look that confirmed absolute verity and finality. Brenda shuffled slightly; the word Gladys had used unsettling her.

'Let's have another look at those photos. You say you found them in a case under your dad's old bed? He must've forgotten them after we'd managed to get him into that care home,' Brenda said, and picked up the pile. She slowly studied each one again then passed them individually to Gladys.

'Dad looks great. He's so proud of his son. Look there, he's pretending to be a muscle man with little Robert posing next to him.' Gladys stubbed her finger on the photograph with the fading colours.

'How many years ago is it?' Brenda asked and, taking the photograph, moved it closer to her face.

'Robert would have been about eight, so that means we'll have been about ten. It's sad really. That'll be the last photo taken of Robert before he drowned. With Mum gone so long and now Dad dead, it's just the two of us left.'

The two stared at the photograph and silence descended in a mist, like the steam that drifted across the top of the distant coffee machines. It was a momentary lapse that dissipated quickly and was gone. Brenda put the photograph back on the pile and took a sip of the milky coffee in front of her. It had gone cold so she put it down again.

'Did you ever tell Dad?' Gladys asked.

'No. I couldn't think of a reason why I should. He looked peaceful in that bed, just staring up at the ceiling. Did you tell him? Did you tell him you knew about us?'

Gladys dropped her head, showing off the tight curls of her immoveable helmet of blue-rinsed hair. When she slowly looked up she was smiling, almost sheepishly. It was as if she was half-heartedly fighting the grin, but couldn't stop it from spreading across her face. 'No. Why would I want to spoil our fun? Why tell him that his good-as-gold life was built around two smart, clever girls; one a daughter, the other her best ever friend?'

Brenda nodded and patted Gladys's hand. Gladys went on. 'Dad loved him so much, much more than he loved me, and then he trod on your dolls. Do you remember him laughing?'

Brenda's eyes sparkled. 'Nasty little boy. We were a much better family without him. Your dad could carry on talking to him in his silly church every day. It was as if little Robert was still alive.'

'Yes, but you did help him get over it, didn't you?' Gladys looked at Brenda and their hands flew to their faces to stop the loud laughs.

'I had to learn about the birds and the bees sometime and you did suggest getting your dad to help. That was clever of you. He was just a man, and they all think with their willies.' Brenda cast her eyes down, knowing that Gladys would disapprove of the word she'd just used, even if it had been almost whispered.

Brenda glanced at her friend to see if she'd been upset, but Gladys was still smiling, still thinking of the good times they'd had.

'Once he'd taken my virginity away, we'd got him, hadn't we?' Brenda went on. 'There was no way we could allow him to marry someone else or have another girlfriend: I'd have had to tell them the truth, wouldn't I? And it worked out ever so well financially.'

Gladys took hold of her friend's arm and stroked it.

'That was very good of you, you know. He didn't want to have sex with you, but he couldn't stop himself. I knew about these urges that men get, so I just thought it best if they could be channelled. If you were able to satisfy them, then we could keep it in the family – you were nearly family by then. You did ever such a good job.'

The two women looked at each other, nodded and pushed their half-empty coffees across the table. They stood up. Almost in unison they patted their bouffant hair, picked up their bags and coats from the chairs and walked out, proud and erect.

***

Aadarsh, sweating and shaking, looked at the bright screen of his phone. A slow flashing red light showed that it had been on record. His eyes moved to a small, oblong, shiny thin card on the seat where the two women had been sitting.

He reached across, picked it up and turned it over. Two young girls, one blonde, the other a brunette, were smiling wildly. To their left was a tall posing man standing over a young boy. The man's face was suffused with pride and pleasure, the boy's expression a picture of happiness.

In the foreground, clothes were scattered as if discarded in a hurry. They included a man's heavy tweed trousers, dark jacket, plain, dark short-sleeved shirt and, on top, a bright, white clerical collar.

Ash slipped the photograph into his pocket as he stood up. He had just one thought. *Who took the photograph?*

SLOW ROAST PORK

S.E. Lynes

I cooked my husband's favourite for dinner last month: slow roast pork. When I told him I was making it, his face lit up.

But when he wasn't home by ten, I took it out of the oven so it wouldn't spoil. By midnight he still wasn't back so I called the police.

'Don't worry,' said the officer. 'He's probably in the pub.'

'Even if he is,' I said, 'he's always back by half eleven.'

He said to leave it twenty-four hours, which I did. But by six the following evening, Pete still hadn't turned up. I called again and they sent a young man and woman to interview me in the back kitchen. They must have got here around eight. I'd put the roast back in the oven on a low temperature sometime in the late afternoon to make sure it heated right through. It hadn't spoilt. If anything it smelled even better than the day before so when the bobbies got here I asked if they were hungry.

'Ah, no, ma'am,' said the chap. 'That's very kind but we're not allowed to eat on duty.'

'Only, I can't reheat it again,' I said. 'It'll go to waste if you don't have some. And who am I going to tell?'

'I suppose I could have a bit,' said the chap. 'I'm starving.'

You should have seen them – like they'd not eaten for weeks. I liked watching them sitting round the table, tucking in. I like it when people enjoy the food I make.

'This is delicious,' the woman said, sandy-haired lass, clean-looking, lovely pink fingernails. 'Is it Delia?'

'I don't know,' I said. 'Might have been. Or Peppa.'

They laughed but I didn't because by then I was getting very worried.

When they'd finished eating, the man got out his notepad while the woman asked me when was the last time I'd seen my husband. The previous morning, I told them.

'Is that your husband's car on the drive?' she asked.

'Yes,' I said. 'But he didn't take it yesterday.'

'Did he mention he might be late coming home?'

'He said he was going for a couple of pints with the lads after work but...'

The two of them exchanged a look. They thought I was making a fuss, I could tell.

'Does he often go to the pub on the way home?' The chap asked, pencil poised, keen as mustard. He had a bald spot the size of a two-pound coin on the back of his head. It was the colour of Spam.

'The Black Boar, he goes to,' I said, clearing their plates for them and loading them into the dishwasher. Pete liked the plates cleared straight away so I suppose I was in the habit.

They asked if Pete went out a lot.

'Yes,' I said. 'I suppose he does. He's a very sociable fellow, is my Peter. You ask anyone. But if you're asking if he stays out all night, then no, he doesn't do that.'

They took down the name of the pub, along with a description of him, where he worked, that sort of thing. I even gave them a photo, taken last year at our niece's wedding.

'His face is a bit ruddy on this one,' I said. 'He'd had a few drinks. But it's the only recent picture I've got.'

They thanked me for the information and the dinner and stood up to go.

'We'll be in touch,' the woman said, with a smile that was meant to be kind but which made me feel even more worried.

On the way out, the chap asked me about my eye.

'That's a nasty bruise,' he said.

'You'll never believe it,' I said. 'I've got one of those chest freezers, you know? My parents had one, back in the day. Always bought a whole cow or a pig to cut up and freeze. It's a lot cheaper to buy meat that way so that's what I always do. Anyway, so I was freezing the pig carcass and whack! The freezer door only bounced up and hit me right in the eye, didn't it?'

They were still laughing when I waved them off. As I closed the door, I wondered if it looked bad, me making light like that, what with Peter missing, but I couldn't help it. It was the stress, I think, making me a bit hyper.

I went into the lounge but I didn't say anything to the twins except that their dad had gone away for work. I always told them that when Pete didn't come home so they were not fussed . They were on the Xbox, trying to get to level five, so I told them to knock it on the head and get to bed.

'Even teenagers need sleep,' I said, switching off the telly. 'Come on, chop chop.'

I was still antsy, so I took a couple of recipe books up with me and that helped me relax. I often settle myself by making a meal plan for the week, so that's what I did, it being Monday. As I said, I love cooking. I slept all right, better than I'd thought.

The next day Pete still hadn't turned up. A policeman called the house to see if I'd heard anything and I told him no, I hadn't.

'I'm afraid Mr Percival didn't go into work yesterday or the day before,' he said. 'And he hasn't been in today either.' His words made me go hot then cold. 'We'll give it another twenty-four hours and then you'll have to come in and make a proper statement.'

I said okay but inside I was in pieces.

I made the twins' packed lunches for college – the leftover pork sandwiches, an apple each and a granola bar. They went for the bus and I went into town to get some groceries.

I was in the supermarket, keeping busy, keeping it together, when I thought I saw Peter over in the booze aisle looking at the cider. I nearly had a heart attack. Once, he'd caught me looking at him in that exact same place and, boy, did I pay for it when he got in. He said I'd been spying on him. I hadn't meant to; I'd just seen him there and the sight of him had stopped me in my tracks, that's all.

Anyway, the man turned around and I saw it wasn't him and my heart slowed down a bit. Still, I picked up some Zantac and took a couple in the car.

We had meatballs in tomato sauce with spaghetti for tea. The twins didn't even ask about their dad so I said nothing. Afterwards, they went up to do their homework and I had a little glass of wine and a ciggie in the back garden. The Cabernet-Shiraz had been on offer in the supermarket so I'd picked up a bottle. I thought if Pete wasn't going to bother turning up, I may as well have a drink – and I wouldn't even have to hide the bottle. The wine was lovely, warm down into my chest. I was still a bit stiff and a drink and a cigarette helped loosen me up a bit.

The next day I had to go and give a statement. Cooking relaxes me so before I went I made some shortbread, an enormous batch of sausage rolls, a pan of soup and I even managed to prepare a joint to put in the oven later. I took the sausage rolls up to the station in my big Tupperware. They went down a storm.

That afternoon, two more coppers came over to interview me again. I have to say, I hadn't had this many visitors in years and I enjoyed fussing them like I used to fuss my friends a long time ago now. These two were both about thirty or so, a man and a woman again. He had brown hair and metal glasses and the woman was very pretty, with dark skin and long black hair. The man had some soup and a pork and apple sauce sarnie but the woman said no she didn't want anything as she was Muslim. I had a joke with the man, asked if anyone ever fed him at home – he was fair wolfing it down.

'Is it all right if we take a look upstairs?' the woman asked.

'The bedroom's a bit of a pigsty,' I said. I'd taken my eye off the ball these last few days. The reasons were obvious but I was cursing myself all the same.

Under the bed they found an almost empty whisky bottle and two empty gin and tonic cans . The policeman held them up and raised his eyebrows.

'What do you want me to say about that?' I asked them. 'It is what it is. I told your colleagues the other day. Peter likes a drink. He's a very sociable man.'

They put the bottles and the cans into a clear plastic bag to take away with them. I didn't know what they thought they'd find. Pete's fingerprints – so what? They could find those on my neck if they bothered to look.

At the front door the man asked how I'd got the bruise on my left eye and this time I had my answer ready.

'Bumped it smack on the chest freezer,' I said. 'Bent forward just as the lid came up. Bang.'

My mum and dad came over for dinner. We had a roast with some oven-ready potatoes, veg, some apple sauce and some Bisto gravy. I love a midweek roast. It's the best comfort food there is and by then I was in need of some comfort.

'Bisto, eh,' said my mum. 'Pete would've gone mad.' She pulled a funny face, trying to cheer me up. My parents weren't making too much of Peter's absence. He did a bunk from time to time, once went AWOL for a week. They knew I didn't like to talk about it, that I found it humiliating.

'He hates Bisto granules,' I said. 'But he's not here, is he?'

Mum bit her lip. 'I'm sorry, love,' she said. 'That was tactless.'

'Slip of the tongue, that's all. Nothing to worry about.'

After dinner we watched *Britain's Got Talent* on catch-up. I relaxed more than I had in years. At one of the acts I laughed so much I let out a snort, which really cracked the twins up. There was a middle-aged woman who'd trained her parrot to sing duets with her; it was hilarious. I suppose I'd drunk most of the red wine. The offer was on all week so I'd got another bottle in.

The next day, the police called to tell me they were treating my husband's disappearance as suspicious. Missing Persons hadn't turned up anything and there'd been no sightings of him since I'd called to say he hadn't come home. My stomach turned over. That's it, I thought. I'll never see him again.

For the next few weeks, I pulled the purse strings tight and told the kids we'd have to live off the freezer for now: pork and olives, bacon and eggs, ham shank and pea soup. I made casseroles for a couple of the neighbours. They'd been so supportive.

By the end of the month, the freezer was pretty much empty. We were having the last of the bacon with baked potatoes and cauliflower cheese.

'Do you think dad will ever come back?' the twins asked me.

'Beats me,' I said.

I knew he was never coming back. Out of doors, my husband was a very sociable man. But at home he was a real pig.

A LAWFUL KILLING

Ross Greenwood

Someone needs to die. No, they deserve to die. That is absolutely clear to me, but nothing else is. I am at the point of waking, yet sleep still has me in its warm buoyant grasp. Almost as if it will never let me go. I feel I should struggle more, to try and escape, but the thoughts of death are taking up every piece of energy I possess. As I sink into oblivion once more, I wonder who is doomed, and whether I am the man to fulfil the task.

***

I bob up to the surface once more, but am no more conscious than last time. However, my thoughts instantly return to the killing. Yes, that person will leave this life by the hand of another. I let my mind wander to my past. It is murky and swirling, but the main players loom large, like phantoms judging me. It can't be my parents; they have always been good people. My mum is still mowing old people's lawns for them, yet she is eighty-two herself. My dad continues driving folk to hospital, even though he has long since given up putting claim forms in. They always wanted the best for me. There is certainly no malice there. Yet, their faces in my dreams are contorted. They seem distraught and let down. Their eyes bulge as their visages whoosh in at me, but they are contortions of pain, regret and remorse. Not anger.

My childhood was happy, I think. Certainly the beginning was. Pictures of summer vacations at caravan parks and snapshots of regular trips to McDonalds light up in the front of my mind. OK, so we never got to go abroad, but my dad was a lazy sod and hardly ever worked. Some bullshit about his back, I think. Actually, now I remember, I was only allowed a hamburger while he chewed his way through a massive quarter pounder. The holidays were good though.

However, as the pictures curl up and wither, the emotions I feel are boredom and mischief. There is sadness too, but not mine. Well, my mum was always crying, so that isn't anything new.

My brother comes next, locked in a cage. Now, he could be the one. A wicked life of waste and gluttony if ever there was. He is rotting in jail for stealing from charities. It's his third time there and won't be his last. Oh, how I wished for his brains when we were young. Never suspecting that inside him a lust for money and respect would blossom and corrupt, leading him to bulldoze his way through the Ten Commandments. Not all of them, of course. He hasn't killed anyone yet, but the rest have been crushed beneath his lawless feet. He would not be missed if he were dispatched.

I suppose that mistake with the air gun didn't help. I thought it would just sting. Still, my brother has done worse since, so in a way he deserved it. I always thought the eye patch suited him. He didn't like me before that, so what did I lose?

Then, there is the one. A she-devil in flames. It must be her. She would deserve a bad end and I would be glad to provide the deadly blow. She has made my life a misery, yet it started so well. The visions clear and I see the folly of our youth. The glorious bright wedding where it began. Happy parents on both sides and our friends looking up at us and smiling. For the first time in my life I could see a happy future that I belonged to. One with children and holidays, careers and potential. If you had told me, just five years from then, that I would gladly crush the life from her with my dying hands, I would have laughed tears of disbelief. Yet it was this woman who took it all from me. I gave her all that she wanted and she still took everything I owned.

Blurred images of my children flash quickly by. It's hard to focus; surely it hasn't been that long? She stopped me from being around, made it so I can't see them. Spiteful cow. After all she said about children needing both a mother and a father too. She is the focus of my rage.

There are others too. All those who have made my life difficult deserve my wrath. There are so many. The teachers with their understanding eyes and lying hearts. I hate all those interfering social services fools, too. They never understood, always took her side, and never helped me. What could I do? It wasn't my fault. The man from the council, well, he deserves pain; and as for the police, well, they were never my friends.

The blackness returns and again I am gone.

***

It's her voice that stirs me this time. It comes from a long, long, way away. As though I am hearing it from one end of an enormous dark tunnel. I can smell her, too, which is weird in a dream. A mixture of Dove soap and the cigarettes she could never give up. The voice is quiet, whispered even, yet I can hear every crystal word.

'I hate you, despise you. You are the embodiment of everything that is wrong with a human. I married a man and lived with a drunken tyrant. I hope our children forget you because I already have. The pyres of hell are too good for your twisted soul, you evil bastard.'

She always was over-dramatic. I hardly drank until I married her. Well, the odd Saturday night maybe, and I always loved Sunday drinking. Sunshine and beer gardens, combined with fags and cold lager. Perfect. Her constant digging made me look for escapes, admittedly vodka was one, but it was her that sent me there. A man has the right to have sex with his wife. Surely that's what it's all about? She used to like it rough to start with; how was I to know things had changed? Her spite is electrically charged, hovering like a malevolent thunderstorm, yet I still slip away.

***

I hear my brother's voice now; it seems like many years since we spoke. There are no images this time, just swirling clouds, grey and white. Again, he talks from remoteness; a million miles off, but the words are clear.

'I forgive you, I hope you know that. I always did and I will do now. We were just children and the choices we made after were our own. That day's madness affected all of us. I'm a changed man, and in a way I feel free. You have released me from the bars I built around myself, so for that I am grateful. You were always the best and worst of us. You should have been a soldier as you were relentless. I have a picture of us; two laughing boys in a race to get Sparkles. I'm straining to catch up and you are laughing over your shoulder, urging me onwards. You got there first, my friend, and I will see you again.'

***

I am pulled once more from the abyss. Somehow I know this will be the final time. It is my mother, I'm sure, but she sounds older now. Her voice is quiet, husky almost, the strength all gone. I've missed her so much, but I saw her last week. I remember the rage that seemed so important and know that it's gone. It will never return as it has been replaced by love. That is how it should be and I am almost at peace.

'Oh son, what did you do to yourself? To us. I just don't understand.'

'Come now, honey, it's too late for all that. It's hard for you, it always would be, but maybe it's for the best.'

'I know, I know. I just want to know why. Are we to blame? Did we do something wrong?'

'No, I don't think so. He was always wild, you know that. I don't think he was ever going to be sat on his reclining chair, smoking his pipe, content in his dotage.'

'He was still my boy.'

'Yes, but maybe it was better this way. At least no-one got hurt.'

'Except him, of course.'

A final vision appears and suddenly I know. That terrible day. I was arrested at the school gates, sodden with Smirnoff. I was eventually released with dire warnings of the consequences of harassment. I would have to go back to court for breaching my restraining order. I'd been given too many last chances and knew I would be sent to prison. I can't face that as inside I am scared. It was a front to hide a lost boy. I'd be no better than my brother, too, and I couldn't live like that. The evil spirit told me to go out in glory and I turned to cocaine, my one remaining friend, to get me out of the door.

There she was at the end of the street, pushing my children in that double buggy I hate. It never worked for me, like many things I guess. I never felt normal or that I belonged in this world, except for that day, with my lady in white.

With screeching tyres and burning smoke, I hammered towards them with retribution in mind. In the end it was the council who had their revenge as a giant pothole jolted the steering wheel out of my hand. The next thing I was parked in someone's lounge. I wasn't sure who was the most surprised. They were sat on the sofa, enjoying pizza, as the walls collapsed on me.

'It's time, love.'

'It feels like yesterday we saw them chase after that ice-cream van. Remember the picture you took?'

'Aye, I do. That was fifty years ago. They never did

get their lollies.'

'No, I'm still a little surprised, all this time later, that he stopped to help his brother up and see if he was okay. There was good in him, wasn't there?'

'Of course, of course.'

'Are we ready?'

'He cried a few months back, Doctor. Is there no hope?'

'I've explained that, numerous times. This is the right thing to do.'

'Pet, we've been through all this. The courts don't make these decisions lightly. Of all people, he wouldn't want to be like this.'

'But I read about people waking up after all this time.'

'Again, we have discussed this. The percentage that wakes is very, very small and recovery has been to a state of severe disability. We believe your son is brain dead now and we, and the court, have agreed it is the right decision to withdraw life support.'

'Yes, Doctor, we are ready. To all intents and purposes, we know he died five years ago. Hold his hand darling.'

'It's done now. I'll leave you. Take as long as you like.'

***

There was a beeping sound, all of this time. It seems I only just heard it, but now, it dolefully slows. The night draws swiftly; the darkness complete. And then, contentedly, I am nothing.

STICKY FINGERS

JT Lawrence

I learnt how to keep a secret when I was three years old. It started on an ordinary day – a sunny Jo'burg afternoon. I was in my mum's arms while she was buying cigarettes from the sweet counter at Checkers. She used to smoke the Dunhill 30s that came in a wide red and gold box, (with gold foil inside!), and a white underside that was perfect for scribbling shopping lists and working out maths problems. When making this smoker's stop after doing the grocery shopping, she'd always let us choose a few little chocolates for the sweetie bowl at home. Maybe it made her feel less guilty about spending money on cigarettes, or smoking around us. Maybe it was just her being kind; even on a teacher's salary she was always generous.

She'd give us each a silver bowl and my older brother and I would be allowed to choose a few different treats. We always went for the chocolates – the other stuff was a waste of time. My favourites were the chocolate-peanut clusters, followed closely by the chocolate-coconut clusters. The bowls were then weighed and paid for: a sweet ritual.

That day, while everyone else's eyes were on the scale, including mine, a little three-year-old hand reached out towards the sweets and, before I knew it, there was a chocolate toffee finger melting in my pocket.

I don't know what made me steal it. Mom had already bought me the chocolates I had wanted (I'm not even sure I liked chocolate toffee fingers). Perhaps I was just born an opportunist. Maybe my kleptomania was inherent to my make-up, along with my bad temper, green eyes and big feet.

Sometimes I wonder if I would still be a thief if that first incident hadn't happened; if I hadn't experienced that hot thrill of having something that didn't belong to me.

If, for some reason, I had resisted that first childish impulse to grab, perhaps my restless heart wouldn't be forever waiting for The Next Nice Thing To Steal.

Was I too young to understand right from wrong? Perhaps. I did show off my loot the moment we got into the car, which makes me think that I didn't know what I had done was wrong. Wasn't it quite clever of me to get something for nothing? I don't remember if I was expecting praise or punishment. I did learn then that I shouldn't show anyone what I had stolen, no matter how urgent the desire becomes. That's when I learnt how to keep a secret.

When I was five I kidnapped two dolls from nursery school. I sneaked them out in my scruffy cardboard suitcase. It wasn't so much 'stealing' in my mind, then, it was more the fact that I loved the dolls so much that I thought they should be living at home with me. Their names were Nadia and Devon. Once the stowaways were discovered, my mother marched me to the teacher to return them, and apologise. The teacher was so very kind about it – not only did she not scold me, but she agreed that, as I was such a good 'mother' to the dolls, I should be allowed to keep them. She was sure that they would be happier with me. Looking back now, I wonder if this confused my developing moral compass.

Whatever caused it, bad genes or bad luck, I am, and (most likely always will be), a thief. It took me a while to admit it, but that doesn't make it any less true. There is no arguing with the two-hundred and sixty-four lipsticks I have stashed under my bathroom sink, or the army of restaurant salt and pepper cellars that take up an entire double-cupboard in the kitchen. In my twenties I referred to myself as a 'collector'. I was making a stand against soulless industrialisation and crass materialism: 'Look,' I thought, 'I can take this without anyone even noticing.'

Row upon row of similar trinkets: my cupboards looked like Andy Warhol installations. I thought I was smart, ironic. I wasn't fooling anyone.

Sometimes I take things for specific reasons. I was at a cocktail party a few months ago and the hostess was this awful person. She had a horsey face and kept guffawing all over the place. She kept forgetting my name and calling me 'love', and I know it was because I'm a housewife and she thinks I don't matter. I turned my back on her soggy canapés but it wasn't enough: I knew I'd have to take something of hers, and I did. She didn't deserve to have the sweet ceramic rabbit miniature I found in her display cabinet, and I was certain he was much happier when he left in my clutch later that night.

It could also be due to nominative determinism. You know, like when your name is Bolt and you become the fastest sprinter in the world. Or Candy, and you become a stripper. Maybe that last example isn't such a good one; that's more like just changing your name to suit your talent. My name is Nicolette, and people call me Nicky or Nick. It's quite funny, I think, and I catch myself wanting to tell people, but of course, I can't.

It's lonely, being a klepto. So much of your existence revolves around your conquests and close calls, but you can never share that part of your life with other people. Last week I took the most beautiful orange and cream silk scarf from Poetry (scarves are one of the easiest things to steal, apart from panties and lipstick) – but I can't tell anyone about it. It has the most charming elephant print on it. I can't even wear it, because if Derek, my husband, sees it, he'll demand to see the receipt.

Sometimes I fantasize about an online dating site that caters to people like me. Of course I wouldn't actually date anyone – I'm happily married! – but it would be wonderful to just meet some like-minded people and share our stories.

Derek keeps giving me more cash. He sneaks it into

my wallet and I pretend that I don't notice. I already have two credit cards that he pays off every month. He has always had so much money. It frustrates him to not be able to pay to make this problem go away. But it's not about money. He doesn't understand.

My best friend, Sylvia, is the only one I can really talk to, but I can't tell her everything either. She is one of the least judgmental people I know, but even she has her limits. I have to be careful to select only the stories I am bursting to tell, and hide everything else, like the fake pearls I took from my sister-in-law's jewellery box on Saturday, and the sandalwood-scented candle I got from the esoteric shop at Rosebank Mall. Esoteric shops are so easy to lift from: they are all too often dimly lit, have poor security measures, and the shop assistants simply don't expect their customers to steal. Bad karma, and all of that.

When I hold back from telling Sylvia for a few weeks she gets this bright look in her eyes. 'You're getting better!' she'll say. Or, 'You've turned a corner!'

She can be so naïve.

She's never really had any money, not much anyway, but I'm sure she hasn't stolen a thing in her life. A few years ago she made me start writing down, item for item, the things I was taking. She thought I was in denial about the extent of my 'problem' (I'm not). But I enjoyed the exercise of recording my acquisitions, and I still do it. I have 12 (stolen) notebooks full of excited entries. They read like accountant's ledgers. The pages are well thumbed: one of my favourite things to do is to go through the lists and remember the moments they brought with them. It makes me feel like a 'collector' again. It makes it more real, in a way. More... honest. The books are stacked underneath our bed. Only Sylvia knows about them.

I met Sylvia years ago at one of Derek's company's functions. They worked in the same building but had never met. I actually introduced them, and now we're all great friends. We've got a lot in common. Over the years she's become part of the family. The kids love her. Did I mention we have kids? A four- and a six-year-old – a boy and a girl (I resisted the urge to name them Nadia and Devon). I'm sure that we look like the picture-perfect family to some. To those who don't know about my habit. Sylvia is like the kids' fairy godmother, always wooing them with gifts and food.

She's like my fairy godmother too, I guess. A couple of years ago I was caught shoplifting a pair of Dolce & Gabana sunglasses from Sandton City. Depending on your technique, sunglasses can be an easy lift, because you end up trying so many pairs on, there are bound to be some floating around the shop, unattended to. You have to do it when the shop is relatively busy – sales are always a good time – and you should arrive with a similar pair to the ones you want to nick, preferably perched on your head. Once you choose a pair, you replace the old ones with the new, et voila, out you flounce with a new pair of shades.

This has worked for me over and over, but on that unlucky day the security guard was paying attention. Perhaps my lipstick was too red: it was Revlon New Cherry. Bold make-up on a shoplifting spree is never a good idea; people don't trust women whose lipstick is too bright. But one gets complacent and neglects the rules. I hadn't been caught for so long that I stopped believing it could happen. Started thinking I had some kind of magical power. Ignored the bad karma of stolen lipstick.

So I made the switch quite near to the exit, and then turned to walk out, and next thing there was a strong hand grabbing me, like a headmaster would yank the arm of a troublesome child. It was shocking, but expected, at the same time. I tried to act confused, concerned, then indignant, but I could see the guard wasn't buying it. He was quiet and kept glancing up at the red LED light of the security camera, as if waiting for someone to come down and give him the go-ahead to slap some cuffs on me. After a perfunctory exchange on his walkie-talkie, he escorted me through the mall and sat me down in a dingy office near the food court. There was another stern-looking man there. All I could smell was Cinnabon.

They weren't sure if they were going to press charges, and wanted to speak to my husband before 'taking any steps'. I gave them Sylvia's number instead. An hour later she had charmed and cajoled the two men into giving me a warning (well, a warning and a lifetime ban from entering the store). She made up this story about how my husband was having an affair and I was having a minor nervous breakdown. I was impressed at what a convincing liar she was – I had never guessed it. From then on she called me 'Sticky Fingers'. She'd poke me in the ribs and say 'Take that, Sticky Fingers.'

The smell of cinnamon still unsettles me.

The next time I was caught I wasn't that lucky. Sometimes I wonder if I actually wanted to get caught. Either way, I guess that it would have happened sooner or later. I mean, I wasn't going to stop stealing, so it was inevitable. My lucky streak, my magical power, wasn't going to last forever. I had had so many close calls over the years, over a lifetime: my Sticky Finger Magic was due to run out.

Derek and I were staying in a luxury hotel in Camps Bay, with a room that overlooked the sea. The kids were with his mother for the weekend, and we decided at the last minute to hop on a plane to Cape Town. We were pretending to be spontaneous: it's something rich married people do to try to keep the relationship exciting. It's weird, because it's like you're pretending to be someone else for the weekend: someone young, childless, passionate, romantic. And you try to reconnect with your significant other, but he is also pretending to be that other, lighter, person, but really neither of you are yourselves. So you drink more than usual and have kinkier sex than usual, but when Monday rolls around and he is pulling out his hair looking for his favourite tie for a meeting and you are wiping toothpaste off your toddler's cheeks and this is your real life and did the weekend in Cape Town actually even happen?

But there we were, in the hotel spa, after a full body Swedish massage and a quickie in the Rasul chamber. We went to our respective change-rooms to shower and before I left I did what I always do – I checked all the lockers. It's like checking a casino slot machine or a basement parking ticket machine for abandoned coins, except that some women are lulled into such a secure stupor by their privileged lifestyles that they don't even bother to lock away their things. I got three quarters of the way through when I hit the jackpot: a shiny new snakeskin Louis Vuitton handbag, with matching wallet and belt. The bag was too big to steal, and I had no need for the belt, so I took the wallet. It was a thing of beauty, not more than a few days old. The fact that it was a wallet meant that they would probably assume that a member of staff took it, for the cash, although I left behind her jewellery. It was gaudy: diamonds and Tanzanite. I held the necklace against my collarbone to see how it would look, just as a matter of interest. It confirmed what I already knew: blue stones are not my style.

A lady in a white spa bathrobe came in just as I was sliding the wallet into my own handbag. I played it cool, pretended that I was doing nothing unusual. I was just a woman putting her wallet into her bag. But, unfortunately for me, the robed lady happened to be the owner of the

Louis Vuitton. It took a while for her to register what I was doing. I think she must have first thought: Oh, look, that lady has the same wallet as me. But then her eyes travelled to her locker, saw the door was open, saw that it had been plundered. Her face, previously scrubbed and blissful-looking, jumped into ferocious mode, and she proceeded to throw the biggest hissy fit I have seen. She was like a toddler on a double espresso. The words she was shouting at me didn't even make sense. I tried to calm her down, explain that it was a misunderstanding. I thought that it was my bag but then I realised I had brought my other bag, so I was putting it back. It's when I saw the jewellery that I had realised that it wasn't my locker. Tanzanite, I said, I never wear Tanzanite. That's what made me realise.

It was an unlikely story, but weaker ones had worked before. People are desperate to believe the best in other people.

But not this manic madwoman. She seemed half outraged, half delighted to have a bit of drama in her day. Despite my constant assurances that she had misinterpreted the situation, she turned and fled the room to call security. I used my towel, still damp from the shower, to quickly wipe down her locker and the things of hers I had touched. Now it was her word against mine.

I glided out and headed in the opposite direction to the noise she was creating at the spa reception. I left through the back door and scuttled my way up to our hotel room. Derek was asleep, naked, on the bed, and I sat on our patio, looking at the sea, waiting for the knock at the door.

It took the hotel manager twenty minutes to figure out my name and room number. It had been staring out at him from the spa appointment book. He knocked softly at first – it was easy to ignore – then louder, and he started calling my name. Derek stumbled out of bed, confused but overly alert, the way you are when your nap is (rudely) interrupted. I threw a gown at him before I opened the door.

The man doing the knocking looked apologetic the moment he saw us.

'Terribly sorry!' he kept saying. 'Terribly sorry to inconvenience you, but could you come down to the hotel reception?'

'What is this about?' Derek demanded.

'Terribly sorry! There seems to be some kind of– I'm sure it's a misunderstanding.'

'Is there a problem?' my husband asked, still pale from sleep.

'There may not be?' said the manager. They looked at each other for a good time, perplexed.

'I know what this is about,' I said. 'Some crazy woman at the spa was accusing me of going through her locker. She was screaming at me... She kicked up such a fuss!'

'Yes,' said the man, clearly relieved that he wouldn't have to make an allegation. Derek sighed.

'I should have complained,' I said to both of them. 'Being accosted like that.'

'Yes...' said the man. 'A misunderstanding. That's what I told her. Will you come down so that we can clear it up?'

I paused. An innocent woman would have flown downstairs to clear her name. I sensed that if I went down there I would get into a vast amount of trouble. Both men sensed my hesitation. The manager's eyes pleaded with me to co-operate, to not make his day any more difficult than it already was. Derek jumped in.

'Well, was anything actually taken?' he asked.

'Taken?' said the man.

'Stolen! Was anything stolen from the woman?'

He paused. 'She's not making much sense – the lady – she's very upset. It's hard to know.'

'So can you please then explain to me why you don't just tell this lady to stop fabricating defamatory stories about my wife?'

I loved Derek so much in that moment. I felt so loved, so protected. He would get me out of this. He started to close the door, but the manager stopped him. Both men were gentle; there was no tussle. The man looked intensely uncomfortable. Eventually he blurted out: 'It's the ring!'

'What ring?' asked Derek.

'That ring,' he said, motioning to my left hand. I looked down and saw a diamond and Tanzanite ring on my index finger. I didn't even remember putting it on.

Things moved both quickly and agonisingly slowly from then. The police were called and I was arrested almost immediately, and charged, but the waiting in between was torture. Hours of staring at the grimy jail cell walls. Hours sitting on cheap cracked chairs waiting for some kind of admin to be done: paperwork to be processed, questions asked, answered and repeated ad nauseam. When they told me that my lawyer was getting on a plane to Cape Town I wanted to tell them – tell everyone – not to bother. I wanted to say, just give me the orange overalls and tin mug and bus me to wherever the hell I'm going to end up. At the time it seemed preferable to waiting for a lawyer to make his way to me all the way from Jo'burg.

Derek had, of course, hired the best lawyer money could buy, and when Mazarakis did finally walk into the beige room they were keeping me in I was very happy to see him. You would never have said that it was a Sunday, or that he had just been on a plane, with his sharp suit and alarmingly clear blue eyes. I, on the other hand, felt that I had aged 20 years in the last few hours. I looked different, felt different: I was a completely disparate person to the woman who had a loving husband and two beautiful children, or the woman who had had a massage overlooking the ocean that morning. My skin was whiter, thinner; my pores larger; my body vulnerable. The enchantment had been broken. I had been exposed for who I truly was.

Mazarakis was calm and measured, and explained what I was to expect in the next few hours, and days. I'd have to stay in custody overnight as they could only apply for bail on Monday morning. He was apologetic at that, as if it was his fault I had stolen the ring. He never asked me if I did actually steal anything – I think Derek must have told him about my 'problem'.

After bail was set, I was allowed to fly home with Derek. He was angry with me, cold, but still sat next to me on the plane, though there were lots of free seats in the first class cabin. It's a terrible feeling, knowing you have let someone down so badly. The exigent guilt settles into your body, your organs become heavy with dread.

We refused the complimentary Graham Beck Brut, and the cheddar straws. They had no place in this new, upside-down world of ours. Derek had a *Business Day* open on his lap but I could tell he wasn't reading it. I could almost hear the thoughts crowding his head: 'What was she thinking?'; 'Why would she risk so much?'; 'What if she has to go to prison?'; 'She doesn't even like Tanzanite!' and, of course, 'What about the children? Who will be their mother?'

Of course, the same questions had been haunting me for years, and I could never answer them. I am dishonest by nature, but this is true: if I could have fed my addiction in a less destructive way, I would have.

During the trial, Sylvia stayed at the house with the

kids. She fed them, bathed them, took them to school. She kept photos of them in her wallet and on her phone to show me when we caught up, in snatched spells during proceedings. She brought paintings that they had done for me, showing us as the perfect little family, standing outside our perfect little house. I couldn't help noticing that the mother in the picture was starting to look more like Sylvia than me.

I was so grateful that she was there to support Derek; he was taking it very badly. She would sit next to him in court, with a brave face, positively glowing in comparison to him. Every time I caught his eye he gave me this pained expression, as if he already knew it was all over.

Sylvia brought me things from home – small comforts: pyjamas, toiletries, books. Even homemade chocolate peanut butter cookies, that she had baked using my recipe, in my oven.

We would have won the case, Mazarakis said so. He said there was absolutely no evidence against me, apart from that damn ring, which he creatively – and successfully – explained away as a 'misunderstanding'.

There was no convincing evidence against me, until on the day of sentencing the prosecutor received a delivery from an anonymous source. It was a large brown box full of notebooks – my lifted ledgers – full of years of detailed entries of all the things I had stolen. Of course, they were in my handwriting, and covered with my fingerprints.

When I recognised the covers and realised what they were, it felt like I had been stabbed in the chest. A quick, nimble blade, between my ribs. In-and-out. And then a slow cold bleeding.

It turned out that I hadn't learnt how to keep a secret at all.

Only one person had known about those notebooks, and where they had been hidden. As the prosecutor introduced them to the court, and they were admitted as evidence, I looked at Sylvia, but she wouldn't return my gaze. It was then that I saw her hand on Derek's lap, and his hand on hers.

And I could hear her voice in my head, saying: 'Take that, Sticky Fingers'.

YOU WILL MEET A TALL, DARK, STRANGLER

Ron Nicholson

'**H**ow peculiar!' Barbara said in a somewhat uneasy tone, her eyes scanning the document in her hands.

'What is?' Joanne glanced over at her friend while carefully pouring cheap white wine into two generous glasses.

'The fact that you subscribe to this astrology rubbish is peculiar enough but have you actually read what it says here?'

Joanne picked up the glasses and walked across to where her friend lounged comfortably on the settee and handed one of them to her. In exchange, she took the typed prediction and glanced down at it. 'What am I supposed to be looking at?'

'About halfway down,' Barbara said. 'The bit about meeting somebody.'

'If you mean the bit about meeting a tall dark stranger, they put something along those lines in every prediction. It's become a bit of a cliché. Nobody believes that line anymore.' Joanne answered with a smile that did little to mask her embarrassment. Joanne and Barbara had been best friends for years and Barbara's opinion mattered to her. The last thing she wanted was for Barbara to think she was in any way whacky.

'But it doesn't say that,' Barbara insisted. 'Read it again.' Joanne frowned and scanned the page. She read it three times to be certain and as she read, Barbara could see a gradual change in her friend's pallor as the blood seemed to drain from her face.

'You're right. It *is* peculiar. It says, '...you will meet a tall dark strangler." She laughed uneasily before handing the paper back to her friend. 'It says "strangler" instead of stranger.'

'If you ask me, it's a bit spooky.' The look on

Barbara's face showed concern. She had begun to worry about Joanne over the past few months. Her personal life and the stress of her job were showing signs that all was not well. Joanne breaking up with Ian after a three-year up and down relationship had damaged her confidence. It was the same old story. He had found somebody younger but hadn't had guts enough to tell her. Joanne had been kept in the dark until the office grapevine eventually let it be known to her. They'd gone everywhere together during their relationship, now she rarely left her flat socially.

***

The prediction had arrived in the post that morning, along with the usual collection of junk mail, and Joanne had glanced through its content, picking out pieces at random that had even a tenuous link to her. Of course, she told herself, the whole thing was rubbish but then, if it wasn't rubbish she would like to be forewarned of anything good that was about to come her way. Her friends at work all swore by the accuracy of this particular astrologist's predictions, so she had allowed herself to be talked into sending off the modest fee.

'It's just a typing error.' Joanne laughed uneasily. 'Like you said before, it's rubbish.'

Since breaking up with Ian, Joanne had gradually felt the need to move on with her life. She managed to convince herself that twenty-five was not too late to make something of her life but if she left it any longer she would lose her nerve and find herself stuck in a rut forever.

It was on a wet Monday morning a month later when Joanne told her boss she needed to escape from work before the long-awaited nervous breakdown arrived. She was good at her job – everybody told her that – but she needed a holiday. The stress was getting to her and if she didn't take time off, that stress would end up breaking her. To her surprise, her boss had agreed to a three-month leave on half pay. To Joanne, it was clear he knew her worth to the company and couldn't afford to lose her permanently. The fact that he was willing to do so boosted her self-esteem somewhat and was just the encouragement she needed. He obviously valued her input more than she had imagined.

***

Two weeks later, she was driving her well-packed Citroen C3 on the busy M26 from London down to the ferry terminal at Dover. The Channel crossing had been smooth but noisy. Luckily, she'd managed to find herself a relatively quiet area of the main passenger lounge where she could lose herself in a Mills and Boon and a latte for a couple of hours.

After a while she looked at her wristwatch and noted she had another half an hour before their arrival. Time had gone by quickly, but there was just enough to visit the duty free shop before the call for drivers to go to the car deck.

Apart from driving on the 'wrong' side of the road and the signs being in French instead of English, there was little difference in being in a foreign country. Leaving Calais was easier than she had imagined it was going to be.

Soon after leaving the ferry port, she spotted the signs for the E402 to Le Havre and Caen, and nervously eased her way into the flow of traffic heading south at exit 23.

***

After about two hours of relatively easy motoring, she found herself just north of Rouen where she pulled off the road at a motorway service station. She filled her petrol tank and allowed herself a half-hour break while she enjoyed a coffee and a baguette. She knew it was going to be a long trip. She'd estimated about four hours for the whole journey this side of the channel and was approximately half way.

As she sat at her table, looking out of the plate glass window at the continuous flow of cars and lorries, she realised that the trepidation she had felt as she left her flat in London that morning was being replaced by a definite feeling of excitement. She was somewhat surprised to find that there appeared to be little difference in the look of the countryside. Normandy could easily be mistaken for Kent with its gently undulating aspect and lush greenery but what excited her at that moment was the fact that she had made the break. Meek little Joanne had done something decisive. There was no turning back now. Her life was about to change.

***

Later that evening, just before dark, she found herself driving up to a picturesque gite situated between Caen and St. Lo. Her friends had told her many times that she could use the holiday cottage but until now she had resisted. Ian had hated travel of any kind and she was aware that she lacked the courage to go alone. Things were different now. One look at the building with its dusty driveway was enough to tell her that she had made the right decision. It was so typically French with its white walls and painted shutters at the windows. She had taken several wrong turns before she had found it tucked away some two kilometres off what passed for the main village road. She couldn't imagine a more isolated but relaxing location to regain her sanity.

The village was small and picturesque. At first glance, there appeared to be no more than twenty houses, serviced by a small general store, but exploring the area later showed that the village was actually quite big.

***

Over the next few days, she managed to use her modest knowledge of the language to start a relationship

122

with the owners of the shop, a nice married couple in their mid sixties. Her awkwardness dissipated as she got to know them and she began to feel at home with the language very quickly.

It was on the third day after arriving that she found herself drowsily listening to the bees pollinating the flowers in the garden as she lounged comfortably in a deckchair. Although devoid of man-made sounds, nature made sure that it wasn't completely quiet. She found herself wondering if the birds had French accents and chuckled to herself at the very idea. She was so into her thoughts that the clearing of somebody's throat startled her.

'Pardon, mademoiselle. I am Gerard.'

She found herself looking up at a tall silhouette of a well-built male. The sun was behind him so she couldn't see his features but if the features matched the voice, she couldn't wait to see his face. She dragged herself out of the chair and stood up. She moved to one side so she could see him clearly and a tingle went through her as he took her hand to shake it. He looked about twenty-eight with slightly windswept dark brown hair. The little she could see of his skin was tanned, telling her that he had either just returned from holiday or more likely that he spent a great deal of his time in the open air. His clean white shirt was unbuttoned at the neck to expose a few wisps of soft looking chest hair and his Wrangler jeans emphasised long muscular legs. His face was ruggedly handsome and the smile was almost boyish as he displayed a fine set of white teeth. His pale blue eyes held her enquiring gaze for the fleetest of moments before embarrassment forced him to look away.

'The owners pay me to look after this house when they are not here. They telephoned me to tell me that you would be here and I come today to ask if there is anything that I can do for you.' The words were said with a tone that oozed sex appeal.

Joanne resisted the obvious temptation and told him that she had everything she needed at that moment. He seemed disappointed so she offered him a cup of coffee by way of compensation. What harm could come of it?

As they sat drinking their coffee at the table in the garden, she became aware that he was avoiding looking directly at her. Was he just shy? If he was, she was finding it endearing.

After finishing the coffee, he went on his way, assuring her he would call by every day to make certain she was okay.

Each day, their conversation got friendlier and he seemed to stay that little bit longer. They became more relaxed with each other and exchanged information about their lives. They were both single with little or no baggage. They enjoyed the same type of music and a love of books. She told him about her job in the city and he in turn told her that he owned a small poultry farm just a few kilometres away. Unlike her, he seemed entirely happy with his lifestyle and she envied him. Every so often, she even found herself fantasising about being a French farmer's wife. Those thoughts made her smile, and blush furiously.

***

By the third week, Joanne and Gerard were going out together on the occasional date. He had first taken her to the cinema in a nearby village and although she had had trouble following the plot, she was happy enough to be holding hands with him in the dark. After the movie, they had enjoyed a simple meal at a local bistro bar. The evening had ended with a kiss goodnight after he had taken her home. She had endured that awkward moment of the first kiss many times in her life. Some turned out to be little more than "okay" but most of them were distinctly forgettable. Gerrard's kiss? Definitely above average for a first attempt. She almost regretted letting him drive off at the end of what had been a perfect evening. For just a reckless moment, she was tempted to drag him off to her bedroom but she was worried that it could scare him away. If it were meant to be though, there would come a time when he wouldn't need to go to his own home. She hoped that it would come soon.

***

One morning, she was at the kitchen sink washing up her breakfast things when she watched him from the window drive into the courtyard in his battered old truck. He got out of the cab and reached into the back of the vehicle. She stopped what she was doing, wiped her hands on a towel, and went to open the door for him.

He stood there with a smile of pride on his face and in his hands was a freshly killed chicken, its feathers still adorning it.

'Look!' he said proudly in his attractive soft accent, lifting the bird high as if it were a trophy. 'I have brought you dinner. I killed it myself just for you with my own hands.'

***

That night, she wrote to her friend Barbara back in England. She told her about the house and the village. She told her about the nice couple who ran the general store and how they had appeared to take her under their wing. Most of all, she let her know about Gerard, dropping a few hints that he was her idea of perfect. But the most important thing that she wanted Barbara to know that she was thanking her lucky stars that it had not been a typing error after all. The act of wringing the neck of a chicken and strangling it could be said to be the same thing... couldn't it? And he was tall and dark.

THE WAGES OF SIN

Lisa Hall

For the wages of sin is death, but the gift of God is eternal life in Christ Jesus Our Lord. Romans 6:23

Her thick, black hair is tangled in the low-hanging branches that stretch their fingertips towards the water beginning to swirl around her body. She lies face down in the river, surrounded by thick, sludgy mud where the tide has gone out, leaving behind only a tangy, dank river smell, a faint smudge of sewage in the air and the woman's naked body bleached a bluish-white by the moonlight. The air is still – crisp and cold, a cloudless sky above meaning that temperatures will drop still further before dawn breaks and the sun rises on another day. The first beginnings of a frost on the riverbank sparkle on the grass as the man stands under the bridge watching her body start to gently bob and sway in the river's current. He didn't think about the branches, or the possibility of her becoming entangled in them when he carefully pushed her off the riverbank and into the water.

A noise from close by makes him start, and he is relieved when it is just a fox, pushing its way through the dense undergrowth that grows along either side of the river, sniffing out its next meal.

A single car passes on the bridge overhead, and he draws closer into the shadows, leaning against the wall graffitied by local teenagers with the slogan, *Make Art Not War*. His breath puffs out in front of him in small, white clouds that drift away on the cold night air. His muscles ache, as he leans against the wall still hidden from view by the dark shadows that haunt this part of the river.

She was heavier than he thought, and he hadn't bargained on having to struggle over a fallen tree that had crashed down across the narrow footpath. He pauses, the only sounds now the gentle in and out of his breathing and the water lapping gently at the mud flats exposed by the low tide. The fox is long gone, chasing after whatever small creature is too slow to escape his sharp claws.

Stealthily he moves forward, peering once more over the edge of the riverbank, frost crackling beneath his feet, to see her still figure; white like marble, drifting gently on the tide. A wave of panic pours over him, beading his brow with sweat. What was he thinking? He couldn't leave her here, like this. This wasn't how it was supposed to be. As he casts his eyes wildly around looking for something, anything, that he could use to cut her free from the branches he notices the tide line on the stone abutment of the bridge. A dark, deliberate marking across the stone denoting where the high tide will reach, almost to the top of the riverbank itself. High enough, that when the tide does roll in, her body will be covered and the force of the strong current that rips along this stretch of the River Medway will disentangle her from the tree branches and she'll be washed miles downriver.

An owl hoots overhead, a short sharp noise that shocks him back to his senses. He turns on one heel and breaks into a jog, the nettles and brambles that line the riverbank clawing at his trousers as he runs.

As he reaches the familiar turning that marks the start of his street, he slows to a walk, chest hitching as he tries to regain his breath. Sweat beads at his temples and prickles uncomfortably on the back of his neck, as he passes the houses of his neighbours, all quiet and still, windows blacked out by darkness. Confident he has arrived unnoticed he gently pushes open the front gate, and creeps quietly along the path to the front door, the soles of his shoes crunching slightly on the crisp, frosty ground underfoot.

Finally, in the warm hallway, lit with the yellow glow of a standard lamp in one corner, he releases his breath in a steady whoosh, holding his shaking hands in front of him, a small huff of laughter expressing his relief. He makes his way into his study, pleased that he kept the small fire alight in the grate before he left, the warmth soaking into his bones. Casting his eyes about the room, the evidence of the struggle that took place only a short while earlier still litters the floor – the carriage clock on the mantelpiece overturned, papers from his desk scattered like autumn leaves across the floor, a hint of her perfume still tainting the air. He bends to scoop up the papers, stacking them neatly on the desk, before taking a seat in the wing-backed armchair and pouring himself a measure of the good brandy from his desk drawer. Tugging the battered Bible on the desk towards him, he flicks through and finds the quote he is searching for. *For the wages of sin is death...*

A tear forms in the corner of his eye. He didn't want to hurt her this evening – but he didn't have a choice did he? He couldn't let her be seen, not dressed like that. And the make-up... It gave her the face of a whore, not the angel she truly was underneath. His heart twists at the memory of her face – ruined by paint and lust – the bluish pallor just visible beneath the fake blush as he rolled her into the river.

And the filth that poured out of her mouth, language that turned his stomach. He shakes his head at the memory, as if to blank it out, the harsh, dirty words she had spoken cutting him to the bone. He did what needed to be done. What Our Lord would have wanted to be done.

He doesn't know how long he sits there, thinking of the splash she made as she hit the water, the way she had held her hands up to him, pleading with him, when she realised what he was about to do to her – before his hands closed tightly around her throat – but fingers of light are making their way through the grimy windows, the sun fighting its way above the horizon, sending streaks of purple and pink into the sky. He gives a small nod, as though accepting some approval, and drains the brandy glass.

'Are you in there?' A light tapping at the door, his housekeeper checking to make sure he hasn't slept all night in the study again. 'It's almost time.'

He checks his watch and realises she is right – it is almost time. Rising, he tucks the Bible into his pocket and stands before the mirror, smoothing his hair to one side and checking his black shirt for any signs of the evening's activities. Reaching for the mantelpiece, he returns the gold carriage clock to an upright position, marvelling at how it wasn't broken when he and Bethany struggled earlier, and picks up the slip of white fabric from beside it, attaching it firmly under his collar. Sunday morning. Time to greet his parishioners.

HIDDEN

KA Richardson

Her scream was loud enough to rattle windows and doors, and caused lights to blink on in the houses opposite.

A dog down the street barked loudly in response.

At two in the morning, it was not a sound anyone wanted to hear.

But they couldn't see her. The neighbours knew nothing about her.

They couldn't see her dark hair hanging around her pale face, or the dark eyes that sparkled even in the dimmest of light. They couldn't even tell he'd already silenced the second scream with a swift flick of the knife in his hand.

She was completely quiet now – her glass-like eyes staring at him as her life's blood ebbed from the laceration across her neck.

There were so many factories on this side of the street: he knew the neighbours would never be able to pinpoint the location.

Slowly the dog stopped barking, and the neighbours' lights went out.

He didn't know if they'd called the police, he didn't really care either way.

They'd never find him in here. No one ever did.

This building was so creepy even the local scrotes didn't come inside.

He smiled: if you were high on drugs this place would seem like a house of horrors – that's why they didn't come inside. They were chicken-shits.

Once upon a time, it had been an abattoir. The air still smelled of old blood, rusted metal and rat droppings. It had been abandoned for about fifteen years now but rusty meat hooks still swung from the ceiling, clanking when the breeze whistled through the smashed upper windows. All of the lower ones had been boarded, then the wood had been pulled off and replaced with metal sheeting. The doors had the same.

Even if the local scruffs had wanted to be in now, they'd have found it virtually impossible. Years ago, under the guise of a council worker, his mam had used a blowtorch to seal all the entrances and metal sheeting.

They were the only people who knew the way inside. The tunnel wasn't on any of the blue-prints. His grandad had built the tunnel when he'd brought him and his mam there to live. No one ever came to visit now.

Apart from the people they occasionally brought inside.

Like the woman now lying dead in front of him.

He didn't even know her name. Had no reason to. He didn't know if anyone would miss her. Didn't care if she had family. He'd found her sniffing around one of the bins to the back of the building – obviously looking for something to steal that she could weigh in for cash. Metal scroungers – they all were, so his mam said.

If the woman hadn't been there she would have lived.

But he couldn't tolerate people around his home. Hated it, in fact.

The one rule he and his mam had was simple. No sniffing around their belongings. There was metal fencing erected around the exterior of the building. The walls outside looked black, like they were covered in soot, but it was the mould that grew on the brick work. What paint there had been had peeled off years before, leaving the bits without black mould looking dirty. It wouldn't have looked inviting to even the most hard-core of adrenaline junkies. Everyone stayed away. And that was how he liked it. No one to see the maggots crawl out of the bins at the back where the flies had made their homes, using the rotting meat to feed their babies.

No one to see them enter or leave via the tunnel that led down to the river bank.

Except her. For weeks there hadn't been anyone – then *she* had come. He'd watched her from his vantage point, searching the back yard, lifting the bin lids, then going white as a sheet when she'd seen what was inside. He'd had no choice but to shimmy down the exit pipe and bring her inside.

And then she'd screamed loud enough to make the hairs stand up on the back of his neck – curly blonde hairs his mother had always said were his baby curls. He was anything but a baby now though. Large muscular arms easily filled the once-white t-shirt he wore. Navy blue overalls covered his legs, with the long arms tied around his waist. And dirty rigger boots covered his feet. He had untidy stubble around the base of his chin and up to his hair-line.

And a scar that went from one ear to the edge of his mouth. The scar was faded now: he barely even noticed it anymore. The only reason he knew it was there was because his stubble didn't grow over the broken tissue so it left a wonky line on the side of his face, like a river through a forest.

He smiled in the darkness, his eyes directing themselves towards the dead woman in front of him.

Frowning now, he knew he had some clean-up to do. Even with the plastic sheeting down, he could see some of the blood had already spilled over onto the wooden floor. And that wouldn't do. His mam couldn't abide mess of any kind.

Carefully he rolled the plastic over the woman's head, staring as the dark liquid sloshed and moved around her hair, dying it from brown to red. It stuck to her face like octopus tentacles as he pulled two of the edges closer and secured some string round her neck to hold the sheeting together.

Moving further down her body, he used butcher's knots to secure the rest of the plastic around her body. His granddad had taught him how to do them, back in the days when he'd worked at this very abattoir. Back when he'd been in awe of everything his granddad did.

The blood inside moved under her back and settled there, leaving a murky red line horizontally around the plastic.

He'd have to double wrap her – it wouldn't do to have seepage when he had to move her outside. Balancing his weight, he grabbed her trussed up feet, and dragged her to the corner of the room, adding her to the pile now congregating.

He coughed a little – they were starting to smell. The carcasses of the dead rats and pigeons he had been stripping and storing there. Those, and the other two large plastic wrapped forms. It was time to take out the trash.

He whistled an eerie off-key tune as he went into the next room along and pulled a trolley back through, the wheels squeaking as loudly as the rats had before they'd met their end. The noise was annoying.

As if it were as light as feathers, he hoisted the latest one onto the cart. Then the bags of animal carcasses and finally the other two plastic wrapped bodies.

The tunnel was dimly lit but he pushed the trolley through with ease, the wheels gliding effortlessly over the wooden floor he'd laid all those years ago when his mam had said she was sick of the mud between her toes. She'd said he was a good boy to lay the flooring by himself. It had made him feel like he was the best son in the world.

Exiting the tunnel, he pushed the trolley back up the

path to the rear of the building, pulling the metal fencing aside with the motion of someone who'd done it many times.

There were two large metal bins alongside the back of the building and he went straight to the one he needed. The plastic on the lid was much more faded around the rim, where his hands had worn the plastic down through use. This one smelled more than the other bin too – he rested the lid against the wall at the back, not even noticing the crawling maggots try and make good their escapes. They were different sizes, some tiny and some huge. They all fed well on the mixed flesh in the bottom of the bin.

The acrid smell spread upwards, causing his eyes to water. Lye was good stuff for helping keep the mass down in the bin, but it's odour was awful. He opened the twist of the bags and poured the dead rats and pigeons inside, on top of the brown slimy mass that had settled in the bottom of the bin. The lye would get rid of them soon enough – he'd learned the term 'alkaline hydrolysis' when he was in his teens and working on a farm not far from where he'd lived. The farmer had shown him how to do it, taught him the quantities required. And then his granddad had torn him away from that job he'd loved and brought him here, to hide in the abattoir. His granddad had said he had to, because of what he'd done. Him and his mam, hidden away where granddad could keep them safe.

He remembered what had happened – it had been an accident. He was being nice to the girl from the next farm over, like she was nice to him. When she'd argued with him over which was the best kitten from the feral cat's new litter, he'd pushed her. He hadn't meant for her to fall from the loft at the top of the barn, and he hadn't meant for her to land on the metal pole the farmer tied his dogs to on a night. His granddad had seen the whole thing and had carted both him and his mam to the abattoir there and then, knowing the farmer would never believe his oaf of a grandson when he told him it was an accident.

Absently, he scratched at his chin. His granddad had been among the last to leave the job at the abattoir and he hadn't gone quietly. He'd shouted and screamed at the men in suits there to lock the doors, and eventually had been led off in handcuffs. The men hadn't seen him though: he'd been in the hiding place his granddad had built with his mam. And they hadn't left the abattoir at all.

Bending his knees, he hoisted the first body up and over the edge of the bin, then did the same with the next two. Opening the smaller container beside it, he tipped four large scoops of the powdered lye into the bin and closed the lid.

Lifting the top to the biggest bin, he stared inside. His mother's face stared back at him, grey in colour with flesh hanging off in places.

'Brought you some visitors, mam. You'll like her. She's dark haired like you were once. I've put her next door. You can be neighbours. And I'll clean up the mess, I promise.'

Tears came to his eyes.

He whispered, 'It's OK, Mam. They didn't find us. Granddad said we'd be safe here forever, didn't he? And we will be. No one will ever find us here. I'll make sure of it.'

He fluffed the cushion behind his mam's head, gently straightened her hair, and patted her cheek, not even noticing the sticky substance her rotting skin left on his hand.

He swiped the tears off his cheeks with the back of his arm, closed the fence behind him, taking no notice of the sign saying 'danger, asbestos inside', and made his way back to the tunnel.

Once inside, he found the latest freshly dead rat in

one of the many traps lying around, and pulled at its fur with his long, cracked fingernails. He sat on the stained duvet on the old bed in the corner, and sank his black teeth into the soft underbelly of the rat, tearing it and chewing slowly. Blood dripped down his chin but he didn't even notice.

He missed his mam. He hated that she was outside while he was in here. But they were OK. They were still together. Like his granddad had promised.

The meat hooks swayed as a breeze rippled through the abattoir, clanking together, and content once more, he closed his eyes and leaned back against the wall.

Now he would sleep.

THE SYDNEY DAHLIA

A.J.Sendall

It was the third time I'd caught her looking at me. This time I held her gaze for a five-beat before turning back to the barman and holding my glass up for a refill.

'One more for the road, Sam?' he asked.

'Sure, and one for the nosey kid in the black and white rugby shirt,' I said tipping my head towards her.

Eddie took my glass and pushed it against an optic, waited for the sight-glass to drain, did it again. He laid the tumbler in front of me, and said, 'You'll need a double if you're going to tangle with her.'

'Why, who is she?'

Without answering, he poured a single malt into a crystal tumbler, walked away and laid the tumbler in front of her, then leaned forward and spoke in a low voice. She turned her head, studied me, then turned away again. She was in her mid-twenties, slightly built with a soft, attractive face free of makeup. What possible interest she could have in a hack journalist old enough to be her father.

Fat Eddie had been running the bar at The Dog and Duck for as long as I could recall. We weren't friends other than when I was drinking and he was serving, and he'd probably served me more drinks than any other barman in Kings Cross. I called in there a couple of times a week, but I didn't remember ever seeing the young woman before. From Eddie's comment and his interaction with her, I guessed he knew her.

After serving two beers at the far end, he walked back to where I was perched on a stool. He wiped the bar with a cloth even though it was already clean and dry.

'Anything you want to tell me, Eddie?'

He looked squarely at me for a moment, then said, 'She's trouble.' He hung the cloth, then laid out beer mats in preparation for new customers.

'Trouble how? Good trouble or bad?'

He turned his back to her, leaned an elbow on the bar, and said, 'You know Luis Two-step?'

'Tall guy with a funny shuffling walk and stooped shoulders?'

'Right. Well, she was Luis's girl.' His eyes held mine making sure I understood.

'How'd she shake free of him?'

'Good question. Luis's in tight with the Lebanese and they don't let nobody go. My guess is that Luis's not happy about it.' He let his words sink in for a moment then said in a lowered voice, 'Be careful, Sam, these are some heavy hitters.' He walked away, like he was nervous about telling me what little he had.

Eddie's attitude, and what he'd just told me raised my curiosity, so I turned and looked around as if casually surveying the bar, wanting to take a closer look at this woman who'd dumped a member of the Sydney underworld. That would take a lot of balls or friends further up the food chain, so she was either reckless or protected. From her looks, I'd guess protected.

When I turned to face her she was no longer there. Five minutes later she hadn't returned. I guessed it wasn't a call to the ladies, and that she'd gone. I shrugged it off and concentrated on smoking and drinking.

Ten minutes later I pushed through the door into the wet September night. It was eleven-thirty, and on most Friday nights at that time the Golden Mile of Kings Cross would be humming, but the cold winter rain had reduced the crowd to a few dozen diehards rather than several hundred revellers.

Cold rain ran down my neck. I cursed the winter, bowed my head, and strode toward William Street, keeping one eye raised for a cab.

'Taxi!' I waved my arm and yelled too loud, drawing attention from a few of the damp tourists and a guy working the door of a nightclub. The silver Falcon swerved into the kerb, its wipers throwing a spray of rain at me as it pulled to a stop. I yanked open the back door feeling lucky to have found a cab so quickly, then I realised it wasn't luck.

I slid onto the back seat, pulled the door shut, pushed the water from my hair, and said, 'If we're going to share a cab I should know your name.'

She continued to stare at me as the cab pulled back into the traffic and continued along Darlinghurst Road. 'Eddie didn't tell you?'

I raised a wet eyebrow. 'If he did, I wouldn't be asking you. I don't play mind games.'

'No, I heard you're a straight shooter.' She lowered her eyes. 'Sorry, I didn't mean it like that. I need to talk with you.'

'What else did you hear that made you curious enough to kidnap me this way?'

Without hesitation she said, 'I heard you're a journalist who has a conscience. I also heard you say what you think – tell it how it is. That you're your own man.'

'Is that why you kept looking at me back at the bar, curiosity about an honest journo? Or were you waiting for me to make a fool of myself trying to pick up a good-looking woman half my age?'

A short nervous snort escaped, like she'd been keeping it bottled up. Beneath the streetwise attitude she was in turmoil.

'And you still haven't told me your name,' I said.

She looked away, but the side window reflected her sadness. 'It's Monica.'

'Okay, Monica, what do you want?' Before she had time to answer I cut her off. 'Wait, let me guess. You have a story to tell about your grubby underworld friends, about life as a moll. Is that it?'

Her jaw set and her eyes hardened. The sadness was gone. I didn't call her a moll to be rude, but to find out what she wanted to say. To needle it out of her. I didn't have time or interest to play word games in a cab on a rainy night with a woman connected to a mid-level underworld hoodlum named Luis Two-step. Didn't matter how cute she was.

'Are you always so rude when you first meet someone?' Her tone was more curious, than angry or offended, and I noticed for the first time that her voice was refined as opposed to street side, which I would have expected.

'Only if I think I am being jerked around. What do you want from me, Monica?'

She buried her emotion behind a cockeyed know-it-all smile, as if the whole world was a joke, particularly me. When she hadn't said anything after five seconds I decided she was just another Kings Cross head-case. I leaned forward in my seat, told the cab driver to pull over. He did as I asked but left the meter running. I turned and looked at her, shrugged, and said, 'Well?'

She lost the pasted smile. 'I've something for you. An exclusive. But not here. I can't talk about it here.'

Like any veteran journalist, I'd heard that line a hundred times before. If it hadn't been for Eddie telling me about her connection to Luis Two-step, I'd have been back in the rain looking for an empty cab.

My hand dropped from the door handle. I said, 'Then where can you talk?'

The cab driver sat passively, the wipers flicked rain, and I didn't know whether to get out into the wet night or go along for the ride and see what she had. When a heavy rain squall hammered the windscreen I leaned back in the seat. 'Okay, one hour. It's all I have.'

Victory flashed across her eyes, then was gone again. She told the driver to take us to Mosman Marina. The cab pulled back into the traffic, I rubbed at midnight eyes wondering if I'd be doing this if she wasn't so easy to look at.

Twenty minutes later the cab dropped us at the marina carpark. We walked to the head of the dock where she opened a security gate with a swipe card taken from her purse. Three quarters of the way down the dock she turned onto one of the fingers and stepped aboard a red hulled yacht about forty feet long.

'This yours?' I asked.

'I wish. It belongs to a friend. I use it sometimes when I want to be alone.'

I followed her below into the saloon where she flicked on the red overhead light used for night sailing. The dim red glow was just enough to see, and I wondered if she'd used it for dramatic effect. I removed my coat and looked around for somewhere to put it. There was a brass hook beside the companionway steps, so I hung it there and let it drip onto the varnished teak grate below.

She lit a cigarette and let it dangle from her lips as she cleared magazines and a laptop from the table, then took a bottle from one locker, two glasses from another and poured drinks without asking if I wanted one. She laid them on the saloon table and sat on the port-side sofa watching me as I sat opposite her.

Keeping the cynicism out of my voice, I said, 'What have you got, Monica? What's the exclusive you have for me?'

After a long moment during which she seemed to be forming her reply, she said, 'Did Eddie tell you I used to hang out with Luis Two-step?' When I didn't answer she went on. 'Luis reacted badly when I left him. It'd be fair to say he's royally pissed and will have me rubbed unless I get away from here. So—'

'—And to get out of here you need a fat pay cheque for your story. Am I right?' She didn't answer, just picked up one of the glasses and swallowed half the whiskey. 'One thing you have to understand right now, Monica, is that if you've got anything significant, and if I'm interested, you'll have to stay local and answer lots of questions. It's not just a case of—'

'—I've written it all down. Everything. Names. Places.' She lowered her eyes. 'All the dark, ugly details.'

'Sounds as if you've been planning this for a while.' She didn't respond, so I asked. 'Where will you go?'

She drained the glass, placed it carefully on the varnished table, then shrugged and said, 'Overseas. Somewhere laid-back. The Caribbean, maybe.'

'In this?' I said spreading my arms.

She smiled properly for the first time, opened her mouth to say something, but before she could, the boat rocked to port as if someone had just stepped onto the side-deck. We both felt it. The blood left her cheeks, and when her eyes met mine they were tense with fear. I put a finger to my lips, then moved from the salon into the darkness of the small forward cabin. I opened the overhead hatch just enough to get my eyes at deck level. The foredeck was clear. I scanned the port side-deck, then flinched at the unmistakable sound of a silenced handgun. I froze, unable to tell if the sound had come from inside or out. All I could hear was the pulsing in my temple. A second or two later the boat rocked again, followed by the sound of quick footsteps on the wharf. I raised my head again until I could see out.

The only movement was the taillights of a car turning left out of the carpark. It was too far to get the make, never mind a colour or number plate.

When I looked back into the salon, Monica was slumped on the sofa. Blood was trickling from a small, dark hole in her forehead, then running through her right eye and down her nose.

***

The cops arrived seven minutes after I called it in. I'd already left the boat and was sitting on a bench at the head of the dock. Two patrol cars were first to arrive. One cop wanted to cuff me but was told not to be a jerk by another. They started to secure the crime scene.

Five minutes later I heard another car come to a rapid stop, and turned to see two men get out of an unmarked car. I recognised one of them as DS Matt Rickman, an honest, if somewhat cynical cop. He made arrests, looked out for his mates and provided for his wife and four kids. Our paths had crossed many times in the past when I was working as crime reporter for the *Mosman Daily*.

They walked over to me. Rickman said, 'What are you doing here, Autenburg? You smell blood?'

'Fucking reporters,' his partner said, then turned away, ducked under the crime scene tape and walked down the dock.

'Good to see you, too, Rickman. And no, I didn't smell blood, I saw it. I'm not here as a reporter, I'm your witness.'

His eyebrows arched, his shoulders hitched, then he said, 'Do you want to tell me what happened here, Sam, or do you want to go to the station and have your lawyer present?'

'I don't need a lawyer, Rickman, I've nothing to hide.'

'Sorry, Sam,' he said with deliberate insincerity. 'Bad time to be riding you when your girl's just been shot. How are you feeling?'

'She wasn't my girl, Rickman. And don't try to finesse me, you're not up to it. Never have been, never will be.'

'So what then? A hooker? Your long-lost daughter?'

I ignored the bait, pulled a pack of cigarettes from my pocket and lit up. After two deep, satisfying draws, I said, 'How come they sent you, Rickman? She's dead, not missing.'

'Perhaps you didn't hear, maybe you're out of touch, but I moved up from missing persons to murder investigations a couple of years ago.'

'Good for you, Rickman,' I said without enthusiasm.

He looked down at me for a long moment, then sat beside me on the bench and in a conciliatory tone said, 'Come on, Sam, let's cut the banter and bullshit. Tell me what happened.'

I told him, leaving out what Fat Eddie had told me about Monica being Luis Two-step's girlfriend, and the part about her having a story to sell. He listened without making notes or interrupting.

'And that's all you saw? Taillights disappearing?'

'That's all. After that I came up here and called it in.'

He pulled at his chin as if deep in thought, then tipped his head and ran his fingers through his oiled and greying hair. 'The thing I'm not seeing, is why a good-looking twenty-five-year-old would pick you up in a bar in Kings Cross and take you to a yacht. No disrespect, Sam, but it doesn't sound likely, does it? What was she after? I mean, she must have said something. Why you?'

'Like I told you, Rickman, she seemed to want to talk

about being a journo. Who knows? Maybe she had aspirations herself. We didn't get that far before someone drilled her forehead.'

***

Just after dawn I left Mosman Police Station where Rickman had taken my formal statement. I went straight back to my apartment, made tea, and then sat in the window-seat smoking, drinking, and thinking about Monica until well after dark.

Ten o'clock that night I returned to the marina and recovered Monica's laptop, which I'd taken from the yacht before the cops arrived, and hidden, wrapped in plastic, beneath a thick shrub at the back of the carpark. I jammed it into my empty laptop case and walked away in the shadows.

As soon as I got home I removed the laptop's hard drive and connected it to my computer via a USB. I figured she'd have passwords on the files, so I ran a piece of software to find recently saved password protected documents, then poured a glass of Laphroaig, added some water and waited.

Before I was halfway down the glass I got a hit. The file name was a string of random characters and numbers. I started up a cracking tool I'd used in the past when I'd forgotten my own passwords, and set it to work. I topped up my glass, slipped a movie into the player and lay down on the sofa.

It was six-thirty the following morning when I woke to find the cursor blinking after the words, 'crack successful'. I opened the file and started reading. After skimming the document for less than five minutes I had to stop, take a deep breath, and take stock. Then I sat at my desk and started reading again from the beginning.

It was all there, the connections between criminal entities, bent cops, who ran what and where. It would have taken Monica months, years even, to get all that information.

149

The overwhelming question was why, and why give it to me? Why not the cops if she wanted to do a deal? Maybe she didn't know who to trust and came to me in desperation. Or maybe she'd approached a cop only to find out they were on some hood's payroll, and she'd been living on borrowed time ever since. Which lead to the question – did Luis know what she'd been doing?

I stood and paced, then stopped and looked down at the street, wondering how much danger this was putting me in. What if Rickman was on the take and he tells Luis Two-step that I was with her when she was killed. I'd always thought Rickman was straight, but who knows. Who really knows anything about anyone at this level? What if the gunman had recognised me? If they had any idea she'd been writing down all of their dirty little secrets, they'd soon put two and two together and come for me next.

After checking there were no more files I'd need on the drive, I copied the protected document to my laptop, then destroyed Monica's hard drive with a hammer. Three minutes later I left the apartment with both laptops and an overnight bag.

***

Annie's Place was a secluded motel four hours north of Sydney. It was no more than a few old wooden huts with deep verandas set beside a lake, but it was where I always went to find solitude, and in this instance, safety as well. The owners greeted me like an old friend. They were as ancient and rustic as the cabins. They gave me my usual spot, and then left me alone.

I switched on my laptop and waited for it to boot up. Monica's computer I'd ditched in a dumpster at a parking bay north of the city. For the remainder of the day I read, then re-read the thirty-two explosive pages. It centred around the unsolved murder of Sonja Hartman, a twenty-two-year-old underworld groupie. Her murder had drawn lots of press coverage, TV, too. It wasn't just because she was an attractive and vulnerable young woman, but because her body was found in two pieces like it had been torn in half. The press soon labelled her The Sydney Dahlia after Elizabeth Short, whose body was found in a similar state in LA in 1947. The LA press had nicknamed her The Black Dahlia, and she was later immortalised by James Ellroy in his novel of the same name. Elizabeth Short's murder was never solved; neither was Sonja Hartman's.

Investigating something like this was way out of my league. For a while I considered handing it over to the cops – but who? There were so many bent cops named in the document that I didn't have faith in anyone, not even Rickman who I'd always thought was straight. He wasn't named, but other cops who I knew he'd worked with were. Some came as no surprise, with others I was gob-smacked. I had to assume they were all tainted, anything else was suicide. Another consideration was that if I went to the cops, I'd probably be charged with tampering with a crime scene and withholding evidence. Who knows what else.

I went out onto the veranda, sat on a rickety chair and lit a cigarette. It was an hour before dark and I had some serious thinking to do. I now knew who'd ordered Sonja Hartman to be killed, and how it should be done. Who did the actual killing came down to three men, all equally guilty in my book. What did it matter which one tied her legs around a tree, which one put a chain around her chest and bound her arms to her sides with gaffer tape, or which one drove the car that pulled her in two? They were all guilty and needed to burn.

What was missing was the reason – the motive. And now Monica was dead there was no witness either. Not that she'd witnessed the murder, but she had – according to her report – heard them planning it, talking about it both before and after the act.

And there was more than Sonja Hartman's murder, so much more. This would blow the lid off the nastiest crock of maggots in Australia. I'd never get a bigger story than this. I could name my price. It was a career piece, but one that would get me killed if my name was on it. The whistling kettle cut into my thoughts.

I made tea and returned to the veranda, my head filling with the obvious, swirling with possibilities as I walked back outside. Since becoming a journalist at age twenty-two I'd always wanted to write fiction. Always wanted time to explore the words and worlds that so often occupied my head. I gazed unblinking across the lake as the pieces formed and aligned in my mind. I opened a new document and started writing.

***

Twenty months after my brief encounter with Monica, I was sitting behind a small table in a bookstore in Melbourne. It was my first book signing, my first public appearance as Johnny Silk. I felt self-conscious, an imposter, because all I'd done was plagiarized Monica's story. I hadn't invented or created it. But I'd used what she'd started, written the story and got it published without getting killed. I'd changed the names of the guilty in such a way that anyone from that murky underworld, or any of those bent cops would know. They'd recognise themselves. It was my parting shot, my salute to Monica, to Sonja Hartman, to all the others. It was as far as I dared go.

The literary agent loved it, the publishers enthused about it, and most important of all, there was no connection between the fictitious Johnny Silk and the missing, presumed dead and unlamented Sam Autenburg. I'd also changed my image with a full beard, heavy rimmed glasses and re-styled hair, sub-consciously modelling myself on a young Stephen King, complete with tweed jacket. All I had to do now was sit back and let the money roll in.

My new image and lifestyle felt good – it had been time to change my old, stale life. What didn't feel good was knowing it took the deaths of two young women to get me there. Some days it was hard to look in the mirror.

My palms were sweating, and I kept my eyes low pretending to do writerly things on an A4 notepad, only occasionally glancing up to see if a crowd was building. It wasn't, but it was only nine-fifteen and the show ran until two in the afternoon. When I sensed someone approach, and then stop in front of me, I wrote two more important words followed by a heavy-handed period, then looked up and smiled at my first fan. My throat was dry, like it was filled with sand. His expressionless eyes held mine as he slid a copy of *The Sydney Dahlia* across the table with his fingertips. 'Would you sign this for me please, Mr Silk? The name's Luis.'

POP DEAD – THE PENSION PAPERS

Pete Adams

A*re you alive?* the letter asked, and Pop looked around, frisked his stubbly face, twiddled the abundance of grey sprouting hair from his left ear, which, if ever he was particularly lost in thought, he could twist into grey dreadlocks (or so his grandkids liked to remark).

Pop wasn't a particularly nervy chap, and on this occasion he was pretty sure he was alive: his ticker had not given up on him, despite many warnings from his doctor, who really was dead. Pop recalled his words upon hearing the news of the doctor's demise, 'Dead? But he ate health stuff!'

But there is only so much lettuce you can hold in one go, and even if it were a dozen cos, stacked, it is not likely to stop a bullet from point blank range.

Bloody inconvenient, though, as Doc was Pop's doctor and, because of his naturally acerbic nature (Pop saw it as an amusing grandiloquence earned by reaching a senior age), he had upset all the other doctors in the practice… and in Portsmouth, to such a degree that they could not be relied upon to sign the form certifying that Pop's life was extant, and not extinct. Pop had upset a few people in his time of *genteel* retirement, more than just the doctors at the surgery. So the pension company and the government had stopped paying Pop's pension all of a sudden on the basis that he was no more and was pushing up daisies somewhere. Daisy was a lovely girl, although their friendship had tailed off along with Pop's performance, since Doc had upped and died, and his Viagra prescription had run out. Had Daisy reported him as no longer functioning?

Well, clearly the thing to do was to get a doctor's signature on the form. Not difficult, he could forge that, but getting it imprinted with the formal practice stamp: that was easier said than done when Pop's Antisocial Behaviour Order, and the restraining order, prevented him venturing within a half mile of the surgery. No other surgery would take him. And even the People's Dispensary for Sick Animals had told him, rather humourlessly, he thought, to stop enquiring about Alsatian and St Bernard-sized Viagra pills.

His *Proof of Life* forms needed to be filled in, stamped, signed and sent off so he could get his pension monies reinstated and at last get his illicit Viagra from the dealer outside the Sunny Rest Home.

So Pop turned his mind to this pressing problem.

His grandson had left his wetsuit in the shed. It was black and would suit his plan admirably. The grandson was as tall as Pop but did not carry quite so much flesh but the material was stretchy, wasn't it? It would be okay. He didn't need the flippers; he would wear his Jesus sandals but would have to wear black socks. It was important not to have anything that would reveal his presence in the dead of the night. He blacked his face with soot and put on the hood and then the face mask. He had tried to remove the snorkel but it was attached securely and every time he pulled it the elasticised strap stretched then snapped the tube back in his face. Never mind, the black eyes would be helpful.

It was about two in the morning before he deemed it dark enough; no moon, no streetlights (the kids had smashed them). It was awkward walking: there was not so much give as he imagined in the wetsuit, and his bum felt so restricted. *Mind you*, he thought, *Daisy would like to see me right now. Dead indeed...*

Pop was a pensioner of action.

Reaching the surgery, he removed the golden syrup and brown paper from his Waitrose bag for life. He always carried this bag, for two reasons. One, it would show everyone he was posh and should be taken serious; and two, if he let go of it he thought there was a chance he might die.

Pop hadn't quite grasped the theory behind the bag for life.

With the screwdriver he always carried (for screwing) he jemmied the lid off the treacle tin, and using his hands he smeared the viscous syrup onto the brown paper. He'd seen this done somewhere: you plastered the window with the syrupy paper and when you smashed the glass it made no sound. He had some difficulty detaching his sticky hands from the paper; and then the paper from the wrong window; and then the side of his wetsuit, but eventually he was ready.

He bent down to get his walking stick and the backside of the wetsuit gave way with an enormous ripping and farting sound as the constrained air and blubber made a bid for liberation and comfort.

Oh well, Pop thought, *I'll get a taxi home.*

He tried to move the walking stick to his right hand, the one he preferred to use when smashing things, but the stick was stuck to the syrup. So he aimed at the brown paper left-handed, missed and hit the wrong pane of glass. Fortunately it didn't sound too loud: hearing loss had its advantages.

Morag the Hag, as the kids called Morag Hughes, the old bat who lived opposite the surgery, was also hard of hearing and her vision wasn't so good either; but ever since the druggies had broken into the surgery and shot the doctor a week or so ago, she'd had difficulty sleeping and watched constantly over the premises across the road. She had sensed something, but was only aware of a presence, a slight movement in the dark, when all of a sudden a huge white mass drew her attention. She didn't realise it, but she was staring down the double barrel of Pop's revealed arse.

After she had collected her infrared binoculars – the ones she used for looking into people's houses – she could see the intruder a little more distinctly. She telephoned the police just as Pop was trying to detach his sticky walking stick from his sticky hand, reporting that she believed the man had a Kalashnikov.

The police, naturally alert following the shooting of the doctor, scrambled the Portsmouth Firearms Unit. Enthusiastically energised, they swung their guns over shoulders, switched on their front lights and the flashing red rear lights, and the blue revolving lights on the handlebars and launched themselves onto their bikes, shouting 'Nee nah, nee nah'. Content in the knowledge that this is what they had trained for, what they kept their tyres pumped up for, they headed to the surgery.

In the meantime Pop was halfway through the window to the side of the treacle and brown paper pane, but was stuck as his walking stick was awkwardly jammed across the frame, and he was disturbed, though not unpleasantly, by a cooling breeze whistling around his naughty bits – which, if he were honest, had been overheating, what with the excitement of the task and their close confinement in neoprene. But, eventually he was through. He immediately headed into reception and waddled to the counter to collect the surgery stamp, stamped his form, and put it back into his bag for life.

He was alerted by criss-crossing of beams of light; he couldn't hear the squeals of brakes as the swat team arrived, padlocked their bikes to a nearby telegraph pole, and set up their positions behind the front boundary wall.

Morag went out into the street to enjoy the party atmosphere, along with her neighbours, most of whom were scantily clad in their night attire.

An officer, clearly in charge of the firearms unit, was busy straightening out what appeared to Morag to be a cardboard tube from a toilet roll that must have become crushed as he cycled to the scene. Having managed to get the tube to resemble a tube, he brought it to his lips and shouted through, 'Hallo, hallo, hallo, what's all the 'ere then?'

There was an eerie silence following the traditional police challenge.

The officer brought the toilet roll to his mouth again and repeated the challenge. Pop had not heard – but he had seen the lights swing as the police officers looked around and their head torches formed an energetic light sabre clash.

Pop realised he needed to think of something quickly, and he did. Whether his plan would work he could not know, but it was a plan; and so he climbed into the big fish tank that took up one side of the waiting room wall, pleased now that he had kept the snorkel. He was sure nobody would see him among the tropical fish that swam in the inch or so of water left. The rest of the water had deluged onto the waiting room lino floor, along with a number of flip-flopping fish.

The firearms officers, edgy, nervous as there had been no response to the challenge, did what they had been coached to do by their American trainers: they opened fire, and the flashes of muzzle fire lit up the street and the resounding bangs were joined by smashing glass. There was silence. Then the windows to the whole facade fell out, followed by a creaking and a groan, as the surgery front door fell in.

'Stop!' It was a sane cry from Detective Sergeant Dixon, who had just arrived, and as the armed officers rested their weapons, he sighed. 'For Christ's sake,' he said, his ears still ringing. 'Okay, let's check out what we have.'

The armed officers leapt into action again, and as a well drilled squad, lined up behind each other, marking time and shouting 'One two, one two, one...' and then launched themselves at what remained of the surgery. 'One two, one two...' crunch, crunch, crunch, their boots trampled over the front door and they progressed through each room.

'Clear!' Crunch, crunch. 'Clear!' Crunch. They crunched into the waiting room, 'Clear!' and then crunched out, not having noticed the huge fish in the aquarium. The detective sergeant wiped his brow with the back of his hand and sighed audibly as he leaned a hand on the side of the aquarium, aware that the strafing of machine gun fire had caused this tropical whale to deposit a number of floating logs on the surface of the water.

DS Dixon wiggled his fingers hallo to the waiting room Jacques Cousteau and Pop realised he had been spotted. All the same, he still tried to hide behind a little rock arch, pushing out a crowd of scared fish, whose neon stripes were flashing like emergency lights.

A uniformed officer was collecting their fallen fishy comrades from the lino and putting them into a bedpan full of water. Some revived, but some were behaving like the logs floating in the aquarium, which Dixon thought would be more appropriately placed in the bedpan.

DS Dixon tapped the glass.

Pop turned his head and saw the detective gesture for him to get out. Pop's left hand was still stuck to the walking stick, but with his free right hand, Pop gestured back, 'who me?', as if he hoped the detective meant the fish.

Dixon nodded, picking up the chair that had fallen as Pop had dived into the aquarium, and with a faux polite wave, indicated that Pop may wish to avail himself of this stepping stone out of the water. Dixon was struggling not to laugh as Pop tried hard, slipping and sliding, to get a purchase so he could raise himself up. Eventually he succeeded. Dixon offered a hand to help him down, and then regretted it when he found himself stuck with treacle to the Kalashnikov walking stick.

A uniformed officer went to handcuff Pop, but Dixon waved him away, not that Pop had noticed: he was rummaging through his bag for life. At last he came up with the soggy *Proof of Life* form. He laid the form over the back of the chair and commenced blowing on it to dry it out.

Dixon did laugh at that and then became angry as the crime scene – *if you could call it that,* he thought – was invaded by a crone in a sagging and not particularly hygienic silk nightdress.

'Morag,' Pop said, except it was muffled as he still had the snorkel in.

'Pop, is that you?'

Pop removed the face mask and snorkel and his wetsuit hood; but Morag was looking at the active bulging of Pop's naughty bits, and this excited Pop even more. There was something about Morag's smile that got to him; maybe it was the way her teeth moved. Her breasts were so alluring as well, in their sagging emptiness, the hint of chilled and prominent nipples. All this visual stimulation combined with the adrenaline rush meant he had no need for the Viagra prescription. If he hurried, he could make out for himself. Life could be sweet at times.

Pop turned to Dixon, 'I'll be with Morag across the road if you need me. And bring my forms when they are dried, please,' and they left together. Pop's left hand was now stuck to Morag's bum, along with the walking stick, and she appeared to be taking great pleasure in that.

Dixon sighed as he watched his dad leave with this old girl.

THE SINS OF MURIEL MCGARRY

A.S.King

By Christmas Muriel had completed all things pertinent to make good her retirement. Documents were meticulously shredded, paper trails deleted and secondary systems checked and re-checked in case of duplicates. Muriel was very thorough. The last task remaining was to dust off her desk in readiness for its new occupant.

She hadn't intended forty-two years of faithful service to end quite this way but someone had to act. Here was Muriel's chance to put things right, to manage things as they should be managed. If she'd learned one useful lesson this last year, it was how little the Company respected her talents. More fool them. It might ruin her spotless reputation but she no longer cared what anyone thought. This was Muriel McGarry breaking out of her mould, making a stand for humanity.

The Board would be waiting to present the compulsory timepiece. She checked her composure in the mirror behind her desk. Not a single brown hair out of place. She applied a coat of coral lipstick and smoothed her powdered cheeks. There hadn't been a day spent at Tamsett's when her manner wasn't tailored to her part. Today would be no different. Nobody should suspect that Muriel wasn't actually retiring, she was being re-born.

Certainly she didn't feel old, being blessed with sound constitution, a testament to a responsible diet and regular purposeful exercise. She cycled the five miles to work from her flat at the top of King's Road. When she dropped the last few remaining files back to records this morning Mr Jamieson had remarked how she looked far too young to be retiring. In fact, he seemed genuinely surprised when she whispered she would soon be turning sixty. This being her last day she didn't beg for his discretion. Everyone but the night-watch would know her true age by dusk.

Emma Perkins from accounts nodded as they passed

in the hall, balancing silicon-pumped sophistication atop impossible four-inch stilettos. The woman spent three months in a hospital bed after attempting a bucket-list wish to skydive. Such gross self-indulgence was not going to propel Muriel into her dotage; she required more rewarding enticements, preferably without a limp.

Muriel had begun her career in the sixties soon after graduating, with honours, from Pitman's Secretarial College. One of her favourite tutors helped organise a temporary placement at Tamsett's head office in the City. She took the position merely to gain experience prior to applying for the Civil Service but the terms and conditions were such she decided to stay, despite her father's hopes. Mr McGarry had always remained in favour of public service.

Tamsett's procedures had rather stagnated in the hundred years since its foundation. Coming bright-eyed into the business at eighteen years of age Muriel discovered a flair for efficient organisation. Sir John Stevens was plain JS back then, having joined the Company that very same month. Although a mere office junior Muriel showed such zeal for innovation that JS begged his father to allow her to act as his personal secretary and the big man agreed, despite her lowly status. Being like-minded they worked tirelessly together innovating the Company's systems and introducing computer-based technologies which their rivals came to envy. After twenty years of diligent service her career absolutely peaked when JS was knighted for his services to British Industry.

The boardroom was crowded. Muriel took her seat meekly, nodding politely at the circle of tight-lipped faces. Forty-two years of greeting them and making them feel at ease with the Company's procedures; mopping up messes, wiping away stains, listing their whims so they didn't throw a tantrum at the tea-girl. Muriel made sure every mistake was neatly blotted up by her efficiency. Oiling wheels within wheels. And not one of them stood up for her when Sir John's arrogant heir concluded his first board meeting with that astonishing announcement. '*I'm sure you'll agree Miss McGarry has been an absolute treasure over the years but I've decided to bring some young blood into the Company. Therefore, I'm taking this opportunity to offer her a very comfortable package so she can enjoy the kind of retirement she deserves.*' And taking to his armchair proceeded to grin back at her like a schoolboy.

There had been no prior consultation. No discussion of her needs. With her face glowing like a beetroot Muriel managed to acknowledge the Board's generosity without hinting at her true feelings. Had the boy but known it her capacity to suppress emotion was chief among the reasons his father so valued her services. Not that she wanted to complain. Right at the beginning JS told her plainly she could never become his wife, and working closely together every single working day seemed fair compensation for not having him always to herself.

Of course, Johnnie later apologised, making every effort to smooth the cracks before proceeding to describe his own good sense for withdrawing from formal responsibility while still in first-class health. The Company pension plan was indeed excellent, and index-linked, '*you can put your feet up and relax knowing you'll have complete financial security.*' Muriel had bitten her lip, suppressing her instinct to straighten his ruffled hair. How could his 'treasure' be dumped so inconsiderately?

However, destiny seemed to take hand. Within the month the measure of her revenge was prescribed by no less a person than Kate Adie. It was Muriel's first inkling of Tamsett's deceit and came during a documentary about a particularly ruthless conflict in Central Africa. The heartrending footage concluded with Miss Adie interviewing the rebel commander, which struck a particular nerve because not a month previously Muriel attended a core meeting with the same urgent-minded gentleman in Sir John's private office. Of course, on that occasion he wasn't wearing desert camouflage or grasping an automatic weapon but listening to his blatant lies made Muriel absolutely steam. If only she had enough courage she might inform the BBC just how he was funding this war.

But once the seed was sown she couldn't let matters rest. Applying every diligence she habitually applied to her work Muriel went through Tamsett's annual transactions with a fine-toothed comb. By examining the movement of funds it didn't take long to confirm the degree of her Company's involvement. Just as Muriel suspected Johnnie was using charitable trusts to disguise the transfer of sickening amounts of capital into investment funds that favoured companies whose sizeable profits were solely derived from manufacturing weapons of war. Worse, quite unwittingly, she'd enabled Tamsett's part, having helped design the very systems he was using to hide their guilt.

That was the day Muriel decided she must take a stand. She began her plan of action by agreeing to the terms of her retirement in principle, but making the addendum that she gave the Company six further months of service, in order to train her replacement. It would take that long, she thought, to doctor the records and facilitate the necessary changes. Of course, Johnnie didn't argue, although his soft sapphire eyes registered obvious relief when reminded she was due a month's sabbatical. It was going to be her first proper holiday in years.

Africa proved seductive. Vast cloudless skies spread across finite amber plains. She embraced the organised tours, enjoyed chasing around in heavy-wheeled four-by-fours after herds of wild beasts not constricted by fences or steel bars. But she longed to go off-piste, to learn something of the people, the survivors of civil war. The day before she was due to fly home she took her heart in her hands and asked hotel reception if they could instruct a taxi-driver to take her inside a refugee camp. It was dangerous: they couldn't recommend such a risk; but neither could Muriel leave without knowing what life was like beyond the gates of her four-star all-inclusive resort.

Coming into a place where few homes had better comfort than four tin walls and a roof was extremely humbling. Packed tight together in straight-lined grids with barely a yard between them meant life was lived in public. Washing hung across beaten pathways, stepping stones bridged the mud and the heat and filth overpowered her senses. Muriel felt faint. Taking pity, her anxious taxi-driver led her inside a wooden-walled shanty bar. Its canvas covered deck brandished an ancient Coca Cola sign and several scrubbed steel tables surrounded by thin-beamed benches. There were no chairs. All Muriel wanted was to return to her cosy hotel but the bar was clean and a kind-faced young lady presented her with a bottle of chilled local beer.

As she sipped politely an elderly man shuffled from a corner to offer her a Polo mint. He smiled, face wrinkled in broken lines. His clothes were threadbare and he smelt of sweet tobacco but his smile grew wider as she accepted his gift. The taxi-driver sloped into the opposite seat and called the waitress over.

'Leah.' He nodded his neat head. 'She speaks good English.'

And they talked.

Leah had been a teacher at high school before the

last war destroyed her life. Muriel listened intently, asking many questions, and when she was finally ready to leave the old man offered his hand for support. They returned to the taxi by way of a nursery where a hedge of silver wire separated the round-faced children from the path. A row of white smiles beamed at Muriel, pressing tiny hands, feet and noses through the mesh.

The old man took her inside, introducing every teacher as the children giggled behind their skirts. The dark backroom that constituted their nursery was a rusty corrugated hut with a pounded earth floor littered with dull plastic toys. A single-ringed stove was heating a vast pan of oil, and the smell of hot-dough cooking reminded Muriel of childhood summers on Blackpool seafront.

Leah appeared, summoned by the taxi-driver. Laughing with the children she explained that the nursery gave the children their one hot meal of the day. That the stove, in fact everything she could see, had been provided by an international charity. But they couldn't afford pens or paper so the children drew their pictures and learned their letters in the dust of the floor.

Muriel cancelled her flight home. Returning to the nursery next day she discovered something which her whole life had been missing. And there was much to do, not least sort out supplies of proper paper and pens. Teaching came naturally and held far better rewards than checking executive expenses. By the time she finally left for England there were tears all round.

With her motives further fuelled Muriel returned meekly to her desk. She hardly expected her final months at Tamsett's to prove so exhilarating. Delving into secrets, diverting hidden funds, clearly the Civil Service had been deprived the talents of a resourceful operator. Johnnie's po-faced heir was so poised with success he barely questioned the transfer papers she asked him to sign, never mind checked the finer details. And Muriel was meticulous. Nobody but the guilty should be blamed when the loss of several millions was finally discovered. All evidence would point to someone on the Board and if they ever came to suspect Muriel McGarry – and she very much doubted they had enough sense between them – senior embarrassment would want to hide it from investors.

Muriel might have been overcome with the handshakes and stilted praise. As Johnnie handed over the timepiece he suddenly became so emotional she wondered if his mind was beginning to fail: that would certainly explain how he managed to ignore his son's many shortcomings.

***

The news hit international headlines during the first week after New Year. Muriel was having breakfast in her new apartment in Kinsa while listening to the BBC World Service. She smiled when she heard Johnnie's shaken voice give the formal statement, composed no doubt by a lawyer.

'We would like to assure our clients that the overseas funds which the press are trying to claim we handled illegally are not under investigation by the fraud squad, nor have we ever contravened any restrictions imposed by the United Nations. I can honestly say that Tamsett's would never be party to such underhand dealings.'

Obviously he was still blissfully unaware of the true extent of her tinkering; she'd given the reporter more than enough evidence to bury the whole bloody company. Salutary to think that whatever the sins of Muriel McGarry, the sins of her lover far outweighed them.

***

All the little ones wore their Sunday best for the party. Their brand new teacher was whisked around the brick-built extension and proudly shown the sparkling facilities, the books, the games, the well-equipped kitchen, as drifts of tiny squeals filled the air. The smell of hot dough cakes announced it was time for the feast to begin. Thankfully there were absolutely no speeches.

THE SHEPHERD'S BOTHY

L J Ross

Ablanket of fog descended, rolling in from the North Sea to settle heavily on the hills and vales of Northumberland. It wound itself through the scattered villages in a cloud so dense the people and houses seemed little more than spectres; ghostly figures passing through the blurry edges of the world.

Through the fog, a line of cars moved slowly along the A1, as if in a convoy heading back towards Newcastle from the north. Detective Chief Inspector Ryan trained his eyes on the red tail lights of the car in front, tugging down the sun shield to protect his eyes from the unrelenting glare of white and grey. Visibility was less than three metres and when he eased off the accelerator to allow a stopping distance, he watched the little red lights disappear again into the mist, leaving him with the impression of being completely alone.

"It's thick as pea soup," Detective Sergeant Frank Phillips pronounced, from his position in the passenger seat beside him.

Ryan's lips quirked.

"I haven't got a clue how far we've travelled. Could be five miles, could be fifteen. I can't see a damn thing."

"I still can't get any GPS signal on my phone," Phillips said.

Ryan huffed out an irritated breath.

"What time is it?" The skies were so grey it was impossible to tell the position of the sun.

"Four o'clock."

Ryan rested an elbow on the edge of the window as they crawled along the road and thought that when the sun set in another hour or so, driving would be even more difficult.

To make matters worse, it was bitterly cold.

"Just so long as it doesn't snow," he said.

* * *

The snow started twenty minutes later, settling heavily on the car bonnet and the parts of the windscreen the wipers couldn't reach.

"Frank, remind me again why I don't move back down south, away from the Grim North?"

Phillips let out a rumbling laugh.

"You'd miss me too much, lad."

Ryan smiled grimly.

"I don't—*shit*!"

The car lurched as he slammed his foot on the brake pedal, swerving to avoid a barrier that had materialised ahead of them, blocking both southbound lanes. Two other cars had careered towards the side of the road, unable to see the bold red 'STOP' signs until it was too late.

Ryan pulled up beside the barrier and pushed open the car door. The wind hit him like a fist to the face but he turned his face against the driving snow and went in search of information.

A man wearing a neon jacket appeared. He wore a thick woollen balaclava underneath his cap, pulled tight to protect his skin.

"What's going on here?" Ryan shouted over the wind.

"Accident, a bit further down," the traffic constable answered, his voice muffled beneath the wool. "You need to follow the diversion."

Ryan peered over the man's shoulder but could see nothing but a wall of white vapour.

"How much longer will you be? Is it worth waiting?"

The constable shook his head.

"Fire and ambulance services haven't arrived yet, so the road will be closed a while longer."

Ryan nodded his thanks and returned to his car. When

he glanced back, the man had gone.

* * *

They followed the yellow diversion signs as far as they could, winding their way through the myriad narrow country lanes which led them further and further into the wilds of Northumberland, away from the city and from civilisation.

"This can't be the right way," Ryan muttered eventually.

"It's been a while since we saw the last marker," Phillips agreed. "Should've followed that other car."

Ryan rolled his eyes.

"Yes, thank you, *sergeant*."

Phillips folded his hands across his paunch.

"No need to get snippy with me, just because you're lost."

Ryan gripped the steering wheel to negotiate another hairpin bend which had appeared in the road ahead.

"In the first place," he said, "my maiden aunt is 'snippy'. If absolutely necessary, I would prefer to be called a 'grumpy bastard'."

"That can be arranged," Phillips put in.

"In the second place," Ryan continued, "we are *not* lost."

They both fell silent, watching as the sky lost all vestiges of light and turned into an oppressive black shroud, relieved only by the flashes of falling snowflakes illuminated by the car's headlights.

They drove like that for another twenty minutes and Ryan was on the verge of suggesting that they pull over somewhere and bed down for the night when, miraculously, a pair of red tail lights reappeared through the gloom.

"Follow that car!" Phillips shouted.

Ryan slanted him a look.

"How long have you been waiting to say that?"

"Years, lad. Years."

* * *

They couldn't make out the colour or make of the phantom car driving a short distance ahead of them but by mutual accord they decided to keep following it. They began to have second thoughts when the car unexpectedly took a sharp right into a single track lane leading up a steep incline.

"Bloody hell," Phillips murmured, trying to visualise a map of Northumberland in his mind's eye. "We must be somewhere in the Coquet Valley."

Ryan set his jaw and gunned the engine, feeling the tyres skid against the snow which carpeted the road. The tracks from the car ahead were already disappearing under a layer of fresh snow but, after some choice language, they finally emerged onto a plateau that led directly through an open gateway.

"Please, God, let it be one of those cosy little boutique hotels."

The outlook did not look promising; a long, ramshackle stone hut presented itself, two of its boxy windows shining a weak orange glow through the darkness. It was impossible to tell if there were any other houses nearby but, as they drew closer, two other cars came into view.

Phillips frowned at them.

"Which car did we follow?"

"Does it matter? Looks like somebody's home. Maybe they'll take pity on us."

* * *

When their knock went unanswered, Ryan took matters into his own hands and burst through the door. The hut consisted of one main room with a solid stone shelf along the back wall and two doors, perhaps leading to a bathroom and the rear exit. There was an enormous stone fireplace, with a fire crackling heartily in the grate. Beside it, two women looked up in surprise.

"Excuse the dramatic entrance," Ryan slammed the door behind them and began to shake off the snow. "We were following the diversion from the A1 but managed to get lost along the way."

"Don't s'pose either of you know where the heck we are?" Phillips asked.

There was a look, swiftly exchanged. Interpreting it, Ryan stepped forward and extended a hand to the closest of the two women, who stood with her back to the fire.

"Sorry—rude of us not to introduce ourselves. I'm Ryan and this is—" he nearly said *Phillips*. "Frank."

If Phillips wondered why Ryan hadn't mentioned they were both murder detectives attached to Northumbria CID, nothing on his face betrayed the fact.

"Aye, don't worry, we're not axe murderers."

There was a long, awkward pause, then both women chuckled awkwardly and the strained sound echoed around all four corners of the hut.

"I'm Mathilda," the woman replied, taking his hand. Her eyes were very dark and in the dim light Ryan couldn't make out their colour. She turned to the other woman, who was now seated on a heavy wooden chest placed to the right of the fire with a thick tartan blanket covering her legs.

"This is Isobel."

Ryan began to unpeel his overcoat.

"Who owns this place?"

"It's a sort of shepherd's hut or bothy, free for people to use if they're out hiking or stargazing so long as they replace the firewood and supplies when they leave. I—" Isobel's eyes skittered across to where the other woman stood gazing into the fire. "We were both caught up in the diversion and decided to drive up here."

Ryan dipped down to remove his boots and noted three other wet pairs sitting neatly against the wall. Phillips was still wearing his boots.

"You drove up here together?"

Isobel began to fiddle with the blanket, folding and re-folding the material between her fingers. Mathilda selected a poker and began to prod the fire back into life.

"No," she said eventually. "We drove separately but we were both heading into Newcastle for the same event."

"Oh?"

"Our friend is going to be married on Saturday. Isn't she, Isobel?"

The other woman nodded dumbly.

"Lucky you both knew about this place, isn't it?" Ryan observed, before taking a leisurely stroll around the room, tracing over the details and noting the placement of the furniture. He scented the air, drawing in the dank, musty smell laced with something earthy and raw.

Three sets of eyes watched him, speculatively.

A gust of wind buffeted against the windows, howling through the cracks between the ancient wooden window frame and the stone walls. The fire dipped and swayed as the cold air swirled around it, then roared into life again.

"This is turning into quite a night," Ryan said quietly. "Mind if I take a seat?"

He settled himself into one of the dusty armchairs beside the fire and, after a moment, Mathilda took a seat on the wooden chest beside her friend. Phillips remained at the door, unconsciously standing guard.

Ryan stared at the fire, watching blue flames lick at a heavy piece of material. A fresh pile of logs rested in a basket to the side, untouched.

The silence was heavy, thrumming with tension until he spoke again.

"On a night like this, anything can happen. All manner

of deeds might go unnoticed, hidden by the storm. Wouldn't you agree?"

Isobel curled her fingers around the edge of the chest, as if getting ready to jump to her feet. Mathilda merely cocked her head, considering the question with interest.

"Yes, on a night like this, things seem unreal; like a fantasy. This hut," she gestured around the decaying walls, "it's like a monument to the past."

"Or a tomb, perhaps?"

Something sparked in her eyes. It might have been appreciation.

"As you say."

"It must have been a very hard life, living here all year round," Ryan added. "Surviving off the land."

"Yes," Isobel looked up from her frantic pleating of the rug. "*Yes*. It would have been a question of survival. Wouldn't it?"

"It's remarkable how times have changed."

"Have they really changed so much?" Mathilda argued quietly. "For all our advances, here we are, still at the mercy of the wind and snow. At times like this, we revert to our most basic selves; to the animals that we still are, underneath all the trappings of society."

"All that, after a simple snowstorm?" Ryan asked.

The window panes rattled in protest against the gale which blew outside.

"Especially after a storm," Mathilda said, willing him to understand. "It's as if God were sending it to blot out His vision, to shield His eyes from the evil that men might do."

"Or women," Phillips put in from his position beside the door.

They all turned to him.

"Just thinking of gender equality," he added with a shrug.

Mathilda smiled and he felt an odd sort of shiver which had absolutely nothing to do with being cold.

"If you believe in God," Ryan continued, "you could argue that He sent a snowstorm to show His anger at the evil taking place. Or, that had already taken place," he tagged on.

"Do you really think so?" Isobel's voice shook. "Do you think He's angry?"

Ryan smiled, like a tiger singling out the weak zebra amongst the herd.

"It certainly seems like it, doesn't it? Of course, there are different degrees of culpability."

"What do you mean?"

"He's talking nonsense," Mathilda hissed. "We are *all* equally guilty before God and we are *all* forgiven."

She took her friend's hand and held it firmly.

Isobel looked between the two of them, then across to the short, barrel of a man standing beside the door.

"What do you think?"

Phillips scratched his chin.

"Well, now, let's see. I'm no expert but an accessory who helps cover up a crime…say, a crime like *murder*, is less blameworthy than the person who committed the deed in cold blood."

"The intention would have been the same," Mathilda shot back. "Both would be equally culpable in the eyes of God. Better to embrace it."

"Whatever has happened tonight must be accounted for," Ryan said flatly.

Mathilda's lips twisted in a grotesque smile.

"And what do you think has happened?"

Ryan unfolded his legs and stood up, suddenly weary with all the talk.

"Open the chest."

Both women gaped at him.

"Didn't I mention? How remiss," he rooted around the pockets of his coat until he found his warrant card. "DCI Ryan and DS Phillips, Northumbria CID.

"Merry Christmas, ladies."

LIFE AFTER LIFE

By Paul D. Brazill

Raymond Kerr watched Mad Eileen stagger out of the off-license with a can of Stella Artois in her hand. The old woman seemed to struggle with opening the beer can at first, before taking a furtive sip. She walked up to the bus shelter, sat down and finished her drink, eyes closed. A few minutes later, the number twelve bus pulled up and Eileen got on. As the bus was about to drive away, Mr Spence, Raymond's old history teacher, ran up the road. Papers spilled from his battered brown briefcase. The driver stopped and Mr Spence got on.

Raymond liked to watch. He liked to watch films – sometimes westerns, sometimes action movies – and he liked to watch television – usually the local news or the History Channel. But he mostly watched his neighbours, gazing out of the window of his bungalow from morning until night. It was pretty much all he could do since his operation. Well, all he wanted to do, anyway.

Of course, the doctors had suggested he take up a little, light exercise. They'd said that part of his problem may even be psychosomatic and that to get out and about would do him the world of good; but Raymond ignored them. There were consequences to his inactivity, of course. Which is why he soon found himself drowning in a cocktail of chronic health problems. Nothing that would kill him but nothing pleasant. He popped so many pills he was a walking chemist's shop.

When his mother died, things only got worse but he was teetering on the precipice of middle-age and he didn't see any point in changing his habits.

He spent the rest of morning sitting in his mother's old leather armchair, looking out of the window and occasionally glancing at the TV. He slept for most of the afternoon and only awoke when he needed to go the toilet.

It was early evening when Raymond saw the red

Ferrari pull into the grove and park outside his bungalow. He wasn't the only one who saw it, either. Curtains twitched. Front doors were edged open.

A well-dressed, suntanned man got out of the car and walked up the path.

The doorbell rang and Raymond struggled out of his chair and down the hall. He opened the door.

'Good to see you, Raymond,' said Trevor Walker, beaming like a lighthouse and holding out a manicured hand. 'Long time no see.'

Raymond grunted a reply. He noticed that Trevor smelt of expensive cologne and he wondered how he himself smelt. He couldn't tell but he guessed it wasn't good. He'd got out of the habit of washing lately.

He walked back into the lounge and slumped into his mum's old armchair, sighing. Trevor followed.

'Sit where you want,' croaked Raymond. His voice was hoarse. He hadn't spoken to anyone in days. He picked up a bottle of Diet Coke and sipped from it.

Trevor sat on the sofa. He looked around the room and sniffed. 'It's been a long time since I was last here,' he said. 'Not since we were nippers. It hasn't changed much.'

Raymond shrugged. 'Mum didn't like change. Neither do I.'

'She was a stern woman, was your mother. All the kids were terrified of her. Your dad, though, he was the life and soul, he was. Your dad and my dad went way back,' said Trevor. 'They were real cronies. Your mum and my mum, well... Women, eh?'

'Do you want a cuppa?' said Raymond, hoping Trevor would say no.

'No, ta. I can't stay long. Busy and that. I just wanted to pop in and make you an offer,' said Trevor. He leaned back on the sofa.

'What sort of offer?' said Raymond.

He shuffled in his chair and glanced out of the window. He saw Mad Eileen almost fall out of the bus. She swore at the driver as it pulled away.

'Well, would you believe, a job offer?' said Trevor.

'Me? You want to give me a job?' Raymond felt his face burning. He shuffled in his seat.

'Yes,' said Trevor.

'But I haven't worked for years. Not since my operation. You know, I don't really do stuff now. I don't do anything. You know?' said Raymond, his voice cracking.

'Exactly!' said Trevor. He clapped his hands, smirking. 'And that's precisely why you're the man I need.'

Trevor got up and sat on the arm of Raymond's chair.

'You know, a couple of years ago I got divorced from Gina?' he said.

'Yeah, sorry to hear that,' said Raymond. He felt uncomfortable with Trevor being so close. He looked out of the window.

'No problem,' said Trevor 'Good riddance to bad rubbish. She was well past her sell-by date anyway. And you know that last year I got hitched again?'

'Yeah, we got the invite. We couldn't make it, though. Mum sent a card, I think.'

'Well, Zoe's the light of my life, she really is, but she's very demanding. And not just in bed,' said Trevor. He winked.

Raymond flushed.

'And she likes the finer things in life. Which is why I've had to buy a massive house outside the city.'

'Sounds nice.'

'It is. Very. The thing is, though, Zoe's a tad...

paranoid. She watches too much reality TV. Crimewatch and the like. So, she wants a top-of-the-line security system installed. Cameras, monitors, the full Monty.'

'Better safe than sorry, I suppose,' said Raymond.

He scratched an armpit.

'For sure,' said Trevor. 'But we need someone to be in charge of security. To keep an eye on things. So I need someone I can trust. Someone without commitments. Someone who can stay twenty-four hours, if need be. And it seems to me that you are that soldier. So, what do you think?'

'Well, I dunno. I'm not exactly…' He glanced out of the window and saw a kid fall off a skateboard. His mother ran out of the house and gave him a slap.

'You can have your own cottage at the back of the house. One room for the monitors the rest is yours,' said Trevor. 'I'll pay you well enough.'

Raymond looked back at the TV screen. *Rio Bravo* had changed to *El Dorado*. Or was it the other way around? 'I'm not sure. I'll have to think about it,' he said.

'You do that. Have a good think,' said Trevor. He handed Raymond a business card. 'Get back to me on Saturday and let me know your decision, one way or the other.'

He stood. 'I'll see myself out.'

Raymond glanced at the business card and put it in his shirt pocket. He looked back out of the window as Trevor drove away and noticed the beautiful young blonde woman in the passenger seat. He closed his eyes.

***

Raymond's tailor-made uniform felt good. He'd never heard of the Italian bloke that had designed it, but he knew it was expensive. And that made him feel good, too. He was sat in the office drinking a cup of cocoa and checking out the wall of monitors. The screens showed different parts of the garden, the front gate and every room in the house expect the bedroom and bathrooms.

He was inspecting the silver, gold and platinum discs that adorned the walls in the hallway. He'd even bought some of the albums himself, though that had been a long time ago. He hadn't listened to music properly for ages, it seemed. He finished his drink and it was while he was putting the empty cup in the sink that he had an idea.

He clicked on the computer, found You Tube. Within a few minutes he was listening to Halcyon Days, the band that Trevor had discovered and managed during the eighties. 'French Windows' had been the B-side of 'I Talk', which had been a minor hit, but Raymond had always preferred it. He closed his eyes. The song transported him to better times.

The song finished and Raymond played it again, a little louder this time. Just as it ended he felt he needed a slash so he rushed to the bathroom. This was one of the long-term side-effects of having his gall bladder taken out.

When he returned to the office he checked the screens and saw the kitchen was lit up. Trevor and Zoe appeared to be arguing again. This seemed to be a regular thing over the last few weeks. Zoe appeared to be even more drunk than usual and after the usual screaming she slapped Trevor. He slapped her back and she threw a wine glass, which smashed against the wall. She stormed out of the room. A few minutes later Trevor followed her.

Raymond was glad he'd started switching off the sound on the security cameras inside the house. Trevor and his wife had a hell of a lot of expensive stuff but it didn't seem to make them too happy, that was for sure. Raymond, however, was as pleased as punch with his new life. He wanted for little and was saving up most of his wages. He had an exercise bike in his bedroom and he'd started using it recently. He was already feeling the benefit.

***

Autumn leaves fell in the garden and Raymond was shedding too. He'd lost quite a lot of weight over the last few months. He was eating better, thanks to the efforts of Trevor's personal chef, and he was managing to go for a jog in the grounds a couple of times each day. He had a trip into town once a week to see a film and had joined a local pub quiz team. He was feeling better and better.

He switched on the laptop and opened his new Spotify account. As Halcyon Days' first album started to play Raymond looked at the screens. Trevor and Zoe were having another slanging match and Raymond was barely paying it any attention when he saw Trevor smash a champagne bottle against the back of Zoe's head. She collapsed to the ground. Trevor stood frozen for a moment and then knelt down and turned her over. Her face was covered in blood. Trevor looked up at the security camera and back at Zoe. And then he screamed.

***

'I'm screwed,' said Trevor. 'I'm really, really screwed.'

He was slouched in Raymond's armchair working his way through a bottle of Mortlach, occasionally glancing at the monitor that showed Zoe's corpse in the kitchen. His nose was caked with the remnants of an ant hill of cocaine.

'We should phone the police. The ambulance,' said Raymond. 'We'll be in trouble if we don't.'

'Trouble?' said Trevor. 'Trouble? I'm already in trouble. She's dead. My Zoe. I told you, I'm completely screwed.'

'So you said.'

Raymond was sweating. The only other dead person

he'd seen had been his mother and he'd been expecting her death for some time. She'd died in her sleep and had looked sedate, calm. But Zoe just looked like a mess of blood. He looked away from the screen. He closed his eyes and tried to control his breathing. He was sure that Trevor was going to ask him to help dispose of Zoe's body and the thought of that made him sick to the stomach.

'Zoe's dad's a friggin' copper for fuck's sake,' said Trevor. 'I'll do big time for this, no worries. I can't go inside, I can't.'

Raymond could feel his new life slipping through his fingers like grains of sand.

They were silent for a long time. Halcyon Days played in the background.

Trevor finished the bottle. He closed his eyes and was silent for so long that Raymond thought he'd fallen asleep. Beads of sweat trickled down his face.

Then Trevor opened his eyes. He leaned over to Raymond and smiled. 'You know what?' he said 'I've had an idea. Maybe you could say you did it? Say she attacked you, or something?'

'Me? Why? Why would she attack me?'

'I don't know, but I'll think of something,' said Trevor . He took another swig of Mortlach.

Raymond felt the room spinning.

'I'll pay you,' said Trevor. 'Make sure you get treated well in the slammer. Get a good lawyer so you go to an open prison, and when you come out there'll be a fortune waiting for you? Zoe's insurance is a packet.'

Raymond thought he was going to vomit. 'I don't know. I mean, it's scary. Prison?'

'Well, it's either that or I get sent down and you end up back home, staring out of the window all day,' said Trevor.

Raymond's head hurt. His stomach turned. He wanted to get up and walk out of the cottage. To call the police. But he just sat and stared at Trevor until he said: 'Can I get a room with a window?'

THE SMALLEST ACORN

April Taylor

Joanne put her key in the door and opened it. The overwhelming fug of heat set her back a few steps, making her hesitate.

'Robin?'

Then she heard Primrose barking from the depths of the house with a high-pitched intensity Joanne had never heard before.

She shouted louder this time.

'Robin, where are you?'

Joanne had walked their retriever that morning before heading for the stately home, but that had been hours earlier. Prim sounded desperate and hungry.

Having let her into the garden, Joanne checked the dining room and lounge, then turned for the stairs. She wanted to call her husband, but daren't. Her hand trembled as she forced herself up the treads. The door to his office stood ajar, and she pushed it gently. A rush of air filled her lungs and left her as a piercing scream.

Robin lay slumped over his desk, a kitchen knife protruding from his back, his working papers strewn on the floor, stained...

The sweet metallic stench made her gag and she struggled to stay upright. But Prim was coming, coming up the stairs, and Joanne turned to stop the dog from bounding into the room. Instead she dropped to her knees and soaked the golden fur with tears.

Police. She had to call the police.

As if on automatic pilot, she led Primrose out into the rear garden, then shut the door. Dialled 999. Why couldn't they understand? Why did they ask all these stupid questions? Then she sat at the dining table. And waited. And cried.

***

When the police eventually arrived it was a relief.

Prim was still in the back garden barking loudly enough to alert the entire neighbourhood.

'I've put the dog in the back,' Joanne said to the man who had knocked.

'So I hear. Good idea. Keep him there.'

'Her.'

'Sorry, her. Can we come in? Inspector Harris has just pulled up so we need to get cracking. I'm Constable Smithson, Scenes of Crime Officer. It's your husband, yes? Where is he?'

Joanne pointed up the stairs. 'Office, second on the right.'

She saw two people coming up the front path. A tall man, very young to be an inspector, she thought, and an overweight woman already panting slightly as she climbed the steps from the gate. She paused to look up at the front of the house. Did Joanne imagine a sneer? The man spoke.

'Good evening. Mrs Price?'

'Yes, Joanne Price.'

He nodded.

'I'm Sergeant Russell and this,' he said, indicating the fat woman, 'is Inspector Harris.'

Joanne realised the expression on her own face was one Harris was used to seeing.

'Yes,' the inspector said, 'a woman. We don't just make the tea now. It is 1975, not 1925.'

Joanne felt obliged to apologise but Harris waved it away.

'Can we come in then?'

***

Joanne found herself shooed into the kitchen. Hearing the inspector lumbering up the stairs, Joanne sat and waited to be told what to do.

Five minutes later, the woman thundered back down and sailed into the kitchen, taking the seat opposite Joanne.

'Right, Jo, any chance of a brew?'

Joanne blinked, put the kettle on, and pulled out the pottery mugs from the cupboard. 'How many?'

'Sugars? Oh, three.'

'Actually, I meant how many of you will want tea, inspector?'

'Just me.'

Silence reigned while Joanne poured the water into the pot, put three huge spoons of sugar in a mug and added a dash of milk. She stood with her back to the policewoman, staring out over the back garden, but saw nothing of the view. It was as if everything and everyone one was on the other side of the cellophane bubble which encased her. Then she shook her head, trying to clear the fog in her brain. 'Can I bring my dog in?'

Harris frowned. 'What kind?'

'Rescue golden retriever.'

'Not one of those little yappy things, then?'

Joanne's laugh came unbidden.

'No, medium size, muddy paws.' She turned to face Harris. 'And my name is Joanne.' Without waiting for another comment, she opened the door and called. Prim bounded in and headed for the newcomer, trying to make friends. Joanne poured the tea and sat down again.

Harris sipped trying to ignore the dog. 'Nice brew, thanks. Now then, Jo, when did you discover your husband's body?'

'A few minutes before I rang you.'

'And where were you before then?'

'At Henwick Hall. I want to do volunteer work there in the gardens and today was a kind of this-is-what-we-do day.'

Harris looked at her, eyes wide, as if Joanne had just landed from another planet. 'Gardening?'

'Yes.'

There was a pause while Harris assimilated this information. 'Okay. What time did you leave for this gardening day?'

'About 7.30 this morning.'

'And your husband was okay when you left?'

Joanne gazed at the woman and sighed, feeling the tears coming, being powerless to stop them. Shock, obviously.

'Yes.'

Harris ignored the tears. 'It's pretty clear somebody didn't like your husband. Any idea who?'

Joanne shook her head and blew her nose. 'No, he's very popular at work.'

'And he works...?'

'Jenkins & Short. They're accountants.' Harris nodded again. 'Can I go upstairs and change?'

'I'll see.'

Joanne expected her to go and speak to one of her officers. Instead, she leaned back on the chair and yelled through the open kitchen door. She had better hearing than Joanne because she understood the burbled reply from upstairs. Prim, hearing her raised voice, pawed at Harris who pushed her off.

'No, not yet. Best stay here.'

'Can I go and walk Primrose, then? I need some fresh air.'

Harris frowned at the dog, the filthy paws, and the mud on her skirt. 'Depends. Where?'

'There's a path through some woods. I usually take her there.' She paused. Harris had finished the tea. 'We could talk as we walk.'

'No thanks,' Harris replied. 'I'm a city girl. Hate creepy-crawlies. Give me a good honest armed robber every time.'

Joanne could have sworn she saw the woman shudder. She stood up. 'We are all God's creatures, Inspector, creepy-crawlies included.'

'That's fine as long as they stay well away from me.'

Harris, Joanne was beginning to learn, had to have the last word.

***

Primrose ran along the path investigating all the bushes and the undergrowth. Joanne breathed deeply, trying to banish the mental picture of Robin with that damn great knife between his shoulder blades, and was aghast that her initial thought was about needing to buy another set of cooking knives. Despite her best efforts, her vision travelled from the knife to the sight of his head turned sideways on the desk and – when she had had the courage to look at his face – the look of surprise in his eyes. She prayed he had not suffered.

Being in the midst of nature helped; it always had. She had discovered from a young age the joy of planting things, watching them grow, tending them and finally enjoying them. From flowers to vegetables, she loved everything about the growing process. She still had a photograph her mother had taken, blurred because Mum had been laughing so much she couldn't hold the camera steady. Joanne had been five years old and the watering can she struggled to carry to her father at the other end of the garden was nearly as big as she.

Primrose's barking brought her back to the present. Silly dog. Would she never learn that squirrels danced round a tree just to wind her up? The laughter helped ease the confusion and uncertainty Joanne felt. Of course, she would be their prime suspect. Her lovely house was being invaded.

Joanne dawdled home to the chaos. She stood by the gate trying to steel herself to go in, gazing at the place she had come to see as her private heaven, hoping that the desecration within would not render it a hell.

***

The police finally left at midnight, taking Robin and sacks of items from the scene with them. Harris said they had finished in the office and Joanne could clean up if she wanted but Harris would be back tomorrow to ask some more questions. Then she yawned and shuffled out without saying goodbye. Sergeant Russell hesitated and turned back.

'Sure you'll be all right on your own, Mrs Price? I can get a WPC to stay with you.'

Joanne shook her head. 'No, I need to be by myself, but thank you.' She gazed over his shoulder to where Harris was negotiating the steps down to the gate. Russell picked up Joanne's unspoken comment.

'Don't mind the inspector. She'll be focused on this.'

'Good. I want whoever did this caught.'

'That's what we all want. Goodnight, Mrs Price.'

Joanne took off her grubby clothes. A bath might calm her down, she thought, turning on the taps. She added the expensive bath salts Robin had bought her, the ones she seldom used because the intense smell made her feel ill. It was so unlike the fragrance from the lavender bush when she brushed against it in the garden. But tonight it felt right to throw one of the cubes into the warm water and soak the day away.

***

Joanne hadn't expected to sleep well, but the relaxing effect of the bath helped her drop off until she woke with at start at 4.30. Against all Robin's house rules, she had allowed Prim to stay with her on the bed, feeling the need to cuddle another breathing being. Hearing her stir, the dog put her nose on Joanne's hand and whined. *Oh well, better start the day.* With the threat of another visit from the overweight policewoman, it promised to be a very long one.

***

It was. Harris, on the doorstep before 9am, stomped in without being asked. She sat down at the kitchen table staring at the kettle. Joanne took the hint.

'Now then, Jo, the pathologist is doing the post-mortem today but he says it might be difficult to pin down the time of death because of the effect of the central heating. Can you tell me why it was turned so high?'

Joanne shook her head. 'No, but I have thought about it. All I can think of is that for some reason Robin shut Primrose in the utility room. I have no idea why. Perhaps someone called and he didn't want her getting in the way or they didn't like dogs. She hates it in there. And the thermostat is in there, too. We have it turned low in summer so the towels in the bathroom dry. I wonder if she caught the dial, jumping up trying to get out.'

Harris stared at the dog, now lying in her basket. 'Possible, I suppose. You left at 7.30 you said. Can anyone verify that?'

'I don't know. Mrs Trent across the road might have seen me go, but it might be early for her to be up and about.'

'I understand you've been married before.'

'Yes. Stephen died in a car crash four years ago.'

'And now your second husband has died.'

Joanne closed her eyes and shuddered. 'I think murdered is more accurate,' she said, tears welling again.

'Bit careless losing two husbands, isn't it?'

'That is a horrible thing to say, Inspector. Stephen

199

was always a hothead behind the wheel. He never maintained the car properly, the police report said. His death was an accident and one he could have avoided had he taken the car to the garage and driven like a normal human being. The Coroner said so.'

'You don't sound as if you regret his death.'

Tears ran freely down Joanne's face and she tried to control the flash of fury at Harris's impassive stare.

'His death was self-inflicted,' Joanne said. 'The two people in the other car were killed by his stupidity. My grief was mixed with anger.'

Harris shrugged. 'So, how did you meet Robin?'

'At an interview. Stephen was a free spender. I needed a job and Robin needed a secretary.'

Harris stifled a chuckle. 'Love in the office, then.'

'Oh no. I didn't get the job. We met a few months later in the park. My flat had no garden and I went to the park every day to see some greenery and flowers. Robin was eating his sandwiches there and remembered me from the interview.'

'What did you talk about?'

'Mostly my love of gardening and animals. He told me he had a lovely garden and a rescue dog. He did all the chasing. Five months later, he proposed. I accepted.'

'And it's been happy ever after?'

'We are very...' Joanne paused and blew her nose. 'Were very happy.' The tension that had been building since the day before burst forth in an uncontrollable fit of hysteria and weeping. She could feel Harris's gaze on her, but the inspector didn't speak. Sergeant Russell came in, his expression one of sympathy.

'You left the front door wide open, Mrs Price,' he began as his phone rang. He went into the hall to answer it.

'It's for you, Inspector.'

Harris heaved herself out of the chair. Russell handed Joanne a clean white handkerchief from his pocket.

'I know she needs to ask questions, but she is so damned heartless,' Joanne sobbed. 'She terrifies me.'

'It's because she's concentrating on solving the case,' Russell replied. 'She's not so bad, once you get to know her.'

Harris waddled through the door, ignoring Russell but zeroing in on Joanne.

'I think you've lied to us, Jo. The pathologist said the last meal your husband ate was some kind of curry the night before his death.'

Joanne frowned.

'Yes.'

'What about breakfast?'

'Robin didn't eat breakfast.'

Oh. So where did you buy the curry? We can check timings with the takeaway.'

'Buy? We never buy curry. We always make it from scratch.' She saw the inspector's eyebrows rise in disbelief. 'Much healthier than those fat-filled horrors you get from takeaways. It was a spinach, chickpea and sweet potato curry from the vegetarian cookbook up there,' Joanne said, pointing to a shelf of cookery books in the corner. 'We opened a nice Riesling to go with it. There's half a bottle still in the fridge.'

Harris's lip curled.

'Oh, give me a few pints down at the pub with a Vindaloo on the way home. That's proper eating.'

'No, Inspector. That's a heart attack waiting to happen if you read the latest research.'

'Unproven rubbish,' the inspector snapped. 'I keep the takeaways in business. Have to, the hours I work. I don't have time for namby-pamby messing about.'

Joanne stared at her. 'Obviously,' she said and felt a glow of satisfaction as the policewoman flushed red.

***

Harris stomped out, muttering about more questions later. Russell looked as if he would rather be anywhere but where he stood. 'Don't antagonise her,' he said.

'I won't be bullied by her. I've done nothing wrong except find my husband murdered. All she is bothered about is closing the case and I am the easiest one to pin it on. I shall ring our solicitor and ask him to recommend someone to advise me.' She saw the sergeant's expression. 'I'm sorry, Sergeant Russell. She scares me. I'm frightened I will say anything to make her stop bombarding me with questions.' Joanne made a visible effort to calm down. 'Still, I suppose we all have to be frightened of something. I gather the inspector doesn't like wildlife.'

'That's an understatement. You should see her at work checking her office when she doesn't think anyone is looking. Spiders and snakes terrify her. Seriously, don't let her get to you. I'll have a word and try to make her back off a bit. She is a good detective, even though she has to be right all the time.'

'What do you mean?'

'It's the general opinion at the station. Harris has to be right even when she's wrong.'

Joanne felt fleeting sympathy for the inspector. She had read all the newspaper stories about how women were kept down, especially in the police force. Harris trying to prove she was as good as the men would be more than an uphill struggle. 'I'll bear that in mind at my next questioning session,' she said, forcing a smile.

***

Joanne was not pleased, but not surprised either, to

find Harris leaning on the doorbell early the next morning. Before opening it, Joanne put Primrose into the utility room. When she did answer the door, Harris pushed past, again without being invited in.

'Not in the kitchen, Inspector,' Joanne said. 'I'm expecting the plumber any moment. Try the dining room, on the left.'

Harris trudged into one of Joanne's favourite rooms but spared no time to stop and look at the elegance of the furniture or the decor. She dropped so heavily onto a chair Joanne winced, thinking it would break under the wretched woman's weight. The vase of roses on the table rocked slightly but did not tip over. She decided to take the initiative.

'What can I help you with this time?'

'Right now, Jo. I'll not beat about the bush. It's time to come clean. Tell me how, when and why?'

'How, when and why what?'

'Very good. However, it won't wash. I know you killed your husband. I suspect, looking at the report on your former husband's death, you did something to his car and killed him, too. And the two people in the car he crashed into. I've got Russell going over it all with a fine tooth-comb as we speak.'

'This is ridiculous. I'm ringing my solicitor.'

Harris steamrollered over her protest. 'You made two mistakes. First, I questioned Mrs Trent. She did happen to be looking out of the window and says she saw you turn and wave to your husband as you left and heard you call out when you arrived home. However, when I asked her for more details, she said she didn't actually see Robin at all, only you waving. A nice bit of theatre for her benefit, wasn't it? The second thing is the radiator in the utility room had been turned off. By you because you shut the dog in there yourself, didn't you? You didn't want her in any distress. All you wanted was to fudge the time of death. Come on, Jo. I know it was you. Confess.'

'That's the biggest load of rubbish I've ever heard. I'm going to make tea. Hopefully by the time I get back, you will have regained your sanity.' She swept from the room, her arm knocking a jar off the sideboard. She didn't stop to pick it up but slammed the door. No way did she want Harris anywhere near her until she had made the tea, which she did, putting the pot, milk, sugar and mugs on the tray before returning to the dining room.

Harris was purple in the face and gasping for air. She had knocked over the vase of roses. Water cascaded along the cherry wood and dripped onto the carpet. Then she tumbled onto the floor.

Joanne watched her for a few moments. She bent and picked up one of the particularly large spiders she had collected in the jar from the sideboard and waved it in front of the policewoman's face. Harris's expression contorted even more as Joanne dropped the spider onto her cheek. Joanne sat on the floor beside her.

'My name is Joanne, not Jo, not JJ. Joanne. Is that so difficult to remember? But that's the one thing you, Robin and Steve have in common. None of you ever listen. All my life I've been treated like a pretty doll without a brain in my head. As if I am incapable of deciding what's good for me and what I want.

'I wanted a dog. Stephen refused in case I loved the dog more than him. That wouldn't have been difficult.' She picked up another spider. 'I'd have loved this spider more than him. He was a bully. A bully and a coward. I decided I'd had enough. I read some books and tampered with the brakes. We only lived a couple of miles from the motorway. I knew they would last until then.'

She paused and shook Harris. 'Stay with me. I haven't finished. You wanted to know the truth, after all. Robin wasn't a bully. He was just oblivious to anything except himself. If he wanted it, we got it. He was a collector of pretty things, gloating over them because they were his. If I wanted something, we couldn't afford it. I'm only here because of Primrose. And yes, she was in the utility room, just like she is now. And yes, I turned off the radiator in there. Thank you for picking up that mistake. I will turn it back on before your people arrive. I imagine your death will mean a stringent enquiry, although knowing the opinion your colleagues have of you, possibly not.

'Where was I? Robin. There he sat revelling over the latest hi-fi catalogues. Going to spend £800 on a music centre. £800. I'm not a wicked woman, you know, truly I'm not. But he wouldn't even spend £250 on a little car so I had some independence. And he lied. I found the paperwork from the rescue centre. He fetched Primrose the week before he first brought me to this house. The dog was the lure to add me to his collection. He never took the least notice of her.'

Her voice brightened.

'Of course, everything comes to me now. This house. The money. Two-thirds of his pension. And now, finally, I will have the life I want. Here, alone with Prim and the garden. My garden.'

Harris groaned and tried to speak. Joanne picked up another couple of spiders and, in the manner of decorating an ornament, she began to drop them on the woman's hands and face. Harris gave one last gasp and lay still.

Joanne didn't hesitate. She gathered up all the spiders she could see and popped them inside the jar. She was three short and decided that was two too many. One she found climbing up the long curtains. The second was in the fireplace. She decided to leave the last one.

Then she walked into the kitchen, opened the back door and scattered the contents on the nearest piece of earth. The jar she returned to its usual home in the pantry. What next? Primrose. Joanne made a fuss of the dog, talking to her as she adjusted the radiator. That done, she put Primrose outside and returned to the dining room.

Concentrating as she never had before, she surveyed the room. Overturned roses, good. Harris having obviously fallen from her chair in the midst of her attack, good. Her weight and lifestyle would be put down as the cause of her heart attack.

Joanne examined the room again. No sign of the final spider. More importantly, no sign of anything amiss other than the body, the overturned chair and the roses. Just one final flourish. She picked up the tray from the kitchen counter top, walked to the open doorway and threw the contents in the air. The broken mugs and spilled liquids made a wonderful mess on the carpet.

'Just remember,' she said aloud, preparing for the ordeals to come. 'You can have the life you want now.'

Joanne Price conjured another bout of hysteria, walked through to the hall, and lifted the telephone.

AN ONION

Joel Hames

1: Tunic

Eric picked his way between the tables, treading carefully to avoid coats and bags hanging off the backs of chairs. The ballroom was wreathed in semi-darkness, the overhead lights dimmed and the spotlights pointed at the stage, but he could see faces turn towards him as he passed, smiles and nods of recognition. He forced a smile onto his own face, relaxed, and found it had stayed in place of its own accord. He might not be used to the acclaim of his peers, but he certainly didn't mind it.

The compere spotted him, tapped the shoulder of the woman beside him, and pointed. She turned to face him, and Eric wondered how much effort she had expended on her own smile. He was aware that Lydia McGrath didn't like him; had been aware of this for twenty years, ever since the incident at the laboratory. Nobody but the two of them knew, and although he considered himself entirely blameless, he was grateful she had chosen to keep it that way.

The compere was smiling, too. When Eric had mentioned the name – a brash young comedian whose success lay more in shock than wit – his daughters had leapt up from their iPads in excitement, begged for autographs, and returned seconds later to the screens, spreading word of the impending encounter across their social networks with a method and a seriousness Eric had found unsettling. They had evinced none of the same enthusiasm when he had addressed the World Health Organisation three months earlier.

They were not present tonight, of course, neither his daughters nor his wife. Attendance was limited to invited industry participants only, without guests or family members. He was pleased enough with the exclusion. Monica would have gushed and preened to an extent he would have found embarrassing; Tabitha and Helen would have spent the evening immersed in their phones and made no attempt to disguise their boredom. The absence of family was, he felt, an entirely satisfactory arrangement.

He had expected to win this award – had not known it absolutely, but had been made aware, from the sly comments and knowing smiles of certain colleagues, that his achievement was deemed worthy of recognition. He was convinced that, thanks to his work, the more severe forms of schizophrenia would be a footnote in the pages of history within a handful of decades. The professional community appeared to concur.

Eric stepped onto the stage, paused for the applause to die, and gave a short speech thanking those who had supported his work. He received the award from Lydia's own hands, and tried to decipher a meaning from the smile she still wore, but there was nothing. For all he knew, it might even have been genuine.

***

2: Outer Epidermis

She stopped, briefly, at his table an hour later, and offered – for a second time – her congratulations. He had been rather enjoying himself until that point – enjoying himself, in part, at her expense and that of the other notables who had played a role in the evening. There was, among the disparate group into which he had been thrown by the whim of the table planners, a general consensus that such events were a waste of time in professional terms, but entertaining nonetheless – an evening away from family, office or lab, with adequate food and plentiful drink, and the opportunity to mock proceedings with like-minded cynics.

They were a young group, but aware, already, of the hierarchy of their profession. Although outside the inner circle, Eric's speeches and papers had drawn him towards the summit, and they were nervous, at first, of making their derision too overt, but as he showed himself receptive to the mockery, the laughter became less constrained. He even joined in, a little, with the occasional acerbic aside during the more tedious speeches. They enjoyed that, and he enjoyed their enjoyment, and had been starting to feel that he might perhaps delay his taxi and stay another hour or two in their company, when he noticed the faces around him rearranging themselves into a semblance of seriousness and turned to find Lydia McGrath standing behind him.

'I just wanted to say, Eric,' she began, and already he was shaking his head and waving away her praise, but she persisted, eyes fixed on a spot above and slightly to the left of his face. 'I just wanted to say I've been thoroughly impressed. I mean it, Eric,' she continued, and his gestures ceased. 'It's really quite extraordinary. You've done more than I would have thought possible in decades, and you've done it all in a year.'

'Thank you, Lydia,' he replied, his voice deeper than he had expected and drained of all the bonhomie it had exuded for the last hour. 'Thank you,' he repeated, the pitch a little higher. She nodded, and took her leave, and his companions returned, within a minute or two, to their laughter and their drinks, but for him, the evening had been soured.

It could have been her award, as much as it had been his. Her imagination, her ability to think of something new when everyone else was combining the same drugs and the same theories in slightly different doses and orders with such tiny variations that these days he could hardly tell one experiment from the next. Doing something different, stripping away decades of orthodoxy, and at the same time stripping away the layers of invented personality, examining and exposing them one by one until only the core remained

– it had been her idea. But it had taken his boldness and practicality to bring it to fruition.

He wondered, for a moment, whether she knew, whether there had been a message encoded in her words that said she was aware of it, of everything he had done, how he had done it, and why, but no sooner had the thought arrived than it was gone. She could not know. If she had known, or even suspected, there would have been no need for messages, coded or otherwise. And he had moved on so much further, in twenty years, than she had envisioned. Had he told her outright that her own work had been the genesis of his, he doubted she would even have believed him.

He tried, briefly, to picture that conversation, to imagine himself confessing all, and her smiling and laughing it away; tried to dismiss the leaden greyness and sense of nausea that had descended upon him with her arrival; but the images that came to him were not hypothetical but all too real. Lydia, in the laboratory, thirty years old, hair tucked behind her ear, smiling as he approached, the smile turning to a frown, hands raised as he encroached too far into her personal space.

He had made a pass at her. But that was all. He had faltered at the frown and backed away at the hands, and the worst that could have been said of him was that he had misread their relationship. That, and the contemplation of infidelity when he was due to marry Monica two months later, but even with the sin compounded to adultery – attempted adultery, he corrected himself – it seemed unreasonable of Lydia to bear the grudge two decades on.

She was not a pretty woman – she had not been pretty then – and part of him had presumed, arrogantly, that she would be flattered by his attentions. But it was not her face or her body that had attracted him. He was spellbound by her intelligence, by the agility with which she jumped from idea to idea, by the simultaneous lightness and depth of thought. He had been in love with her mind. It had been so many years, and still she carried that grudge, and yet somehow, when things had been at their worst with Monica and he had been spending six nights each week in the Town House and the other on the sofa, he had entertained hopes that one day he would be returning to that Town House in Lydia's company. But he had barely seen her; two-dozen instances, perhaps, in all that time, despite her frequent visits to the university. (She worked for a private institution now, but one with deep links to her alma mater). But even in those fleeting moments, he had seen nothing to suggest that lightness and depth had deserted her.

The phone in his pocket buzzed. His taxi had arrived. He thanked his fellow guests for their company, and took his leave.

***

3: Inner Epidermis

The girls were still up. They were sitting on the sofa watching television. Monica was on the leather chair reading a book. A very wet young man was shouting and gesturing wildly on the television screen while behind him, other young men and women were trying to push each other off inflatable rafts into a swimming pool. Neither his wife nor his daughters had heard Eric enter.

He toyed with the idea of going straight upstairs and waiting there, naked, on the bed.

After a moment's consideration he dismissed the notion. Monica would not, he felt, appreciate the surprise. Decades ago, perhaps – perhaps, too, two years back, in the flower of their reconciliation, but not now. His feelings about this were ambivalent. He appreciated Monica, certainly; she was as beautiful now as she had been when they married, she was a good mother and a patient and understanding wife, and he felt a nostalgic pang for the days when they had made love frequently and without thought. But a nostalgic pang was as far as it went. He was fond of his wife and he found her attractive. He did not love her.

He coughed, and Monica turned and smiled as she saw him. The girls did not acknowledge his presence until they found their view of the television blocked by their parents' brief embrace, an interruption met with a vomiting sound from Tabitha and a cry of 'Get out of the way' from Helen. He led Monica back to the leather chair and perched on one of its arms.

'So?' she asked, eyes wide in anticipation. He had told her of his expectations. She had been searching his face for a clue since the moment she had seen him.

He nodded. 'I got it. Greatest contribution in the field of mental health, research category.' He spoke casually, each word qualifying those that had preceded it, but he smiled as he spoke. He had been gratified to win the award, and he knew that Monica would be delighted, and not solely for the reflected glory. She was delighted for him, an endearing trait that he had spent decades attempting to understand and years trying to strip away to what he assumed was an ultimately egotistical core. He had failed on both counts. Her pleasure in his success was as incomprehensible to him as it was genuine.

He noticed, suddenly, that the shouts from the television had died away, and looked up to find the girls standing before him, identical grins on their faces.

'Well done, Dad,' said Tabitha, and Helen nodded.

'Yeah, great job. We're really proud of you.'

They were easier to decipher than their mother; for all that they had inherited her blonde hair and fair complexion, there was more of him in the girls than there was of Monica. Tabitha wanted the car on Saturday; she was meeting friends in town, and had struck a deal with Helen whereby the younger sister would be permitted to tag along if she supported Tabitha's campaign to borrow it for the afternoon. He had overheard them discussing the plan before he had left that evening.

'You'll have to do better than that if you want the car,' he replied, and enjoyed their frowns and their shrugs of denial. A warmth descended upon him. For a moment, for the rest of the evening perhaps, he would not be thinking about Lydia McGrath. Tomorrow he would hand the keys to Tabitha with a stern warning about concentration and common sense, watch her reverse jerkily out of the driveway onto the busy main road, and spend the next four hours worrying about the safety of his daughters. They noticed the smile spreading across his face, ceased their protestations, and returned to the sofa and the rapidly emptying rafts. Monica leaned over to kiss him on the cheek.

Perhaps they would make love tonight after all.

***

4: Outer Scales

The girls were dismissed to bed with less than the usual objections half an hour later. The rafts were empty, the victors having been reduced to a single champion through a complex process that involved crawling through dark, narrow tubes with rivers of water running through them.

The television was still on, a violent drama that Monica had fallen into by chance some weeks earlier and was determined to see through to its end. But they spoke to one another, briefly, during intervals in the action. Monica sipped at her red wine, he at his single malt. It was a gently companionable evening, an evening for logs in the stove – it was early in September and still too warm for that – and his wife lying back across the sofa and across him – they were too old, their bodies too vulnerable to inexplicable aches and sudden, sharp pains. And then Monica mentioned the Town House. (It was always capitalised, when she spoke of it, partly to distinguish it from their home, partly to elevate it from what it was: three narrow floors, a tiny patch of garden, no driveway or garage; partly, he felt, as a reproach to him for buying it in the first place, although she had never expressed these thoughts directly).

'Any sign of a tenant, Eric?'

They had not had a tenant in the two years since he had vacated the property, they had not even managed a viewing, but he was reluctant to sell. He had purchased the Town House nearly ten years earlier, when his teaching hours had increased and his research had entered a critical phase. It was, he had explained, ridiculous to endure the hour-long journey (worse, in the mornings), up to four times every day, when he could sleep half a mile from the lab and the lecture rooms. His seniority within the faculty brought with it certain responsibilities, a need to be more closely entwined with the university community. He would not spend more than a night or two each week there, three at most. His father had passed away and left more than enough money to purchase a property outright; prices would only increase in the years to come. The Town House made sense on every level. He hadn't known, at the time, how it would become his refuge from a failing marriage, hadn't known either that when that marriage somehow, miraculously, revived, it would become something else entirely.

'No,' he replied, in a tone he hoped would put an end to the subject. He dealt with the letting agents directly, not wishing to burden Monica with the details. She had no reason to burden him in return. The outgoings were small enough and his salary now high enough that rental income would be a bonus rather than a necessity. In the meantime, the Town House had its uses. He had insisted on a rent that deterred even the wealthiest and most determined. Tenants were an inconvenience he could do without.

It might have been the tone, it might have just been a desire on Monica's part to avoid uncomfortable conversation – the Town House was part of a past in which he had "abandoned" her and the children, as she had somewhat dramatically put it during the crisis which precipitated their reconciliation – but she chose to move on, steering into more agreeable waters. He allowed himself to be led. The past was behind them, and he had enjoyed a singularly successful evening crowning a remarkable year. Monica drained her glass, glanced at the empty bottle, disappeared into the kitchen, and returned a minute later with another, an obscure northern Italian red that had been a gift from a student hailing from that region, and that, he had discovered a week after her graduation and return to her native land, was worth more than he made in a week's teaching. He and Monica had been saving the bottle for a special occasion; that Monica deemed the evening worthy of the wine made it more special still. He set down his near-empty tumbler and accepted the offered glass.

The programme had come to an end but still they sat, and drank, in silence broken by the occasional easy observation. She leaned back and closed her eyes, and he took the opportunity to look at her in the minute detail he usually reserved for his professional subjects. He nodded to himself; he was right. Monica was a beautiful woman, the decades had been kind, and if the bond they shared was less intense than others might have been, was (on his side at least) borne of tenderness and shared history, and a fascination with the unknowable, then that was still something worth savouring. Emboldened by the wine, he rose awkwardly to his feet, saw her open her eyes and smile as he approached, leaned down and kissed her with a passion he had not felt in months.

***

They made love urgently, belying their years and their familiarity, each of them astonished and a little awed by their own inexplicable fervour. They made love in the living room, on the sofa recently vacated by their daughters, and ignored the chafes from the age-roughened upholstery and the zips and hard corners that had always been so insistently present. They refreshed themselves with cold water and the dregs of the Italian wine, and made love more slowly in the bedroom. Again he gazed at her, at the entirety of her, at her back and legs and breasts and hair, and she returned his gaze with such intensity that at any other time, even with Monica, even inside her and drowning in her, he might have felt a self-consciousness that distanced him from the moment. Instead he felt nothing but that desire, that passion, a new crisis between them, unexpected, but welcome nonetheless.

She fell asleep lying against him. He listened to her breaths soften and lengthen, and closed his eyes, and the stars revolved around him with new and unexplored possibilities.

***

5: Inner Scales
He woke an hour later, thirsty and with his head throbbing painfully. Monica had shifted slightly, opening up an inch of space between them, and he moved carefully, extracting his limbs from the bed with the precision of a palaeontologist unearthing the bones of an ancient beast. He crept from the room and down the stairs, and it was while he was filling a glass with ice-cold water from the fridge that he glanced to the countertop and saw there a letter topped with the name and logo of the letting agent.

217

He stared at it until he felt a chill across his hands and realised he had overfilled the glass and the water was spilling out across the kitchen floor. Concentrating on dealing with one matter at a time, he wiped and dried the floor, drank the water, and poured himself another glass before reaching for the letter.

He scanned its contents, observed its creases, and relaxed at once. He had seen this letter before, read its contents, which were bland and unimportant, folded it and placed it in his back pocket, from where it must have fallen and been found by Monica. It contained a brief summary of developments in the local market. Nothing that could disturb the still-fragile construction of truth and evasion on which their reconciliation was built, nothing that could disturb the strange new state which, he felt – and was sure she felt, too – their lovemaking had awakened. He tossed it in the bin and returned, with his glass of ice-cold water, to the bedroom.

Yet now, he could not sleep.

The evening spun behind his eyes. The moment his name had been called. The conversations at the table. The return and the ninety-seven minutes (he had glanced at the clock and taken note of the times) of sex that followed. Lydia McGrath handing him the award. His taxi ride home, leaning comfortably on the faux-leather seats and drinking in the moments that had gone before. The absurd television show with its absurd wet young people. Lydia McGrath congratulating him at the table.

He could not escape her. He tried to force his mind back to Monica, lying naked beneath him, but the scene was interrupted by Lydia's face as she gazed past him and told him again how impressed she had been by his work. And the sudden lurch, the nausea that had engulfed him as he realised this was his triumph, this, not the lump of engraved Perspex she had placed in his hand on the stage. The recognition – but she had recognised only his achievement, not her own place in it. For all he had never admitted it to himself, it had been Lydia always and at every point, every decisive moment, not just the Town House but the decision to remain at the university, to teach, because only by teaching could he continue his research – their research, he had told himself – the avenues he had chosen, the experiments he had undertaken. A life of work, to prove and to justify, and Lydia to share in his victory. There had only ever been one goal, and he had reached it, and she was no longer there.

What had he done, in his quest for the unattainable?

And beside him, now snoring gently, lay Monica, who offered him suddenly something so much more than she had, something approaching the sublime he had always sought.

Had he simply been searching in the wrong place?

There was still time. He did not know how, but there was still time to correct his life.

He woke Monica gently by kissing her on the cheek.

'I've just remembered there are some things I need to take care of. At the lab. If I go in now I can get everything in place and come home early tomorrow.'

'Hmm,' she replied, and settled back into sleep. He dressed quietly and allowed the car to roll backwards onto the road before he started the engine. At that time of night, the drive would take no more than fifty minutes.

It was 2am.

***

6: Core

He was woken by a sharp pain in his left temple and an accompanying ache that seemed to span the whole of his spine. He knew at once that something was very wrong.

He opened his eyes. It was dark, and silent. He could

not place himself, could not orientate himself, did not know for certain whether he was sitting, leaning, or even lying down. He tried to move his right foot, and a jolt of pain shot through him so hard and so unexpectedly that he gasped. The act of gasping hurt even more.

A light swept by and illuminated his surroundings for a few seconds before fading away. A few seconds were all he needed.

He was in the car, still strapped in the driver's seat. The car was on its side. The glass from the windscreen was gone, which accounted for the breeze, although the window beside him was miraculously intact. The bonnet had buckled and compacted so that the front of the car was far closer to his face than it should have been. One of his legs – the one attached to the foot he had tried to move – seemed to be twisted into an impractical position. A five-foot long metal pole, part of the trampoline he had loaded into the car a fortnight earlier and not yet managed to dispose of, had slipped forward and was jutting out through the space the windscreen had once occupied. It had taken the easiest and most direct route to its current position, which was to enter the back of the driver's seat and the back of the driver and slide through them both until friction or some unseen obstacle had brought it to a halt. He could not see anything to his rear, but judging from the length he had glimpsed in front, there might be as much of a foot of the pole still behind him.

His first thought, once the pain had subsided enough for him to have any thought at all, was that there was no way Tabitha and Helen would be able to take the car tomorrow. He could not recall precisely what had happened – there was a memory of a sign, another car, perhaps, a moment of confusion over which lane he was supposed to be in.

He had drunk far too much. He had drunk a little whisky and far too much wine, and crashed his car, which was entirely his own fault, and it seemed likely that he would die as a result of it. He did not know how long he had been unconscious, but he could hear nothing except the wind, and if he could judge from the lights that had passed by, he was some distance from the road. If help was coming, he would have heard it by now. Without help, he could not survive long.

He should not have come out at all. He should have formulated a plan and waited until morning. What had he hoped to achieve in the middle of the night? What could he have disposed of or released without consequence? He had been heading for the Town House to end it all, he recalled, but what had he meant by that end?

He knew what he had meant. He had meant to release the subjects. An absurd notion. Release was impossible. They knew him too well, even if they were drugged and set loose hundreds of miles away. He had found them in different places, scattered indigents, male and female, young and old, all poor, friendless, and – the critical common factor – all afflicted by schizophrenia. He had lured them into the car without difficulty, fed them, befriended them, offered them warmth and shelter 'just till you get on your feet'.

There were four of them left. There had been five, but Amira had proven difficult, had fought the experiments, had refused food and water. Amira was buried in that tiny patch of garden behind the Town House. Carlos, Sophie, William and Emma remained. They too fought from time to time; scratched him, when he was distracted, and shouted obscenities when he wasn't. But underneath all the violence was, he felt, an understanding; they were part of something bigger than themselves, something bigger than him, bigger even than Lydia McGrath, whose genius had been the spark of it all. They would be stripped to the core, layer after layer shrivelling to dust as it was exposed to the light. Between them, they would show the world the way.

That had been the plan, at least. But he was dying in his car beside a road from which nobody could see him in the dark. He would be found, when daylight came, but his work would remain incomplete. And how long until someone decided to look in the Town House? How long until the shock had passed and it occurred to Monica that she could sell it? He had meant to feed them tomorrow; they were low on water too, and however loud their shouts, nobody would hear them from the basement. Nobody even knew about the basement; a trapdoor under a rug, metal lining, soundproofing, all his own work in the odd stolen half-hour. Amira's death had been a necessary step, but one that had pained him at the time and still pained him now. That Carlos, Sophie, William and Emma would suffer the same fate because he had chosen to drive after a large scotch and a bottle of expensive red wine caused him as much anguish as his own impending demise.

The cold was closing in. He had to do something. Summoning his last reserves of strength, he twisted to the side and dragged his fingers across the window.

***

7: Tears

It had been a dignified ceremony, Monica felt. Notable figures from the field had come to pay their respects and offered soft words in sombre tones. The attendance from the university had not been quite what she had expected, but then, for all his brilliance, Eric had never been an easy man to get on with. Lydia McGrath, of whom he had never spoken fondly, had seemed almost stunned, her face pale and tear-streaked, her words spoken quietly but without reserve.

Monica had only met her twice before, but she always been a little suspicious of Lydia McGrath.

As for Monica herself, she would recover, was already recovering. The girls would take longer. They had never been as close to their father as Monica would have liked, but they had been touched, as had Monica, by his final dying gesture. A "T" and an "H", for Tabitha and Helen, ghostly shadows of his fingers traced in the mist on the window beside him.

A week had passed. It was time to start planning, to gather herself and take stock of where she was and what she would do. There was a pension from the university, a modest sum due from the life insurance company, still revenue from his work that would be paid for ten more years. There was the Town House too, of course. She could finally sell it. But she could wait a few weeks for that.

There was no rush.

I'VE GONE

Anita Waller

It came as something of a surprise when she walked down the stairs and into the kitchen to find a note from Kevin, propped up by a mug.

I've gone.

No kisses, no protestations of his love, nothing. Gone? Her recently asleep brain did a quick chug to life. Did he mean gone to the shops for milk? Gone for the day? Gone for eternity?

After three years of blissful marriage anyone would think she would know what the rather cryptic note meant. She didn't.

She picked up the offending mug and carried it across to the ever barren kettle. It needed water in it. Didn't it always need water in it? She filled it, switched it on and moved to the fridge. That's when she really hoped he had gone for some milk because they were right out of it.

I've gone. She leaned across the sink unit and peered out of the window. It was pouring with rain and she looked to see if she could spot him, bottle of milk clutched in hand, dodging the puddles. There was no sign of him and she resigned herself to a cup of black coffee.

She called his mobile phone because she really didn't want black coffee but it went straight to voicemail.

'Hi,' she said. 'Hope you've gone to milk a cow or something. Love you.'

She expected him to ring, but for the rest of that Saturday she heard nothing. They had actually planned to go to the antiques quarter to look for a desk so by the time late afternoon came around she was feeling pretty uptight about the situation. No Kevin, no milk and no desk.

Feeling increasingly fretful, she rang him twice more during the course of the day but her own phone remained silent.

By midnight she started to feel sick. *I've gone* was starting to take on a whole new meaning. It meant *I've gone*.

She didn't sleep much that first night; instead she watched the crude red lights on her alarm clock blink past each hour and when she got up Sunday morning she felt angry as well as puzzled. That's when she saw the second note propped up against the same mug, the one with elephants on it.

Don't try to contact me, it said. She screwed it up and threw it at the wall.

'Chance would be a fine bloody thing' she yelled, then sat down with a thud as tears overwhelmed her.

And now she really was puzzled. Why had he gone to the trouble of sneaking back in the house to leave this second note – why not just push it through the letterbox?

Shaking as she did so, she picked up the now crumpled note and spread it open, trying to smooth it back into a reasonable piece of paper. It told her nothing; no clues, no ideas. She phoned him once more and was surprised to receive an automated message saying the number was no longer in use. With a new crippling fear deep in her chest she realised he must have cancelled his service.

She spent the next couple of hours ringing round their friends, all to no avail. Inexplicably he'd literally disappeared.

And then, to add insult to injury, she had to fetch some milk. She couldn't stomach any more black coffee. She picked up some other essentials while she was there; the Garibaldi biscuits that Kevin loved and which were always an automatic purchase she put back on the shelf with a mumbled 'Get your own bloody biscuits.'

She paused before going back into the house, and looked around her. She felt as though – oh, she didn't know.

Something felt not quite right. She inserted the key and pushed open the door. There was a further note on the hall stand.

Stop worrying, this one said. He'd been in the house again. She went back outside and scanned around but couldn't see anything strange, nothing out of the ordinary. And still something felt out of kilter.

Her head was buzzing and her stomach growled. She couldn't concentrate on anything beyond making a coffee with milk in it. Normally Sundays they spent doing the odd bit of housework and generally just chilling out with a pizza or something; their plans for this particular Sunday had been to set up the small box room as an office for her and by now she should have been polishing her new desk. But she wasn't. And as it was 7pm on a Sunday evening there was no chance of getting a desk now.

Instead she was sitting like a wimp on the settee wondering what to do next. Go to the police? She can't. They'll laugh at her. He's actually been in touch, albeit by notes, so he's hardly a missing person; he's just missing.

And then she knew what was out of kilter. His car. His beloved Ford Capri, a gleaming white monstrosity of a car that he washes and shines every weekend without fail was still sitting at the kerb, newly polished for its trip to the antiques quarter.

He adores that car and sometimes, most times, she thinks she takes second place to it. And that's why it's out of kilter; it's sitting outside their home when he isn't inside their home.

She went to get the spare car keys and opened the front door. Seriously spooked, she peered outside. She looked up and down the road before stepping out. Crossing to the car took a monumental effort. She peered inside. Nothing. She opened the door – with the key, no fancy locking system on a Capri – and slid behind the steering wheel. She reached across into the glove compartment and pulled out the couple of items he kept in there. Insurance document and the owner's manual – nothing new.

She swivelled round and looked in the back seat but there was nothing. The car was in its usual immaculate condition; the only worrying thing was that it was actually here and Kevin wasn't.

She climbed out of the low slung vehicle, locked it and headed back to her door. It was open.

She stood for a moment trying to remember if she had closed it when she went down to the car and couldn't for the life of her decide. She tentatively pushed it and it swung wider. One step inside. Two steps. She shivered. The air around her was freezing cold. She reached out a hand to touch the radiator. It was hot.

Moving carefully through the hallway she stopped at the kitchen door. It was closed and she couldn't remember closing it. She rarely closed it because sometimes the handle stuck and it needed screwdriver activity to repair it. She reached out to touch the handle and very carefully pressed the lever. Slowly she opened the door.

'Kevin!'

He smiled at her and remained seated at the table. 'Hello, you.'

She couldn't speak. She didn't know what to say. So she cried.

The tears rolled down her cheeks and she sobbed. She pulled a chair away from the table and sat down, resting her head on her arms and allowing her hair to spread across the table top.

'Don't cry, sweetheart,' he said. 'Don't cry.'

The tears stopped instantly and the anger flared.

'Don't cry? Don't fucking cry? Where the fucking hell have you been? And why all these ridiculous notes?'

'I don't like to hear you swear.' His tone was mildly reproachful.

'And I don't like to get notes that say *I've gone* with no bloody explanation,' she screamed. 'I was scared, Kevin. What's going on? Are you back for good? 'Cos there are no Garibaldi biscuits, I can assure you.'

She realised how ridiculous she sounded and the tears started again. Once more her head dropped to the table and he let her cry. She eventually stood and moved towards the kitchen worktop. Tearing off three sheets of kitchen roll she mopped her tears and blew her nose. He sat and stared at her waiting for her to calm down.

'So,' she said. 'Start talking.'

'I've come back to you,' he said. 'Did you get your desk?'

'No, I bloody well didn't get my desk!' she yelled, aware she was starting to sound like a Billingsgate fishwife.

'You're swearing again,' he said.

'And are you back for good?' she demanded. 'Or am I going to get a note tomorrow morning that says *Fooled you*?'

He smiled the slow sexy smile she had fallen for when she first met him. 'I'll always be with you,' he said. 'Never doubt that. I love you, with or without Garibaldi biscuits. You're mine and always will be.'

She stared at him. His answers were good, she granted him that, but they weren't telling her anything.

'So where have you been?'

'Does it matter?'

'Too right, it bloody matters. Have you been with another woman who's now decided she doesn't want you? Hmmm? Is that it? And I want the truth, Kevin. No bullshit.'

'No bullshit, my love. No, I haven't been with

another woman, I wouldn't do that. I got into some trouble. There's a man called Pete Danvers. You don't know him, so just listen. He's not a good man, Laura, and I owed him some money. That's where I've been, with him. Remember that name, Laura; remember Pete Danvers. He's evil.'

'How much did you owe him? And have you paid him?' She looked troubled. 'We've about £5,000 in the savings account…'

He smiled. Once again her heart flipped. She loved his smile.

'It was about £20,000 but the account has been settled. That's why I've not been here. I've been sorting it, but I didn't want you dragging into it.'

She stood and began to move towards him. He held up a hand. 'No, don't touch me yet, Laura. I'm not worthy. We have to rebuild a relationship. I let you down by doing what I did and before we can be close again I have to recover from the guilt I feel.'

She hesitated, not quite understanding the situation. She still wanted to hold him in her arms but she also still wanted to shout at him, to punish him for putting her through the two days of misery that she had suffered.

She sat back down and once more he smiled.

'Do you want a drink? Something to eat?' she asked, aware that he looked a little grey.

He shook his head. 'No, I'm fine, thank you. But you go ahead; you look like you need something. And I am sorry, sweetheart. I'm here now and I wish I'd never had to leave. I love you.'

'When did you leave?' she demanded. 'Why didn't you tell me you were going if you love me so much?'

'I left Friday night. I had a text just after you went upstairs to bed. It wasn't a good text so I took the problem far away from you. I thought it was for the best.'

'And you left that stupid note saying *I've gone.*'

He didn't answer, just smiled at her.

'I could hit you,' she said, her voice quite cold and matter of fact. 'Hit you really hard. I've even been out to the car, just to check that you weren't dead, sitting behind the steering wheel.'

Once again the smile.

She felt, for a moment, that he really wasn't taking her seriously and the tears started to prick her eyes once more. Couldn't he see how worried she had been? Didn't he realise it was the first time they had been apart for three years? She reached for some more kitchen roll and dabbed at her eyes.

'I think I hate you,' she said.

'No, you don't. And these two days of my absence have meant that you'll now have a life free from fear. I've sorted it, so it's all been worth it.'

She switched on the kettle and waved a mug at him. 'You sure you don't want a drink?'

He shook his head. 'No, I'm good, thanks. It wouldn't help –'

'What do you mean?'

For the first time he looked uncomfortable. 'I mean, I'm thinking clearly and so I don't need to calm down with a cup of tea.' He knew he was waffling and she could see he knew it.

'Okay.' She looked at him carefully. 'Are you still lying to me?'

'I have never lied to you.'

Her expression was inscrutable. 'Isn't omission lying?'

'I've told you now,' he said simply.

'So the debt is definitely paid?'

'Definitely.'

'How?'

'I took a gamble.'

She felt sick. Not only drugs or whatever had caused the massive £20,000 debt, but gambling as well. 'Kevin…'

'Laura, it's over. Look, make yourself a cup of tea and come and sit back down at the table. If you have more questions I'll answer them but I just need you to remember the name of Pete Danvers. You'll do that for me?'

'Of course I will, but why? Is he likely to turn up here?'

Kevin shook his head. 'No, he isn't. But one day you may need to tell somebody that name, so just remember it. It's a "just in case" kind of memory.'

She picked up her phone, went to notes and typed in the name. 'I won't forget it now.' She smiled at him for the first time.

She was starting to feel not quite so angry with him and shelved any more questions until another time. She noticed he still wasn't looking too good and placed some biscuits on the table. Not Garibaldis.

He didn't take any, just sat and watched as she dunked the ginger nut in her tea.

'So, what now?' she asked.

'I'm going to court you, make it up to you for what has happened over the last couple of days. I'm not presuming anything, Laura, and I'll sleep in the spare room tonight. We'll start afresh tomorrow. I need space, need to get my head around things. I can't do that with you in the same bed as me. Is that okay?'

'I've managed without you for the last two nights,' she said coolly, 'so I guess another night won't matter. And I'll sleep better knowing you're back, anyway. As you can imagine, I didn't sleep too well last night.'

Inside she seethed. She felt cast aside. Why didn't he want to sleep with her? His reasons didn't ring true. She would give him tonight in the spare room, but tomorrow night he would either be in her bed or in the Capri.

At nine o'clock she stood and wished him good night. They had remained at the kitchen table, occasionally chatting and occasionally having quiet moments. He repeated several times how much he loved her, but she couldn't say it to him, not yet. He had killed something between them. She prayed it would come back because if it didn't...

She showered and put on her oldest and most comforting pyjamas, listening for him climbing the stairs. She heard nothing and presumed he was giving her time to settle before going to bed in the adjoining room.

Mentally exhausted, she read for a short time before switching off her light and falling asleep very quickly. Her last thoughts were that she would deal with any further issues after a good night's rest.

Her sleep lasted until 5am. The banging on the door was loud and she reached out to the other side of the bed to tell Kevin someone was at the door.

She felt emptiness and then she remembered he was in the other room. She put on her slippers and dressing gown and walked out on to the landing, calling for Kevin as she did so. Once down in the hallway her brain finally kicked into gear and she approached the front door with caution.

A glance through the spy hole showed her an ID card being held up to it.

'Yes?' she said, aware her voice was squeaking. 'What do you want?'

And where the hell was Kevin? Why hadn't he heard the loud banging too? It must have woken half the street up.

'South Yorkshire Police. Are you Mrs Greystone? Mrs Laura Greystone?'

'Yes,' she said. 'I asked you, what do you want?'

'Can you open the door, please, Mrs Greystone? We need to speak to you.'

She unlocked the door, leaving the chain fastened. Opening it as far as it would, she peered out. What the fuck had Kevin done that would bring police officers to their home at this ungodly hour?

'Thank you, Mrs Greystone. Can you take the chain off, please?' A female officer was standing behind the man and holding out her ID. 'PC Carter, Mrs Greystone. Can we come in, please?'

She took off the chain and looked backwards towards the stairs. She hoped she would see Kevin coming down them, but she didn't.

She stepped aside as the two police officers came through the front door. They looked at her enquiringly and she pointed to the kitchen door, thankful that it was open. No screwdriver needed this time.

They waited for her to follow them and DI Sutherland – she could vaguely remember the name on the ID – waved her to a chair.

'Sue?' he said to the PC who had accompanied him. She nodded and moved towards the kettle.

'Mrs Greystone, Laura,' he began, 'is your husband Kevin Greystone?'

'Yes, he is.'

Her anger was threatening to overwhelm her. She knew he had been keeping something back. The police arriving at 5am proved there was more to his story than he had told her.

'I'm sorry, Laura, but I have to tell you that his body

has been recovered from an old warehouse down near the canal wharf. He has been shot.'

She stared at him. 'Impossible!'

'We believe it happened in the early hours of Saturday morning.'

She smiled. 'It can't be him. He's upstairs in bed. We were chatting till about nine last night and then I went to bed. He slept in the spare room so he didn't disturb me.' They didn't need to know the real reason.

Sutherland looked across at PC Carter, who was pouring milk into the drinks.

'Can you go and get him, Laura?'

She nodded. 'Of course. I'm surprised you didn't wake him, all that noise you made.'

She stood and moved towards the hall. Sue Carter left the drinks and followed her. They went up the stairs together, Laura feeling quite put out that she had to be accompanied. What if Kevin was naked?

She opened the door of the spare room and switched on the light. The bed was empty, the covers as smooth as she had left them when she made up the bed two weeks earlier.

'He must be on the sofa,' she said and turned to go along the landing.

Sue followed her back downstairs and into the lounge. The curtains were still open – Laura hadn't even thought about closing them when she went to bed. She looked around and the room was exactly as it had been before Kevin's arrival.

'But…'

'Laura, come back into the kitchen.'

Sue gently led her back to Sutherland. She looked at her boss and shook her head.

'Laura, we need you to come with us to identify your husband's body. Here,' he said and handed her a mug of tea.

'Did you know where your husband was? Does he do this a lot? Go missing for a couple of days?'

'He wasn't missing,' she whispered. 'He was here for two hours last night. We talked...'

'Is there someone we can call for you, Laura?' Sue asked gently.

'You think I'm making it up, don't you? We sat at this table, had biscuits and a drink and talked.' Sutherland looked towards the draining board. There was one mug.

'Sue will go with you while you get dressed, Laura, and then we'd like you to come with us. We just need you to identify Kevin and then we can get on with the job of finding his killer.'

She shook her head bewildered. 'But you're not listening. He was here with me last night.'

Sue led her towards the stairs once more and waited patiently while Laura found some jeans and a top.

'This is silly,' Laura said as they headed back down the stairs, 'but I'll go along with it just to prove it isn't Kevin. If the body that you have was killed in the early hours of Saturday morning, and Kevin was here last night, it kinda proves it can't be him.'

'So where is Kevin?'

'I have no idea. But he was definitely here yesterday.'

Half an hour later they were at the morgue. She stared through the window at the sheet-covered corpse, completely unafraid. She knew what she knew and it couldn't be Kevin. She heard Sutherland say 'we're ready' into a microphone and the lab assistant slowly rolled the sheet away from the head.

As if in slow motion Laura fell to the floor and a doctor was summoned. She came out of the faint and began to cry.

'But how? How can that be Kevin? If it is him – and I'll give you that it looks like him – how could he have been killed when you say he was, and yet have been with me yesterday?'

A box of tissues was handed to her and she dabbed at her eyes.

'Trust me, he couldn't have been with you yesterday, Laura,' Sutherland said gently. 'Could you have maybe dreamt it?'

Could she? She had had no sleep the previous night – could she have fallen asleep and dreamt it?

She needed to get out of there. She shrugged. 'Maybe. Maybe I did dream it. I don't know. Can I go home now, please? I need to grieve for my husband.'

Sue took her home and followed her into the house but Laura asked her to leave, saying she would be okay. She needed to think. She didn't agree that it had been a dream. It had been real; Kevin had been in that kitchen with her.

As Sue walked back to the police car, Laura locked the door and leaned against it. She waited a couple of minutes and then opened up the notes in her mobile phone. Pete Danvers. That had been no dream. That had been Kevin telling her the name of his killer.

She headed upstairs. She wanted to wash the stench of the morgue from her so she switched on the shower before going into the bedroom.

On her pillow was a note. *I've gone.*

But this time he had added three kisses.

THE BRIDGE

Simon Maltman

Part 1

I opened the door into my small and let's say minimal office at just after half nine that morning. As usual, I had made the short journey on the metro from Chodov to Pancrák, grabbing a takeout coffee and the morning papers on the way. I opened the blinds and sat down at my desk. I leaned back and felt fresh and ready for the day.

At that time, we had lived in Prague for about three years and it still felt new and exciting. Grace had been offered a job as a translator in the British embassy and instead of maybe getting married – at the grand old age of twenty-seven, we had set off for an adventure somewhere new instead. I had worked as a journalist in Belfast and the idea was for me to write some freelance stuff there when I could pick it up, knowing that Grace had a good wage coming in. I didn't find that much work, but a few investigations led me into the realm of private detection and I just kind of fell into it. There was enough trade, mostly from ex-pats, to keep things ticking over and I found I really quite liked it.

I lit a cigarette and put one foot on the desk, opening up my copy of *Czechia Today*. There were a couple of calls in the morning – the tying up of a recent case and some others, dealing with bills and invoices. His call came at exactly midday.

'Is that Mr Cairns? Mr Christopher J Cairns?'

'Yes, speaking,' I said, stubbing out a cigarette.

'I would like to speak with you in regards to the handling perhaps of a new case.'

The accent was Czech, a man's, perhaps approaching middle age. I considered my reflection on my mobile screen as I lifted it off the desk. I wasn't looking bad, though my beard needed a bit of work and my gelled black hair could do with a trim. I pressed record.

'Yes, certainly I could discuss this with you. What does

it involve?'

He paused and I could hear a thin intake of breath. 'It would be something that is in your usual remit I feel, though I would prefer not to speak on the phone.'

'I see,' I said evenly and shrugged. 'That's okay. Would you like to meet somewhere to discuss it then?'

'Certainly. I could come to your office or meet you in the centre some place?'

'If you're thinking today, I was going to head into town this afternoon actually. We could meet at two, say Café Franz Kafka, in old town?'

'Yes, Mr Cairns, I will see you then.'

'Okay, oh, what's the name?'

'Stein. Bernard Stein.'

I stepped off the metro again about one o'clock and bought a frankfurter from a vendor on my walk round to Old Town Square. It was a warm April afternoon, my checked short sleeve shirt and black jeans felt comfortable enough, but T-shirt and shorts would have been better. Back in Belfast, if we had a few dry days in spring, tops were off and the employment 'sickness' levels would rocket.

I lit a cigarette walking up Staroměstské nám, as I turned the corner and the medieval old square appeared in front of me. It never ceases to impress. It is the best preserved square of its kind in the world, I'd say. The old buildings loom proudly over the cobbled streets, cafés and restaurants jut out from canopies, menus on stands offering frothy pitchers of Prague beer, schnitzel and guláš.

I walked up towards the Old Town Hall and could see a crowd gathering beneath the Astronomical Clock. Every hour it was the same. There were always at least fifty tourists, waiting for the hour to change as the clockwork apostles march outwards and the little skeleton chimes the bell. It seems like midnight on New Year's Eve every hour.

As I neared the centre of the square, there was quite a bustle too for this time of year. It's always busy, but there seemed to be more of a squeeze that day – maybe Prague was just getting fuller day after day. There seemed to be more tour guides too, walking past with their umbrellas held high, incongruous in the sun, shepherding tourists forward. They always reminded me of the sixties show The Prisoner and the inmates with their umbrellas and Butlin's-style clothes.

'Mr Cairns?'

I turned in my seat, at a small table on the street front of the café. I hadn't sensed him approach.

'Yes, glad to meet you,' I said, standing. We shook hands and Stein smiled, but his cold brown eyes surveyed me deeply. He was a little smaller than me, dressed in a full dark suit and he didn't seem to mind the heat. I'd say he was around fifty, with short curly black hair, clean shaven, and with three thick creases on his brow.

'Can I offer you a drink?' he asked with a small flourish of his hand.

'Yeah, please, I'd take another Americano, thanks.'

He swiftly went off to the counter inside, and I sat back down and lit a cigarette.

He returned promptly and set the drinks down with a fleeting smile.

'Thanks,' I said. He took out a fully stocked leather cigarette case and fingered one out as he shot me a lingering stare. I leaned back and flicked some ash into the glass ash tray.

'Thank you for meeting with me at short notice,' he said, then paused to inhale deeply. 'There is a somewhat urgent matter that I would like to share with you.'

'Certainly, that's fine. I've just tied up a few cases so I'm available to start on something new as soon as tomorrow, if it's something I can agree to.'

'Good, good.' He scooped out two sugar cubes and dropped them into his coffee. They broke up the thin brown swirls on top and he lifted his teaspoon, turning the drink a muddy black. Taking his time, he sipped it cautiously and stared at me again with a brief smile. 'I think you will be quite interested. Let me explain a little. I work for the government, Mr Cairns.' He looked around him and lowered his voice slightly, although there was nobody seated at the tables next to ours. 'I have some documents that I must show you. I would like to–'

He was interrupted by his mobile phone droning on vibrate in his pocket. 'I am terribly sorry,' he said and snatched it out, looking to see who the caller was. His face contorted for a flash and then he offered an apologetic smile. 'I must take this, I'm afraid.'

'Stein,' he said and then went on to talk in what I was think was either German or Czech. He said very little, appearing to be answering the caller's questions at the start, then asking a few of his own. I did not register any farewells when he ended the call and slipped the phone thoughtfully back into his pocket.

'Mr Cairns, I am very sorry for wasting your time like this and I am very keen to talk with you further, but I am afraid I must leave you now,' he said, taking out another cigarette and lighting it. 'There is a most urgent matter that has arose and I must attend to it immediately.'

'That's fine, I understand,' I replied with a shrug. 'We can meet again.' I was going to be in town anyway, so it didn't matter much. He interested me, I was curious.

'I appreciate your patience,' he said and stood. I got up

too, pushing my chair backwards.

He offered me his hand and I took it. 'Would it be an inconvenience to meet again this evening? This matter is really also quite pressing.'

He released my grip and reached out an open envelope from his inside pocket and offered it to me. I leafed through it, trying to appear disinterested. There looked to be over seven thousand Koruna, more than about two hundred quid.

'This would be a retainer, if that is acceptable to you,' he added and took a few quick puffs on his cigarette.

'Yes, that should be fine,' I answered nonchalantly. 'Where and when?'

He thought for a moment then asked, 'Do you know the approach to Petrin Hill? There is a small rose garden with some benches in the corner. I am sorry for the element of secrecy, but it would be a quiet and pleasant place where we could have our conversation.'

I thought for a second. It was unusual but I wanted to know more. If I didn't like things I could just not take the case and give him back his money. 'That's grand,' I said. 'I can do that. What time?'

'Ten o'clock?' he asked, taking a step back.

'Yes, I'll see you then.'

'Goodbye, Mr Cairns,' he said and offered a half wave as he turned and strode away. I could see him reaching for another cigarette as he went.

Part 2

'Steak and chips,' I said as she leaned round me for a kiss. Grace is tall, blonde, and still way out of my league.

'Yum, I'm starving,' she said, peering over my shoulder as I turned over the onions and mushrooms as they sizzled beside the steaks.

'It'll be about ten minutes,' I said and added in a few

herbs from the jar.

'Great. Thanks, love. I'll get the plates.'

We enjoyed a quiet meal with a glass of beer each and a little Art Blakely on in the background. It wasn't often we could take our time over dinner.

At a quarter to nine, Grace had changed into her gym stuff and came into the living room where I was catching up with the BBC news channel.

'I'm off to my class then.' She bent over and kissed me on the cheek.

'Have fun. I've got that meeting so it'll be about midnight I'd say for me.'

'Okay,' she said, walking to the door, and then said turning, 'Be careful, won't you?'

'Always,' I said casually. 'See you later.'

I looked back to the TV, and another story involving Brexit and the gloomy forecasts for the foreseeable future. I was glad Grace had her languages and we could travel where we liked. I was glad for my Irish passport too.

There was a sharp knock on the door and I presumed Grace had forgotten something.

As I approached the middle glass pane, I saw two dark outlines on the other side. I opened the door to find two men in dark suits, both sporting sullen expressions. The first wore a fine old-fashioned hat with a rim, and the second an equally old-fashioned and ugly moustache.

'Hello. Can I help you?' I asked.

'Yes,' said the first. 'Mr Cairns, we would like to come in and ask you a few questions.' He flashed a badge.

'What's this about?'

'Please, if we could come in?' He didn't trouble himself with a smile.

I led them in to the living room, but we all remained standing.

'You met with a man today. A Mr Stein,' the first stated.

It wasn't a question, so I didn't answer it. *Moustache* glared at me then *Hat* pressed on.

'What did he talk to you about?' His expression didn't change.

'We didn't talk about much at all. Look, he wants to discuss a possible case, but I don't know anything about it. If I did, I probably wouldn't tell you anyway, not until I see some warrant or papers telling me that I have to.'

I wasn't trying to sound particularly tough and from their undisturbed stances, I hadn't come across tough either.

'You accepted from him a large sum of money. What was this in exchange for?' he went on crisply.

'Like I said, I'm not saying anything more until I see something official. Can I have a look at that badge again? What's your name?' I added, trying to keep up my nerve.

The first man looked at me coldly and licked his lips. He abruptly turned and the second followed. I walked behind them to the door and they both turned when out on the steps.

'We will talk with you again,' said the first firmly.

'We?' I asked. 'I thought your buddy was mute. Be seeing you.'

That time I was trying to sound tough. I closed the door then leaned my back against it, catching my breath.

Part 3

I approached the rose garden close to ten. I had been pretty much chain smoking from when I got off the metro and stubbed the most recent cig out on the black fence surrounding the garden. There were a few people around, walking on by, mostly in pairs. No one was in the garden except a lone figure sitting on one of the benches.

A couple of streetlights had just come on after the daylight had started to fade. Even so, it was still dark and it wasn't until a few steps in that I was sure it was Stein. Petrin Hill stood tall behind him, the replica Eiffel Tower at the summit, surveying the city. He was sitting to the side, a Trilby hat hanging partly over his face.

When I was just a few yards away I was almost certain he was dead. I stopped suddenly and felt as if my feet were sinking into the dry, dusty earth below. Acid seemed to flood my stomach and my head burst with adrenalin. I searched all around, pulled my feet, spinning, gripped by fear. My body then stiffened, poised.

There were trees behind the benches but I could see through them and there was no one else there. I relaxed my muscles slightly. I moved on and stood before the body, a shell. The face was grey and the eyes like a set of disused traffic lights. I forced myself to sit beside it and I lifted up the hand. It was cold, quite rigid, and I could find no pulse.

I looked up at the body and for the first time noticed a small, reddish brown stain on the jacket. I edged the jacket away with two fingers and found the shirt beneath was saturated with blood. I slid to the side of the bench, as far as I could go, and pulled out my mobile.

I jumped up and pressed in numbers, my whole body tingling with an unpleasant sensation. When I spotted a book jutting out from his lower jacket pocket, I stopped dialling and put the phone back in my pocket. I glanced around me before reaching over, plucking out the book and stepping backwards again. It was a collection of short stories.

Protruding from page 411 was a small brown envelope, much like the one Stein had given me earlier. Impulsively, I carefully lifted out the contents; one folded white sheet. I opened it out and found it was some kind of official document, written in a foreign language. There were only two words I recognised on it: Christopher Cairns.

It was almost eleven when I arrived at her apartment. I was as close to the word 'frantic' as I have ever been. My type of investigations did not usually involve dead bodies with government documents that had my name on them. There were plenty of things that I know I should have done like calling the police or even taking the document for Grace to translate. I didn't do any of them; I especially didn't want to involve Grace.

'Hello, is Becky in?' I asked, attempting to appear casual.

The stocky thirty-something man eyed me with caution and replied in a Czech accent, 'Just one moment please. Who can I say is calling?'

'Oh, it's Chris Cairns.'

He closed the door to and went back into the apartment. I lit a smoke and tried to calm myself down.

***

After a minute, she came to the door. She wore a smart blue dress, her usual style for wearing to work. Becky was English, in her twenties, and pretty. I had worked with her briefly at one of the local papers, soon after I moved to Prague.

'Chris, this is a surprise.'

'I know. I'm really sorry to barge in on you. Would you have five minutes, it's pretty important?' I threw down the half-smoked cigarette and stood on it.

'Of course, come in,' she said, looking concerned. She opened the door for me. I walked past the guy seated at a table in the living room and she showed me through into the kitchen.

'Can I get you something, coffee?' she asked as we both sat down at the breakfast bar.

No, no, thank you. Can you close the door?'

'Okay, sure. What's this about? I haven't seen you in ages,' she answered, closing the door slowly, then swiftly returning to her stool.

'I know, I'm sorry,' I said, gathering myself and lifting out the envelope. I set it in front of us and she looked down at it with a blank expression.

'I just need five minutes. I know you're fluent in a couple of languages and I need something translated. If you can, please?'

'Sure, I'll try. What is it?'

'Look, it's better I don't tell you much. It's… well, an official document. I just need to know the gist of it.'

She looked pained and brushed her long brown hair to the side. 'Are you in some kind of trouble?'

'Please,' I said, 'just take a look.'

She looked at the envelope as if it might jump up and bite her on the nose, but picked it up and slid out the letter. She quickly unfolded it and read it silently. I stared at her face, searching for a reaction. Her lips moved as she scanned the document, a few wrinkles appearing on her forehead, 'It's in Czech. I can read it,' she said absently.

As she read on, her face went a little pale and her lips stopped moving.

'What does it say?' I asked, my voice cracked and harsher than I intended.

'Just a second,' she said in almost a whisper.

'What does it say!' I begged, trying not to shout.

'Wait a second!' she snapped.

Just then the door opened, and the guy looked round the door at us. 'Everything okay, Becky?' he asked, looking directly at her, a firmness to his voice.

'Yes, yes, everything's fine,' she said looking up, trying

to sound chipper. 'Chris has just had some bad news here.'

'Aright, I'll just be next door,' he added evenly then closed the door and left.

I watched her patiently as she read the rest of the sheet then set it down.

She reached her hand to her brow and spoke very quietly. 'You have to call the police, Chris,' she said, facing down at the table.

'What does it say?' I urged, almost desperately.

'You are in trouble. What have you been doing?'

'Nothing,' I said and shook my head. 'What does it say about me?'

'You're being investigated. It looks like it's quite serious. They're considering warrants, even one for your arrest.'

I felt sick. I had felt sick all night long, but this was total nausea. I said nothing.

'You need to ring them now,' she said and lifted out her mobile, passing it to me.

'No, I can't.'

'You have to,' she hissed. 'Or I'll have to do it,' she added gentler.

I considered her with disdain and stood up.

'I'll go. Just don't call anyone. I'll sort things,' I said almost mechanically.

'I have to call them,' she said, holding the phone up with a shrug, rising from the counter.

I shook my head again and looked her in the eyes, my body almost limp now. 'At least wait five minutes.'

The streets were quiet. Bodies moved past me occasionally but I hardly noticed them. My eyes were searching for only uniforms or flashing lights. I ambled through the centre of Prague, passing the Apostles and their skeleton. I found myself walking on and then I crossed the street beside the macabre and favourite tourist attraction The Museum of Torture.

I allowed myself a wry smile. Maybe it was a nervous smile – I don't know what I was feeling. I had no plan, nothing more than one foot in front of the other. I looked over to The Charles Bridge, curving out in front of me. A thin mist hung over it. The cobbles were silent after the day's tourists and caricaturists had long departed. I began to walk across the bridge. I had never seen it empty before.

There was a slight chill on the air, and after throwing down a cigarette, I held my arms close to my sides. I walked on. I only sensed the approaching steps as the blade passed easily into my side.

My shirt is suddenly wet as the knife is pulled from me.

My body heaves and seems to pull apart like cracked glass.

I fall forward. I'm on my knees.

The metal feels cold as it enters my back.

THE MOTH JAR

Jim Ody

Asurreptitious glance at the computer screen clock told me I was free to leave for the day. A silent hooter sounding in corporate bedlam where, for most, there were contracted hours. But these were seen as a guide to minimum working hours, for those with a slack work ethic and no ambitious tendencies.

My time as a clock-watcher was now over, thanks to promotions and responsibilities. The memories still fresh of counting down the minutes, and leaping up as if receiving either an electric shock or some epiphany, just as soon as the magical 5:00pm appeared. However, at some point the revelation hits you that a little extra effort results in promotion, pay rises and a better standard of living. In a similar theory of the well-worn saying of "looking after pennies and the pounds will look after themselves", so it could be said that if you add a few extra hard minutes here and there, you will receive hours of pleasure in return. It is easy for me to say as I delegate and reap bonuses quite unapologetically.

I looked at my lonely office. I was not the sort to adorn it with my academic accolades, nor pictures of my handshaking of celebrities, so apart from a couple of family photographs, the walls were uncharacteristically sparse.

Having earned my stripes, I was able to leave when I wanted to. I had hit, and smashed through, that threshold that silently winked at me, and with a secret handshake said, get the work done to a decent standard and you can come and go as you please. So that is what I did. With little care, I left an open-ended Out Of Office message that was vague enough to suggest I may be checking emails up until midnight, or may also be deciphered as: I might never check them again.

It was two in the afternoon on a Friday. I had overseen the winning of a large contract, so could negotiate as many free Friday afternoons as I wanted. This contract was worth millions. I was suddenly a corporate king with the meal ticket that everybody wanted.

I looked down at the picture on my desk, taken in the Caribbean the previous summer. My wife Laura, as slender as ever, blonde and showing her bright white teeth as she smiled, looked gorgeous in a sprayed-on dress. Next to her my eight-year-old daughter Bobbi grinned, an ice cream melting in her hand.

'See you soon,' I said under my breath, wheeling back on my chair.

I grabbed my jacket, but held it over my shoulder as the weather was seasonably warm. I raised a hand to a couple of my team as I left the office, mainly the ones who weren't jealous of me. These were not the ones silently thinking of ways to murder me, without ever having the balls to follow through with their morbid fantasies.

One of the females, a pretty brunette called Mel, looked slightly concerned as she waved fingers at me. I smiled back – she deserved that at least.

I had just gone through the doors and slowed for the lift, when I heard the doors behind open and a voice call my name. 'Tom?'

I looked round to see Mel stood there, straightening her skirt. 'Do you fancy going for a drink?'

'What, now?' I replied, my jacket still clung to my shoulder as my right hand automatically went towards my left hand.

'Now. Or later, whatever?'

I realised that I was turning around the wedding band on my finger. I don't know whether this was through unspoken love, or perhaps some illusion of love that I was trying to make disappear. 'I would like that, Mel, very much, but…' I couldn't say any more and let the words hang there, their weight too heavy to follow with anything flippant. Even a joke seemed grossly inappropriate.

I saw her eyes glance to my fumbling hands. They were filled with a sadness that was disappointment, but as much for me as it was for her. This was perhaps a joint burden that we silently shared.

'I understand… *Laura.*'

I nodded. My lift arrived, the doors opening to show another member of senior management. I nodded at him, and of course he reciprocated.

I turned back but Mel was gone.

How did I feel? How *should* I feel?

Love wraps you up tightly, engulfing you in emotions so strong you almost suffocate. Perhaps it is possible to feel the light touch from another love, whispering upon your cheek like a breath of fresh air.

I nodded to the security guy, who was polite but with little charm. I wondered again whether he provided any real security other than the jurisdiction to slightly man-handle unauthorised personnel, or escort employees on their dismissal walk of shame from the premises – the latter I always thought to be a real perk of the job. He seemed bored and acted like this was community service. Perhaps it was.

My car was less than twenty-feet away from the building, another proof of status, up there with the disabled and heavily pregnant employees, senior management got to park their flashy cars like a game show reveal of *look what you could've had.* Perhaps our portly figures from rich food, or the weight of our thick wallets, gave justification to us not having to fight for a space like the rest of the employees. My car was a Range Rover. I didn't need a Range Rover, but it cost me nothing but a small amount of tax per month, so why not? It was slightly more palatable in silver, rather than a Chelsea-wives white, or a footballer's black.

The sun could not hide in a cloudless sky, so I was forced to put on my sunglasses. I often shied away from their usage, that being one of a few acts of self-consciousness that I had, often happy to roll the dice with my eyesight and a life of crows' feet, in order to feel at ease. Some consider dark-glasses to be cool, which says a lot about our society today. When we feel covering up the part of us that sets us apart from others is considered aesthetically pleasing, then it could be said that we are losing our grip on the important things in life. It is also said that cool is but one letter away from fool, so there you go.

Before I started up the V8 motor, I sent off a text to Laura. 'Just leaving x.'

Now in our late thirties, we had been married for a vast number of years, but I still felt that I was an incredibly lucky guy. I was not always struck with random acts of romance, but that day something told me I should do it. So a few streets away, I pulled in next to an independent florist, and made a fuss about choosing a small selection of flowers that I knew not the name of, only how beautiful they complimented each other, the same way that I felt a family photograph of Laura, Bobbi and I did.

I sang along to The Stones on the radio whilst drumming my hands on the steering wheel to "Honky Tonk Woman", and grinning like the village idiot. I only lived another ten minutes away in a new housing estate on the edge of town. It was on what was once a green belt of land that for fifty years the council had promised would not to be built on, but finally the financial pull had been too much, and a handful of years earlier a dozen houses, including our Victorian copy, was erected. Money and over population once again trumping the environment.

***

I opened the front door, and called to Laura, part of me knowing that we had a couple of hours before I had to pick Bobbi up from school.

'Laura? I'm home!' I called, slightly in a sing-song fashion, but got no answer. Of late she had not been herself, so perhaps this was the real reason for this off-the-cuff romantic gesture. It's funny how you do things, to later realise that there was probably a reason for it.

The place seemed empty without Bobbi running around, the sound of her giggles bouncing off the walls.

I walked up the stairs, clutching the flowers to my chest, my heart rattling my ribcage, the way it had done a lifetime earlier when we had first met. Anticipation meets anxiety.

There was almost an eerie feeling as I walked slowly down the landing towards our bedroom. I peaked in the door and saw Laura lay under the covers, a single crisp white sheet over her lithe naked body. She smiled coyly, then grinned at the flowers.

'For me?' she asked in a half whisper. I nodded and pointed to her. 'For me?' I whispered. She nodded and drew back the sheet.

Liberated from my clothes, she welcomed me warmly as we were entwined as one. This tender act seemed even more poignant than normal, and at one point she smiled as a tear escaped onto the pillow below. We have all known of love, but this was something I couldn't believe others had ever experienced so intensely. The clichés are there, dog-eared, creased and stained, but this doesn't make them any less truthful. A Polaroid of passion, this was a teenage fantasy I never thought would come true.

Between the love of my wife and the love of my daughter, I had no room for anyone else.

***

Afterwards as silence fell upon us, Laura closed her eyes and drifted off to sleep. Her breathing rhythmic and deep, she was an angel sweetly off someplace else. I left her peacefully recharging her batteries as I went downstairs and put on a pot of coffee.

At that point, the doorbell went.

I did up my jeans, and slipped on a t-shirt. I opened the door to expect to see the postman with a parcel for me to sign. He certainly didn't need to see any of my naked body, he wasn't paid enough.

It wasn't the postman, it was Mel. She stood there as a picture of innocence.

'Tom?' she said, in a way that she almost sounded like she required me to confirm this for her.

'Mel. Hi. I… Are you okay?' I glanced behind me out of habit, then back at the attractive lady at my door.

Ignoring my question, she asked, 'Is everything alright, Tom?' I paused, which made her look all the more concerned. If this was her way of coming on to me then it was certainly one of the more unorthodox methods, and not one most people would choose.

When I didn't respond, she added, 'Can I come in?'

I took a step back, looked up the stairs, then ushered her into the lounge. My head was spinning, and a kick-drum had replaced my heart. What was I doing? Nothing good could ever come from this situation.

'Look, Tom.' She touched my arm, which made me freeze. 'Things have been difficult. I know that, but I am here if you need someone to talk to.'

We both sat down. Mel on the side of the sofa – Laura's side – and me perched in my chair looking at her, not knowing what to say. I was unclear of her intentions; or perhaps deep down I knew. The air became thick with tension and a wave of vertigo had me grabbing for the arm of the chair. Her lips moved in slow motion, and the tip of her tongue came to rest in the corner of her mouth, possibly in suggestion.

'Sorry?' I said, realising that I had missed what she had just said to me. The words floated over my head, never making it anywhere near my ears. Above her, a picture of a smiling family looked over our liaison.

'I didn't know whether I should have come here.' She glanced down at hands that trembled, wringing with nerves, maybe a little adrenaline pulsing around her body.

'It was very thoughtful of you,' I said, glancing up out of the lounge door again.

She ran her hand through her hair, then in a quick movement she must've felt vulnerable, and tugged a few strands back down by way of a shield, or a comfort blanket of hair follicles. 'It's just... you never talk about it.'

'I... I'm not sure I, er.' I got up. 'Excuse me for a minute.' I strode up the stairs, wondering just what I was getting into. I walked towards our bedroom, suddenly filled with dread and guilt.

Laura sat in her trousers and bra, buttoning up her shirt. 'And what, may I ask, is she doing here?' At first I thought that she was cross, but then I saw the side of her mouth twitch. I think she was amused because she saw me squirm.

'Laura, I... I don't know,' I stammered, placing a hand gently on the side of her neck, and sliding down her shoulder and clavicle.

She looked up suddenly with cold eyes. 'Yes, you do, Tom. She wants you.'

'I...' I started, but was unsure just what to say. 'Go to her,' she said shooing me away. She lay back on the bed, suddenly purring with seduction. 'I'll be here when she's gone.'

I walked away, backwards at first, then spun around and headed back downstairs.

Mel was sat more comfortably now, and I swear she had undone one of the buttons on her blouse. Her breasts appeared to be straining the buttons more than I had remembered. I looked away, my eye catching the clock, and without even being completely conscious of it, I knew there was still plenty of time before I picked Bobbi up from school.

'Everything okay?' Mel asked again. This was a recurring obsession for her. It was also odd that she didn't think it strange to come to the house of a married man, lounge out on his sofa like some truck-stop whore, then ask him whether everything was okay. For a second I wondered whether this was some elaborate set up that Laura had coordinated to gauge my reaction, or perhaps some sort of spicy threesome she had orchestrated. Deep down I knew I was far off the mark.

'I heard voices,' she said. 'Is someone else here?' I felt my heart sink. To lie would do me no good with either woman, but was this really a time for the truth?

'Look, I was talking to Laura. I'm fine, so... you know, maybe you should go.'

Mel looked up and swallowed hard. 'Tom,' she said, shuffling forward and grabbing my hand. 'You know that Laura is dead, don't you?'

If it weren't for the look in Mel's eyes then I might've thought that she was joking, except people don't joke about that sort of thing, do they? Something was happening in my stomach, a deep hole was appearing. My throat was contracting, and I was gulping for air.

'No,' I muttered barely audible, and with no conviction. 'I was upstairs talking to her. We were... she just...' Mel was up on her feet and pulling me close to her before I could fully understand. My legs were weak twigs and my body a dead weight, unable to stay upright. Colours flashed like a kaleidoscope being twisted by a child. I couldn't make out any of the shapes, my world was unrecognisable, but the feeling of her body against mine was familiar.

'Laura!' I shouted, my eyes filling up. 'Come down here!' I ran to the stairs calling her name, now a child without control of his emotions. I stomped up the stairs and towards the bedroom.

'Laura!' I screamed.

Laura was laid on the bed, her skin pale and her eyes lifeless. Slowly her head turned towards me, her dark eyes looked almost hollow. 'My poor Tom,' she muttered resigned, blood trickled from the corners of her mouth.

'What... when...'

Laura raised her finger to her lips. 'Let me go, Tom. Later on we can be together.'

I sat on the bed, with my back to her, my head heavy in my hands and my heart broken into a thousand pieces.

My heart suddenly leaped, my eyes shot open, and I turned back to her fading body. 'Bobbi? What about Bobbi?' I asked desperately. Laura's body finally faded away with her shaking her head. 'Nooooo!' I screamed loudly, my throat raw as I punched the wardrobe door. The door swung open to reveal its empty contents. All of Laura's clothes were gone. Cleared out long ago.

***

I heard Mel before I saw her. She grabbed me again, but I shook her off, pushed past and went into Bobbi's room. Her things were there, but it was too clean and tidy. Everything looked about right, so maybe she was still here.

The calendar was two years out of date, and the month was wrong by a couple, but kids aren't as bothered about time as adults, are they?

'She's gone too, Tom,' Mel said quietly. 'That was the month and year it happened.'

'This can't be happening!' I said, holding the top of my head with both hands, worried it might explode with over sensory-reaction. 'But I saw them. I have… I know…'

'It's not unusual to be like this, Tom. Our mind is a very clever thing, and yours has been protecting you for over two years.'

'No, look, wait.' I fumbled in my pocket for my mobile. 'I took this last week when we were at the park. Look it…' but of course the picture showed the park with no one else in it. Another showed an empty seat on a park bench, three in fact, and a small footbridge that I had taken five shots of because of the wind, then the sun in Laura's eyes, and Bobbi distracted – but these were now five very similar photographs of a bridge. Nothing more.

It was hard to imagine that I could ever endure a worse feeling in my life. This had to be rock bottom and I could see no way out.

'You took a few months off after it happened. Do you remember that?'

I shook my head.

I walked slowly down the stairs, Mel followed close behind. I almost wished she would push me, let me tumble down headfirst and land like a discarded action figure, limbs bent in positions only yoga masters could successfully execute.

I was now in a thick daze, completely numb. I walked out of the back door and down to the bottom of the garden. Ignoring the dead flowers, and the unkempt grass neglected years ago, I strode forth; the magnetic pull was too much.

'You had feelings for me, Tom. That is why we were

here.'

I turned to her, and suddenly anger was firing through me, burning in my veins. 'I should have been with them!' I spat. 'It was all your fault!'

The door to the shed was locked. The key remained close to me at all times, hung around my neck. I pulled it out.

'And this helps, does it?' she asked. 'You blame me, because I knew how to treat you better than your wife!'

'You were nothing more than a whore!' I spat and swung open the door. I pushed my way to the back of the large brick building, past memories idly sat, or lent against other unwanted items that once had a use before my life changed forever. The large hemp sack lay hidden behind old boxes. I was no longer put off by the smell or the flies, as I reached over and pulled off the top of the sack.

The dried-bloodied face of Mel stared back at me. Lifeless and shocked.

I looked behind me, but Mel had now disappeared too.

I rubbed my hand through my hair and felt the tears in my eyes. Flashes of memories switched back and forth between naked passion with Mel in a hotel room, and my family in a car, surprising me with a visit at work... stolen kisses and quick breaths as a lorry ploughs into the side of the car splitting it in two and killing my wife and daughter instantly. The agony and the ecstasy.

***

I stumble back to the house sobbing uncontrollably, remembering the doctors shaking their heads at me, the policemen offering me useless condolences, and the months of therapy and mind-numbing drugs.

Tears drip as I reach into the back of the cupboard in the kitchen retrieving the bottle of the illegal tablets. I had promised a number of people that it would never come to this, but I always knew that reality would bite, and I would have no choice.

I swig down a glass of ice-cold water to speed up the effects of the tablets rushing into my bloodstream. I sit down and look at the two pictures in front of me. I rip up the photograph of Mel in anger, the pieces snow down onto the floor like confetti.

My vision begins to blur as I look at the picture of my wife and child. My thumb caresses their faces without feeling. My breathing is suddenly strained, and my head is swimming. The darkness engulfs me.

'See you both soon...' I barely manage, and like a moth in a jar, I give up the fight for oxygen and accept my fate.

JIMMY JIMMY

Steven Dunne

'James. No that's my first name and my surname. James James. Nice, eh? You think I can believe it? My dad's idea – bastard. Jimmy Jimmy! One of his favourites. I can still remember him singing it to me. Never spoke to me. Never. Not a chance. Never said, "Hey, Jim, come and watch the match. Hey, Jim, come and have your tea." He always sang it – "Jimmy Jimmy" – then fell about laughing. Big Undertones fan, see. You know the song? *Jimmy Jimmy oh.* Drunken old fart. He left when I was five. Good riddance I say, if that's how serious you take yer parenting. Too late even then. Damage done, eh? He should have booked me into the nuthouse right then and there. Ha, ha.

'You know what's weird? You must be the first person *ever* not to laugh at that. Not sure how I feel about that. Good, I think. Been too much laughing at my name. Two sugars, thanks. Mmmmm, lovely. That chases out the cold alright. Any biscuits? Rich tea – that it? Thought you lot were on good money.

'Hey, beggars can't be choosers. First time I've heard that gag. Hilarious.

'Where was I? Oh yeah, the die was cast. Everywhere I went people were singing that song at me. Wasn't having school. No way. Couldn't face it. Besides, if education's so fucking good for me how come all the fucking teachers were so depressed. Answer me that. So I jacked it in when I was fourteen. I mean really jacked it in. Left and never went back, not like some of the sad sacks who walked out of lessons then spent all their time walking round the site giving it V-signs at all the classrooms cos they really wanted to be in there but were scared they'd be... invisible. Wankers.

'Sorry. Okay, I'm getting to it. What year is it now? No, I really don't know. 2016. Shit. Coming up for five years. I been on the streets for five years. Mum kicked me out when

I was fifteen. I'm twenty now. I think. Where the hell does it go? There's your childhood Jimmy Jimmy now fuck off and find a clean vein.

'Okay, the tea was good. I'm warming up now, brain's starting to work. You want to know about Neeta. Let's see, it's February now. Is it? Two months then. We met just before Christmas. Good time of year for the homeless. And the worst. People walk by with that look in their eye. Not like summer. When the sun shines, they pass by and they almost envy you – so much you don't get the spare change. *Hey, you don't need it, not when you're leading such a healthy outdoor life, no ties, no responsibilities, no mortgage.* Weird, right. But Christmas is different. You don't see much envy then. Just pity. *Thank fuck I'm not like you. Thank fuck I don't live in a box. Here's a quid and thanks for reminding me I'm so well off. Ha, ha.*

'Neeta, yeah. I'm getting to it. Shit. Pull that blind down, will you? So I was in some doorway, down from Fat Cats, listening to the music in my box. Computer box, it was. Well sturdy. None of your rubbish. So I'm under my layers and the cadge had been okay for a couple of weeks so I had a couple of quid. You see pre-Christmas is better because people still got the hope and expectation but after the misery takes its first bite, after the presents have been opened… Yeah, sorry. Off the point. Right. Well I'd done okay, enough for a couple of Special Brews. And the second one was really hitting the spot. I had my box over my head, a good one mind, computer box, I think. They're the best. Oh, I've said that. Sorry. The point is it was proper cosy as far as these things go. I even had a little night light going. So I was sweet for the night.

'Well, you know that kind of thing can't last. Sure enough, couple of minutes later the world comes crashing down on me and someone falls on top of my box. Night light spilled hot wax all over me, my box is crushed and, worst of all, my can gets knocked over.

'Thirty seconds of effing and blinding later – well, you think you're under attack don't you? Wouldn't be the first time some pissed-up blokes have given me a kicking to make sure I'm paying attention when they tell me to get a job. So I'm all clenched, ready for a rumble, you know, even though best thing is just lie back and take it cos if you fight back, it's that much worse cos they really put one on you. But it's not pissed-up blokes; it's pissed-up Neeta instead, legless and sprawling all over me.

'And I mean I'm not best happy cos my gaff's just been wrecked and my dinner's been spilled, but turns out she's in the life, same as me. Got kicked out same age as me. And she's pretty, oh yeah, let me tell you. And, best of all, she's got half a bottle of vodka left, the other half already flying around her bloodstream. Got it from some punter, she said and she licked her lips so I'd know how she got it without being told. Don't ask, don't tell, right?

'And she's sharing so we tuck in some more but she's had her fill so I get the lion's, right? Yeah, good stuff and all, not the shit you get down Aldi but the good stuff with the funny writing on it and strong too. Sweetest bottle I ever had. Man, I didn't feel the cold for a week. Mind you, I couldn't feel my legs for a couple days either. Unexpected mind fucks I have known. Ha ha. Happy days.

'Okay I'm getting there if you can't guess the rest. We team up. A couple. Inseparable like. Yin and Yang. Justin and Britney. Ha, ha. That's what we called ourselves. And we done alright on the cadge too. I mean, you normally score more on your lonesome cos people think you're all alone in the world. I mean, boo fucking hoo, right. But Neet was so pretty and being a Paki you get your liberal guilt digging its hands in its pockets cos she'd tell punters she was legging it from her dad and uncle in Bradford cos they'd found some sixty-year-old perv in Karachi who was willing to marry her in exchange for a set of curtains. Ha, ha.

'And things were going good. Spring was just round the corner so the life gets a bit easier innit? You can sleep down by the river next to the courts–

'Okay, okay. I'm getting to it. How about some more tea with a slug of whisky in it? I know CID always keep half a bottle on the go in some filing cabinet or other. Seen it on the telly. No? Just the tea then and don't go so easy on the sugar this time.

'So that last night, we'd been drinking all day – White Lightning. Goes well with fish. Ha, ha. And by ten o'clock we were starving. So Neet says, let's go stand outside a curry house cos punters always over-order and then, cos they're mean bastards, they always get the rest to take away. We might get some guilty fat stiff hand us his leftovers. Smart, right?

'So we heads off to the Taj but it's late and it's midweek and virtually empty. There's just some old geezer in, white with a small white beard, well-dressed, tugging on a glass of wine. So after a couple of minute's window-licking we can't take the smell no more. You know what it's like with Indian grub. You smell it, you gotta have it. Hell, even talking about it gets your juices going. So we're thinking about where we might go, pooling our shrapnel see if we got enough for a bag of chips when the Indian waiter pops his head out.

'"The gentleman inside would like to buy one of you a meal," he says. Weird or what? But before I can share my thoughts with Neet, she's through the door and sitting at his table before I can get a word out. I mean, quick on her feet or what?

'So the geezer pours her a glass of wine and Neet

throws it down like it's lemonade and he pours her another. She does the same and I'm thinking the geezer's gonna realise his mistake and tell her to fuck off. But he doesn't, he orders another bottle of wine and I start to realise what's going on. The old guy is going to get her legless and... Well, you know the rest.

'So I stay and watch and they drink and their meal comes and they eat and they drink some more and Neet's hanging on his every word like he's God or something. Plus the old man leaves half of his meal which Neet finishes off. I mean, waste not, want not, right?

'Eventually the guy pays so I go to the door to wait and they come out arm in arm. And I realise that Neet's going to hang on to this old fart and milk him for as much as she can get. Clever.

'So they walk out and straight past me as though I don't exist and Neet's laughing at his jokes and hanging on his every word and they walk to his car – a tasty old Jag, by the by – and off they drive into the night.

'Why do you think I'm shaking my head? Course I'm upset. That was the last time I saw my Neet. The last time. Give me a minute, will you?

'No, I had no idea she was dead. Not for days. I don't get the morning paper as you can imagine and I don't watch telly. Can't watch telly, I should say. Ha, ha. So I looked for her. All our usual spots – the shop doorways, the chippie, the town hall steps. One night I'm walking along and I seen the paper in a newsagent window: "Search for Aneeta Desai's killer widens". I mean shit, that knocked me for six, I can tell you. I had a bit of shrapnel so I buy the paper and read what happened to her. Poor Neet. Beaten and strangled. That's shit. She never deserved that. Never. But here's the thing. I check the date on the paper and it's exactly one week since I seen her leave the curry house with the old geezer.

'Go to the police? You're joking, right? You lot aren't gonna listen to a single word I say, am I right? No maybes about it, Inspector, and you know it. So I realise If I'm gonna find out what happened to my Neet, I've got to do it all myself.

'Yeah, you guessed it. So that night I go and I sit in a doorway opposite the Taj and I wait. Sure enough about half nine that same car pulls up and the same old geezer steps out. I'm only yards away but he doesn't see me. I mean, they never see me, his kind. It's like I don't exist, right. And in he goes and over to the window to watch I goes. And it's like I'm reliving that night all over again. The old geezer orders the same bottle of white wine, orders the same meal and sits down to chew on a poppadom.

'Next thing I know the waiter pops his head out. You know what's coming, don't you? Well, you're right. The waiter says the exact same thing he'd said the week before. The old man would like to buy me a meal. I'm well gobsmacked and I don't know what to do. I mean, I stand there and think about it and the more I think about it, the more I realise that this guy was the last to see Neet alive and I realise if I don't go in and speak to him, I might *never* know what happened to her.

'So I go in and I drink and I eat. And the geezer talks like it's going out of style. But I don't hear anything cos all I can think about is Neet. That she was here a week ago in the same chair drinking the same wine.

'So I pluck up the courage. "You don't remember me, do you?" I said. "I was here last week with my girl".

'"Oh, but I do remember," he said and that freaks me out a bit.

'But I get my shit together and I asked him. "What did you do with her, you pervert?"

'He stops smiling then, alright. He knows I've got him. But you know what he does then? He laughs and I mean like a proper nutter and says, "Her? I screwed her then I killed her." His exact words, mind. You want to write them down. I mean it. And I'm reeling cos I kinda knew already but hearing him say it makes it all crash in on me. Neet is dead. He killed my Neet. And my fists start clenching and I'm thinking my Neet should be avenged and I can see he's starting to get nervous. He looks at his watch like he's waiting for something. So I order another lager to keep him waiting, make him sweat and he gets more and more agitated. He calls a waiter over and whispers in his ear and the waiter disappears to bring the bill.

'But before he gets back, the old man turns to me and says, "I think we should go outside."

'"What about the bill?" I said.

'He smiled and pushed back his chair. "Don't worry about that," he said. "I've taken care of it."

'So I down the lager, but I'm worried. What if he's got the same plans for me as he had for Neet? I tell him I need the toilet and I nip out the back. I find the waiter and I hiss at him to call the police. Urgent. To his credit the waiter doesn't ask why, just nods and goes to pick up the phone so I take a piss and when I get back the old man's gone.

'I run outside and there he is next to his car, surrounded by you lot. And, for once in my life, I'm well glad to see you. And here we sit.'

Silence.

'Thank God that's off my chest. Inspector Brook, is it?'

***

Inspector Brook stood and smiled. 'You've done the right thing, Jimmy. Now, just one more job. Sergeant Noble will walk you through it.'

'Name it.'

'We're holding Mr Jenkins next door–' said DS Noble.

'Is that his name?'

'That's his name and he's told us everything,' said Brook. 'Now we've organised a line-up. Just to be thorough, you understand?'

Jimmy took a deep breath. 'Of course. I'm ready to do my duty.'

'Good for you.' Brook switched off the tape after the formalities and Noble opened the door of the windowless room and ushered Jimmy outside.

The young man held up an arm to the light. 'Jesus. That's bright.'

'Yes, sorry,' said Brook, stopping in the corridor outside another door. He opened it and ushered Jimmy through.

'This is weird,' said Jimmy. 'Will he be able to see me?'

Brook smiled reassuringly and pointed to a cross on the floor. 'Right there. Face the window.'

Jimmy stood and held his arms in front of him. 'Bright in here.'

Brook left but Noble waited by the door. A young man appeared. Then another. And another. Four young men, all around Jimmy's age and build stood next to him.

'Hey, guys. What's going on?'

The light brightened and Jimmy shielded his eyes.

'Put your arm down, Jimmy.'

Jimmy lowered his arm but screwed his eyes to filter out the piercing light. 'How can I ID the guy with this in my face?'

'Don't worry.'

There was silence for a few moments. Jimmy stared the best he could at the window but nobody appeared. Then a voice on speaker. Brook's voice.

'Okay, John. Number Four. You can let the rest go.'

The other young men filed out without a word leaving Jimmy stranded. The sergeant kept his eyes on Jimmy. 'This way, Jimmy.'

Jimmy turned to look behind him. The number four was behind his head. 'Wait. What is this?'

The door opened and two uniformed officers marched towards Jimmy, one unhooking handcuffs.

'What are you doing?' He grappled as they span him round but was unable to resist and the cuffs snapped on his wrist. But though restrained he managed to wriggle free and ran to the blank window, squashing his face against the glass, not sure whether anyone was in the room beyond. 'Wait! You don't understand. It's not my fault. Don't you see?'

The officers got a better grip and hauled Jimmy through the door. Brook was coming the other way to join Noble.

'Inspector, it's the old man you want.'

At that moment a uniformed officer escorted Mr Jenkins from the adjoining room. The old man looked up nervously on seeing Jimmy.

'Him,' screamed Jimmy. 'This is all his fault.'

'Mr James, you'll be charged with the murder of Anita Desai,' said Brook. 'These officers will caution you and arrange for representation.'

Something changed in Jimmy's expression. The tenacity he needed to survive on the streets turned his face to concrete and he stopped struggling, eyes dead, staring back at Brook. 'Murder? Nah! That bitch killed herself. Neet was dead the minute that dirty old man invited her to his table. Don't you see? The sorry-assed bitch dumped me for a fucking curry. And you know what was worse. When she was filling her face, she didn't look at me once. Never gave me a second's thought. Not when she was eating and not when she came outside. Like I was invisible. Me. Just a wink would have done it; and she would be alive today. But no. She. Couldn't. See. Me.'

Jimmy became agitated again, struggling to be free. 'You did this,' he shouted at the old man who was scuttling away, gaze to the floor. 'This is on you.' But the old man was gone and Jimmy's legs buckled and he began to sob uncontrollably, able only to summon one last appeal to Brook. 'It's not my fault,' he whined through the tears. 'She dumped me for a plate food.'

'And a human being is dead,' mumbled Brook. The uniformed officers dragged Jimmy James kicking and screaming in the direction of the custody suite.

'People have died for less,' observed Noble. After a few seconds, he turned to his superior with a grin. 'Poor little Jimmy, wouldn't let go.' Brook stared at him, his face blank. 'The Undertones? No?'

'You can explain it to me over a meal, John. I'm buying.'

'Meal?'

'All this talk of curry. As Jimmy said, you've got to have it.'

BE CAREFUL WHAT YOU WISH FOR

Peter Best

S ammy Carmichael took a deep breath, counted to three then relaxed her shoulders. She let her breath out slowly and tried her hardest to count from ten backwards. Nothing, not a thing. The relaxation technique she had used since her mother taught her as a child felt so strange this time. Normally it worked, but not today

Slowly, she made her way along the plush red carpet towards the art deco mirror that took pride of place in the hallway of Carter's, one of New York's finest restaurants. She stopped and looked at her reflection. Her eyes were tired, dull even, she thought. Not what they were six months ago when she first set foot in this charming place. She had been happy then: she had her whole young life in front of her; a life to be filled with adventure and happiness; not like today. Today, her life was filled with nothing but fear and dread; and it showed.

She straightened her skirt, took one more deep breath and readied herself to enter the bar to meet a man named Don Hart; a man she hated more than anything in this world. Sammy knew he had a question to ask her; a question that would shape her life forever. Also she knew what her answer would be, because how the hell can you refuse a man who is one of the biggest and most heartless mafia bosses the island of Manhattan had ever seen.

***

Thoughts whirled around in her head as she moved away from her reflection. She was in a mess and she knew it. To be honest, the same mess she had been in since the day she met her so-called boyfriend. That is if you could call a man who, at the age of sixty-five, was forty years her senior, a boyfriend. A boyfriend she didn't even want.

'So, why did you agree to have dinner with him?' Monica, one of her friends, asked her in disgust when she first told her of her dinner date. Sammy didn't answer, but her friend knew exactly what the answer was. Like many young girls her age Sammy had been fascinated by the façade of the mob and totally taken in by it. But now, six months later the mask had fallen, and she wanted out.

Of course, Sammy would never forget the day Don Hart walked into her life. It was at Macy's, the largest department store in the world; the jewellery department to be precise, where she worked behind the counter. Apparently, he wasn't even looking for jewellery at the time; he was trying to get to menswear but somehow turned right instead of left. He stopped in his tracks when he realised he had made a mistake but as he looked around him to get his bearings, he noticed her.

There she was, Sammy Carmichael. She looked radiant as ever and for the first time since his wife died many years ago Don Hart looked at another woman and just knew he wanted her in his bed.

'Who on earth is that?' Sammy, unnerved by the way he was looking at her, whispered to Monica when she moved up to her side.

'Who is that, you ask? Girl, you know nothing,' she whispered back. 'That man is Don Hart and, if I were you, I would run a hundred miles whenever you see him.'

'Why?'

'Because he is a mean son of a bitch who will see you are dead if you ever cross him. So stay away if you know what is good for you.'

However, that was easier said than done, as Sammy found out when Don Hart moved forward.

'I would like to buy some earrings, if I may.'

Sammy gulped. Suddenly she felt a certain apprehension. However, she still managed a reply. 'Of course sir. Are they for your good wife?'

'No, they're for you.'

'Excuse me!'

'As I said, they're for you.'

Sammy's eyes widened as she heard his reply. She was stunned as well as mystified by his unexpected answer. *Why would he want to buy a complete stranger like me earrings?* She stuttered an answer. 'I... I'm not sure if that's allowed, sir; taking gifts from our customers.'

'Don't worry if it's allowed or not,' he replied. 'I want to buy you a gift: something pretty to go with the pretty face you have.'

Sammy was worried and at a complete loss as to what to do. She looked sidewards to Monica who answered with a slight nod.

'Which ones do you prefer?' the man asked her.

'I, I guess I like these ones here,' she said pointing to a plain pair, and one of the cheapest.

'No, they're no good. I think I should buy you these,' he said as he pointed to a pair of pearl earrings, one of the most expensive.

'No, sir, I couldn't really.'

'I don't see why not. Wrap them up nicely so I can give you them this evening.'

'This evening! I don't understand.'

'I would like to take you out to dinner if you would be so kind as to accompany me?' he said raising his eyebrows in anticipation of her answer.

'It will be in New York's finest restaurant, Carter's,' he said, encouraging her answer.

'Then I will be delighted to accept,' she said softly, immediately regretting her decision. She was simply too scared to reject this bizarre man in front of her.

***

The evening was quite pleasant and she was enjoying the flair of the restaurant, although she was still very uncertain about this strange man. Strangely enough she was a little taken in by his charisma and that relaxed her somewhat. However, she still knew in the back of her mind that he was a criminal and this scared the hell out of her, even as it fascinated her too.

As dessert was served the inevitable happened. Don Hart took a smile on his face and handed her the nicely wrapped package containing the earrings. She took them gracefully and put them in.

'You look beautiful,' he whispered as he moved his hand towards her face wanting to gently stroke her cheek; but as he did, she pulled back quickly.

Don's expression changed from happy to sad in a split second. He slowly removed his hand and took another sip of his wine without saying a word.

'I'm sorry, I just can't,' Sammy said as she felt her face flush. Don never asked why or spoke to her about it again, but he knew he had made a mistake. Sammy was a lady and ladies need time.

***

As the evening slowly drew to a close he walked her to his car and instructed his driver to take her home.

'Will I see you again?' he asked, as he was about to close the door behind her.

'Call me,' she replied and he did, the very next day, and so it was after a short time Sammy Carmichael became known as Don Hart's girlfriend; and boy did her life change.

However, it wasn't just her life that had changed. Don himself changed a great deal. His charming personality was long gone and replaced by his true self. Not just this, her work in Macy's was a distant memory.

'I don't want to have any girlfriend of mine working as a shop-girl,' he told her.

'But I'm happy working there,' she protested and at this very moment the back of his hand hit the side of her cheek, knocking her heavily to the floor.

'Never, ever disagree with me again,' was all he said.

Slowly she picked herself up as a trickle of blood ran from her lip. She knew this man was mean and that he ran his firm through fear. Now she really got the message, just like everyone else did around him. He pays you; he owns you and you will do as he says without question, or feel pain in one form or another.

The other problem was, he was frustrated. During the last six months he showered Sammy with gifts, bought her the most beautiful jewellery and in his mind he treated her like a queen. But now he had had enough. Many times he tried to get her into his bed and many times she refused. Now he was going to take what he wanted. In his eyes, he loved Sammy and he wanted her to love him back, but if this love would not come from her own free will then he would simply take it.

Again she felt the force of the back of his hand and she was sure it was not going to be the last time. He stood above her, undid his belt, pushed her onto his bed and then the pain hit her as she blacked out, but not before she found out just how much a monster this disgusting man really was.

***

Sammy hated her life. Many times she even considered ending it all, but she even feared that, too. She was, without a doubt, in a dreadful situation; but at least she had one ray of sunshine in her life. This ray of sunshine came in the form of Rebecca and she just happened to be the wife of Don's son, Louie.

If you ever got to know the story of Rebecca, you

could easily say it was very close to Sammy's story. The only difference was Rebecca fell head over heels for Louie and would do anything for him. But, as they say, love is blind and she was, without a doubt, blind to what Louie was doing behind her back. He had affairs from the day they wed, according to Rebecca when cloud of love finally cleared from her own eyes and she realised what was happening.

Of course, Rebecca being a fiery type of person wasn't going to have it and when she found out what he was up to, she blew. The fists started flying, but Louie, being a championship boxer in his younger days was no match for her petite figure. He let rip with a left hook followed by a right jab to her jaw. That was that, he thought, when he stood over the unconscious body of his wife.

'Fucking slut! If you were anything near a half decent fuck perhaps I wouldn't have to play the field,' he shouted at her, even though she was in no position to hear him.

'And don't think you're clever enough to fool me about your own stupid affairs either,' he continued, just before he let his right foot hammer into her ribs.

So that was how their marriage continued. Louie continued his so-called friendships with other women and Rebecca had no option but to put up with them. However, Rebecca simply bided her time and every time her ribs hurt she knew she would have her revenge someday.

***

As for Sammy, Rebecca, was very concerned for her friend, especially when she overheard Don telling Louie the night before that he was going to propose marriage to her.

Sammy was petrified when she heard this news and didn't know what to say when Rebecca asked her what her answer was going to be.

'I guess I have no option. I will have to say yes.'

'Well, listen honey,' Rebecca said, grabbing her hand. 'I can understand your choice and if you do marry the son of a bitch I will be right with you all the way. But that's not all you have to worry about. The word on the street is that he has been messing with the Rossi brothers from Brooklyn and they aren't too happy. Apparently he's tried to muscle in on their numbers racket. The thing is, they aren't just going to lay down and let him get away with it.'

'Jesus Christ,' Sammy exclaimed. 'There will be a bloodbath: the Rossis are just as evil as Don.'

'That's what everyone is worried about and Louie said they don't hang about either.'

'What does all this mean?'

'It means if you agree to marry the bastard you won't be married for long, the way things are looking.'

***

So that's how it was for Sammy as she walked into Carter's to meet the man she hated most in the world but was about to marry. The words of her friend Rebecca were ringing through her head. *Agree to marry, as it won't be for long. Then you will have your freedom.*

'Ah, there you are my darling,' Don said in a charming way; the way he always acted when seen in public. He stood as he moved forward to greet her with a kiss.

'Hello, darling,' Sammy replied turning her head so he could only give her a peck on the cheek.

'Aw, don't be like that,' he said. 'We have something to celebrate today, something very special.' He was smiling but Sammy noticed the smile suddenly change as his face took on another complexion as he quickly put his hand in his inside pocket of his jacket and pulled his gun.

Don took no notice of Sammy's cry as she fell to the floor after he pulled her violently out of the way, the shot from his pistol just missing her head. He also missed the man running through the bar towards him. He took aim again and fired. The man went down with a loud scream as the bullet entered his shoulder. It would have been in the centre of his chest if Don had not already downed a few bourbons, causing him to miss his target.

'Where are my fucking bodyguards?' Don screamed in anger as he took aim at a second assailant rushing towards him. This time he did not miss and the bullet hammered right into the man's chest.

'I said, where are my fucking bodyguards?' he shouted once more with venom. 'Where the fuck is Jake?'

'I'm right behind you,' a voice said. Don turned around to face his friend and companion since his childhood days. He was angry with Jake, though the look on his face showed not anger but fear as one of his most trusted men in the world pointed a pistol into his face and pulled the trigger.

Don Hart's body jerked backwards before it fell into a heap next to the grand piano where only a few moments before an old musician from the Bronx played his tunes.

***

'Oh my God, what the fuck have I done?' Jake shouted in frustration as he stood over the body of the man he had classed as his brother. 'Forgive me, my friend, I had no choice.' He then looked down towards Sammy quivering with fear under one of the tables.

The first assailant, who had now picked himself up off the floor, was clutching his shoulder trying to stem the flow of blood from the bullet wound. He winced with pain as he slowly moved to retrieve his gun of the floor. Blood started to flow again when he stumbled towards the dead body of Don Hart.

He then placed the barrel into what was left of the dead man's left eye socket and fired one single shot blowing the back of his skull away from his head. Screams were heard again as he looked towards Jake crying.

A state of shock had taken over and the assailant knew this. His target was now dead, the trademark shot through the left eye of his victim had been made and all he had to do now was make his escape. Then he realised the job had only been half done when saw Sammy under the table shaking with the shock of what she had just witnessed.

'You finish the job,' he commanded Jake. But Jake was traumatised, staring into space. The assailant said no more. Again he winced with pain as he lifted his gun and pointed it towards Sammy's tearful face as he pulled the trigger back. She screamed again as she heard the shot being fired but it was the wounded man who fell to the ground dead and not her.

Sammy looked towards Jake. The pistol that had just shot the assailant was still in his hand. The look of pain etched on his face told Sammy his story. He was guilty of treason and he felt it hard. Again, he turned to look at Sammy before putting his gun back in the holster hidden inside his jacket. He stepped over the man he had just killed and slowly walked out of the door.

By the time Detective Harry Deadman arrived, the screaming had stopped and was replaced by heavy sobbing. He greeted his colleague John Churchill with a terse nod. John was well known in the police force as being a walking encyclopaedia when it comes to knowing who's who in the world of the New York's Mafia. Both men looked down towards Don Hart's left eye, or at least where his left eye should have been.

'What do you think John; the Rossis?' Harry asked his right-hand man, already knowing his answer.

'We've got to be looking that way. I know the two

other stiffs worked for them, to do their dirty work.'

'What else have we got?'

'Nothing much apart from this young lady here,' he said as he pointed to Sammy who was still sitting under the table sobbing. 'Her name is Sammy Carmichael; she is, or was, I should say, the girlfriend of Don Hart before his so-called bodyguard decided to put a bullet in his face.'

Harry looked down towards Sammy, knelt down beside her and softly called her name. She turned slowly as Harry smiled at her.

'Miss Carmichael, we need to talk.'

***

Some twenty minutes or so later Harry, John and Sammy were sitting in a small coffee shop on Fourth Avenue. Sammy still in a state of shock hardly looked up from her cup of coffee.

'Sammy,' Harry asked her gently. 'We need to find out what exactly happened back there so we can try and bring the Rossi brothers to justice for killing Don Hart; I know you were close to him.'

'I wasn't close to him,' Sammy replied quietly. 'He was a bastard.'

Harry didn't reply to her comment, but instead asked another question. 'Some witnesses have just told me it was another hood who killed Don Hart. As yet we do not know who this man is. Do you?'

'It was Jake Sullivan,' Sammy answered.

Harry looked at Sammy with some disbelief. 'Are you sure? Jake Sullivan and Don Hart have been like brothers all their lives.'

'I'm telling you, it was Jake Sullivan. I was just as surprised as you but he was the one who pulled the trigger.'

'So where is he now?' Harry asked.

'I don't know; but he saved my life. One of the other men was just about to shoot me. He had the gun right to my head and I could have sworn he was about to shoot me then Jake shot him dead. He fell right in front of me, the gun still in his hand.'

'Then what happened?'

'Well that was it, really. Jake just put his gun away and walked out.'

'Okay,' Harry said still puzzled. 'I can understand them wanting to get at Don Hart, but what would they gain by killing you?'

'I don't know,' Sammy answered. 'I'm scared; what do you think will happen now?'

'It's hard to say. Possibly because Don Hart's dead, his son Louie will take things over. If the Rossi brothers are behind this, obviously Louie Hart will be next on their list.

'And Rebecca!' Sammy cried out.

'Who's Rebecca?'

'She's Louie's wife,' Sammy replied. 'If the Rossi brothers wanted me dead then they will want her dead too. We've got to warn her.'

Sammy stood up and barged her way past Harry and ran towards an empty phone booth at the other end of the coffee house. She quickly dialled the number of her friend and then grasped the handset tight.

'Come on, come on, pick up will you.' She let the phone ring and ring; no answer! Sammy put the phone down and rushed out of the cafe in a panic.

She looked up Fourth Avenue at a sea of yellow cabs. *One of them must be free,* she thought but, as always this time of day, the traffic was at a snail's pace. 'Damn!' she shouted in frustration, deciding to run the six or seven blocks to where Rebecca lived. *It's not far, ten minutes tops,*

***

Harry ran out of the coffee shop directly after Sammy. He called for her to stop but she had disappeared into the crowd, and then he saw him.

Jake Sullivan was standing on the street some twenty yards away, gun pulled and aiming at Sammy. If Harry took the easy option he could have simply pulled his own firearm and taken a shot at Sullivan, ending it there and then. However, the shot wasn't as easy as it looked and he knew he had more chance of missing and killing some bystander. Quickly he came up with his next idea. He simply ran at Sullivan shouting and screaming as loud as he could have.

Jake's instinct told him to run for his life up the sidewalk back towards Carter's Restaurant. Despite his large size Harry could move himself and was not far behind Jake. Jake knew he urgently needed an opportunity to escape. As luck would have it, he spotted a way to make a diversion.

Two men at each end of a coffin were finding it extremely difficult lifting the heavy weight of the body of Don Hart. As big and strong as they were, all four men struggled to carry him the short distance from the restaurant door to the waiting hearse parked on street. Harry had already given permission to clear the crime scene and Hart's was the first of the bodies to be taken out by the quickest way possible; straight out the main door and across the sidewalk, even if it was crowded with New Yorkers going about their business.

It was an upper class lady walking her poodle who was the first to notice a man sweating profusely running along the avenue with a pistol in his hand. She gave out a scream which made some others look. At once one man selling newspapers shouted 'GUN.' Then panic!

Screams and more shouts were heard as people started to run in all directions falling over themselves. Jake

Sullivan knew this was just what he needed. He drew level with one of the men carrying the coffin. His gun was already in his hand and all he needed to do was put it against the young man's back and pull the trigger. He fell instantly to the ground, dropping the coffin hard to the pavement below. The wood cracked as it fell to one side. The lid came away exposing the faceless head of Don Hart. More screams were heard, this time from another young lady who had the misfortune to be walking just where the coffin had landed. She dropped her bag of shopping, spewing apples and oranges onto the sidewalk. The people who were running with panic in their eyes ran even harder. It was chaos and that is just what Jake Sullivan needed. He saw a gap in the crowd and went for it, running as fast as his legs could take him. Looking back, he saw that his ruse had worked and Harry Deadman was left cursing his head off.

***

'Christ, I don't believe this. How the hell did he get away? The guy must be pushing sixty.'

'Because he's a sly old bastard,' John answered his colleague, gasping for breath. 'Always has been but I'll tell you one thing: this is not adding up.'

'I agree,' Harry said also panting for breath. 'Sammy said this guy had saved her life; now he's pulled a gun and tried to kill her. Why the change of heart?'

'I don't know – but I do know where we will find out. Sammy said she wanted to warn Louie's wife Rebecca she's about to be hit. I suggest we go to her condo on the East Side.'

'You know where they live?' Harry asked.

'I sure do, I've staked out that little shit Louie on many occasions and I will bet you a cent to a dollar that is where Sammy is heading; and Jake Sullivan won't be far behind.

***

Sammy was in a hell of a state when Rebecca let her through the front entrance door.

'Oh my Lord, what on earth has happened to you?'

'You've got to go quickly, get out of town,' Sammy stammered. 'It's Jake, he done it all and–'

'Whoa, slow down, Sammy, take it easy. One step at a time and tell me what is going on.'

'Don's dead!'

'What!'

'Don's dead. Jake's shot him in the restaurant and now he's coming after you and Louie.'

'Well, look who we have here!' Louie said walking into the room holding a bottle of Champagne. 'I take it Jake fucked up, did he?'

At first, Sammy was puzzled at this comment but soon understood what had happened.

'You bastard, you horrible bastard! I thought it was the Rossi brothers but it was you, wasn't it?'

Louie simply sniggered before he answered. 'Close, it was me and the Rossis together.'

Rebecca gasped as she put her hands to her mouth not believing what she had just heard. 'What are you saying? Why?'

'What else could I have done? Listen, my father tried to fuck the Rossis over and it didn't work. It's been coming for a while and my father was too stupid to notice it.'

'And you and Jake have joined them?'

'We didn't have a choice; they would have killed us both and anyone else who stayed loyal to Don. But for me it was different; we made a deal. With Don out of the way I get to keep the legitimate side of my father's business and the Rossis get to run everything else.

'Well, I never thought I would see the day,' Rebecca replied with venom in her voice. As much as she hated her husband she was still stunned as to how low he would go. 'My husband, the great Louie Hart has just had his own flesh and blood killed so he can turn his back on crime and become a legitimate businessman.'

Sammy joined her friend and also showed her bitterness towards Louie. 'So why did you want me dead? Was that also part of the deal?'

'Listen! Since the day you and my father met you have done nothing but take everything he has. Jewellery, the best clothes money could buy, you wanted it all; and leeches like you don't stop. They keep going until they have bled their victims dry. I had to put a stop to it. Let's face it, as soon as my father would have put that stupid ring on your finger you would have gotten everything if he survived the attack. I wanted to make sure that didn't happen so I ordered both of you dead. Anyhow, you should think yourself lucky. Since my father is dead, there is no need to kill you now. By the way, everything my father had will now come to me and you get fuck all, and believe me that is how it's going to stay.'

Louie grinned a grin of triumph. He turned to look at his wife's face. 'And you, my dear, don't you even think you're going to get a dime off me once we're divorced. You are nothing but a slut in my eyes. And cheap sluts who cheat on their husbands get nothing from me; not a dime.'

'I don't want a thing off you. You can go and rot in hell as far as I'm concerned. And yes, the sooner we are divorced the better.' Rebecca would have carried on with the onslaught given half a chance but the back of Louie's hand hit her so hard she fell against the wall before sliding to the floor.

Louie took a big swing with his left leg and kicked Rebecca hard in the ribs. Sammy screamed as Louie kicked at his wife again and again. Finally, he stopped and knelt down beside her gripped a handful of her hair. 'And you don't forget. Once I find the name of the man you are fucking I will rip his balls off and shove them in your mouth. Do you understand?'

He pushed her head away knocking it hard against the wall before turning around to look up. When he did he just caught a glimpse of the champagne bottle hurtling towards his head. He never had a chance to move out of the way as Sammy crashed the bottle full into his head. Champagne shot out from the neck of the bottle drenching her as once again she lifted it above her head then, through fear of the man, brought it down again using the same fiery force as before. This time she heard his skull crack; but still not sure if he was dead, she did it again and again.

Once she was satisfied that his body was not moving and would never move again she turned to her friend, letting out a cry when she saw her plight.

Sammy knelt down as Rebecca stared ahead at something. Sammy followed her stare and looked towards Jake Sullivan standing above them, his gun in his trembling hand pointing it at her.

It was Sammy who spoke first with only one word. 'Why?'

'I messed up,' Jake answered. 'I'm sorry, I'm a coward, I know. I should have just let the other guy finish it all, but it just wasn't right. I couldn't let him do it. Afterwards I went to Central Park and sat on a bench to collect my thoughts. I realised I had to finish the job or Louie would hunt me down like a rat and my life would be over. But now you've killed him I don't know what to do. The thing is, you're going to spend the rest of your life in the pen for smashing that bottle over his head and don't think you can plead innoc–' Jake never finished his sentence. A bullet hit his arm, the force of it spinning him round. The second bullet went straight into his chest.

Harry Deadman stood at the doorway to the room, his pistol in his hand. He looked down at what was below his feet. Jake Sullivan and Louie Hart were dead.

'It's quite clear what has happened John,' Harry explained to his colleague when he followed him into the room a few seconds later. 'I saw it with my own eyes. Jake Sullivan beat Louie Hart over the head with that Champagne bottle just before he turned the gun on me.'

John was in total disbelief at this blatant lie and Harry knew it. John turned towards the two women on the floor. They were both in a bad way.

'Is this correct, ladies? Did Jake Sullivan kill Louie Hart?

It wasn't instant but both women slowly nodded their heads indicating this was the truth. Of course, John still did not believe it, but as far as he was concerned at least two more of New York's scum had been wiped of the face of the world.

'So let that be it then.' Rules had been broken, lies had been told, of that he was sure, but one thing: justice had been done.

***

Two months later Rebecca Hart was asked to attend the offices of William Drakemore, Attorney at Law, on the sixteenth floor of the Empire State Building on Fifth Avenue and Thirty-third.

Her broken ribs had been fixed and all the cuts and bruises to her face had long disappeared and she was looking radiant. Nevertheless, she was a little apprehensive as to what the outcome of this afternoon's meeting would be.

Sammy went with her for moral support and they

both sat in front of a large mahogany desk occupied by a Mr James Morgan.

'I have some news for you, Mrs Hart. As you have been advised, the estate of your father-in-law Donald Hart was left to your husband, Mr Louie Hart. For obvious reasons we do not need to go into how your husband met his untimely end, but because he did the estate went automatically from your husband to you, being his lawful wife. As you stated, you had no wish to carry on running any of his enterprises so you instructed us to sell his business for the best possible price.'

'That is correct, Mr Morgan, and I believe this has now been completed,' Rebecca answered.

'Indeed it has,' he replied. 'This morning I signed off the last property to be sold and I am sure you will be in agreement that we at William Drakemore have succeeded in obtaining a very good deal.'

He then wrote down a figure on a slip of paper and passed it over the table to Rebecca. 'This is the final figure for all the property and businesses that were originally in Donald Hart's name. Each one has been sold and, if you are in agreement, I can write you a cheque now for that said amount. Less our fees, of course.'

Rebecca looked at the slip of paper but showed no emotion. However, when she showed it to Sammy, the former shop girl's eyes widened.

'So, Mrs Hart, are you in agreement?'

'With a figure of seven million, three hundred and twenty-six thousand dollars Mr Morgan I am more than happy.'

And so five minutes later the two women entered the lift to take them down to ground level, with a cheque stashed safely in Rebecca's Pocketbook ready to take to the bank.

'I think we should celebrate with a bottle of the finest Champagne this evening,' Rebecca said to Sammy.

'Yes, I think you are right, we shall,' she answered as she linked her arm in her friend's.

Rebecca looked into her eyes, those happy smiling eyes Sammy had when she first came to New York from New Jersey in the search for some adventure in Manhattan. She moved her lips to hers and gave her a long sensual kiss, a kiss she hadn't given for such a long time. She slowly pulled away, smiling at Sammy.

'He never did find out who I was having the affair with did he?'

MY OWN EGGSECUTIONER

Tess Makovesky

Vernon Russell stole my life, not once but twice. I'm sitting here in an overstuffed chair watching him die. Knowing there's nothing I can do to help him – or myself. The rise and fall of his chest grows shallower with every halting breath. His face is the colour of old newspaper, yellow and grey. Blood trickles from his mouth, oozes sluggishly from the scissors where they stick out through his shirt. It takes me back to when I was six years old.

I can still remember the mess that day when I got home from school. Blood and broken glass all over the floor. A space in the dust on the mantelpiece. And my Dad lying by the hearth, curled and twisted like an autumn leaf. I remember wondering why he'd chosen such a funny place to go to sleep, and why all my efforts couldn't shake him awake. The village bobby found me when he investigated the open door at half past three at night, still clutching my Dad's hand. He had to pry my fingers off. 'Come on, Andrew, let go, there's a good lad. He's gone, lad, he's gone.'

Yes, he was gone, and so was our Fabergé egg. It was the only thing of value the family had ever owned – a reminder, Dad said, of Great Aunt Irina who'd smuggled it out of Russia at the end of World War Two. It was one of my favourite stories as a kid. Dad would sit me on his knee and point to the egg, and tell me again how his father and uncle had travelled the railways of a war-ravaged Europe to bring the old lady back.

'Some friends of the family had taken her as far as Austria, but they couldn't travel the rest of the way, so Grandad and Uncle George got travel permits and went out there themselves. It took them nearly two weeks because the trains kept being diverted to make way for all the troops, but one of the friends stayed with her until they arrived. She was already in her eighties then, and she had nothing but the clothes she stood up in, a fur-collared coat and a blanket given to her by the Red Cross. The blanket was searched at every border post and revealed nothing more than some black bread and wurst and a jar of sauerkraut, but nobody checked the coat.'

I knew the end of the tale by heart by then, but never tired of the final twist. 'Go on, Dad. Tell me about her coat.'

'She'd had the egg divided into lots of separate segments, and sewn them into the heavy fur collar herself. They didn't have metal detectors in those days and although they stripped her and searched her pockets, nobody thought to feel around her neck. So she kept the egg hidden, just as she'd hidden it from both the Russians and the invading Germans for the entire duration of the war.'

And I would squeal with excitement and demand to see the egg. Dad handed it to me with the greatest of care and even at three or four years old I matched that care, holding it as though it was a real egg ready to crack, and trying to see where it had been taken apart and put back together again. You couldn't, of course. It was so exquisitely made that the joins were invisible. I stroked its glossy golden surface instead, and learned my numbers by counting its tiny gems.

***

The blood oozes more slowly now and Vernon's breath bubbles in his throat. I know it won't be long. 'Don't do this, old man,' I say, but without much hope. The scissors have penetrated his lungs, might even have nicked his heart. How could he survive all that?

Irina died too, soon after leaving her motherland, but Dad said she was happy when she went. 'She'd saved the egg, you see. It was given to her by the Tsar just before his arrest and he'd told her to keep it safe. She was a distant – very distant – cousin of his and she was lucky to escape the Revolution with her life; she moved to a remote village in Siberia and kept chickens and ducks. All her fine possessions – her clothes and paintings and jewels – were left behind or sold, but she always kept the egg. She hid it in an old goose-down quilt at first, and then behind a loose stone in the well, and she was happy because she'd handed it on, not to some soldier at bayonet point but to her own kith and kin.'

She'd have been a lot less happy if she could have seen the result, I think, with her great-nephew knifed to death and the egg vanished as though it had been boiled and eaten by the thief. Not to mention what's happening to me.

Without that egg, without my Dad, I had nothing left. I was brought up by another Irene, a relative on my mother's side, in a great barn of a flat where the few sparse pieces of furniture had to shout to one another and my room didn't have so much as a picture on the walls. Not like Vernon Russell's place, with its leaning towers of antiquities and crazy piles of junk. The date carved over the fireplace downstairs reads 1659 and some of the stuff must have been accumulating ever since. One man couldn't collect all this, even if he started the day he was born. Vernon's an antiques dealer, of course, and only buys to sell, but judging by the chaos here he buys far more than he ever sells. Buys, or begs. Or steals.

***

A bell rang as I walked in. Not the usual tinny chime of a shop door-bell, but a deeply resonant note; a clock bell, perhaps, or some great sonorous thing. It sounded oddly fateful – 'Abandon hope all ye who enter here' – but there was no reason to think it applied to me. The shop smelled musty: old polish, old paper, unwashed hair; but it was hardly a place of doom. A teddy-bear grinned at me from the top of a pile of books, and I saw friends galore on the groaning tabletops. Here a James Bond book I'd had as a boy. There a poppy mug like the ones Irene had. Here Darth Vader, hissing gently through a speaker hidden beneath his robe. There a Wedgwood vase. And there, on his desk, the egg.

I'd not set eyes on it in over thirty years but I knew exactly what it was. That burnished softly gleaming gold, those tiny pearls, the cluster of rubies and emeralds at the top. I could have picked it out of a line-up of fifty others with barely a second glance. As soon as I saw it I lost my rag. Here Vernon Russell sat, fat and self-satisfied, surrounded by his worldly goods like a spider in the middle of a web. Where I'd had nothing, he was surrounded by polished wood and precious glass, silver and porcelain and ancient stone. Where I'd lost my only kin, a photograph in a silver frame stood on his desk – Vernon with a little more hair, laughing and relaxed in the arms of wife and child. Like a matador's cloak to a bull, the photo was propped against my egg.

Inside I was a volcano, boiling with molten rock and steam, but outside I stayed icy cool. 'Carl Fabergé, if I'm not mistaken.'

He followed the direction of my gaze, and smirked. 'Ah, yes. A particularly fine example if I do say so myself. Rare, too. There were only two made in that precise style and one of those is at the Hermitage. Of course, this one has a price tag to match... I'm Vernon Russell, by the way. Purveyor of antiques and fine *objets d'art*.'

He's a purveyor all right, I think – but only of bad dreams and other people's misery. 'I'm not interested in buying it,' I said. After all, it was mine to start with. 'I am interested in where you got it, though.'

'Hmm, let me think.' He scratched the end of his nose; a gesture liars make, or so I'm told. He was lying all right. You don't forget where you laid your hands on something as precious as that. He just didn't want to say.

The volcano, stoked by his hesitation, blew its top. I could have buried the egg in his head, but didn't want to have to clean bits of brain matter off the jewels. 'I'll save you the bother, you fat bastard. I know exactly where you got it, because it's mine. Had it all this time, have you? Can't bear to part with it? It's a pretty thing, isn't it, even if it was bought with my father's death.'

'No, no,' he protested, his breath coming faster than it had. No doubt he thought I was a lunatic; perhaps he was right at that. Dad's death did something to me, all those years ago. Mad Andrew, the kids at school called me, in whispers when they thought the teacher couldn't hear. Maybe I was living up to the name at last.

'Don't bother denying it. I can see the evidence right here.'

Vernon stroked what was left of his hair. His hands shook, then disappeared beneath the desk.

'Got a gun down there, have you? Or a knife – the one you used on my Dad, perhaps. Well you're not going to do the same to me.' I didn't have a weapon, hadn't come prepared, but on the table beside me was an ebony sewing box. The silvery contents gleamed: thimbles and needle cases, buttons on cards, and a pair of scissors with handles of deepest black. I grabbed them and thrust them towards his chest.

***

He doesn't have a gun. As the blades sink deep into folds of flesh his hands come up in belated self-defence. Both are empty. He whimpers, tries to pull the scissors out, before realising that to do so will only cause more pain. 'Why?' he mumbles. 'What have I ever done?'

'You know what you did,' I yell, but already I'm having doubts. If he didn't have a weapon, he wasn't trying to kill me. And if I was wrong about that, then maybe I'm wrong about everything else. It's hard, though, to let go of the solution that presented itself. I need to talk, to convince myself. 'You broke into our house, years ago, and stabbed my Dad and stole our Fabergé egg. This one right here on your desk. My great-aunt brought it all the way from Russia, and you took it from us, and took my Dad from me.'

'No,' he says again, but fainter now, and he mutters something I can't catch.

'What's that?' The blood's starting to seep out round the scissor blades, staining his shirt in scarlet trails. I gaze at it, and feel myself go faint. There's a monstrous tartan armchair by the desk. I lower myself into its welcoming curves, put my head between my legs.

He's still muttering; that awful bubbling wheeze. 'Not me. Only bought it... two years ago. From... someone else.'

I reach across, take his shoulders and shake him like a dog. 'It must have been you. Who else could it have been? And what were you doing underneath that desk?'

He coughs, sprays terrible bright red blood across my hands, but his grimace could almost be a smile. 'Shop alarm. Police are on... their way.'

Crap. I'm caught red-handed, literally, and he's fading away and still hasn't told me what I need to know. I've no idea if he was telling the truth or not. He could be a brazen murderer, or a fence. Or an honest man who bought something he liked from someone he didn't know.

I should have one last go at getting him to talk, but his eyes have glazed over and his last breath rasps in his throat. I don't need the village bobby to tell me he's gone – or that I'll never know who really killed my Dad. I pick up the egg and fondle it. There's a smear of blood, shocking red against the gold, so I wipe it off on my sleeve. How proud Great-Aunt Irina would be that I've saved it for the family again. How proud Dad would be that I've avenged his death. Except that the egg will be taken as evidence the minute the police turn up. And I've rushed in like a fool, and murdered my only hope. Answers, that's what I needed, not another death. Answers he could have given me. The name of the man he bought the egg from; the name of that man's source. A trail I could have followed, but is now as cold as gold.

***

Vernon Russell stole my life, not twice but once. This place may look like a relic of bygone times but it's got a security system that's bang up to date. The alarm's brought metal shutters on doors and windows rattling down. I'm trapped in here with the man I've just killed. And outside the sirens wail.

ONE LAST JOB

Alex Walters

They always chose a place like this, and Rigby always hated it.

He wasn't a snob. But he had standards and a budget hotel in a business park at the arse-end of some post-industrial northern city didn't come close to meeting them.

It was deliberate, obviously. Reminding him who was in charge, as if he needed telling. They held up the hoop and he dived through it. He didn't delude himself that there was any equality in this relationship. Sure, he had the skills, but they had the money. However good he might be, there were always others who could match him.

He was surprised it had lasted as long as it had. The big clients – the really big ones – usually moved on after a year or two. They didn't want you getting too close, finding out too much. Eventually, the phone stopped ringing, and that was that.

That was fine. He had enough of a reputation to keep moving. It was like any freelance work. There were busy periods and quiet periods. It was nice to have repeat business, but you were a fool if you thought it would last forever.

Sweet was late again. But Sweet was always late. More gamesmanship. Not that Sweet was a big player, whatever he might want you to think. Another minnow, a bit closer to the centre, but no more important. An errand boy.

Rigby was well into his third beer before Sweet turned up. He usually limited his drinking at these meetings, just to show willing, but if the bastard was forty-five minutes late what could you do?

'Traffic,' Sweet said. 'Shall we go straight in?'

And a good evening to you, Rigby thought, *and I'm sorry I'm late.* He followed Sweet through to the restaurant. He didn't know whether Sweet was his real name. If not, it suggested an unlikely sense of humour. It would be hard to think of a less appropriate pseudonym for the thin-lipped figure sitting himself at the table, preparing to order his usual salad and sparkling water.

They ate largely in silence. The meal was just another part of the ritual. They could have done the business in twenty minutes in the bar, but Sweet seemed to enjoy the discomfort, the interminable stretching out of the evening. Rigby resigned himself to it, and polished off his steak with as much enjoyment as he could manage. Sweet made no attempt to initiate conversation, and responded monosyllabically to Rigby's half-hearted efforts.

Over coffee, Sweet finally got down to business. He glanced around as if there were a danger of them being overheard, though the only other diner was a solitary woman picking disconsolately at a plate of pasta. That was the other reason they chose places like this. There was nowhere more anonymous than this kind of business hotel. It was full of transients who were literally here today and gone tomorrow. No-one cared or noticed who you were. Rigby always stayed over simply because it was less conspicuous. Who'd eat in this place by choice?

Sweet fumbled in his briefcase and pulled out a manila envelope. 'OK,' he said in that toneless voice. 'One more job.'

That sounded ominously final, Rigby thought. Maybe this was where he got his marching orders. 'One more job?' he echoed, with an emphasis on the first word.

'Another job,' Sweet said, as if correcting himself. He opened the envelope and extracted a thin sheaf of papers, face down.

'How long do I have?'

'A week. Seven days.'

Sweet Jesus. They never made it easy, did they? He'd tried to tell them how much preparation was needed to do this properly. But they never listened. That was how mistakes got made. 'Go on, then,' Rigby said, after a pause.

'This is your target.' Sweet turned over the papers and slid a photograph across the table.

Rigby was looking at his own image. It was a good likeness, though he couldn't even guess where it had been taken. 'Is this some kind of joke?'

'No joke,' Sweet said, in a tone that suggested he barely knew what the word meant. 'We're terminating your services.'

For Christ's sake, Rigby thought. *They've brought me all the way up here just to tell me that.* 'If you say so,' he said, finally. 'Well, thanks for the business.'

'I don't think you follow. We are literally terminating your services.'

'I don't understand—'

'As I say, you have seven days. We don't care how you do it. Jump under a train. Off a bridge. Sleeping pills. As long as it's relatively inconspicuous and we're not implicated. We prefer to keep our hands clean.'

Rigby swallowed the last of his coffee. 'You've more of a sense of humour than I thought. On the dark side, though.'

'No joke,' Sweet repeated. 'You've become sloppy lately. We need to let you go.'

'Now look—'

'After the last one, we had the police sniffing round. No real risk, but too close for our comfort. I'm guessing you didn't even realise.'

Rigby thought back. The last job had been a tricky one. Another where they hadn't given him enough time. But he thought he'd handled it well enough, all told. 'That's crap'

Sweet held up his hand. 'Enough. We've made our decision. But even in these circumstances we like to treat people fairly.'

'What the hell are you talking about?'

'It's straightforward. You know too much about us. So we're offering a deal. Your last target is yourself.'

'This isn't funny.'

'It's not meant to be. We'll pay you, of course.' Sweet made a show of reading the typed notes attached to the photograph. 'You have a dependent sister.'

It wasn't a question, but Rigby was unsurprised. They'd have done their due diligence before taking him on in the first place. 'What about her?'

'Motor neurone disease, I believe. A terrible affliction. She'll be taken care of for – well, as long as she needs to be.'

Rigby started to speak, then stopped. 'You're serious, aren't you? You're really fucking serious.'

Sweet shook his head sadly. 'I'm never not serious,' he said, as if this might be an occasional source of regret.

'What happens if I say no?'

'You've seven days to decide. We thought that was reasonable. If you've not acted by then, we'll have to handle things another way.'

'Meaning?'

'We'll take the necessary action ourselves. I can't promise we'll do it as cleanly or as painlessly. And, of course, your sister will have nothing but what you can leave her.' Sweet consulted the notes again. 'Which, frankly, won't last her very long.'

Rigby stared at him. 'What if I talk to the police?'

Sweet allowed himself a thin smile. 'Not with your history. And if you try, you'll regret it.' He paused. 'And your sister will regret it even more. We can be ruthless if our security's at stake. I'm sure you understand. And please don't think we won't find you. You know our resources.'

'I–'

Sweet picked up the photograph and pushed himself to his feet. 'Good evening, Mr Rigby. It's been good doing business with you, too. I'm sorry it had to end in this way. But when you've thought about it, you'll realise we're offering a fair deal.' He gestured towards the reception. 'I'll sort out the bill before I leave.'

Afterwards, Rigby sat staring at the blank table. Perhaps Sweet was simply insane, or had been joking after all. Perhaps it was all just a bluff. Or a warning, a coded threat. Perhaps.

Eventually, he rose and left the restaurant, heading back upstairs. Back to the solitude of his box-like room.

Back to the first of seven endless, sleepless nights.

A STRANGER'S EYES

Paul Gitsham

Pain. It yanks me from a deep and dreamless sleep.

There's a tearing, ripping sensation on the left side of my face as I turn from the sunlight lancing through the window. The pillow is stuck to me and as I lift my head, its weight sends lightning bolts through what I realise must be a cut just below my hair-line.

I am disoriented. Where am I? Nothing feels familiar. It's morning – of that I am certain, but nothing else. Did I go out last night? I must have done. I have no memories of it.

No clue where I am, what day it is or what I did yesterday. I'm not even sure who I am. All I know is that I feel sick, my mouth is horribly parched and I have a nasty head wound. I can't hear properly on the left side. Mustering all of my willpower I finally yank myself upright, part of the newly formed scab remaining on the bloodied pillow. Somehow my feet find their way beneath me and I head instinctively for the wooden door at the far side of the room. Stumbling through it, I figure that I must be in some sort of hotel room.

Holding on to the toilet bowl, I find that I no longer feel sick. Rising shakily, I stare at my reflection in the mirror above the sink. I was right about the laceration. Long and deep, it slices into my left temple. Matted hair sticks to the clot. It must have happened some time ago, for it's stopped bleeding. I look at my reflection. No flicker of recognition in the eyes. A chill runs through me. Without knowing how, I feel certain that this isn't a hangover; this is no chemically induced temporary amnesia.

'Who are you?' The voice is cracked, unfamiliar.

The face staring back would comfortably fit any man between the age of twenty-five and forty. A little pasty perhaps: the complexion speaks of fluorescent lights and computer screens, rather than fresh air and sunshine.

I look at my hands. They are soft, not calloused; the fingers nimble rather than strong. They are covered in blood. Stepping back I see more of my reflection. A slim man of average height wearing a white button-down shirt and a pair of black trousers. The front of the shirt is covered in blood.

There is a dull aching in my ribs – have I been shot? Stabbed? I yank the shirt open, ignoring the buttons pinging into the sink. I see bruises, fresh by the look of them, but no gaping wound. No visible source for all that blood. I look again at my face – the cut is nasty, angry looking, but there's no way it made that much mess.

Again, I catch the reflection's eyes. Nothing. I feel the panic start to rise. My legs give way and I'm falling backwards into the shower. My last thought as the world fades around me echoes in my mind.

'Who am I and what have I done?'

***

Am I dreaming?

I must be dreaming. Fragments of memories come and go. Nothing makes sense. Time has lost its direction. What happens after, now happens before. What has already taken place is yet to be experienced.

I'm confused. I don't know where I am, what I am doing or what I have done. All I know is that I need to run. Fast. Get away from this stinking alleyway my instincts tell me and I obey.

My head hurts. A throbbing, burning, howling pain that starts in my temple and radiates outward. There's blood in my eye but I daren't stop to wipe it clear.

As I step off the kerb, something heavy in my right hand bangs painfully against my knee. I ignore it, no time to stop; instinct tells me to shove the object into my pocket.

Now the lights are well behind me, their vibrant, flashing colours fading away, the only illumination a full moon and a flickering street lamp. My surroundings are even more run-down than the alleyway I've... escaped from? I slow to a walk.

Rounding a corner I spy a dismal hotel with an empty parking lot. If not for the glowing neon sign in the shuttered windows I'd assume it was closed. The sign is a toothy-looking rodent, the name beneath reading 'The Des ert Rat Motel'. Closer inspection reveals another unlit letter 'S'. Whether it has been broken by accident or to correct the spelling mistake, I can't tell. Regardless, it draws me on with a feeling of refuge and safety.

I become aware of a throbbing ache in the palm of my left hand and look down. The keys have pressed into the flesh. A large plastic fob matches the sign in the motel. The faint impression of a second letter 'S' implies that the wordsmith is at least consistent.

Room 24 is upstairs. The lobby was empty and I feel relieved. I don't know why but it seems important that nobody saw me. Entering the room I head straight for the bathroom. The sight that greets me in the mirror takes my breath away. Blood, all over.

A splinter of memory surfaces, then disappears too quickly for me to examine, nevertheless a sudden urge hits and without knowing why I find myself prying up the top of the toilet cistern. A loud splash, the chink of metal on porcelain and my right pocket is suddenly lighter.

A feeling of dizziness runs through me and I crash through the door heading towards the bed. My last impression as the world dissolves is of a pair of eyes, staring.

***

The cold tiles of the bathroom against my face rouse me this time. Memories rush back – but only as far back as my earlier awakening. Parts of the dream still cling. Clambering awkwardly out of the shower, I shiver. But not from cold. I'm scared. Of not knowing who I am or what I am or what I've done.

I pat my pockets, searching for clues. Nothing: no wallet, no keys, no phone. Think! I'm in a hotel room, where would I keep ID? I cross back into the bedroom. A small suitcase sits on a chair by a desk.

Why do American hotels supply a refrigerator, a kettle and a microwave – but not so much as a complimentary teabag or coffee sachet? *How do I know I am in America?* The flash of insight evaporates as soon as it has deposited this nugget of information.

Opening the case I find socks and underwear, and a couple of inexpertly folded shirts. A crumpled pair of jeans have clearly been worn, but remain clean enough to wear again. A balled up T-shirt smells of airports and jet lag. I clearly travel light.

I'm not sure why, but I am certain that I've come a long way. Therefore, I must have money, documents. The pockets of the jeans are empty, but feeling around the bottom of the case I find a zip. Pulling it open I reach inside a pocket in the lining and tug out a thin envelope containing US dollars, crisp and new. A zip-up leather purse contains a handful of coins and more notes, this time British pounds. Unlike the dollars, they are worn and tattered, as if they have been sitting in the bottom of a pocket, rather than a cashier's drawer. They feel more natural.

Even if my memory is flaky, the logical part of my brain seems just fine. Was I in the UK recently? If I've just flown in then I must have a passport. I run my hand around the pocket but find only fluff.

I look at the door. It's flimsy; poor protection against

a burglar. A single key, attached to the garish fob I remember from the dream, sticks out of the cheap lock. Maybe the hotel has a safe. I should go and ask at the reception desk.

I make for the door then stop, remembering the blood. I need to shower and change first.

I rub my eyes. There's a strange, yet familiar smell on my fingers; a sort of burning. Fireworks? Another scrap of the dream resurfaces and before I know it, I'm back in the bathroom, prying up the lid to the toilet cistern. I plunge my hand into the water. There it is; heavy, metal. With mounting horror I pull out the object that I remember from the dream.

The nausea returns and I barely make it to my knees before I'm heaving into the toilet. The fear is back and stronger than before.

Once again, the world is leaving and I'm falling.

***

I'm back in the alleyway, the smell of un-emptied bins mingling with the odour of stale beer and a burning smell that reminds me of childhood firework parties. I'm lying on my back, the left side of my head is ablaze with pain, the ear ringing, yet everything else is shockingly silent. I struggle to sit up, then wish I hadn't. The man to my left is slumped against the wall. His still, lifeless eyes are wide-open in surprise. The bullet hole between them oozes blood, black in the darkness.

In front of me a second man lies on his stomach, a huge pool of liquid spreading out from underneath him. He too is dead. Nobody alive could be that still. Terrified, I scramble to my feet. My chest hurts, the ribs bruised and battered. There's a clattering noise as I drop something. Without thinking I pick it up. It's metal, warm to the touch. I look down.

The gun gleams in the reflected glow from the upstairs windows of a Chinese restaurant. The full horror of the moment strikes me and I freeze. What just happened? Why are there two dead men beside me? Why have I got a gun in my hand?

Leave! Get away! The part of my brain that still functions issues commands. My body obeys. I start to run.

***

The final image from the dream is of eyes; brown, wide, staring. Who do they belong to? As I rinse the bile from my mouth, bits of the dream float in and out, mingling with the earlier memories. But instead of answering questions, they merely lead to more. Did I shoot those men? If so, why?

The face in the mirror tells me nothing more. Do the answers to my questions lie in the hotel safe?

The shelf in front of the mirror has a disposable plastic cup, a tiny, plastic-wrapped cake of soap and a sachet of shampoo. Beside them is a see-through zippered plastic bag with a small tube of toothpaste, fold-up toothbrush and dark blue flannel. No razor blades: it's designed to be carried in hand luggage.

I fill the sink and tear the soap open with my teeth. Soaking the flannel, I take a deep breath and gingerly start to wipe the blood off my face. Ten minutes later I appear more presentable than I feel. I'll claim I fell over and ask for some sticking plasters for my scalp when I go down to reception.

A knocking at the door throws me back into panic.

'Police! Open up!'

Whatever I have or haven't done, the last thing I want to do is explain it to the police. I look frantically around the room for an exit. There is only one door and one window in the whole suite. The police are behind the door, so window it is.

I stuff the gun into the waistband of my trousers. If I take it with me, I can hide it. If I return it to the toilet

318

cistern, it'll be found. I grab the jacket hanging on the back of the door to hide the bloodstain on my shirt.

The pounding at the door hastens me towards the window. I'm one floor up with nothing but a couple of plastic trash cans to cushion the fall. The car park is empty, save for an empty police cruiser, its light slowly rotating. Its insignia, Las Vegas Metropolitan Police Department, opens up a whole load more questions, but now is not the time to dwell on them.

Steeling myself, I pull the window open. A hot, desert wind blows in. Clambering onto the sill, I lower my legs over the edge. I look down and wish I hadn't. Ten feet, I tell myself. That's all. I guess I'm six feet tall. Add another couple for my arms and that leaves only two or three feet. Easy. Hanging by my fingertips I look down again. The distance between my feet and the ground still looks like ten feet.

A crash against the door makes my mind up for me. I let go.

***

A deafening blast and a sear of intense heat across my temple and for the briefest of seconds I lose all sensation except pain. No sight, no touch, no hearing, just pain. Excruciating pain, as every nerve in my body cries out.

And then I'm back. The left side of my face is numb, my hearing almost all gone – it's as if I am wearing one half of a pair of ear-defenders. I double over, gasping, as the punch empties my lungs of air. Somehow I keep my grip on the gun. Even as the man behind me collapses to the ground, I continue to wrestle with his partner for control of the weapon. Who he is, I have no idea. I don't even know what I'm doing here in this alleyway.

Face-to-face, teeth bared, we wrestle over the deadly piece of metal. We both give one last yank and that's it. A massive bang, a huge concussive blow to my chest and I'm falling backwards. I look in horror at the huge patch of blood spreading across my shirt.

But the blood isn't mine. The gun is still in my hand, warm and smoking. Opposite me my assailant lies; face down, a growing pool of blood under his body…

The pain in my head resurfaces and I slump backwards…

***

My disorientation as I awaken is less than before and I immediately roll to my feet, my left ankle howling. I ignore it; just another entry in the litany of complaints my battered body is making. I start to run, limping, putting as much distance between me and the hotel room as I can. Between me and the police. Already, the flashback is fading and I cling desperately to the details; finally all that remains is a single image. Brown eyes. Staring. Scared.

In daylight, the area surrounding the guesthouse is even worse than I remember. Slowly though, the empty, boarded up shops give way to better maintained properties, the graffiti disappears.

I find myself outside a small diner – what the British would call a 'greasy spoon'. My stomach rumbles. The plate glass window allows me to compare my reflection to the customers inside. With the jacket hiding my shirt I am not much scruffier than those drinking coffee and tucking into the three-dollar breakfast special. The smell draws me in.

The babble of voices drowns out a TV that nobody is paying any attention to. I join the queue, squinting at the menu above the zinc serving counter. Waiting my turn, I catch a few words on the TV and glance over. It's me. The photo is clearly a few years old, but it is definitely the man from the bathroom mirror. A ticker runs across the bottom of the screen, accompanying the voice over. I stare in shock, only processing a few words. Known drug dealers... shot dead... alleyway... strip-club... Chinese restaurant. The picture zooms out, revealing a British passport. I strain to hear the details. Mark Radisson... 36 years old... holiday maker... recently laid off... My name means nothing to me. I wonder what I did before I was made redundant and why I am here in Las Vegas on vacation.

'Hey, watcha want, honey?' It's the second time she's asked; the middle-aged server's expression is a mixture of boredom and irritation.

'Coffee,' I manage.

'That it?'

The smell of bacon and eggs makes my mouth water, but I feel as though every eye in the room is on me. I grab two sorry-looking, Danish pastries from the plate on the counter-top.

'To go, please,' I mumble, hoping my British accent doesn't make her curious.

It doesn't. This is Vegas, she's seen everything.

Four bucks. I drop a ten and leave quickly. Nobody even glances in my direction.

The look of surprise on the two police officers' faces is almost comical. The two guns that they yank out of their belts aren't. Within seconds I'm face down on the bonnet of their patrol car, my hands cuffed behind my back. The Miranda rights being read to me fade away as if the volume is being turned down.

**

I exit the strip club, the taste of over-priced, watered-down beer sour in my mouth, a cloud of smoke following me onto the street. What am I doing here, I ask myself for the thousandth time.

I'd been saving for the trip for three years; a tick on

321

the list of things to do before forty. A week in Vegas. First class flights, a five-star hotel, gambling, high-class strip-clubs and a helicopter flight over the Hoover Dam... Six weeks ago I'd finally booked it.

Then the cutbacks. Efficiency savings. Now, I'm an IT manager with nothing to manage. The five thousand pounds sitting in my 'Vegas Account' is all I have to my name. I should cancel the trip.

But then an idea forms. Phone calls, favours called in, outright begging and there it is; a letter of invitation to CES the world's biggest electronics show. In Vegas. On paper I'm affiliated to my friend's company. I agree to distribute information packs for their latest product. At the same time, I'll hand out copies of my CV.

More phone calls. The flights are down-graded to economy class, the hotel switched to the Desert Rat Motel, the three grand spending money cut to five hundred, the helicopter cancelled.

For three days I wander around the Vegas Convention Centre. The leaflets for my friend's new broadband router are received with polite smiles. My CV is received with empty smiles. Most recipients at least wait until I've walked away before tossing it in the bin. Most, but not all.

The show closes with all its usual razzmatazz. At least that's what it says on the news. By now I've over-stayed my welcome, my credentials politely, but firmly taken from me. I have forty-eight hours to kill before my flight home. I'm down to my last two hundred dollars, hence the free-entry titty bar next to the Chinese restaurant. Tomorrow, I'll hit the strip. I've heard that some of the casinos lure you in with a complimentary ten-dollar gamble and free entertainment.

The metal-reinforced door slams behind me, abandoning me on a darkened street, lit only by the glaring neon of the bar's sign and the glow from the upstairs windows of the closed Chinese restaurant next door. At the far end of the street, I see the glimmer of lights. Civilisation of a sort, or at least somewhere I can get a taxi.

Turning at the sound of the voice as I pass the alleyway is my big mistake. But I'm a Brit, I'm from out of town and I'm pre-occupied.

'Got a light, buddy?'

'Sorry, I don't smoke.'

The pause in my step is just enough for them to flank me. Black, white, Hispanic, I don't know. All I see is the gun.

A flick of the wrist and I follow them into the alleyway. Give them what they want, my mind screams. I have less than fifty dollars in my wallet and I hand it over without complaint.

The one without the gun takes the cash then throws the wallet on the floor in disgust. 'That it?'

I nod, terrified.

He frisks me. I have nothing else. My phone doesn't work here and is with my passport and tickets in the hotel's safe. The rest of my money is in the security pocket of my suitcase. He pauses at my left pocket, then pulls out the hotel key. He shows it to his friend.

'Three blocks away, no security. He's a tourist, I bet he has more money in his room.'

I'm in more trouble than I thought. Walking me back to my hotel and forcing me to get money are not the actions of rational men. And then what? A bullet in the back of the head?

The one with the gun turns to his friend. Before I know it, I'm moving. Almost immediately I regret my impulsiveness, but it's too late. I punch the unarmed man and turn to grab the gun. Surprise works in my favour and I manage to get both hands around the weapon, wrestling for control. Behind me I hear the grunt of the man I hit as he staggers back into the fray. There's a deafening explosion and an eruption of pain in my left temple. Who pulled the trigger, I don't know, but I hear the thud of a collapsing body behind me. Blood is pouring into my eye, but I still see the look of horror on my opponent's face. We continue to struggle for advantage and then there is a second explosion…

***

An unemployed tourist with bogus credentials is removed from CES for harassing delegates. Then, covered in blood from two dead drug dealers, with the murder weapon in his waistband, he attempts to evade arrest by jumping out of a hotel window.

Even I can see why I am handcuffed to a hospital bed facing two homicide charges. The doctors agree that my head wound comes from the nick of a bullet, the concussion explains the blackouts, amnesia and ringing deafness in my left ear. The over-worked, under-paid public defender who has just left suggests it may bolster my plea of self-defence. He sounded unconvinced and uninterested.

Exhausted, I fall into a troubled sleep…

***

Now the whole story is replayed, in glorious Technicolor; from the moment I am called into my boss' office, his face sympathetic but resolute, to the frustrated wandering of the massive convention centre, then the depressing pseudo-eroticism of the strip-club and finally the desperate struggle in the alleyway between the club and the Chinese restaurant, the light from its upstairs windows the only illumination.

The light from its windows…

Those staring brown eyes that have haunted me

every time I pass out swim into view...

There's a connection. A vital connection, I'm convinced of it. Those eyes...

I wake with a gasp, sweat pouring off me. I reach for the intercom button, but my hand is restrained by the handcuff. I yell for a doctor as loud as I can.

***

Three months later.

The official glances at my scarred forehead but says nothing. Armed police look over, then away. I pass through the double doors and into the throng of waiting people, below a sign reading 'Welcome to Birmingham'. At last the nightmare is over. Suddenly, I'm engulfed in hugs, Mum, Dad, and my sister. Flashes around me and shouted questions announce the presence of the press. I don't care.

I give a silent prayer of thanks to the seven-year-old boy five thousand miles away who couldn't sleep, whose brown-eyes stared out of his bedroom window above his parents' restaurant. Too scared to tell his parents what he'd seen in case he got into trouble, he'd told the police everything when they'd asked.

I don't even know his name.

DANGEROUS ACTIONS

M.A. Comley

Joanne sighed and her friend Beth folded her arms and tapped her foot. 'Look, I've told you why I deleted my Facebook page. Why do you keep hounding me about getting another account?'

'Because you need to start bloody living again.'

'Who says? I'm fine as I am, Beth.' Joanne sipped her glass of wine to avoid her friend's frustrated glare.

'Okay, let's look at things logically here. What if I got run over by a bus tomorrow, who would come and visit you then? You can't keep yourself locked away like this, that's all I'm saying. You need more in your life than the weekly visits I can give you, hon.'

Joanne's chin dropped to her chest. Deep down she knew Beth was right but it was hard after what happened to trust someone again after all these years. 'You know why that is: my horrendous experience with Mark would put anyone off dating for life. Surely you can see that?'

'I'm not poo-pooing what he did to you because it was bloody disgusting, but look at it this way, he's still winning.'

Joanne shook her head. 'How the hell do you work that one out?'

'He's laughing at you because you haven't put the trauma behind you. You're existing in your own little cocoon.'

'I know, but it's hard. Can't you put yourself in my shoes for a change?'

Beth sighed. 'I try to, love. Personally, I wouldn't let the psycho, or any other man, have the power over me that he seems to possess over you.' She took the glass from Joanne's hand, placed it on the table, then gathered Joanne's hands in her own. 'Maybe getting out and about more would help you regain control of your life. Don't let the bastard dominate every minute of your day the way you've let him over the years. You're not getting any younger. Didn't you tell me not so long ago how desperate you are to have kids?'

Joanne nodded. 'I am. However, what man in his right mind is going to give me a second glance nowadays.'

'Stop that! You're beautiful.'

'Am I? Maybe you've got used to seeing the scars on my face but to me they're a constant reminder that my boyfriend, someone whom I cared for deeply, despised me enough to try to end my life.'

'I know. My heart bleeds for you, but the scars have faded over time – at least your external scars have. Anything lingering on the outside can be covered up by make-up, hon.'

'I wish it worked that way up here,' Joanne said, pointing at her head.

'What harm would it do creating a Facebook page, eh, just to test the water. I bet you'll receive hundreds of friend requests within the first week. Go on, let's do it together now?' Beth nudged her elbow into Joanne's ribs.

Sighing heavily, Joanne agreed, fearing if she didn't back down her life would be a constant struggle, fending off Beth's persistent badgering every time they met up.

Beth leapt off the sofa and danced around the room. 'Yay, this day will mark– no pun intended, forget I said that… This will be the beginning of a new life for you once you've taken this ginormous first step.'

'You're nuts. What do we do now? It's been years since I looked at any form of social media.'

'Right, first of all we need a photo.'

Joanne's eyes widened. 'Are you serious? I can't do that, not looking like this.'

'What utter rubbish. Stop putting yourself down all the time. An old photo will do. Where do you keep your albums?'

Joanne's gaze drifted to the bookcase behind Beth, who turned around and grabbed an album off the shelf. She returned to the sofa and sat down beside Joanne. Opening the album, she flipped through the pages and stopped at one photo in particular. 'Well, there's not much to choose from. I forgot you're one of these people who'd rather be behind the camera than in front of it. How about this one?'

Joanne swallowed hard. The photo was of her and Mark on a Caribbean beach, arm in arm, smiling broadly as if they were deeply in love. Which they had been once upon a time. 'You want to use that one?'

'Yes. Don't worry about Mark, I'll crop him out of the picture. You look stunning in this one, hon. You should go for it.'

'I'm not so sure. I look far from beautiful now, Beth.'

'Just stop it! I've had enough of your self-doubts. This exercise is about building up your self-esteem again, okay?'

Joanne nodded. She could do little else when her friend was adamant about a project.

'Scissors? I can cut it, can't I? It's not like you're brooding for him, are you?'

'No, I'm not. Do what you like with it, I'd forgotten it was in there,' she lied. Every now and then she flicked through the photos, looking into Mark's eyes, searching for some kind of clue she might have missed when they'd been a couple, hinting at the amount of evil which existed beneath the façade. She'd been a fool to fall for his charming ways. He'd treated her like a lady at the beginning of their relationship and like an absolute whore at the end of it. She shuddered, a cold shiver running up her spine.

Beth's hands covered hers. 'Are you sure it's okay to do this?'

'I'm fine, just a little chilly. I'll make a coffee while you dismember the photo and set up the account.'

'Good idea.'

When Joanne returned to the lounge, carrying two mugs of coffee, Beth was busy tapping on the keyboard of Joanne's laptop. 'How's it going?'

Her friend turned the computer her way. 'See for yourself.'

'Wow, that was quick. I must admit, I do look good in that pic. What happens now?'

'We wait for all the dozens of friend requests to come in.'

***

Over the coming week, her Facebook page proved to be Joanne's most visited site on her computer. In that time, she had accepted over one hundred and fifty friend requests from both men and women. On Thursday, Beth came to dinner as usual. After their meal they rushed to open the laptop.

'Oh my God! Look at all the activity on your page. Why haven't you answered these messages?' Beth asked, her mouth dropping open in awe.

'What messages? I didn't see any messages. I accepted the friend requests like you told me to, but I didn't see any messages.'

'Look at this at the top of the screen, click on the icon and all your messages will show up. There might even be some in your 'other folder' from people who you haven't befriended yet. Let's see what juicy hunks lie within.' Beth clicked on the first message and burst out laughing.

'Wow, oh no. Get it off my computer. How disgusting of someone to send me pics of their genitals. I think I'm going to be sick.'

Beth laughed. 'It happens all the time. You tend to just ignore the weirdos. Hey, now this one looks interesting. This is what he says: 'Hey pretty lady, thanks for friending me. I'd certainly like to get to know you better, maybe meet up in the flesh in the near future?' What do you think of him?'

Joanne shrugged. 'He's all right I suppose. The blond Adonis isn't really my type, though. I'm surprised he's not gay – they usually are.'

'You crack me up, girl. Well, if you don't fancy him I certainly do.'

'Go for it. Get in touch with him and arrange a date.'

Beth laughed. 'It's you he has the hots for, not me.'

'Pretend to be me. When we used to go out clubbing the men always used to think we were twins. We had a laugh back then, leading the guys on, I seem to remember. Have you still got that brunette wig?'

Beth swept her long blonde hair over her shoulder. 'I have, as a matter of fact.'

Joanne laughed. She could tell Beth was seriously contemplating hooking up with the guy. 'That's settled, no more excuses. Message him back and get a conversation going.'

Beth's fingers flew across the keyboard. 'Hi, thank you for your lovely message, it would be great to know more about you. Who knows where that might lead in the future.' 'Is that it, or should I add anything else?'

'That's a start. Let's see if he responds, if he doesn't, then we'll just put it down to yet another weirdo encounter.'

Her friend hit the send button and they waited, watching the screen like hawks. Suddenly a notification came through. 'Damn, that was quick,' Beth said, opening the message. 'Sure, I'm Peter Warner, but you know that already. I'm a warehouse manager for a local DIY store. I'd love to meet up with you and get to know you in person, rather than online. I don't bite, I promise.' The message ended with a smiley face.

'He does sound kind of cute,' Joanne admitted.

'Ah, I sense someone changing her mind here.'

'Not at all. I'm truly not ready to meet anyone just yet. That shouldn't stop you from arranging to meet this guy. Pretend you're me and then if you like him after a few dates you can tell him the truth. You'll have him hooked by then, so it won't make any difference. You're stunning; the guy would be foolish not to fall in love with you. What are you waiting for?'

'If you're sure. God, I'm really keen now. He sounds wonderful. Okay, I'm going to respond. 'Hi, Peter, okay, I'm up for meeting if you are. When and where?'

The message was answered immediately and a date was set for the coming Saturday.

'Sounds fabulous, I almost envy you now– I said, almost!' Joanne gave her friend a shove. 'Why don't you drop by here before you go out? I'll help you get ready. The rendezvous point is closer to my house anyway. What do you think?'

'That would be amazing. We'll do that.'

***

Saturday evening soon came around and Beth arrived at five-thirty straight from her job at the supermarket.

'Shoo. The water is hot. Go and have a bit of a soak in the bath. I'll bring up a glass of wine to put you in the mood,' Joanne said, taking Beth's bags from her hands and pushing her up the stairs.

'You're too good to me. I wish it was us who were going out. I miss our girlie nights out on the town.'

'What? Are you having second thoughts about this?

It's not too late to call it off if you are.'

Beth shook her head. 'Not really. I'm just disappointed to be leaving you behind when you're so excited.'

'Don't be ridiculous. I'm just pleased that you'll be having a good time.'

A couple of hours later and Beth was dressed and ready to thrill. One final look, side by side in the hallway mirror. They would definitely pass as twins. Joanne kissed Beth on the cheek. 'Have a wonderful evening; play it cool. Don't give too much away on the first date.'

'Listen to you! Anyone would think it was me who hadn't had a date in God knows how long instead of you. I'll ring you when I get home.'

'You do that. No matter what time of night or morning that is, I doubt I'll be able to sleep properly until I find out all the gossip on this chap, anyway.'

Beth left and Joanne settled down to watch a romcom DVD she'd had her eye on for ages. The film turned out to be such a disappointment that she fell asleep halfway through it. She woke up at eleven-thirty and wondered how Beth was getting on with the hunky Peter. Twelve, one and two o'clock arrived and there was still no word from Beth. In the end, Joanne gave in and went to bed, smirking at the thought of Beth getting lucky on her first date.

The following morning, Joanne left it until eleven before she rang Beth's mobile. It rang and rang but remained unanswered. Joanne gave up and called Beth's home number instead. But when that went unanswered panic set in. She sent her friend a text message: 'Call me ASAP, let me know UR OK.'

She paced around the living room, awaiting either a call or message, but nothing came. Sometime around mid-afternoon, Joanne blew out a relieved breath when her phone tinkled that she'd received a message through Facebook. 'Thank God.'

The message was from Peter. 'That wasn't a very nice trick you played on me. You'll both be sorry now.'

Joanne dropped the phone as if the metal casing had just scalded her palm. She placed her hands over her face and sobbed. 'Oh God, Beth, where are you? What have we done?' Once her mind had stopped spinning, she picked up the phone again and rang the police, begging them for help. Two female officers appeared on her doorstep within the hour.

'I'm so scared. Please help me find her,' she pleaded, letting them into the house.

The three of them sat at the kitchen table and Joanne went through every single detail she could think of concerning their interaction with Peter.

'Can you show us the conversation you had with this man on Facebook?' the younger officer asked.

Joanne flipped open her laptop and logged into Facebook. She swivelled the computer towards the officers who read it with interest. One of them even jotted the message down in her notebook. 'Okay, this is what we're going to do. We'll see if we can find any CCTV footage around the area they were due to meet, we'll also try and track this Peter down via Facebook and pay him a visit. It might all still be innocent, so please don't worry too much at this point.'

'I'm trying not to, but it's hard, especially after his last message to me.'

The officer studied the message again and shook her head. 'Well, that certainly has a more sinister tone to it. Leave it with us for twenty-four hours and we'll get back to you.'

Joanne sighed. 'That long? Anything could happen

to Beth in that time.'

She walked the officers to the door. 'Try not to worry. We'll get back to you soon.'

Alone again, Joanne's mind raced non-stop for hours. Every ten minutes she rang Beth's number but there was still no answer on either phone.

At six, she turned on the evening news. The last story had a breaking news banner running underneath it: 'A body has been found down by the canal. Police are at the scene now.'

Joanne burst into tears. The canal was very close to the rendezvous point where Beth and Peter had agreed to meet. No, please don't let it be her!

Her mobile tinkled that she'd received a message. She quickly grabbed the phone and opened it. 'The police have just been to see me. Why did you send them here? If you want to know what happened to Beth, you should come and see me. If you tell the police, you'll never know the truth.'

Without any thought for her own safety she sent a message back, agreeing to meet Peter. He replied instantly, giving her the address of where he worked and told her to meet him at the warehouse in an hour.

Joanne paced around the room, trying to decide whether to tell the police or not. She decided against it and set off for the warehouse.

The huge doors were open when she arrived. 'Hello? Peter, are you here?' she called out.

There was no response. She ventured inside the building, the interior was darker than she had anticipated and fear squeezed her heart. Suddenly a figure came out of the room nearest to her. 'Hello, Joanne, nice of you to meet me.'

Her heart sank into her stomach, she recognised the voice. How could she have been so foolish. She glanced over her shoulder but he'd already moved towards the door and was in the process of shutting it.

'Where's Beth?' she asked, her voice quivering.

He laughed. 'I think we both know the answer to that. Don't tell me you didn't see the news tonight?'

Tears pricked her eyes. He was referring to the body found by the canal. 'You bastard. How could you do that to Beth?'

Before she could move he pounced on her. He hooked his forearm around her throat in a stranglehold. 'You really shouldn't have tricked me like that. Thought you were being clever, didn't you?'

'We didn't mean to do it. Who tricked who anyway? Your profile was false. Why? Why do this, Mark?' she pleaded with her ex-boyfriend for answers.

'Revenge. I deserve revenge for what you put me through.'

'I didn't do anything. It was you who tried to kill me.'

'And I would've succeeded too if that do-gooder hadn't come to your rescue. No one is going to prevent me finishing off the job now though.' His grip tightened. Her airway was slowly closing.

Joanne started kicking at his shins and tried to pull his arm away from her neck, but his grip tightened even more. Dizziness took hold and she felt her legs failing beneath her. Then everything went black.

***

She woke up a few hours later in a hospital bed. At the end of the bed she saw one of the officers who'd called to take down her statement.

'Hello there. How are you feeling?'

'Groggy. Am I alive?' she asked breathlessly.

'Of course. We rescued you before Mark could do

any really damage.'

'How? How did you know where to find me?'

'We visited Peter, or should I say Mark, realised he was nothing like the profile picture you showed us, but we needed more proof before we could make an arrest. Our sergeant told us to put you both under surveillance, sure that he would contact you again.'

'Thank God. So you followed us to the warehouse. Please tell me you've arrested him.'

'We have, I can assure you. He won't be released from prison again, not in the foreseeable future anyway.'

'But when he does get out he'll come after me again.'

'There's only one way around that: you should consider changing your name, move to another area.'

She sighed heavily. 'Tell me, the body they've found down by the canal, is it...'

The curtain around the bed was suddenly pulled back and lying in the bed next to her was Beth. Joanne pulled the sheet back, rushed over and hugged her friend. 'How did you get away from him? Oh my God, I can't believe you're still alive.'

Beth's voice was croaky when she spoke. 'He tried to kill me. I pretended he had succeeded. He didn't wait around long enough to see if I was dead or alive. The police decided it would be a good idea to run the story through the media, in the hope it would flush him out.'

The officer stood up. 'Right, now you girls have been reacquainted, I'll let you recuperate.'

Joanne rushed forward and hugged her. 'I can't thank you enough for listening to me and taking on the case: not every police officer would have done that.'

The officer's cheeks burned. 'You're welcome. Get well soon, girls, and be careful who you make friends with on Facebook in the future.'

Joanne climbed back into bed and reached out a hand for Beth to take. 'We'll never be that stupid again, will we?'

Beth smiled. 'No one is ever worth that kind of risk, ever.'

***

Six months later both the girls turned up for Mark's trial. He glared at them through the whole experience and shouted derogatory things at them when the judge passed sentence. He wouldn't be released for another twenty years. By that time Joanne would make sure she'd changed her name and address so there would be no way on earth he'd be able to track her down ever again.

CAPTIVE

Stephen Edger

1

A helium balloon. That's the last anyone saw of Daisy Bloomhelm. Six years old, an only child, and all anyone will remember is that sodding balloon. She didn't even like Peppa Pig.

'I should have been watching her,' her mother told the police. 'I only took my eyes off her for a moment.'

Try fifteen moments.

Better still, try fifteen minutes.

Fifteen long minutes where Daisy was vulnerable. Fifteen minutes where any weirdo could have been watching her, touching himself, hoping nobody had noticed him sitting in the car across the road from the park.

'My little girl knew not to talk to strangers,' her mother claimed. 'Daisy knew better than that.'

She's right, of course: Daisy did know better than that. She wasn't stupid. She knew she shouldn't speak to strangers, especially when they offered sweets.

What Daisy didn't know was just how true her mother's warnings had been; not until it was too late.

He seemed so kind at first. He had a puppy with him and he invited her to stroke it. Daisy loved dogs, she'd always wanted one as a pet, but her mother had always said their house was too small. This little one was soft, white and fluffy, and bounced up and down at her feet.

'What's its name?' she'd asked him.

'She doesn't have one yet. I'm not sure I can keep her. I work during the day and I have nobody around who can take care of her for me. She likes you. Would you like her?'

Of course she would! But then she thought about how her mum would react. 'Mum wouldn't let me keep her.'

'That's a shame. Gosh, look, she loves you. You're really good with her. You should name her. What name do you think she'd like?'

Daisy thought carefully, rubbing the puppy's ears playfully. 'I like the name Ruby. You could buy her a red collar.'

'That's a great name. I like the name Ruby too. It's settled. From now on, she will be known as Ruby. Thank you for your help. What did you say your name was again?'

Daisy hadn't told him her name, but she didn't hesitate in answering. 'I'm Daisy.'

'Hello, Daisy. My name's Tim. Do you live near here?'

'Not far.'

'Say, I wonder if you could do me a huge favour, Daisy… would you mind walking Ruby for me? I need to make a really important phone call. I don't live very far away. If you could walk Ruby back to my house, you'd be doing me a massive favour.'

Daisy knew she should have told him no, and walked away at that point. But Tim seemed so nice, and she really liked playing with Ruby. 'Okay.'

Tim passed her the lead, and took her hand as they walked away from the park.

Every story has a beginning, a middle and an end. Daisy was the beginning.

***

2

Her eyes are transfixed on the large metal door.

His words echo through her memory: *touch it and you'll get an electric shock, and then I'll punish you.*

There is no handle on this side of the door. He has a remote control that he uses to open it. The lights are on, which means he is on his way. She rubs her fingers over the names etched into the soft walls. She knows every nook and crevice. She has memorised the names. *If* she ever gets out, she will tell someone about the years she has spent in this prison beneath the ground. She will tell someone about the girls who have come and gone at one time or another. She will recite the list of names.

Megan, Paula, Emily, Alice, Poppy, Chloe, and Ellie. *If…*

She continues to watch the door.

Today is shopping day. He will be through the door in a moment with the same straw bag he always uses. Yesterday she requested milk, eggs and bread. He never buys everything she asks for. He always leaves something out. He always passes it off as forgetfulness in his advancing years, but she's certain now he does it to exert more control over her.

Sometimes he brings her books to read, but it usually means he wants to try something different. Sometimes he is rough with her, but other times he is gentle. She has stopped fighting his urges.

It's been lonely since Ellie left the cell. She was there one night, and gone the next morning. He bores easily, and tires of girls who are too compliant. Michelle has just enough fight in her, and he likes that.

She hears the outer door creak open. It is barely a metre wide, and she is sure he must crawl through the space to get to her. She has never managed to see how many other doors and tunnels extend beyond that narrow space. Nobody has ever discovered the cell, despite hours of screaming. Even if she managed to get through the large metal door, and managed to crawl through the next passage, she doesn't know how or if she would get any further.

The metal door to the cell whirs open. She clamps her eyes shut, and pulls the duvet up to her chin. He watches her from the doorway, before stepping inside the small room. The motors hum as the door slides closed again.

He kicks the side of the bed. 'Breakfast. Get up, Michelle.'

She opens her eyes again and pretends to stretch her arms above her head. She knows not to speak until he asks her a question. She pushes back the duvet and takes the bag of groceries from him. She puts the cold items in the fridge.

'We're going to have a new guest joining us tonight. I want you to make her welcome, and show her the ropes. You need to make her understand the rules, if you don't want to see her hurt. Okay?'

She averts her gaze. 'Yes, Tim.'

She can feel his lecherous eyes on her as she drops two rashers of bacon into the frying pan on the hot plate.

He puts his chubby hands on her shoulders as the bacon sizzles and spits. 'You seem tense. Is everything okay?'

She flips over the bacon. 'Fine, Tim. Thank you.'

'Good. I brought you a new book.'

She closes her eyes to stop a tear escaping. She doesn't want to think about what he is imagining. 'Thank you, Tim.'

'I thought you could read some of it to me after breakfast.'

She grits her teeth. 'Certainly.'

***

3

He lies back on the bed, a satisfied look on his face. 'I enjoyed that. Go and make us a tea, there's a good girl.'

After all this time in his dungeon, he still calls her his girl. She can't be certain exactly how long she's been his prisoner, but she conservatively estimates ten years. He never celebrates her birthday, and daylight is just a faded memory to her. She only has fragments of a life outside these walls.

She pushes herself off the mattress, and moves back to the small kitchen units in the opposite corner. She puts a pan of water onto the hotplate. Her legs ache, but she cannot show him the pain he has inflicted; it isn't worth the hassle it would cause.

His large chest is covered in grey hairs now. He didn't always look so old. She doesn't know what she looks like now; he has never allowed mirrors in the cell. He carefully wraps the condom in tissue, before sealing it in a small bag and dropping it to the floor. He used to transfer the bag to his coat straight away, but he has become lazier in recent months.

She pours the boiling water into his cup, and swishes the teabag around, before adding milk and sugar. She carries it back to the bed and hands it to him.

It's now or never.

As he reaches for the handle, she flicks her wrist, splashing the steaming liquid over his face and torso. Then, quick as she can, she cracks the mug against the back of his head, and reaches under the bed. She pulls out the small shank she fashioned from the springs she managed to tear from the mattress. She jabs the sharp point into his neck, but it barely breaks the thick wrinkled skin.

He roars and covers the spot with his hand. 'I'll make you pay for this.'

She jabs the spring at his neck again, but it still doesn't penetrate. She repeats the stabbing action, using his neck like a pin cushion. He yelps with each prick, but is waving his arms around, trying to grab her wrists.

Now what?

It is too late to stop. No matter what happens from here, if she doesn't escape, the punishment will be worse than ever. She scans the cell for anything she can use as a weapon.

She darts across the room and picks up the greasy frying pan, and charges back, swatting it at his chubby hands. He is yelling her name, and his face is growing redder as his anger boils. With all her might, she slams the frying pan into his face. His nose cracks, and for a moment he falls backwards against the bed. He won't be out for long. She's passed the point of no return.

***

4

She trembles as she watches him on the bed.

Is he really unconscious? Or is he just pretending to trick me?

His nose is a bloody mess, and he's making no effort to stem the flow of blood.

Move!

His jacket is hanging from the back of the chair by the kitchen table. She reaches into each pocket, feeling for the small remote control.

Where is it?

She checks the pockets again but they are empty, save for his usual brand of cigarettes and a lighter, neither of which are going to keep him incapacitated. She searches the cell.

Did he hide it somewhere when I wasn't looking?

She tries to replay the memory of his actions when he'd come into the room. She'd been so nervous about her planned attack that she hadn't been paying much attention. Her eyes fall to the floor.

His trousers!

Of course, why didn't she spot them sooner? He must have put the remote in his trouser pocket. She edges closer to the frame of the bed, conscious that he could reach out for her at any point. On her knees, she pulls his trousers closer. The first pocket contains a squashed handkerchief. She discards it, and moves onto the second pocket: nothing.

Where is it?

She straightens and slowly turns to stare at him. His left knee is poking out underneath the thin blanket on the bed. A glimmer of black catches her eye. She reaches for the blanket, and ever so carefully pulls it off his legs.

He's wearing shorts.

The thumping of her heart is all she can hear. She takes a deep breath in an effort to steady her nerves, but the adrenaline is flowing freely now. She presses her knee onto the mattress. The bed frame creaks, but he doesn't stir. She lifts her second leg onto the mattress, so she is sitting astride him. Still, he doesn't stir. Keeping her eyes fixed on him for any sign of movement, she slides her hand along the bedsheet, towards the pocket of his shorts. She pushes her fingertips in. They brush against hard plastic.

It's there.

She pushes her hand further in, using her fingernails like tweezers to grip the edge of the remote. It's only the size of a packet of matches, but it's caught on something: a crease in the shorts?

She leans closer to the shorts, allowing her fingers to sink deeper into the pocket. She studies the position of her hand in relation to the shorts. Because of his body position, the control is stuck between the curve of the material and his inner leg. She grips it as tightly as she can, and jiggles it slightly.

Just a little more, and you're free.

The remote wobbles, and releases. She grasps it with her free hand, and for a moment, she is elated.

And then his chubby hand shoots up and around her wrist. 'You're going nowhere, you ungrateful bitch.'

***

5

She tries to pull her wrist free, but his grip is too strong.

Where did I put that shank?

She searches the mattress with her free hand, as he pushes himself up. Her fingers brush nothing but sheet. He pulls her wrist towards him, and then slaps her hard across the face. Instinctively, she tucks her face behind the arm he's still squeezing. Her cheek stings, but she continues to search for the thin wire.

He shuffles over the mattress, and stands, pulling her onto the floor as he strides across the small cell. 'Did you really think I'd let you leave here?' He snatches the small remote control from her fingers, before kicking her in the stomach, releasing her wrist in the process.

She rolls into a foetal position as he kicks again.

And again.

And again.

He steps over her, and heads into the small kitchen area, turning on the hotplate. 'You thought it would be good to scold me, did you? Let's see how you like it when I burn the skin from your face.'

I need to do something. I can't wait for him to kill me.

She spots the coiled spring. The thin blanket is in a heap on the floor from where he dragged her, and the spring is tucked between two folds. His back is to her as he checks the temperature of the hot plate with the back of his hand. She rolls over, and grabs the spring in one motion. He turns at the sound, but she remains curled up so he won't suspect.

'What you don't realise, Michelle, is how much the world has changed out there. You're safer in here. I look after you, and how do you repay me? With betrayal. I have to punish you now. You realise that, don't you? You've driven me to this. I don't like to hurt you, but you need to be disciplined. You've got to learn that I only keep you here because I love you, and I want to protect you.'

He stomps over, and pulls her up by the hair, dragging her towards the hot plate. She tries to fight against his pull, but he's too strong, and her feet have no grip on the laminated floor. She could beg for forgiveness but she doesn't want to give him the satisfaction.

Standing behind her, he wraps his arms around her middle, trapping both her limbs. He lifts her up, and forward, but she fights with all her strength to keep her upper body vertical. He loosens his grip, raising his right arm, and grabs the back of her head forcing it down towards the hotplate.

But her right arm is freed in the process, and he hasn't realised what she's holding. She grips the spring tightly, and drives it into his eye. The flesh is soft, and the spike tears through his iris. He immediately drops her, screaming, and she is able to push herself away from the counter and back to the floor. His hands are over his face, as he howls in pain.

Move, move, move.

The remote control is on the countertop. She lunges for it, and the motors whir to life. He recognises the sound, and stumbles unsteadily towards the noise. The door slowly grinds open, and she dives through the gap, hitting the close button in the process, as he reaches for her.

***

6

There is silence as the motors stop turning. She collapses against the metal door, relieved when no electric current passes through. She is in virtual darkness, and closes her eyes to encourage them to adjust to the lack of light.

She shudders at the sound of Tim's anguished cries.

'You need me, Michelle. The world you knew died a

long time ago. You don't understand how dangerous it is out there. You need me!'

She can just about see the small hole he crawled through earlier, and she knows she should be through it already, but she remains leant against the door, quietly listening to his howling.

Now he knows what it was like for me every night.

She remains still, taking short breaths until the ache in her gut passes. She doesn't want to remember what she did to him.

'Michelle, I'm in trouble… please? I need you. You can't leave me down here.'

He is still trying to control her, even though she has defeated him.

Ignore him. He's trying to trick you.

'Please, Michelle… I pulled out the spike… I can't stop the blood… I'm feeling weak… I need a doctor. Please, Michelle… I still love you.'

He's lying. He knows he's beaten, and he's desperate.

'I forgive you, Michelle… and I'm sorry… let me out, and I swear we can leave here together… we'll go to the hospital, and then I'll let you go…'

She clamps her eyes shut and covers her ears.

She silently recites the nursery rhymes her mother used to sing to her.

You can do this!

She lowers her hands and is relieved that he has stopped calling to her. She crawls unsteadily across the concrete floor, her eyes focused on the hole ahead of her. There is no door covering the gap. She reaches into the darkness, but there is no door within touching distance.

Where's the door? I know he opens a door here somewhere… where does this tunnel go?

The tunnel is narrow but if he can fit through it, she knows she can too. She flattens her body, and pulls herself into the black, keeping her fingers outstretched for the door she knows is there somewhere.

She has crawled for five metres when her trembling hands finally touch something solid. There is a small frame of light around the two sides of the wooden covering, but nothing indicating the top or bottom of the frame. Her fingers rub against the pane, searching for a handle, or mechanism that might be used to open it, but all she can feel is the grain of the wood.

Think! How did he get out of here? What did it sound like? Don't panic!

She bends her legs towards the sides of the tunnel, her toes looking for anything to use as leverage, but the concrete is cold and rough, there are no divots she can push off. She takes a deep breath and pushes the wood with all the strength she can muster, but it doesn't move.

What doesn't go back, must go up.

Her fingers scrabble for the edges of the pane, but the gap between the wood and the side of the tunnel is too tight. Pressing her palms against the wood, she pushes out and up.

It has to move. How else did he get out?

She screams as the hatch remains unmoved. There is nothing else for it, she needs to ask him. She has to go back.

***

7

The relief at being out of the tunnel is palpable. Although the darkness is suffocating, there is light escaping from beneath the metal door. She crawls over to the door, and places her ear against it.

There is no sound coming from within.

She gently taps on the metal. 'Tim?'

She holds her breath as she waits for him to answer, but there is only silence.

There must be a second remote. That must be how he lifts the wooden hatch.

'Tim? Can you hear me?'

He still doesn't answer. He's either tricking her, or he's hurt worse than she thought. There is only one way to know for certain, but she doesn't want to open the door. If he is lying beyond the door, playing dead, she'll have no way of escaping him. But, if he is dying, the longer she waits, the less chance he'll be able to tell her how to get out.

This isn't fair! There has to be another way.

'Tim, please answer me. I've come back to get you some help. You need to tell me how to get the next door open, then I can call for an ambulance for you. Don't be silly. This is the only way.'

Answer me, damn you!

She presses the button on the remote, and the motors shatter the silence. Tim is lying across the entrance, with his eyes closed. The side of his face is caked in dried blood, and there is a small puddle where his hair rests on the floor.

Jesus! I killed him?

She crouches down at his side and bends her ear closer to his nose. His breathing is shallow, but he is alive. Just.

She cradles his head in her lap. 'Tim? Can you hear me? I need to get you some help, but I don't know the way out. Tell me how to lift the second door.'

He mumbles.

'What's that, Tim? You're in a bad way, but I can get you help. Please, tell me how to get out. Is there another remote? Or a handle somewhere?' She realises her legs are shaking. 'Come on, Tim. If you really love me, you'll help me.' She leans closer to his mouth as he mumbles again.

'If I tell you… you'll leave me.'

'I won't. I'll get you help. You need a doctor urgently.'

'Do you swear? You… won't leave me here?'

She crosses the fingers on one hand. 'I promise.'

'There's a box… on the wall. It… contains a key.'

She gently lowers his head to the floor. The room outside her cell is better lit now, from the light pouring through the open door, and she can see the box on the wall. She runs to it, and opens the small door at the front.

A look of confusion descends. 'There's a code, Tim. It wants a password of some sort. What is it?'

He doesn't answer.

'Tim? What's the password for the box?'

'It's… your… name.'

She eagerly starts typing. M…I…C…H…E…

The box buzzes and a message appears: *INCORRECT PASSWORD.*

She turns back to him. 'Are you sure it's *my* name? The password should be five letters.' She recites the other names that were etched into the wall by her bed, typing their names in one by one: Megan, Paula, Emily, Alice, Poppy, Chloe, and Ellie. 'It's not opening, Tim. It must be someone else.'

She hears him gently laughing, as the sliding door's motors hum to life. She looks at her hands.

Where's the remote? Why don't I have it?

As she stares through the closing gap, she spots the remote between his fingers. Before she can react, the light disappears, and the motors fall silent again.

She races towards the metal door and thumps her fists against it in desperation. 'What's the code, Tim? If I don't get you help, you'll die in there. Tim!'

She hears him laughing through the door. 'You were always my favourite… you never forget your first…'

She hammers the door again. 'Tim, what's the code?'

'You were reborn… when you came here.'

'You'll die in there, Tim. Is that what you want?'

'I'll never let you go.'

'Tell me the code, Tim. I don't want to die!'

Silence.

She yells for all she's worth, but it is in vain.

Daisy was the beginning of the story, but Michelle is the end.

LEFT BEHIND

Nick Jackson

The following was retrieved from John Edwin's work laptop on May twentieth this year. It is reproduced verbatim, without corrections. Whilst neither the Society for Psychical Research nor the West Yorkshire Police makes any comment as to its veracity, this is being released in the hope it will aid the ongoing investigation.

19 May, 7.58 pm

My shift begins with Marco talking me through the handover document. That's our one-page baton from the I.T. Help Desk's day shift to its night shift. Marco trained me before moving to another team in January, and I was glad when he returned. Sometimes I consider telling him what happens after they leave, but I like Marco, and I don't want him to think I'm going mad, the way others do.

A quiet day, I'm told, just the *twelve* critical incidents.... I laugh, and he's fooled by that. It's a high-pressured job, but these people are a good bunch. I know what you're thinking: 'I.T. nerds have the social skills of a Dalek', but during the day it's a fun place. During the night, however, these people have gone home, and then it's just me.

Then it's no fun.

Goodbyes are exchanged, and the guys leave. I watch their slow walk to freedom through the large open-plan office, voices fading at the far end of the room. A swipe of a fob against the lock – a red L.E.D. flashes green, like a traffic light – and they're gone. With a click, the door shuts behind them, sealing me in. And I'm left behind.

Left behind, and alone.

8.14 pm

Of my friends who didn't leave for university last year, I'm the only one with a job. I should be grateful, but I hate being here now. When I tell people, they think I just want attention. I get flustered easily nowadays, so the nice lady in

Occupational Health suggested keeping a journal, so people will understand why I feel this way.

So people will know why I'm scared.

The first hour drags. When there were two of us we'd lark about on *YouTube*, but watching piano-playing cats by yourself isn't as entertaining. There are always emails though. Eleven today, on the subject of lunchtimes. I guess nobody remembered that mouths are used for more than eating.

I've not had a call yet. I'll be here twelve hours, and won't get more than a dozen in that time. Through the day, the phones never stop. Through the day, we're the team that fixes your problems, the heroes who find your lost files, the villains who ask if you've turned it off and on again. But through the night we action tickets and reset passwords. Most callers work from home then anyway, so there's nothing more we can do.

Nothing but wait for the end of one day and the start of another, through nights that get longer and longer.

9.03 pm

Jerry the security guard makes his first round. Every hour, he walks the building's nine floors, of which we're on the second. Jerry's pushing forty, which sounds ancient, but he's got that reassurance where you feel nothing can go wrong when he's around. Reminds me of Dad, before he left.

We'll talk about the footy, and transfer-market rumours, then he'll go check the other floors. I trust Jerry. He never told anyone about that time he found me in the lift, red faced and screaming.

It's starting to get dark.

My desk faces west. On three sides, I'm surrounded by glass (the fourth is meeting rooms) and in the summer I'll see the sun sink in front of me and rise behind me. When I started last year, I liked watching the clouds burning away, the window-frame silhouettes stretching then fading into the carpet, the shadows deepening... And hours later, after the tiredness and the dark numbed me, the vending-machine coffee and energy drinks revived me, I'd catch the first pale wash in the east windows and the shadows would recede, and that light would return.... Now I dread the sun going down. I dread those shadows.

I know what's coming.

9.24 pm

I notice the first temperature drop. This is how it starts.

There's a thermometer on my desk but its red line does not change, as if it's accusing me of inventing this as others have done: like Hans, the I.T. department head; like the police; like Mum. And when I'm back on days – when I can sleep without the tablets – then I almost think I did imagine it. Until the nightshifts come back around – three days of twelve hours – until it starts again. And not even this crappy thermometer believes me.

So I'm writing everything down. I want someone to know, in case –

I can hear voices. I'll check the landing.

9.28 pm

Nobody there. It's possible others are in the building, aside from me and Jerry. Marketing are on the floor above; they often work late.

It's possible.

9.56 pm

It is really dark now. Rows of abandoned desks roll out behind me like furrows in a ploughed field at night. Orange fireflies are monitor power buttons on standby. The last light is fading outside with the impatience of dusk.

At the end of my row is the breakout room, where a hot-drinks machine will warm my chilled hands. Movement-activated ceiling lights follow me, like those glowing paving stones in that Michael Jackson video.

On my return there's an email, from Kevin Dwight. I already know its contents. His BlackBerry sends one every night I'm on:

How many calls received?
How many tickets closed?
How many still outstanding?

I remember when he interviewed me for the job. There were questions like: *Who do you admire? What is your ambition?* Kevin's ambition was to attend a World Cup Final – though he said he'd have to stop supporting England to get there – which made me laugh, and five minutes later we shook on it. The perfect manager; always available by text or email, even when he's meant to be relaxing on the team away-day.

The last of the day has gone. Streetlights cast white pools into an empty world. In the surrounding buildings – another office complex ahead, an apartment block behind – lights go out, lights come on, as people leave work and return home.

It is night time. It is their time.

10.15 pm
I don't have long to wait.

During the day, my laptop connects to a second monitor, for remote-accessing other computers. At night, that extra screen is a redundant black mirror on my desk, facing the rest of the office, and reflecting a square of white that a few seconds earlier was not there. The ceiling light in the far corner is on. Then it goes off. On again, off again.

Once activated, they should stay lit for ten minutes, yet this does not. And how can it be activated anyway, when there's nobody here except me?

I try ignoring it. But the monitor's flickering reflection won't stop – on again, off again – as though, like a Morse code message, someone wants my attention.

10.30 pm
This is how I try to ignore that light.

Alongside the office is our car park, where a streetlight's glow settles like fine snow on the smoking-shelter roof known, in honour of the desk's chain-smoking Casanova, as Jed's Shed. From my window, I search the vast space for any parked cars, for any sign others are in the building. It is deserted.

The stillness outside reinforces the solitude within. For distraction, I explore nearby desks – the ephemera of personalities that I know – and at first it helps. A monitor, covered in garish post-it notes. A *Star Wars* mug. An RSPCA mouse-mat. Tissues, tablets and cough mixture, clustered together in a Superdrug shrine… But then I see Kevin's sound-board, where a crayon steam-engine drawn by the son he adores is surrounded by photos of his loving family, and it's a reminder of what I no longer have.

Sometimes, when she thinks I'm out, I hear Mum on the phone to Dad. Saying how things could be good again, if it were the two of them. They'd have fun again, the two of them. Be happy, and free. The two of them.

Three desks from mine, Denise Carson's favourite book, *Labyrinth*, passes the night. Denise once said that when she retires she'll move to Carcassonne, where the novel is set. Last November, she started learning French. The mother hen of the team, I doubt there's a person here who hasn't confided in Denise; certainly I've talked to her often about

361

things at home. Many times I'd roll my chair over for a chat – though, if I'm honest, it was as much to do with the proximity of the person sat opposite her.

Cathy Harrington.

Thoughts of her are the one distraction I don't need. I drop into my chair, spin round…

And face that flickering light in the corner.

There *could* be a perfectly rational explanation. And, though I'm sure there isn't, I now have to check.

As I near the corner the light goes out. I wait, but it stays out. We're often told how I.T. problems suddenly fix themselves when we answer the phone; we'd joke that the equipment was scared of us. Now I'm scared of the equipment – and it's no joke.

Because I've still no idea what set off the light. Nor can I explain why it feels so cold near there. When Jerry next visits I'll ask him to check the temperature settings, in the hope he will find an explanation. In the hope I can prolong this denial.

We all do it. We're so unforgiving of others for their self-deceptions, but how often do we lie to ourselves? For two years, Mum's taken every antidepressant going, but we both know the cure isn't something to swallow with a glass of water; the cure needs to walk back through the door and tell her he's home – or she needs to change the locks. I've been though every emotion for my absent dad: I've cried for him, prayed for him, hated him and wished him gone forever; for my mum though, I've just slowly ceased to exist, a stranger she lives with but nothing more. Except, perhaps, a burden? Dad was bored, he said, that's why he left. Bored of us? Of fatherhood? If even my own parents can't love me, how can I expect anyone else will? Which leads me to my own self-deception. To my foolish belief that *I* could ever have a chance with Cathy.

I've always found beautiful women intimidating, but with her it was different right from the start. Cathy was already the desk's senior analyst when I joined, which meant often she'd be in charge. I soon began scouring the new rota each month, praying to be assigned to her weekend shifts. You see, Cathy never treated me like the nervous kid I was around her. And she'd owned every fibre of my heart since the day we met.

I'd collect snippets about her likes and dislikes. At Christmas she got tickets to see *Aerosmith* this summer, and whenever her ring-tone would belt out *Walk This Way* we'd all sing along, for her amusement. Her favourite perfume, *Classique*, reminds me of roses and vanilla, and summertime; the bottle, curved like a woman, reminds me of her. My whole day would be judged good or bad by whether she smiled at me. I longed for Cathy to enquire about my life, to show I existed in hers. I ached to ask her out. Like that could ever happen, when even saying hello left me tongue-tied.

Unlike Jed Farley. Everybody knows a guy like him, and wants to be him, and envies him, and fears him. Jed was charm itself to your face, but he would remember things you wish he'd forget, like that night in Revolution when –

There's something outside.

I can hear wheels *clack-clacking* over concrete slabs.

It's coming from the communal area, between here and the car park. I hurry to the window, peer out – almost head-butting my reflection – but I already know what it is, and also that I won't see it. I never have, previous nights.

That sound is gone. But it will be back.

11.05 pm

Jerry promised to check the temperature settings. He won't find anything though. It warmed up right before he arrived.

When I asked him if there was anyone else in the building he said no. He joked about noisy spirits keeping me up, but although I laughed, it was a little too forced and a little too late. I think he suspects something.

I didn't mention the talking I heard earlier. Of course, it could be that others *were* in, and they have since left.

It could be that.

11.42 pm

A text from Urfan, my best mate on the desk. My best mate full stop, since my former best mate is at Loughborough University with a new life and new friends. My eyes drift to the monitor opposite mine, and the action figure atop it. I open his away-day text:

Everyone is getting drunk! Now you would fit right in, and I could take pictures

to remind you how funny you look! ;-)

He's referring to my first pay day. Most of the team headed to Revolution and I followed like an eager puppy.

I've tried hard to forget that night.

Urfan wasn't there, but he was in the following Monday when I confessed what happened. He gently said, 'This is why I do not drink.' The only time you'd see Urfan excited – apart from when Bradford City beat Chelsea in the Cup – was on his Xbox. The *S.S.X.* snowboarding games were his thing (his action figure on the monitor, a woman clutching a snowboard, is from the games: Elise, I think she's called). Hours we'd spend trying to get the top scores, but he never could master the Alps wingsuit level.

He did make it to the team away-day though. The idea was Kevin's: an outward-bound centre, with orienteering, an assault course, two dormitories, one barbeque – and a fridge full of beer. I was to go too, but then I knackered my knee and –

That light in the corner is back on.

I won't look at it. Until Jerry arrives in twenty minutes, I'm staying right here.

20 May, 12.14 am
Jerry doesn't arrive.

I've never known him be late. He could've nipped for a piss but it only takes a minute. I also need one; however, I'd have to go towards that light.

It's been on for thirty minutes now. That's impossible, unless somebody's over there. But there's nobody.

There's just me. Alone.

Kidding myself that I'm alone.

12.40 am
And still Jerry does not arrive. And still that light does not go out. Only continuous movement can keep it activated. I know this, because I've been so rooted to my chair, afraid to move, that the light above me *has* gone out. Before I typed this, my laptop monitor had entered sleep mode. There's only that light in the corner, and –

It flickers, twice. The third time it does go out, and somehow that's worse, because as I stare at that corner and try to decipher the pitch black, for just a second I *think* I see....

Rising from my chair awakens the light above me, and I yell when it bursts back on. I laugh, rub my face, notice the wetness on my cheeks, and stop laughing. But it's got me moving again, and I see there's nothing in the far corner except shadows.

I need the loo and I can't wait. After I've been, I'll visit reception and check Jerry's okay.

12.56 am
I cannot find Jerry anywhere.

I'd nipped to the loo then went down to the lobby, to the reception desk where he passes the night when he's not on his rounds. The monitor screens illuminated an empty chair. I shouted his name. Nobody answered. I checked the screens. Nothing moved.

It felt like I was the only person in the entire building. In the entire world, even.   Then I heard a distant ringing. My phone.

I ran back upstairs and answered it before the ringing stopped. The caller was angry I didn't pick up sooner. I almost told him why, but he was too interested in the work he'd locked himself out of to care, so I reset his password and he hung up without a thank you. Well, screw him. Screw him and the rest who cannot go to bed at a time when nobody in their right mind is working.

So here I am, at four minutes to one in the morning – absolutely not in my right mind – updating this.

1.06 am
When another hour ended and still no Jerry, I went looking again. It only took a moment. The lobby was as empty as before. I didn't linger.

I don't like it down there, in the dark.

1.07 am
I hear footsteps.

It could be Jerry, but here's the thing: most of the floors are carpeted and therefore silent. You'll hear footsteps in the restaurant and lobby, but that's two floors below, and I've just come from there. So, who's making that noise?

This time I'll only go as far as the landing.

1.16 am
I need a moment to stop shaking.

Okay. I'll try to tell it exactly as it happened. Nobody was on the landing. I opened the stair door, shouted down. Nobody replied. But then, from behind me, a sound that fills me with absolute dread. The rumble of the lift doors opening.

I haven't told anybody about what happened in the lift when Jerry found me that time. Not even my counsellor.

It goes back to the night it started, thirteen weeks ago, when I couldn't take the stairs, so instead took the lift... when I was inside it, and the doors refused to open.

Later the building manager, Mr Velázquez, apologised. 'Helvetia, she's a new building,' he said. 'Some of the equipment is still bedding in, you understand.' I pretended to understand, pretended it was okay, but it wasn't. I was in there, alone, for twenty minutes. And that was fine, that was not the problem. But what happened next, when suddenly there came the unbearable heat, those terrible cries, that nauseating smell of flesh cooking, what happened when I was no longer alone in a trapped lift is something I will never understand.

My screams had brought Jerry running. By the time he prised those doors apart I was a wild-eyed, shrieking wreck. I told him afterwards it was claustrophobia. Jerry wasn't fooled, but while he never asked me what happened, a few days later he did confess the heatwave that erupted from the lift nearly flattened him.

So, a rumble. The lift doors open –

And out steps Jerry!

There's been a power cut in the plant room. He's trained in maintenance as well; he's been down there fixing it. He lost track of time, but as soon as he finished he came straight up in the lift to check on me.

Only after he leaves does it occur to me that the plant room is underneath the building. So if Jerry was in there, then who was making those footsteps?

1.48 am

Another temperature drop. The thermometer still refuses to support me. But I feel it. Through my skin, in my bones.

That *clack-clacking* noise again, outside. Louder, closer. Though it speckles goosebumps along my arms, it's my ringing phone that makes me jump.

This caller is nicer than the last. She's actually apologetic – even though I'm paid to be here – but it's good to hear a friendly voice, and for a short while I feel better. For a short while.

2.11 am

I don't notice it at first. Partly because most of this floor is laid out behind me, I don't see it. But I sense it.

In the far corner, the light is still off. The air's cool, but not like earlier. There are no noises from outside, no footsteps or voices from within. All seems to be as it should.

That's when I notice it.

Red to green. Red to green. Down the far end of the room – visible only because it's so dark – the door's L.E.D. light changes, as though somebody's swiping a fob over the lock. Nobody is there and yet still it keeps alternating: red, green, red, green. The door does not open. Nobody enters. Just that light, faster, faster. A blur.

Until finally it stops: point made. There are others here.

2.24 am
Why am I here?

It's easier than the alternative, I suppose. We're accustomed to the path of least resistance, and it requires something huge to push us to the point of no return. A matter of life and death even.

I've tried speaking to the department head. Hans sympathised, said it must feel like being trapped down a well, but everyone wants to help.... Yet nobody can.

I've attended interviews. Lots of talk: about fresh starts, new challenges, exciting futures.... Lots of talk.

I've been seen by Occupational Health, so concerned were they about my wellbeing, and since then a counsellor.... Again, lots of talk.

And I have written the letter, three times. Each one lists different reasons, not one gives the whole story, because no-one wants the whole story. Is quitting a sign of strength, or weakness? What does that make me? Where does that leave me? Unable to answer the question of why I am still here.

Unable to see a way out.

2.39 am
Urfan's latest text arrives. The one I've been dreading.

I do not wish to be the bearer of bad news, but Cathy and Jed have gone outside for a cigarette, and she does not smoke. I fear you were too late asking her.

Cathy. And Jed.

Two friends having a natter? I can tell myself that – but who am I kidding? The fact Cathy avoided relationships with work colleagues made no difference. The fact Jed lived with another woman made no difference. The fact, most of all, it is none of my damn business anyway makes absolutely no damn difference.

I fear you were too late asking her....

Of course, I blame Jed – even though my cowardice was not his fault – but I need someone aside from myself to hate, so I blame him for that, as I blamed him for what happened in Revolution when I got pissed and shared my feelings for Cathy. I felt betrayed when he then told her – although I've no proof that he did – yet blaming him for sabotaging my chance was easier than admitting I never actually had one. I never had a chance, but the cruelty of hopeless love means we don't see further than our dreams. So I blamed him, and I hated him, and now I'll never get to say I'm sorry.

Cathy and Jed have gone outside for a cigarette....

Is that when it happened? Is that how? The fire investigator's report could only speculate. Certainly the gas canister's pipes to the water heater were 'deficient'; a clinical word for what stole the lives of sixteen people when the leaking gas ignited, when the canisters exploded, when the fire engulfed the outward-bound centre thirteen weeks ago.

I do not wish to be the bearer of bad news....

Oh, Urfan .... Could you ever know how much your final text hurt me?

I thought my stupid jealousy was pain enough; but later, when I heard about the accident, when I realised this was the last I would ever hear from you.... No more us playing *S.S.X.* together. No more you teaching me to skateboard, wheels *clack-clacking* over paving stones. I fell off last time, walloped my knee so bad I could barely walk, and Kevin said I'd have to miss the away-day the following week and cover the night shift instead. Your skateboard saved my life – and ruined it forever.

2.50 am

The voices return. But now they are loud enough for me to hear words. A man and a woman. He asks how her language lessons are going, and she replies in broken French.

I don't know where they're coming from, but I know who they belong to. Jed and Denise.

3.21 am

When Jerry dropped by twenty minutes ago I hid. I didn't want him to see me crying.

What would I say? Nobody believes me. It's either some post-traumatic workplace bereavement, or I'm missing a father who may be dead for all he stays in touch. Even the police, when they saw the texts, wouldn't listen. They contacted the phone company, but Kevin and Urfan's numbers are no longer in use and won't be for years. Their phones were destroyed in the fire, so it's a glitch. Like when a sent text repeats several times. I'm being haunted by a *glitch*.

But that is not what scares me.

Denise's favourite book vanishes before Jerry arrives. So too Kevin's photos, and the figure ready to snowboard down what used to be Urfan's monitor. These things were packed away thirteen weeks ago, returned to grieving families. I'm the only one who sees them now, the only one who receives their texts. The only one visited by the dead.

But that is still not what scares me.

It isn't a fear of their intent. It's a fear of *mine*. You see, in life they were my family, after my real one fell apart. They were my friends, when my old ones moved away. They were my entire world – and now, now they are gone. My world is gone. And what remains is simply too painful.

What remains is me, alone.

I attended their funerals. I wept bitterly. For my best mate, who will never complete that Alps wingsuit level. For my unrequited love, who won't see Steve Tyler sing *Walk*

This Way live. For my boss, there's a seat at a World Cup Final he will never fill. For the kind lady I confided in, she will never taste the fresh bread and fine wine of Carcassonne. And for Jed, whose dreams I never knew because my petty resentment stopped me from knowing him. I said goodbye to each of them, in crematoriums and at gravesides. I said goodbye to those who befriended me when I had no one. All I needed was to feel wanted, all I wanted was to be needed – to be part of something – and for a time I was. An all-too-brief time. Now they are gone, and it's just me. And none of our dreams will be fulfilled.

Besides Marco and those few who returned from other teams, the rest of the Help Desk is new. They call me "lucky". The "survivor". They'll never understand that I don't feel lucky, they'll never appreciate that I'm not surviving.

And they will never know how much I wish I had gone on that away-day.

3.44 am
There. That's it. The final truth.

This is what I've been afraid of. My acceptance. I knew it was coming. When the sun goes down, when the shadows grow long, when I have so much time to think.... It horrifies me. But also, it releases me.

All those letters I wrote and tore up, I realise now the problem wasn't how I explain it to others, it was how I explain it to *me* – and now I have.

And now, finally, I see a way out.

Through the east windows, the first hint of daylight comes from far-off clouds now darker than the surrounding sky. But it no longer holds the promise of salvation. I no longer want salvation.

I just don't want to be left behind anymore.

3.50 am

This time the thermometer does not deny the truth.

A tiny square reflects on the opaque monitor, but not from the far corner; now it's the light over the door. One by one they activate, all the way from the entrance to my row. But when I look, nobody's there.

I watch, and I wait, and still nobody's there.

I shiver. Breathe out clouds, like the dead of winter. Breathe in roses and vanilla, and summertime.

As realisation hits me, I stare at these words I just typed. The letters swirl, but I don't wipe away my tears. Then I look to the second, blank monitor. Then I see, reflected in it, the shape of her.

The shape standing right behind me.

She was not here a moment ago. She is here now – she who died three months back – she is right behind me. I won't turn round because of what I will see. But her reflection is so pure, so beautiful, and so undamaged by that awful night, and I cannot tear my gaze from it even as I feel a hand upon my shoulder, a hand which, from the corner of my watering eye, is nothing like the hands of the Cathy I knew and loved and still love, and the fingers of that hand in my blurred vision are dried twigs, cracked and burnt, and whilst I cannot stop writing this, for I must tell it all, and though I dare not turn round, I don't want her to leave me again and I don't want to be alone anymore, and I pray she will not go

go
go

go

go

go
go

go
go
gone

There is no more. Helvetia's security software shows John's fob was not used to leave the building. All the windows are sealed. When the security officer checked, approximately twelve minutes after this journal's final entry, the floor was empty.

John Edwin never returned home.

If you have any information as to his whereabouts, contact details are available below.

HORROR

Roz White

The night was cold – well, cold once she was outside the club. Breath steamed suddenly from her mouth as an involuntary gasp shook her slender frame and she shuddered in the chill night air. Around her, streetlights competed with garish neon, even at this late hour; beyond the pavement where she stood shivering, cars still flew past, though not as many as earlier.

Well, that might make getting a cab easier, I guess!

She opened her bag and dug for a purse – then grimaced sadly. *Looks like I'm walking, then...* she rattled the purse experimentally, more in hope than expectation, but it remained steadfastly near-silent, with only the faintest sound of chinking coins. She already knew that she was out of notes.

Bloody good night though... Where are they?

The chill of the night was dispelling the heavy fumes of alcohol in her head by the moment; but it was too late to go back inside: she knew from other nights that this place didn't allow re-entry, and besides, hadn't she just proved that she was broke? She lifted her long, shapely legs, carefully marching on the spot in a vain attempt to get... well, not warm, she was hardly dressed for warm – maybe simply *not freezing* would do? She wrapped bare arms around her chest, covering at least a portion of her rather exposed cleavage in the process, though that was far from her mind. Her dark-shadowed eyes glanced down to her shoes, and she reflected glumly on their own impracticality for walking.

For the second time, she wondered where her friends had got to, and what was taking them so long. She pulled out her phone, drawing the attention of the doorman who had only just now let her out of the place. But the screen was dark – there were no messages. She bit her lip as she stared at the thing, wondering what to do. *We were all pretty much finished. Nobody had money any more. I could've sworn they'd said they were on the way out!*

Doubt began to gnaw at her. She knew what she ought to do – she ought to message them all and ask what was happening. But suddenly she didn't want to. Didn't want to risk more rejection, more upset, more... loneliness...

This was supposed to be getting me over him, after all! And it's worked... kinda...

But the bravado and confidence she had so effortlessly deployed within the club's suddenly safe-feeling walls was dissipating even as her body temperature dropped in the cold, stark reality of the chilly night air, and she found it impossible to even unlock the phone and find where her mates had gone.

Am I really so easy to simply leave behind? She could feel the tears beginning, and frowned fiercely to herself. *I don't want to go there... really, seriously don't want to go there!*

She rattled her purse again, aware now that the bouncer was staring curiously at her as she stood there undecided. *Maybe enough for a bus,* she told herself, and fervently hoped it was true. *Well, it'll be up to the bus station anyway. There's a cashpoint: I can get a bit more out, enough for a cab home.*

She looked at her feet again, encased in their strappy, glittery, made-for-dancing-not-walking party heels. There was likely to be a world of pain tomorrow, she just knew there was. The pavement around her glistened wetly, as if to add insult to injury, and the doorman's glances had hardened into a stare.

She slung her bag back onto her shoulder with a sigh and took a few tentative steps out into the night.

***

Once away from the garish lights of the club, darkness crowded around her – both within and without. She had no coat, little money and not a lot else beyond a clear sense of direction: she knew the bus station was up the hill a way, even if she didn't know precisely where. *It's hardly a problem,* she told herself, *all I have to do is find somebody to ask.*

Her eyes began, quite subconsciously, to seek out friendly figures. But she found none – come to that, figures of *any* sort were few enough. But those she could see were, to her suddenly suspicious eyes, far from suitable to ask directions from.

What's he doing in that doorway?

As her steps took her closer, she automatically moved towards the kerb – until a car hurtled past, catching her in its wake and almost sucking her into the road. She tottered unbalanced for what felt like long, long moments, before taking a step back towards the looming wall of the building and the shadowy doorway ahead. The patch of darkness she *knew* she had seen move just a moment ago was still there – but now she could see nothing in it, so dense were the shadows and so poor was the light. She felt a shiver run through her, and it wasn't just from the cold.

Her eyes seemed glued to the darkness ahead, making her impervious to anything else. *How do I avoid this?* She wondered, even as her route took her closer and closer. It took a supreme effort to drag her gaze away, to look somewhere else, anywhere else. Risk assessment took over, weighing the pros and cons of moving closer, crossing the road, a hundred other factors – the litany of womanhood when walking alone from time immemorial. Where can I go? What do I do if..? How do I just stay safe..?

I'm all alone out here…

One hand slid into her bag even as she tried to remain calm and look casual. But she didn't carry pepper spray, or even an alarm. She knew this, yet still she searched blindly for them, even as one part of her mind silently berated other parts for *not* having them. *But it was just a night out,* she told herself – and in her head the voice sounded plaintive, as if merely making excuses. *What was going to happen that needed something? I was safe…*

I was safe when I was with the rest of the gang, she corrected bitterly. *Maybe not so bloody safe now!*

The shadow shifted suddenly – she saw it, there was no mistaking it. Her mind went into overdrive; she hurriedly looked around, registered a gap in the passing traffic and darted out into the road, heading for the other side. Her toes were already beginning to hurt, and her ankles felt strained – yet she pushed herself to go faster, to get across in one piece and put the relative safety of the traffic between her and whatever was lurking in that doorway. *It's probably perfectly innocent,* she told herself even as she skipped onto the far pavement and felt an undeniable surge of relief. *Yet all the same…*

A car surged past, sounding its horn for reasons that escaped her, but still making her jump. Her heartbeat pounded in her temples, her breathing came hot, ragged and rapid; she looked around frantically, seeking any sort of solace or comfort – but there was none. The nearest oasis of light was up the street still, too far away for her to be certain just what it was. *Anything's better than nothing,* she told herself as she fought to get herself back under control. *I've got to go past it anyway.*

She risked a look back over the road. From the doorway, a figure in a dark hoodie appeared to be staring at her, and she felt her blood run cold. It merely matched how the rest of her already felt. She forlornly wrapped her arms around herself again and hurried on as well as her shoes would let her – which wasn't very quickly at all. Her calves were already aching, and even her thighs were starting to protest.

At least I've got tights on, she acknowledged with a wry smile. *Think how much colder I'd be if I'd gone with the bare legs as well!*

It was not really a huge amount of comfort.

***

The bright, almost acrid, light spilling onto the pavement ahead of her resolved itself slowly into the window of a convenience store. Her steps slowed as she drew closer: partly from the pain shooting through her legs and feet with every step, but also from a vague, ill-defined sense of dread and apprehension. *Get a grip,* she told herself. She didn't seem to be listening, however. She took in the cluster of cars parked outside, noting that a good number of them appeared to be taxis – or rather, minicabs. You never got into a minicab unless you'd ordered it – that was basic, Personal Security 101, a Golden Rule even. Never, never *ever*, no matter how dire the circumstances. The internet was awash with tales of what happened to girls who *did* do such a stupid thing. The problem was, if the cars were here, where were their drivers?

There was really only one answer, of course. And her path took her right past their own refuge against the night.

Shit, shit, shit, shit, shit... She was trembling, and it wasn't only from the chill of the wind that was getting up. Her stomach churned, and her knees were about to buckle under her, she just knew they were. She was sure she could feel what little energy she had left ebbing away, even as she stood and wondered what to do next. She turned slightly, trying to see back along the other side of the street, to where that darkened doorway had been. *But what am I trying to see? What am I even looking for? And why?*

But a movement further down her own side of the street rapidly answered all those questions. A dark, hooded figure was walking steadily closer, and her panic rose within her once again. She looked back frantically towards the brightness of the shop – a shop full of unknowns, and to her mind that suggested some sort of peril, though she knew she would never be able to explain precisely why.

Caught! Caught between... between... there was something about that figure coming closer that scared her to the core. She just knew somehow it meant danger, and didn't wish her well. It was not a feeling she wished to put to the test; but the alternative was to go closer to that brightness, and risk the reaction of a whole *bunch* of potentially worse scenarios.

But she had to do *something*. Standing and slowly freezing in the middle of the pavement – whether that freezing be from fear or from the weather – simply wasn't an option. Slowly, almost but not quite with gritted teeth, she forced her tired, complaining legs into motion once more – towards the light. *After all,* she reasoned, *if there are a whole bunch of them in the same place, what're the odds of them* all *being willing to gang up on me together? There'd be one decent one among them, surely?*

Wouldn't there?

There was a change in the light up ahead – it was accompanied by the sound of a door opening, rattling on its hinges and banging into something inside the shop. Men spilled out – three of them, all looming large in the gloom of the streetlamps, big, menacing, with their arms waving and their voices loud. She strained to hear words – and heard them in a language she didn't even recognise. Any hope she might have harboured of rescue or succour faded in a sudden rush of unreasoning, inexplicable, unjustifiable tabloid racism and terror of the unknown. Instinctively, she stepped as quietly as she could (which given her heels wasn't very) towards the shadows of the other, darkened shopfronts, seeking the very sort of doorway that she had been so keen to avoid only a few minutes earlier.

Just wait, hide... get round them, wait till they go away, they won't be here forever, they've got to be going somewhere, surely? Her thoughts tumbled over each other in their haste to be at the forefront of her mind, feeding her fright and pushing reason into the darkest recesses of her psyche. The men seemed to have taken root like trees in a gale at the edge of the kerb, their arms still flailing like branches and their voices raised above a storm that wasn't there, shouting and laughing (or she presumed it was laughter) right in each other's faces, in a way that made her quail. She was about to slip into a dark doorway when, from the corner of her eye, she caught another glimpse of the figure striding up the street towards her. And ahead there was only the bright, shadow-banishing glare of the shopfront. She blinked back a tear as panic overtook her. There was nowhere safe to go.

Her attention snapped back to the men at the kerb as one of them bent to open a car door; with a final shout and a wave, he folded himself into the driver's seat and slammed the door behind him. Her pulse quickened; if only the others would do the same! To her amazement, as if they had heard her, the remaining two separated amid much noise and the shining of teeth in the darkness of the street, strolling with impossible slowness towards minicabs of their own. More shouted banter; more laughter before they finally, unbelievably, climbed into the cars, shut the doors and started the engines. She watched them in a kind of hypnotic state, unable to tear her eyes away and yet still all too aware that another source of worry was approaching up the hill. She needed to move, she knew she did... yet she remained rooted to the spot, concealed in a patch of shadow between the streetlights.

As the last taxi finally pulled away and thus rendered itself beyond a capacity to harm, she heard the fateful footfall from lower down the street. Her mystery follower was almost upon her. Galvanised into action, she darted from her hiding-place, not caring what anyone thought about her sudden appearance, so great was her desire to simply get away. Her legs protested, her feet screamed in agony at her – and she didn't care. She wasn't even concerned if she appeared less than casual – it would only reflect her inner state, after all, as her thoughts whirled faster than she could catch them and her instinct for survival at any cost overrode even common sense. She hurried on as fast as she could, and prayed as fervently as she was able that she had misinterpreted everything, that her pursuer would turn into the shop and she would continue up the hill to the now-visible lights of the bus station unmolested.

Never again, she told herself sternly – and for the moment at least, she believed it. *Never again! No more late nights, no more going out alone, no more not having the money for a bloody cab home… no more going out half bloody naked, either!* She added as a chill gust raised goose-bumps on her expanses of bare, exposed flesh.

She hurried onwards, her stomach refusing to settle. *Only a few more minutes,* she told herself, turning the words into a mantra of hope and relief all in one. *I'm nearly there… just a few more minutes…*

As she reached an intersection and was forced to slow and check for oncoming traffic, she also risked a look back over her shoulder, brushing her hair from her eyes as she did so. Her knees almost buckled as relief washed over her – there was nobody in sight. The light from the little shop still shone like a beacon in the night, but she was past it and any peril it might have held. Her mystery stalker – or so she

wryly described him, even as she realised there was no truth
and probably quite a lot of slander in the term – had
vanished, presumably having turned into that same oh-so-
handy shop, the only one that appeared to be open. In the
distance, almost a world away, she could still see the lights of
the club she had vacated so recently – but there were no signs
of any other revellers having left. She blinked away another
tear as the traffic cleared enough to let her cross. *No more so-
called mates from the look of it, either.* She found that thought too
sad to consider, and also found herself hoping that an
explanation would be forthcoming in the morning.

***

The bus station was warmly lit, its ancient bulbs giving a
yellower, friendlier light than the bright white neon of the
shop down the hill; as she pushed open the doors, she felt
the welcome touch of warmth on her skin as well, and
enjoyed it for a long moment before letting go of the door
and stepping fully inside. *Safe at last – made it!* The thought
echoed round and round her mind as she slowed the frantic
pace that had brought her here, and she almost dared to
relax. *Not so far to go now. Get some cash, see if the late bus is
running… Get a cab if not.*

Suddenly all her troubles, worries and panic seemed
to flow out of her – she had a plan, she was somewhere warm
and well-lit, and all the terror began to ebb away. A trace of
her usual confidence returned; she looked around, spotted a
group of lads hanging around in a doorway by the long-
closed kiosk, and much of *that* vanished once more. But there
had to be officials around here somewhere, she reasoned:
drivers, inspectors, that sort of thing. She somehow *knew* –
in a wholly illogical manner – that she was safe here. Or safer
than out there, at any rate.

Keeping half an eye on the youths, she strolled across
the concourse, keeping as far away as she could from them

and hoping that they somehow, miraculously, hadn't seen her. The cashpoint was at the far end, of course – after all, nothing was ever easy! But as her flesh warmed and her eyes adjusted to the light levels, she felt... alright. Maybe not brilliant, but definitely alright. She had a plan, and it was one she could stick to.

The lads showed no interest in her as she reached the cashpoint and fumbled in her bag for her card. The place was not actually as active as she had thought it was, she realised, as she pushed notes into her purse and stepped away from the machine. Not many buses standing outside; most of the windows around her were dark, also implying a distinct lack of people. Unexpectedly, she shivered again.

Maybe I'm not quite out of the woods yet after all...

She shook her head to clear the cobwebs, and stepped – feeling real pain at every step now – towards the destination boards up on the far wall. Her heart leapt – there was a bus! Stand six... Where was stand six? She turned, pivoting on one foot and regretting it instantly; then she located her goal and tried her best to walk without falling off her heels, so acute was the agony all up her legs. *How did I ever get this dumb? God but I'm never, ever, doing this again! Stupid, stupid, stupid...*

Her bus stood like a silent cliff, two decks of welcoming metal and diesel fumes. She climbed aboard, handed over money to a sallow-faced, dour driver who looked as if he desperately needed a shave, and took the closest seat – simply to avoid having to walk even a single pace further. The seat was warm, and even if it didn't quite mould itself to her form, it was close enough for her to be totally and utterly grateful for its comfort. As she sat and awaited their departure, she felt her last few knots of tension ease; her legs turned to jelly beneath her but she didn't need them for at least another hour; even then, it was a short and easy walk back to her own front door – and then to her bed at last. Tomorrow was another day, and something within her *knew* that it was going to be a better one.

***

As the engine coughed finally into life, an unnoticed figure in a dark hoodie looked up from the rear of the bus, and settled his gaze upon his newly-arrived fellow passenger.

MARY AND JOSEPH

David Evans

J oyce passed the foaming pint over the bar. 'And a merry Christmas to you, Joe.'

'Thanks, love.'

He took hold of the glass, walked over and placed it on the table by his folded up cap then shuffled into his regular seat in the best room of the Horse and Strumpet. It was actually 'Trumpet' but Joe always referred to it that way. The first sip he always considered to be the best and today was no exception. As the beer ran smoothly down his throat, he took in his familiar surroundings. His eye was caught, in fact it was almost put out, by the buxom blonde who'd just entered the bar. She was obviously supported by a structure designed by a civil engineer and he smiled as he imagined its catastrophic failure.

'Don't you dare let your mind handle something your body can't.' Mary had slipped unseen into the seat beside him.

'God, you frightened me to death, Mary.'

'Very prophetic, Joe.'

'You took your time getting here.'

'Looks like I just got back in time.' Mary chuckled in the same manner that Joe had been unable to resist more than fifty-three years before.

'Listen, if I can't enjoy a bit of window shopping at my age, then I've got nothing left.'

'As long as you don't take a test drive.'

It was Joe's turn to chuckle. He stifled it as one or two in the bar turned to stare. 'I love Christmas, you know,' said Joe, 'but it won't be the same this year.'

'It'll be all right. Off to our Sandra's for the day tomorrow. Billy will be there with his two.'

Over the general hubbub of bar room conversations the unmistakable strains of 'White Christmas' clamoured for attention.

'Remember this, Mary?'

'Ooh, you mean that soppy old film we saw years ago?'

Joe took another mouthful of Tetley's best. 'Actually, I was thinking of our Alfred... when he borrowed Dad's pipe and those false ears and did his Bing Crosby impression.'

Mary laughed, 'Aye, that must have been about 1953. He was always good for a joke, were Alfred.' Her laughter slowly transformed into a sigh as her thoughts carried her back to the best room of her in-laws' terraced house. Paper chains strung diagonally across the ceiling; a coal fire roaring in the grate, the only day of the year she'd ever seen one lit. Despite rationing, the table was full. The radio was tuned to the Light Programme in time for the first Queen's speech.

Joe brought her temporarily back to the present. 'Remember that first Christmas in our own house.'

'Of course.' Mary drifted back in time once again. 'It was a lovely house, only two bedrooms but we were cosy.'

'Your mother came round that year along with my mum and dad.'

'He was full of mischief your dad.' Mary's eyes twinkled. 'He set up Billy's clockwork train set in the room and plonked the cat down in the middle. Nearly drove it demented.'

'God, that seems like last year; instead it must be over forty.' Joe's eyes moistened slightly. 'Where's it all gone?'

'Hey!' Mary was insistent, 'None of that now, Joe Ritchie.'

'I'm sorry, Mary. I'll just have a bit more of this medicine.' He finished his pint then looked across. 'Can I get you a glass of white wine?'

Mary smiled at him. 'Best not.'

390

He stood and made his way to the bar for a refill. Waiting to be served, Gladys Grimshaw sidled up beside him. Gladys was in her early sixties but thought everyone took her for ten or fifteen years younger. Always plenty of powder and paint, hair coloured regularly and dresses shorter than they should be. It was probably the lines around her mouth and the appearance of her hands that betrayed her true age.

She slipped one arm under his. 'Now then, Joe,' she said, patting his sleeve with the other. 'How are you faring?'

'Oh, not so bad, Gladys. I didn't see you there,' he lied. Her strong sickly perfume had given her away long before she'd spoken.

Gladys gripped him tighter and in a low voice asked, 'What are your plans for tomorrow, then?'

'Going to our Sandra's for Christmas lunch. The kids and all, you know.'

She went up on tiptoe to be closer to his ear and whispered, 'You know you're welcome to hang your stocking up next to mine, any time you want.'

As he turned and bent down slightly to listen, he was offered a close view of Gladys's main assets which she was not averse to making a show of. 'Er … thanks.' He gave a nervous cough and glanced back towards his seat. 'But I'll be all right as I am. It's very kind.'

'You always were a considerate man, Joe.' To his relief, she released her grip. 'Don't forget, though, call round anytime.' With a well-practised wink and a large smile, she moved gracefully away and disappeared into the other room.

'Another pint, Joe?' Joyce brought his attention back.

'Thanks, Joyce.' He handed his glass over. 'That was a narrow escape.'

'Has she got her eyes on you?'

'She's too fast for me.'

'Still,' Joyce said, placing the beer on the drip tray, 'at least it's comforting to know you can still pull!'

He nodded towards the pumps. 'I'll take that as a compliment then; from someone who does it for a living.'

'Cheeky bugger.' She laughed.

When he'd settled back in his seat, Mary waited a few seconds. 'What did that trollop Grimshaw want, as if I didn't know?'

'Just interested in my welfare.'

'I'll bet. Don't you let her get her hands on your superannuation.'

'She's not getting her hands on anything of mine.'

'Glad to hear it.'

They sat there in silence for a minute or two before Mary tugged his arm. 'Here, remember that fancy dress party Betty invited us to one year.'

'Boxing Day, wasn't it?'

'That's right, and you hired a kilt and full highland dress.'

Joe's face lit up. 'I looked pretty good in that.'

'You did too. A good pair of legs you had in your day.'

'What d'you mean, "in my day"? I still have. Made Betty's Christmas that did.'

Mary chuckled again. 'Especially when she asked you if anything was worn under the kilt and you said, "No, everything's in perfect working order."'

'That was the year we nearly brought old missus Walters to a premature end.'

'God, I nearly never forgave you for that. Fancy doing your impression of the last turkey in the shop to an eighty-five-year-old woman.'

'That made her Christmas,' Joe said proudly. 'Her

last one too, poor old soul.'

Just then, the door opened and a plump woman of around fifty, accompanied by a tall weedy-looking man, swept in.

'Oh, no,' Joe groaned softly, 'That's all I need.'

He kept his head low and took another mouthful of beer. Too late: she'd spotted him.

'Hello, Joe,' she greeted loudly. 'How are you doing, love,' lowering her tone and oozing false concern.

'Fine, Jackie.' Joe smiled.

'D'you know, I was just saying to Walter...' She turned to her companion. 'Wasn't I, love?'

'What's that?' Walter dared to say.

'Well if you'd listen, I'll tell you.'

Suitably rebuked, Walter stayed silent.

'No, I was only saying to Walter the other day, how we'd not seen you around as much.'

'Oh?' Joe took another sip.

'Yes. We were wondering how you were.'

'I'm fine, thanks.'

'Because you know there's been so much of this flu around this winter. We've both had it dreadfully, haven't we, Walter?'

Walter dutifully nodded but said nothing.

'Shocking it's been. And it's seen so many old folks off. Old Mrs White in Gas Street only last week.'

'Aye, I'd heard.' He only said something to stop himself smiling.

'Well you ought to look after yourself, you know. You are looking after yourself, aren't you? Eating well, keeping warm?'

Joe stretched back in his seat and patted his stomach. 'You should know me better than that. I can cook as well as any of them fancy TV chefs.'

'Oh I don't doubt it, but you hear of people just losing the will, letting themselves go, d'you know what I mean.'

'I do, Jackie, love, and I appreciate your concern, but I'm looking after myself all right. Trust me.'

Walter coughed, as if it was the ritual he had to go through before he dare interrupt her.

'Oh, I am sorry,' she continued, 'whatever must you think.'

Joe put up a hand in acknowledgement and gently shook his head.

Walter finally summoned up the courage. 'Shall I get some drinks in, love?'

'Of course, Walter. No need to ask, you know what I'll have. And a pint for Joe too.'

'Er… No thanks, Jackie. This'll be my last for tonight.'

'Are you sure, love.' Her tone adopted the sickly, patronising one Joe detested.

'Thanks, Jackie. Merry Christmas to you… and you too Walter.'

'Okay… Well…' She seemed to take the hint. 'If you really are sure?'

Joe nodded a thanks and she swept away towards the other side of the bar with Walter in tow.

'God that woman gets right up my nose.'

Mary chuckled again.

'I don't know how Walter puts up with it. I'd have walked out years ago.'

'I know, Joe.' Mary squeezed his arm. 'But you're a real man. That's why I've loved you all these years.'

'I don't know, Mary. Am I really that old and decrepit? I look in the mirror in the morning and I see someone resembling my dad.'

'He wasn't a bad looking man, your dad.'

'No, but I mean, I see an old man. But in here...' Joe tapped his temple. 'I'm twenty-one. I still see things exactly as I did over fifty years ago, yet people don't seem to take me seriously any more. Take that patronising old sod.'

'Jackie, you mean.' Mary looked puzzled.

'Yes her. Am I looking after myself? Do they think we revert to childhood when we reach a certain age? I'm sure I never viewed my dad like that – or my mum, come to that.'

Mary smiled and snuggled closer to him. 'No, Joe, I'm positive you didn't'

'If it's not people thinking I'm going back to childhood, then I've got to contend with that piece of mutton, Gladys, thinking I'm a randy teenager again.'

'What d'you mean "again"?'

Joe looked at Mary about to respond but when he saw the expression on her face he laughed.

'Personally,' Mary said, 'I blame HRT.'

They sat in quiet contemplation for a few more minutes before Joe drained his glass and announced he was off home.

'Good night, Mary, sleep well.'

'You too, Joe,' Mary said softly. 'I'll be looking out for you.'

He raised himself slowly from his seat and took his empty glass back to the bar.

'Cheerio, now, Joyce. You have yourself a lovely Christmas.'

'And you, Joe. Take care.'

She watched as the old man turned up his collar, put his cap on and made his way out into the cold night air.

A customer leaned over the bar. 'Who's the old fart, then?' he said.

'You just show a bit of respect,' Joyce retorted. 'Joe's been a regular here longer than you've been in long trousers.'

The drinker shrugged and, taking another slug from the lager bottle, turned back to his friends.

It's going to be hard for him this year, Joyce thought, *his first Christmas on his own. Sometimes I feel she's still with him at that table over there.*

LOVE YOU TO DEATH

Lucy V. Hay

The day she returned to their little cottage, old Edward Barton didn't know what hit him. Literally. (It was, incidentally, a wrought iron poker from the coal buckets by the Rayburn).

Bitch!

When Edward awoke again, the day had ended. His head banged. A hand flew to the back of his neck: blood, thick and tacky, congealed there. He attempted to sit up. Sharp pain, needle-hot, shot through his skull and shoulders like electricity. It set his teeth on edge, bringing hot bile to the back of his throat.

He blinked: once, twice, three times, as he tried to lift the stupor from his brain. Edward sprawled in his favourite armchair by the fire. But like the pain in his head and shoulders, everything else felt wrong.

The cottage was too cold. His bare toes were blue; he was just in a trousers and shirt. Untended, the Rayburn had gone out. The firebox was just full of grey ash, no logs crackled there. The radio, usually on, was off. Its muttering of clipped vowels in educated voices was silent. The room was in darkness; the overhead lights were off, as was every lamp.

Both windows on the left of the room were open; the curtains billowed in the breeze. He could smell the rain falling softly in the garden beyond, onto the peaty earth just a few feet away. Edward wanted to stand, shut the windows, and close the curtains. Relight the fire. Stoke the Rayburn again.

But he knew he wouldn't.

She's back.

Mrs Barton sat in the corner, on the diagonal from him. She perched on Edward's father's old milking stool, which seemed appropriate for the old cow. A slash of moonlight illuminated only half of her face.

The years had not been kind. Her long, greying locks fell about her face. She'd barely cut it in their fifty-odd years together. Edward had loved her hair when he was a lad. He'd run his fingers through it as he wooed her with words he'd had every intention of pursuing... Until life got in the way. Not to mention her dark scorn; her skyward eyes; plus her ever-curling lip and cruel, lashing tongue.

'You're awake, then.'

Her voice was just as Edward remembered. Girlish, not womanly: reedy, whiny, petulant. Hers was the timbre of a spoilt child. Mrs Barton craved constant attention and sulked when she deemed what he considered her due not enough.

And it was never enough.

'Aye.' Edward replied. He tried to shift in his chair, but every bone in his seventy-six-year old frame creaked in protest.

A slow smile spread across her wizened features. 'You don't seem surprised.'

Edward regarded his wife with undisguised resentment. He'd seen that smirk of hers plenty over the decades. It was the one where she felt she'd bested him, caught him unawares. Mrs Barton had worn it a lot before she'd had to go. She'd taunted him constantly: *you're not a real man, Eddie.* She liked games; it was a power play he'd felt helpless to resist. He would fall right into her hands... Yet she got to play the victim, of course. *Women!*

'I always knew you'd come back for me eventually.' He coughed. Blood flecked the back of his hand.

'Two of a kind, you and me.' She leaned forward. Now that slash of moonlight revealed something in her hands, resting on her lap.

His father's old shotgun.

Edward Barton sighed, resigned to his fate. 'Get it over with, then.'

But that smirk was back on Mrs Barton's face. 'Oh no,' she counselled, 'You and I are going for a little walk, first.'

Edward extricated himself from the chair with difficulty: the effort made him woozy. Mrs Barton rose with him, her hands on the gun, always pointed level with his belly.

'Steady now,' she advised.

She was already in a sou'wester and gumboots, but she didn't let him pause to pull on his own wellies, or a coat. Instead she indicated to him to turn around, with a nod of her head. Edward did as he was told.

She pressed the two barrels of the shotgun into his lower back. 'Off you go, then, boyo.'

She took him through the cottage's back door, out into the night beyond. He hissed as cold mud worked its way between his bare toes. The darkness was still, only the odd bark of a fox breaking through the country air. She took him through the garden, past his prized vegetable patch. Past the old, mouldering stable block that hadn't housed horses in years. He trudged his numb feet past the hen coop, all the chickens long dead. She marched him away from the smallholding. He and Mrs Barton had tended it so lovingly, back in those early years (when they'd still had hope).

Now, all gone.

The ominous face of the scarecrow loomed out at Edward. They were on their way past Farmer Bryant's cornfield behind the cottage. He knew where they were going: out towards the moor, beyond the headland. Edward shivered against the drenching mizzle and the feel of mud between his frozen extremities. Edward placed his hands under his armpits. Rain soaked through his shirt and trousers. He was still a strong man, the knot of his muscles tight in his bare arms.

'Do you remember our wedding day?'

The question was incongruous. Edward almost didn't answer, before he realised it might be an effective ploy to distract Mrs Barton and grab that shotgun back off her.

'Of course I do!' He tried to soften his voice. *Women could be flattered, couldn't they?* 'You looked beautiful. Like an angel.'

That much at least was true... But that was before she'd become the embittered and ever-disappointed Mrs Barton. Just an eighteen-year-old girl, that young woman he'd fallen in love with had had the bright eyes and optimism of youth.

They both had.

But she poked him in the back with the shotgun again, forcing him forwards by a few more steps.

'You really remember, Eddie? 'Cos way I recall, you were off your face on the ale by three o'clock.'

'Maybe I knew what I was letting myself in for?' Edward growled, before he could stop himself. He tensed again, thinking this might be enough for her to pull the trigger.

To his surprise, Mrs Barton laughed as they neared their destination. 'Happen you did.'

Edward blinked as rainwater made its way down his wide, balding forehead. In front of them, next to the boggy marshland, was a spade. It stood bolt upwards in the earth like the sword in the stone of Arthurian legend.

X marks the spot.

Edward grasped the handle with both hands. Could he hit her with this before she shot him? Was it worth it?

'Don't go getting any funny ideas,' Mrs Barton

declared. She always did have a knack of knowing what was going through his mind. 'Now, dig.'

Edward did as he was bid. He carved at the boggy ground with the spade, the hard steel of the blade hurting his bare feet. Despite the soft earth, going was tough. The hole filled with water as quickly as he carved chunks from it. After twenty minutes of slow progress, Edward fell to his knees. He started to scoop up fistfuls of mud with his bare hands. Mrs Barton stood over him, the shotgun primed and waiting, her expression impassive.

'It was all your fault, you know,' she said.

Edward looked up at her, still on his knees. Wistfulness struck him now, along with a feeling in the gut that was not quite so easy to process. Regret? Or guilt? He wasn't sure.

'It was no one's fault.'

Her piercing gaze never left his. 'But it might've been different, if it hadn't been just us, all those years?'

Or it could have been worse, Edward wanted to say, but didn't. It was all too late now, anyway.

His hands were as numb as his feet, but still Edward kept digging. He hooked them into claws, scraping more and more earth to the side of him, a human-sized molehill.

Finally, after about an hour and a half of this torture, the grave was excavated. The body inside was smaller than he remembered, but it had been a long time. He looked at its form, wrapped tightly in tarpaulin.

Weary and fatalistic, Edward stood. He could no longer feel his fingers, hands, toes and feet, nor much of any of his limbs. Even his chest felt like dead weight, as if Mrs Barton had killed him already.

Surely this was it, her revenge?

But she wasn't done. 'Unwrap it.'

Edward clambered into the waterlogged grave. His

frozen hands made him clumsy. It felt like it took an age to peel the tarpaulin away, shivering in the dark and rain. Finally, what was inside was revealed.

How long had it been, three years?

Waxy, mottled skin. Sunken cheeks. There was a hole in the chest, concave and ringed by dark, dead blood: a gunshot. The body had been partially preserved by the peaty earth. It was also badly decomposed, bone showing through in places now. The clothes it died in were rag-like, strings of rotted fabric.

Around its face, wisps of her long, grey hair remained.

Edward looked up sharply, expecting to see Mrs Barton standing above the grave... But she was gone. He touched the back of his head: blood still congealed there.

Had he fallen perhaps, hit his head?

A guilty conscience must have manifested a vision of his dead wife, driven him to unearth her. Edward knew he'd find the shotgun where it had always been, in his father's gun cabinet. He'd not touched it since that fateful day he'd been unable to take Mrs Barton's abuse and daily humiliations any longer.

This realisation made way for practicalities. He had to cover up the body again, before anyone saw it.

The old man attempted to hoist himself out of Mrs Barton's final resting place. The peaty, bog-like earth broke away underneath him. He slid, ungainly, on top of his late wife's corpse. An inappropriate laugh wheezed from him, else he would have screamed.

Then her bony arms locked around him.

The mud he had carefully excavated began to pour back into the gravesite, falling on top of them, a freezing weight.

Edward thrashed against the cadaver, his own arms pinned against his sides. Mrs Barton had only been a small woman in life, but in death she was able to grasp hold of her husband and not let him go. His face pressed next to her decomposing lips, a parody of a loving kiss.

Now Edward screamed.

But not for long. The mud covered them both in seconds.

FASTBALL

Alex Shaw

London, United Kingdom.

Aidan Snow sipped his espresso, as he listened to the Today Programme on Radio 4. The main news of the morning centred on the fleet of Russian warships, which had entered the English Channel, bound for Syria. As the clock ticked around to eight, the headlines were read again.

'The Russian aircraft carrier, *Admiral Kuznetsov*, has crossed international waters in the North Sea, with seven other vessels, early this morning. It is the largest Russian military deployment since the Cold War...'

Having been a member of Boat Troop within the Special Air Service (SAS), Snow knew more than most about the capabilities of the Russian navy. Whilst the *Admiral Kuznetsov* was an aging, Soviet-era vessel, it could still act as a mobile airfield for fifty warplanes. Snow sighed. The world was a peculiar place, where big boys played with their toys, in the hope of impressing everyone else. Russia's diminutive president was flexing his muscles again, pretending it was still 1980. First, annexing Crimea, then, invading eastern Ukraine, and now, propping up a failing dictator in Syria; Putin was relying heavily on the old KGB playbook.

Snow finished his coffee, and was in the process of popping another capsule into the machine when his secure Blackberry vibrated. Snow hit the 'pour' button on his Nespresso, and then, opened the email on his phone. It was from Jack Patchem, his boss at the Secret Intelligence Service (MI6). Both the email and the espresso were strong and short.

> *Aidan,*
>
> *Five has requested you be immediately seconded to them for a fastball. You are to be at the following address by 0930 today.*

Snow frowned. 'Five', as the Security Service (MI5) was known, had their own operatives, so why on Earth would they need him? He knocked back his coffee, grabbed his go-bag, and left his London flat.

Manor Royal Business Park, Crawley, United Kingdom.

The office was empty, save for a large desk and a pair of leatherette executive chairs, which had seen better days. The cream-coloured walls had white patches here and there, the ghosts of whatever corporate art had once adorned them, before the travel company had gone belly-up, and pulled out of the UK. Snow sat on the guest side of the desk, and studied a digital image on an MI5-issue tablet.

David Finn drummed his fingers on the scarred desk top. "Do you see now why I asked for you?" Snow nodded, without looking up, as he zoomed in on part of the image. Finn continued in his estuary-tinged accent, "The man you are looking at goes by the name of Ruslan Pavlov, but we believe that to be an assumed identity."

"Your assumption may be right." The man in the image resembled someone Snow had met eighteen months earlier in insurgent-controlled eastern Ukraine. That man had been a fanatic, a commander in the Russian-backed militia of the Donetsk People's Republic. Snow swiped left, and inspected another image of the same subject.

"Do you have a name for me, Aidan?"

"Oleg Kredisov."

"Good." Finn smiled. "That's what we have, too."

Snow studied the flat features of the man, who had tried to kill him in Donetsk. The hair was neater, and the clothes were civilian, but the heavy eyebrows, dark eyes, and wide jaw were the same. He was standing outside what looked to be a modern, detached house, and had a cigarette in his hand. "Where was this taken?"

Finn pointed toward the grubby window. "About a

mile that way."

"He's meant to be dead." Snow slid the tablet back across the table. "The last time I saw him he was sitting in a civilian car, which had been hit with a rocket propelled grenade."

"An RPG? Are you sure?"

"I fired it."

"That would explain the burns on his left arm."

Snow had been sent into Donetsk to locate and rescue a British student taken captive by pro-Russian insurgents. After finding the youth, he had barely managed to get them both out again. His report had been classified, but, in it, he had named Oleg Kredisov as the commander responsible for running the illegal detention camps. He was a member of an ultra-nationalist party, which believed the Kremlin was too soft on the west. "How did you get his name?"

"I can't tell you."

"So, why am I here?"

"I need you to positively identify Kredisov." Finn nodded at the tablet. "That isn't good enough. I need you to eyeball him."

"And if it is Kredisov, why is he here?"

"We got wind of something being planned, something big. Our signals intelligence picked up increased chatter. We were lucky, and pulled up an address. He was filmed entering and leaving that address three times over the past five days."

Snow leaned back in his chair, and folded his arms. "What is he planning?"

Finn sighed. "We don't know."

"So, when do you want me to ID him?"

Finn checked his watch. "Now would be a good time."

***

Finn's team gathered for their final mission briefing in the 'Superior Holidays' meeting room. Snow glanced out of the window, and noted the empty office was on the grandly named, Fleming Way. Snow hoped the targets would be shaken and not stirred, when members of the Metropolitan Police Service Counterterrorism Command (SO15) broke down their door.

"We keep it simple," Finn addressed Hughes, the SO15 team leader and then the rest of his men. "Alpha One makes entry via the front of the target address, whilst Alpha Two secures the rear. Once inside, Alpha One will secure all suspects."

Hughes, dressed in full midnight-blue tactical coveralls and body armour, bobbed his head. "Agreed."

Finn turned to a pair of female MI5 officers. "Golding and Lyons, once the x-rays are secured, you are to start your search of the house."

"Yes, boss," Golding, the shorter of the two women, replied.

"Snow, at this point, you will enter the target address, and make your formal identification of 'Suspect One' as Oleg Kredisov."

"Fingers crossed," Snow said.

Finn cut Snow a curt smile, before he stood, and declared the briefing over.

Having left his own Audi in the deserted car park, Snow found himself sitting in the front passenger seat of Finn's anonymous Vauxhall. The midmorning traffic was light, and the drizzle kept away pedestrians, as the convoy of undercover vehicles crept the mile to the target address in Crawley's Vancouver Drive.

"How many x-rays are we expecting?" Snow asked.

Finn grinned at Snow's use of the military term for 'suspects', "We've got three, including Kredisov."

"That's an odd number."

"Odd, as in not even, or odd, as in strange?"

"Both."

In four minutes, they were on target. Finn parked the Vauxhall in Auckland Close, directly opposite the target address. Seconds later, two unmarked VW people carriers, concealing the SO15 officers, screeched to a halt outside the detached house. A further non-descript Ford Mondeo, carrying Golding and Lyons, stopped behind them. The doors of the VWs opened, and, quicker than Snow had expected, the SO15 men streamed out. The entry-man held 'the persuader,' and without warning, slammed the battering ram into the uPVC front door. It gave on his second attempt, and the team filed swiftly into the building, weapons up. "Armed police!" was shouted as the team vanished through the doorway.

Finn tapped his left hand nervously on the steering wheel, before he put his right hand to his ear. "Okay, confirmed." Finn leapt out of the driver's seat, followed closely by Snow. They entered the hallway, where an officer stood at the bottom of the stairs.

"What have we got?" Finn asked.

"All three of them, sir." The officer inclined his head left. "In the lounge, first door there."

Finn took Snow further into the house. The carpeted hall led to a door, which gave way to a gloomy living room. Dark purple curtains were drawn over the window, preventing most of the daylight from penetrating. The main source of illumination came from an oversized television, which was hooked up to a PlayStation. On the floor, in amongst discarded takeaway pizza boxes and coke cans, three figures lay face down, their arms secured tightly with flexicuffs. Everything was silent, except for the sound of heavy boots moving around upstairs, and the disembodied voice of The Rock jabbering away on the console game.

"We got them all, sir," Hughes said. "They didn't try to run."

"Can you turn them over?" Finn asked.

"It'll be a pleasure."

Snow watched as each of the x-rays was rolled onto their backs. The first two Snow didn't recognise, but the third he did. Snow met Finn's expectant his gaze. "Yes, that's Oleg Kredisov."

Kredisov eyes narrowed, before fury flashed across his face, and he spat in Russian, "*Suka!*"

"What did he say?" Finn asked.

"He called me a bitch."

Kredisov continued to bark at Snow in Russian, it wasn't anything he hadn't heard before and he allowed himself a smile.

"Sir, we've got something up here," a voice called. It could have been either Golding or Lyons, Snow didn't know.

"Coming." Finn left the lounge, and bounded up the stairs. Snow followed, curious to see what the discovery was. At the top of the stairs, two SO15 men backed into the tiny bathroom to let them pass. Golding poked her head out of a doorway, and beckoned Finn inside. He was about to ask what she had found, when his mouth dropped open. It took several long seconds for Finn to find his voice again. "Don't touch anything. We'll have bomb disposal check it out."

Snow stepped into the bedroom. On the floor, laying diagonally, was a large, oblong-shaped, wooden packing case. The top had been removed to show a slightly smaller olive-drab, green metal box.

"What is that?" Finn asked Golding and Lyons.

"It looks to be some type of missile," Lyons stated. "But, I don't want to get too close to it."

Snow moved forward, and crouched over the box. He recognised the writing, but didn't believe what he was seeing. "That's an FIM-92 Stinger surface-to-air missile."

Finn let out a sigh of relief. "I think I can say we've had a result!"

"Did you know they had this?" Snow asked.

"No." Finn rubbed his hands together, and repeated himself, "This is a major result."

Thames House, London

Snow sat in the observation chamber, looking into the interview room and its occupant, Oleg Kredisov. The other two Russians who had been with him at the house had resolutely refused to speak, and were now pretending not to understand English. Hindered by their rules of interrogation, Finn and another officer, Marsh, had switched their attention on to Kredisov.

"You may as well come clean now, Oleg," Marsh said. "We've got the Stinger. What was the target?"

"Your mother." Kredisov's English was heavily accented. "Your mother was target."

"As a stand-up comedian, you are a bit crap, old son, aren't you?"

"As a terrorist, he's a lot crap," Finn added.

Kredisov furrowed his brows. "What is crap?"

"You are," Marsh said, with a polite smile.

"I'm going to take a wild guess, Oleg. You were planning on using the Stinger we found to bring down a passenger jet."

"I know nothing about that rocket," Kredisov grunted.

"You expect us to believe that, Oleg?" Marsh said flatly.

"I do not care. Believe what you like. I am here as a tourist."

Finn tried not to laugh. "A tourist?"

"Yes, I go to all the sites, south of England is very interesting place – Bath, Stonehenge, Brighton, Beachy Head."

"How did you get hold of the weapon?" Marsh asked.

"I do not know. Perhaps it was in Christmas cracker. Pull it, and POP, it is there."

The door to the observation chamber opened, and a bespectacled man, holding a sheet of A4 paper, entered. He had a sheen of sweat on his large brow. "Oh, he's in there," he exclaimed aloud to himself, before he noticed Snow. "And you are?"

"Aidan Snow, I'm from Six." Snow used the colloquial term for MI6.

"Edmond Huet." He paused, and pushed his heavy spectacles back up his nose. "You saw the Stinger?"

"I did."

"We have a problem." Huet hastily exited. A moment later, Snow saw the interview room door open, and Huet beckon to Finn. The pair then re-entered the observation room. Huet nodded at Snow. "Is he cleared to hear this?"

"Yes, Aidan is," Finn replied, with a bemused frown. "Edmond, what is it?"

Huet looked at both men in turn, before he took a deep calming breath. "The serial number of the Stinger you found tallies with one of two stolen three years ago."

"Oh shit." Finn leaned against the wall, his face

losing its colour, as the implication hit him.

"What?" Snow couldn't conceal his surprise. *How the hell did a pair of Stingers go missing?*

"We need to immediately close Gatwick," Finn said, recovering his composure. "Edmond, get hold of Gatwick control, and the Civil Aviation Authority. I'll take this upstairs to Burstow. We have to presume, until we know otherwise, the second Stinger is in play."

"I want to help," Snow said. "Tell me what you need."

Finn nodded. "Okay, thanks. I could use your eyes; you may see something we've missed. Edmond, after you've spoken to Gatwick, set Aidan up at a computer, and get him our surveillance footage."

***

The office was open plan, with the exception of a glass-walled meeting room in the centre. Snow sat at an empty desk, and scrolled through the surveillance footage of the address in Vancouver Drive. Snow didn't know where Five had hidden their camera, but the image was surprisingly clear, and showed the front of the house, square on.

The address had been under surveillance for ten days. Snow started at the beginning and moved forward, speeding the footage up, until he spotted movement. For the first two days, he saw only one man enter and leave the address, whom he recognised as being one of the Russians in custody, but, on the third day, a transit van reversed onto the drive. The Russian helped the driver open the rear doors, and they unloaded something into the garage.

Snow paused the footage and zoomed in, but the van and the shadows blocked his view. He squinted. *Was that a Stinger packing crate?* He let the footage run again. The van drove off, leaving the Russian to close the garage doors. Snow rewound the tape, and took a screenshot of the van and its number plate, and sent it to a printer, before, once more, cycling through the footage. Kredisov and the other Russian being held arrived, but apart from that, the only other visitors to the address carried post, or pizzas.

"Coffee." Finn placed a mug in front of Snow.

"Thanks. Any updates?"

Finn shook his head despondently. "No. To be honest, it's like looking for a needle in a haystack. It could be anywhere, but at least they don't have any targets to shoot at – Gatwick's on lock-down."

"What about the van?" Snow retrieved the photo from the printer.

"I had a car tail it into Kent. It stopped at an address in Rochester. The house is rented to a Polish national, who fit the description of the driver."

"Did your team search the van?"

"We had no reason to; it wasn't the van we were interested in - the driver seemed to be legitimate."

"Gatwick notwithstanding, there are three airports within an hour of that location. Kent International, Ashford, and Rochester."

For the second time that day, Snow saw Finn's face lose its colour. "Shit…what if they were planning to hit two airports?"

***

Snow left Thames House, and drove south out of London. There was nothing more he could do at Five. He'd just be getting in the way, as all hands sought to track down the transit van, and, potentially, the second Stinger. The afternoon traffic was heavy, as workers attempted to escape the city. Snow also needed to escape, so he headed for the coast, and the house his parents kept in Worthing.

Radio 4 played, as he drove. An announcement said

due to a bomb scare, all flights into Gatwick had been diverted, and all flights out were suspended. No doubt news crews had flooded the scene to capture images of armed police patrolling the area. However, a closed Gatwick meant traffic and tailbacks on the M25, A24, and the M23.

Snow sighed, he'd have to go cross-country, via Sevenoaks and Tunbridge Wells. As he continued to drive south, something started to nag Snow; an overwhelming sensation something wasn't right. He thought back on the events of the day. Five knew somewhere two rogue Stingers existed, but Finn had not known Kredisov's group were in possession of at least one of them.

Was it luck they had discovered the single Stinger, or something else? Where had the Intel on Kredisov come from, and why had the Russians made no attempt to evade arrest? Kredisov, at least, was battle-hardened, so why was he happily sitting, unarmed, eating pizza with a stolen surface-to-air missile in the room above his head? Snow didn't have answers to any of these questions, and it irked him.

The clock ticked to five, and the evening news program started. The progress of the Russian fleet had now been knocked off the top spot by the news of Gatwick's closure. The BBC had dug up an expert on aviation security, and he gave his considered opinion. The expert discussed several previous security alerts, and what this new scare may, or may not, mean for air travellers.

Ultimately, however, the media didn't know the real story. Snow knew behind the scenes his old Regiment, the SAS, would be on standby to swoop in, should circumstances necessitate their presence. The expert finished his spiel, and the news switched back to the Russian fleet. A reporter, live at Beachy Head, stated the fleet should be visible within the next hour, off the East Sussex coast. Something again nagged at Snow. *Where had he heard Beachy*

Head mentioned before? Then it came to him, Kredisov had named it as a place he had visited. Was this just a coincidence? Snow still couldn't see a connection but on a whim, he decided he'd go there, and try to catch a glimpse of the Russian fleet for himself.

***

Snow managed to find a space in a lay-by, and parked his Audi. Stepping out into the breeze, he strode over the undulating grass toward the cliff edge, where a crowd had gathered. He spotted a TV news crew interviewing a man, who had a large pair of binoculars strung around his neck. Snow moved away. He had no desire to be famous, and looked out to sea. He saw a smudge of black smoke, which seemed to be getting larger.

"It's bloody awful isn't it?" a voice said. Standing next to him, now, was a grey-haired rambler. He, too, had the requisite pair of field glasses. "Look at the filth coming out of that thing; it's like it's on fire!" The hulking shape of the *Admiral Kuznetsov*, Russia's only aircraft carrier, appeared through the smoke. "If you ask me," the elderly rambler continued, "it's nothing but a provocation, having them sail in our waters! I bet the Russians wouldn't allow the Royal Navy to mess about near St. Petersburg."

Snow gave a non-committal nod, as the other ships in the convoy became clearer. They were much nearer to land than he had expected. The Russian ships, escorted by British warships, looked out of place in the English Channel, grey smudges on a navy-blue sea.

"And imagine if something goes wrong with any of them? We'd be blamed, and then, it would be World War Three! He's already got his bombers buzzing us!"

A thought struck Snow. "Can I borrow your binoculars for a moment?"

"Of course."

Snow raised the lenses to his eyes, and the warships swam into focus. He could see ratings on the deck of the aircraft carrier and a couple of jets. The smoke swirled in front of the *Admiral Kuznetsov*, again, obscuring the deck. Snow shifted his focus to the other ships, and started to lower the binoculars, but then something caught his eye—a shape not at sea but on the land.

Snow panned to his left, and saw a white transit van parked on the grass, overlooking the cliff. The van rocked slightly on its suspension, as the driver climbed out. A face filled Snow's vision; it was the same driver he had seen on the surveillance tape. And then Snow understood everything. He hurriedly handed the binoculars back to the rambler, and started to walk towards the van.

In between him and the van, the ground dipped. Unseen for a several strides, Snow increased his pace, until he crested the rise. He was now no more than twenty feet from the van, and its back doors were open. Focussing on nothing but the doors, Snow sprinted across the uneven grass. He arrived at the van, took a beat to compose himself, and then peered inside.

The cargo space was empty. Snow crept around to the far side of the van. Moving away, and toward the edge of the cliff, he now saw the driver. An olive green, box-shaped cage rested on his shoulder, with a tube protruding out over his back. Snow shuddered; it was the second Stinger.

The driver continued to walk toward a path, along the edge of the cliff. If he ran, could he get there in time to stop the Stinger from being launched? Once he was seen, that would be it. There was only one course of action available to him.

Snow slipped inside the van, and released the hand brake. It started to silently roll forward, toward its owner.

Snow stayed low, leaning over the passenger seat to minimize his profile. The van picked up speed, and he held the wheel with a firm grip, as it bounced over the grass. The driver stopped at the very edge of the cliff, and shifted his shoulders to adjust the weight of the Stinger. Snow had no choice; he had to stop it from being fired.

He twisted the key in the ignition, and the engine came to life with an angry groan. The driver turned his head, as Snow floored the accelerator. The driver's eyes became wide. He froze – his brain yelling that he was about to be hit, but his body unable to move...

Snow threw himself out of the open door, as the vehicle struck the driver, sending him, the van, and the Stinger over the edge of the cliff.

Snow rolled, sky and grass swopping places several times, before he came to a stop. He lay still, and listened. There was a thud and a crunch of tearing metal, as the van hit the rocks below, but no explosion. Snow rose to his knees, and then to his feet. Behind him, there were concerned shouts from onlookers. He ignored these, and followed the tracks torn into the grass by the van's tyres. He stared over the edge. The van had landed on its nose, concertinaed. It lay on its side. Next to it, on a stretch of sand, was the Stinger. The body of the driver was nowhere to be seen.

Snow pulled out his secure Blackberry, and dialled Finn's number. "Stand down. I've found your missile."

***

Thames House, London.

"I don't believe the plan was ever to hit anything," Snow said. "I think the idea was to fire off the Stinger in the general direction of the Russian ships, so their radar would ping it as a threat."

"How can you be so sure?" Finn asked.

"The Stinger uses an auto-director to search for its target - a heat source, for example, a jet engine or helicopter turbines."

"So, it couldn't hit a warship?"

"Not unless it was fired without guidance. The heat source isn't intense enough."

"Surely the one we found in Crawley was going to be used against a passenger plane?"

"Perhaps." Snow paused to sip the MI5 machine coffee; it tasted faintly of soup. "Where did you get the Intel about Kredisov and his group being in Crawley?"

"I can't say."

"My guess is it was purposely fed to you. Kredisov was sacrificed to cause a diversion."

"So, what were they trying to do? Create a 'false flag' situation, where the Russians would think they were under attack? That makes no sense."

"Does anything? We know Kredisov is a card-carrying member of an ultra-nationalist party which insists Putin is too soft on the west. What better way to force his hand than to attack the Russian flagship?"

"That's enough theories for one night." Finn let out a yawn. He'd been running on caffeine and a prayer for the last four hours, since Snow had prevented the attack. "I'm just glad I requested your secondment."

"Please don't make a habit of it," Snow replied, as he finished his coffee.

***

THE RETREAT

Jane E. James

Day One: They Don't Sleep

I watched them arrive in a velvety smog that clung to their perfect silhouettes and I realised dismally that I was different to them, and always would be.

As they came walking down the drive, it also became clear the three women had already bonded during their three-hour car journey. I could tell this by the secretive way they smiled at each other without having to say a word. The division came as no surprise. They were from the north of England while I was from the south, and because of this I'd had to travel up alone. Although I am by nature a loner, I'd hated arriving first and having to clumsily match up rusty keys to stubborn doors. Being first might have afforded me the luxury of exploring the Old Vicarage alone – but I hadn't the courage to claim the best room for myself or venture onto the isolated moor.

The four of us had been friends on Facebook for a while but it had been my idea to arrange this week-long writer's retreat. That was forgotten about, though, the moment Beth decided to take charge and, rather than book the coastal cottage in Cornwall we'd previously settled on, she insisted we come here instead, to this rambling five-bedroom house perched precariously on the northern edge of the Yorkshire Dales.

Although the Old Vicarage had been described as 'having character' for me it lacked warmth. The challenging drive through a free-ranging, unfenced herd of bored cattle who refused to move out of the way, followed by a hair-raising descent down a slippery hill hadn't exactly endeared me to its remote location.

Although I knew I was close, the house still took me by surprise when I happened upon it. It appeared out of nowhere with a grey ethereal mist clinging to its chimneys and there was something sinister about its shuttered windows. I don't mind admitting the silence of the place unsettled my city girl senses. It soon became clear though that Beth, Laura and Denise did not share my reservations. Their exclamations of delight followed them around the rambling house as they dived first into one room and then another with me lagging behind; already the slow, awkward one of the four.

We all thought we knew each other but until today none of us had actually met in person. Even so, our faces were as familiar to each other as our closest friends and family. Paranormal best-selling author Beth, with her swishy blonde hair and green cat-like eyes was the pretty, popular one. Gothic horror writer Laura, was a head taller than anyone else and had a severe pony tail that made her look fierce; yet she was generally the kindest one of the three. Then, last but by no means least, came supernatural Kindle star Denise, who laughed a lot and had a potty mouth. In comparison, I was the short, dumpy one and, unlike me, they were way more attractive than their author photos. They were already quite famous and I was just starting out; a regional crime writer who was scared of her own shadow. Because of this, I suspected they would overlook me just as much in real life as they did on social media. I had never really been important to them.

That first night, everyone but me stayed up late. Convinced I wouldn't be able to compete with their lively discussions on the craft of writing I retired early to my smaller-than-anybody-else's bedroom, intending to finish a short story; my contribution to a charity crime collection of dark tales being produced by my publisher. The room was chilly, despite the heating being on full blast, and my fingers grew numb with cold. Stopping at 2,000 words I was surprised to find it had gone midnight and I could no longer hear the sound of my friends' tinny laughter echoing below me. *That's strange*, I thought, *I didn't hear them come upstairs.*

I climbed out of the austere metal bed and ignored the picture of Christ on a cross nailed to the wall. My bare feet squeaked on the wooden floorboards as I went to investigate. Why I didn't simply pull the covers over my head and ignore the silence, I'll never know.

The landing was eerily lit and even colder than my bedroom and I could see the doors to the other three bedrooms were wide open. Without prying I could tell that they were all empty. Hesitating at the top of the stairs I listened again but only silence greeted me. Could they have fallen asleep in front of the wood-burning stove? Although I knew this was unlikely, I made myself go downstairs to check, drawn like a moth to the light shining underneath the living room door. Imagine my surprise then, when I pushed open the door and discovered the big dusty room was empty. Not only that but everything had been tidied away. Every cushion had been plumped and straightened and not a wine glass remained behind. This was definitely not the behaviour I expected from Beth, Laura and Denise, who normally relied on PAs and housekeepers to take care of their every need.

Something was not right. I could feel it in my bones and in the icy air that spiralled out of my mouth. But I knew they couldn't have just vanished. So, where were they? At this point it did cross my mind that their disappearance might be part of an elaborate trick meant to frighten me. If so, it was already working. On that daunting thought, I decided to go back to bed. I'd rather hide under the covers than give them the satisfaction of scaring me half to death.

Creeping along on tippy-toes, I headed once more for the stairs, blindly clawing at the hateful cobwebs that clung to my face. They seemed to come from nowhere.

That's when I noticed the cellar door was open and knew straight away that something was amiss. Having followed the other three into it earlier, I knew it was cold, damp and spooky down there. I hadn't been in it three minutes before imagining walkers lost on the dales might have been taken there and tortured; never to be heard of again.

Peering warily down the concrete steps, ignoring the ominous creaking of the door on its rusty hinges, I heard a shuffling sound and quickly flicked on the light switch. To my relief, a trickle of gloomy light appeared and at first glance everything was as it should be. No ghouls or demons lurked below. Not even a mouse was visible. But I could not see all of the cellar from here and, wanting to be 100 per cent sure there was nothing down there, I toyed with the idea of going further down the cellar steps; knowing I never would. Then, I heard it again... that swishy, sloppy sound, like a lazy foot being dragged along the floor. My whole face stretched in fear when I realised I was already staring at what had made that noise.

Their faces and bodies might be hidden silently in the shadows but I immediately recognised the three pairs of bare feet lined up by the wall. Although my heart was in my mouth, no matter how much I wanted to I could not move away from the cellar door. From here I could smell my friends' claustrophobic perfume. The sickly-sweet aroma reminded me of rotting meat and I wondered why I had not noticed this before. As my eyes adjusted to the dim lighting, I was at last able to make out that each woman stood facing the wall with her head hung low; like a child sulking in a corner. Not once did they glance up to acknowledge they were aware of my presence. I honestly think I would have passed out from sheer fright if they had. Their toes were abnormally grey and like dead people they were creepily still.

So much so I began to wonder if I had conjured up the entire scene in my head. Was I sleepwalking? Was I in the middle of a bad dream? Why else would these three intelligent women be standing like frozen statues in the cellar, never once talking or moving. Why weren't they tucked up asleep in their beds?

Having held my breath for too long, I greedily sucked in air and was horrified to see one of the women's heads (Beth's I think), start to turn in my direction. I'm sure my heart stopped beating for a terrifying second or two. Catching a glimpse of wild straggly hair and a black dilated pupil, I slammed the door on this abominable sight and fled back up the stairs; never once daring to look back over my shoulder.

***

Day Two: They Can't Eat

I was doing clumsy lengths of the indoor pool when they came in. It didn't surprise me to see that all three women, with their immaculately straightened hair, wore incredibly tiny bikinis, showing off china-white skin and flat stomachs. With my old-fashioned swimsuit and ugly swim cap, it had never been more obvious how out of their league I was. With unsmiling faces, they walked into the water together, not pausing, as I had done, to acclimatise to the temperature. Straight away I noticed the bruising on Laura's body and the cut above one eye. Strange, but I couldn't remember them being there yesterday.

As they swam toward me, each mimicking the other's identical breast stroke, I changed direction at the last minute; heaving myself up and out of the pool to avoid a collision. So far this morning, not one of them had spoken to me. Nor did they appear to be communicating with each other; except perhaps in a weird telepathic way.

Last night, after I had fled upstairs, somebody had

tried the handle on my bedroom door. Luckily, I'd had the foresight to lock it after me and whoever it was gave up after a few attempts. Naturally enough, I didn't get much shut-eye after that. Enough was enough and I made up my mind to leave the next morning. I left the house as soon as it was light, only to discover my car tyres had been slashed. Filled with an increasing sense of dread and convinced somebody was keeping a close eye on me, I glanced up at Beth's bedroom window to see a trio of still shadows observing me through the glass.

During breakfast I made every effort to get back on a normal footing with them, chatting nervously about my plans for the day as I pushed scrambled egg around my plate, too sick with worry to eat. Instead of joining in with the conversation, they stared queasily at my plate and even turned their noses up at the pot of coffee I made them.

After my swim, I'd taken my phone up to the east bedroom to see if I could get a connection. So far, I hadn't been able to ring home at all. I couldn't even log on to social media or send a text message. So, as advised by the holiday manual, I stood on the window sill and placed my phone close to the catch on the sash window but still couldn't get a solitary bar. Sighing, I climbed back down, noticing for the first time that Beth hadn't unpacked her case. Curiosity piqued, I took advantage of my friends' absence and checked out the other bedrooms. Here, the story was just the same. None of the women had taken out so much as a toothbrush. Even more worrying was the pile of mobile phones I found in the basin of Denise's en suite bathroom. It looked as if they had deliberately been left there to drown in a puddle of water.

When I caught sight of them walking back from the private pool complex, which was situated close to the house,

I noticed that the cows in the field ignored them; yet this morning one of them had angrily stomped its foot at me. I hated the strange way the three women seemed to glide through the grass, rather than walk. The rest of their movements were jerky and unnatural, as if their heads no longer belonged to their bodies. I also noticed Denise no longer laughed at every little thing the other two said, that Laura's fierce expression now suited her and Beth's eyes were full of spite. This realisation terrified me so much my hands shook as I trawled once again through the holiday manual. I didn't really know what I hoped to find but when I stumbled across a paragraph explaining the owner would call to see us on the first full day of our stay, I felt such relief.

That afternoon, while the others were holed up in Beth's bedroom doing God knows what, I remained in the garden, kicking rotten fruit off the grass and hoping to come across Penny, the owner, before they did. Today, I had no heart to enjoy the sudden crispness of the leaves on the trees or the golden autumnal hues evident in the hedgerows. The cawing of the crows, which had somewhat perturbed me when I first arrived, no longer made me anxious, even when the birds boldly followed in my footsteps, no doubt having fun at my expense. What did worry me though was the occasional snarling noise coming from the surrounding woodland. It sounded like no animal I had ever heard before.

By 4pm I knew Penny wasn't going to show and began to fear that something may have happened to her. I was certain she was not the type of woman to let her holidaymakers down. I also knew I was soon going to have to go back inside and face the others. By now the sky had darkened and the mist was starting to make its steadfast appearance. There was something about the uncurling fog that held me spellbound and as I allowed it to settle creepily around my shoulders, I saw something black and dramatic emerge from the woodland.

From a distance of thirty feet away, I watched a menacing creature pause in its prowling to turn and stare in my direction; its savage lip curling up to reveal yellow canines. I'd heard rumours of a black beast roaming the Yorkshire dales but never expected to see it; nor be seen by it. Bigger than the largest of dogs, its shoulders slunk low as it crawled out of the woodland; orange eyes appeared like two burning lumps of coal. I had no idea what name was given to this type of wild cat but I could tell it was powerful enough to maul an adult human to death.

Fortunately, the beast didn't appear the slightest bit interested in me and soon dissolved mysteriously back into the mist. I sensed that its insidious appearance was no accident. The black beast was as much a part of the mystery enveloping our retreat as we were. Not wanting to come across it again, I hurried back inside the house; unconvinced I was any safer within its formidable walls.

Much later, I found myself sitting by an unlit fire, listening mawkishly to the wind howling down the chimney and jumping each time a twig or stone flew up against the window. So much for a relaxed time away, I complained inwardly. Rather than concentrate on my short story, I had spent the last hour biting my fingernails down to sore bloody stubs.

Earlier, I had bumped into Laura on the stairs, an occurrence made doubly awkward by the fact she was on her own and still wouldn't acknowledge me. I was shocked to discover that the bruising on her body was now migrating to her face. There was also freshly congealed blood around the cut on her eye and the sickly rotten meat smell was as prevalent as ever; so much so I had to hold my breath until she reached the bottom of the stairs. I didn't have to wait long to find out the reason for her sneaking around alone, because when I came downstairs again I discovered my phone had disappeared from the window seat where I left it. By now, I guessed it must have joined the others in the sink. The lack of signal might have made the phone unusable, but the absence of it made me feel more isolated than ever. I was becoming increasingly fearful of this house and its occupants.

A clap of thunder and a flickering of the lamp beside me soon had me out of my chair and I scurried like a frightened mouse into the kitchen to search for candles. The idea of being without light in this house at night filled me with such terror that I couldn't stop shaking. I found a half-burnt candle in a drawer but just as I managed to light it the electricity went off. This was the last straw! Tomorrow I was getting out of here. Car or no car. Until then, I had to weather one more night. Not knowing how I would get through it, I felt my way upstairs; cradling the candle's flame from sudden drafts. On the landing, I paused to listen out for sound coming from the other three bedrooms.

I felt it long before I saw it. Its sleek black outline meant it was almost invisible. But its long black tail whacking against the wooden floorboards alerted me to the fact that it was lying right outside Beth's door. If it hadn't blinked when it did, I wouldn't have recognised its orange eyes in the darkness. Flattening my back against the wall, I watched the wild cat bare its teeth at me, dripping saliva onto its glossy paws. As I backed away, it followed my painfully slow progress along the landing and only abandoned its guarding stance once it realised I was no longer any threat. Just before closing and locking my bedroom door behind me, I saw it curl up on the floor outside Beth's door and begin to purr like a domestic cat.

***

Day Three: And They Won't Let Her Leave...

Although the disturbances ended abruptly at 2am, unnervingly followed by the disgusting sound of vomiting from nearby rooms, I couldn't be sure their persecution wouldn't start up again. At 8am the diluted winter sun was finally showing through cracks in the clouds, and I felt I could at last unwind my stiff limbs and breathe again.

I should have been lugging my case downstairs but fear prevented me. All I could think about was the warning I had received.

As before, the terror started with somebody turning the handle of my bedroom door and when that wouldn't open, they progressed to raking their nails down it. A truly blood-curdling sound that had me on the edge of my bed for the best part of an hour. By then my solitary candle had burnt out and only a partial moon kept me company but I could still sense shadows moving around on the landing. Eventually, I had crept over to the door and put my ear to it.

'What do you want?' I called out in a voice that didn't seem to belong to me and I recognised this was because I hadn't spoken to a living soul in days. With trembling fingers, I slid the key out of the lock but when I put my squinting eye to it, I realised what a terrible mistake this was. The distorted vision on the other side was more horrific than anything I could dream up for one of my novels.

A few seconds was all it took for me to make out the withered faces of Beth, Laura and Denise peering back at me and I stepped away so fast I actually went sprawling across the floor, twisting my ankle and grazing my elbow. Retreating like a beaten dog to the furthest corner of the room, I buried my face in my hands and started to sob.

'Go away. Leave me alone,' I whimpered noiselessly, not wanting to give away my whereabouts in the room. But although I tried not to think about what I had witnessed, all I could see when I closed my eyes was their glassy-eyed stare. Five minutes later a note with childish handwriting was pushed under the door. *We won't let you leave*, it warned. One look at my packed suitcase would have told them my plan.

By nine o'clock I was ready. Instinctively, I knew that once I left my bedroom there would be no going back. So, with a shaky intake of breath, I pulled open the door and took a brave step forward onto the landing. As I did so, I felt my face stretch out of shape with horror at the carnage that was in front of me. The wild cat was dead. Fact. But not naturally dead, if that made any sense. Sprawled out on the floor outside Beth's door, the animal's corpse had decayed almost beyond recognition. But no matter how dramatic its death might have been, this level of putrefaction couldn't have happened overnight. Already, its black glossy coat had turned an unhealthy shade of grey and its splintered bones poked up from a disembowelled belly. Although there were no longer any predatory eyes left in its shrunken head to observe me creeping quietly down the stairs, I remained on edge anyway in case one of the bedroom doors creaked upon as I passed by. Convinced either Beth, Laura or Denise was about to jump on my back and maul me with their discoloured, loosened teeth, I felt sick with fear and an awful sense of foreboding. My ordeal wasn't over yet, I could tell. The worst was yet to come.

The worst was waiting for me in the kitchen. Beth, Laura and Denise – all sitting around the table like Stepford wives – looking hauntingly gaunt. The warning I had been given last night was about to come true. I was sure of it. But when I moved unintentionally, creating a swishing anorak sound, I couldn't believe it when not one of them stood up to challenge me. Although I was still scared out of my wits, this knowledge gave me the confidence to start edging toward the door. That's when I realised their soulless eyes weren't even trained on me. Instead, they were focused on the laptops in front of them and without once looking up they persisted in furiously tapping away at their powerless keyboards. Their once glossy hair now hung lifelessly down their backs, I noticed, and Beth's previously talon-like nails were shredded down to nothing and the remains of her red nail polish appeared like splashes of blood. Their downturned faces reminded me of spoilt children used to getting their own way. And no words appeared on the black screens in front of them.

When I reached the gravel drive, a quick glance over my shoulder confirmed I wasn't being followed. So far, so good, I thought, but as soon as I got to the top of the steep incline, I paused for breath and looked down at the house. I felt ridiculously pleased to discover how small and insignificant it appeared; swallowed up as it was by the huge valley that surrounded it. From here, I could just about make out the doll-like figures of Beth, Laura and Denise who had come outside to see me off. They were too far away to do me any harm but I sensed their faces were screwed up in confusion; as if they were sorry to see me go. I raised my hand in the smallest of salutes and then turned my back on them; painfully regretting ever wanting to be like them.

I must have tramped for three miles without seeing another dwelling on the horizon. Having found a gnarled piece of wood, the perfect size for a walking aid and fending off inquisitive cows, I didn't pause anywhere too long, just in case. Until I reached civilisation, and by that I meant a city – not a hamlet or even a town, I wouldn't feel safe.

When I eventually stumbled upon a sign for Richmond, which turned out to be only another two miles away, my sagging energy levels received a huge boost. For the first time in days I felt positive and almost broke into song.

At the same time, I noticed the battered Range Rover poking out from a jagged rock ledge some fifty feet below. It was hidden by dense woodland and nobody driving by would ever know it was there. As all of my calls of 'Is anyone in there?' went unanswered, I felt I had no choice but to make my way down there to see if anyone had survived the crash. It was a tricky descent and at times I grew frightened I would tumble to my death and have my tongue pecked out by crows. But after everything I had been through I was determined to survive, so I clung desperately to clumps of wet moorland grass that sliced my fingers, until eventually I did make it to safety. Driving me on was the knowledge that I might not have been able to help Beth, Laura and Denise but I could save these poor crash victims and be a hero for once.

When I made it on to the same rocky ledge as the car and took a first tentative peek inside, I was deeply shaken to discover this was no conventional accident. The discovery wiped me off my feet and left me shaking, crying and screaming in the chilly afternoon air. It must have taken me a good fifteen minutes to get back up again. But get up again I did. Because I needed to start piecing together the terrible tragedy that had happened here. The biggest giveaway was of course the dead wild cat slung over the dented bonnet of the car, crushed and partly decapitated where it had impacted against the rock.

Beth would have been driving too fast as usual and ignoring all of Laura's responsibly barked directions. In the back, Denise would have been laughing at all their jokes; more desperate to fit in than I had ever been. I can imagine Beth reaching for a lipstick as they drew closer to the house; wanting to look her absolute best on arrival. In that split second, the wild cat must have run across the pot-holed farm track; snarling with fear when it realised too late its destiny. Together, cat and car would have plummeted off the road into the booby-trapped canyon below, bouncing sickeningly from one outcrop of rock to another; before finally impaling itself on the lower branches of an ancient woodland tree.

Peering through the driver's blood-splattered window, I swallowed a mouthful of vomit and then gagged some more. An unbuckled Beth had gone straight through the windscreen and her bloodied head now rested sentimentally against the wild cat's body; as if they were already the best of friends. 'Where had it escaped from?' she might have asked herself on the slow-motion way down.

Laura's battered head was buried in the dashboard but her body remained in a brace position. She might have been sensible enough to prepare for the crash but nothing could have prevented her being crushed to death by Denise in the back seat.

It took me longer to work out what happened to Denise because her injuries were not immediately obvious; but I suspected she may have bled to death. An agonising demise brought on by a jagged piece of branch that pierced one of her lower organs.

The loss of three such incredibly talented writers would be felt by many; myself included. But in light of their unconcealed disregard for me, I couldn't resist being amused by the fact that in death they now resembled the ghosts and monsters they once wrote about. Sales of their books would no doubt rocket and they would be remembered in the publishing world for many years to come; but eventually their celebrity status would fade.

I had always known I was different to them and now I knew why. I am alive, I am pleased to say, while they are dead. And from this day on, I will be as famous as they were, if not more so; because unlike them I still have a great many books to write.

They might have died on the way to the Old Vicarage but with one last book to finish, the three career-minded women had been determined they still had a writer's retreat to attend. And so they had.

OUT OF RETIREMENT

Mark L. Fowler

'What!' I said. 'Murder of Albert Jenkins? Too much of an eye for young women,' I said. 'Same as the rest of them. Taking me where? I'll be blessed.'

There wasn't much point going to the police station because they didn't listen when we got there. Two of them in a room you couldn't swing a cat in. The young devils charged me with killing Albert Jenkins. I'd have raised them with some respect for their elders.

Seems that someone with too much mouth and too little sense let on about me and Albert seeing a bit of each other. We're no spring chickens, but it's still not a criminal offence, at least not in my book.

They let on how I turned a bit sour when I saw Albert coming out of the Admiral's Club with that Hilda Preston. (She's barely old enough to be drawing pension!) Now I don't deny I might have said one or two things, but nothing undeserved. Seems they heard me dishing out home truths and saw me buying rat poison. What of it? And even if I did say, 'Hanging's too good for the likes of Albert Jenkins,' it doesn't prove I poisoned him.

'I believe you visited Mr Jenkins late that evening,' says this copper, like he's already made his mind up. I was in two minds whether to let him feel the back of my hand for his trouble.

'When I visited Albert Jenkins *late that evening*,' I said, 'it was to give him his ring back. I told him he could keep it for one of his young trollops who would let herself be bought for a bit of fool's gold.'

'What happened next, Miss Wilson?'

I said, 'What do you think happened next? I told Albert Jenkins to keep out of my way in future, and to sleep with an eye open.'

Well, this copper's wearing out his pencil writing it

all down. Then he says, 'You didn't share a coffee with Mr Jenkins?'

Enough was enough. 'Would you share a coffee with someone after you'd thrown an engagement ring in his face!'

I know I shouldn't lose my temper, but I'd heard enough from that insolent wretch, and I gave him a backhander or two. Couldn't have lived with myself if I hadn't. Next thing I've got three of them manhandling me into a cell. I tell you, I never thought I'd see the day it took so much muscle to get a poor defenceless old lady behind bars.

Reckon they thought they'd leave me to cool off. But what with the uncomfortable bed and me with all my errands to do... Well, by morning I was livid. I didn't let on at first, of course. Thought I'd see how the land lay. But when this suited bit-of-a-kid started asking the most rude and personal questions – well, I'm afraid I saw red. I had a damned good try at fetching his eye out, and I'd have had it clean out of its socket if he hadn't pressed one of them alarm buttons and had half the police station running in to help. I can tell you, I was quite pleased with the mess I made. I'm not as young as I used to be.

Anyway, that did it. Next thing they brought out the white coats and the needles, just like before. Then this doctor comes to see me, up at St Jude's. Smart looking chap, and didn't he know it. Brings this great thick file with him too.

'What's that?' I said. *'This is Your Life?'*

It was, too. All my records going back donkey's years, things they reckon I'd done. Things they locked me away for. What they never seem to take into account is what those men did to *me*.

Take George Robinson. He'd have had me at the altar back in 1959 if he hadn't tried out his wares on that skinny tramp from the factory. I thought, in the circumstances, that a couple of ripped throats was being merciful. I'm only flesh and blood, you know. But some people don't get any luck in this life, because blow me down, if the same thing doesn't happen the minute I'm out and breathing free air. Ned Jacobs and that farm tart, making a proper fool of me. I followed them to the old barn and made use of that petrol Ned's father was saving for the shortage.

Made a cozy little blaze and no mistake.

But that's old business. It's what happened this morning that's got my goat.

The doctor shows me this bit of paper. 'Looks like you've come out of retirement, Miss Wilson.'

I let it go. I thought: *Whose heart will* you *be breaking tonight?* He had that twinkle about him. You know the kind.

'I'd like you to read it and tell me what you think, Miss Wilson,' he says, in that oh so smoo-oo-ooth voice. Reckons I wrote it last night after one of those psychosessions or whatever he calls them. Looked a bit like my writing, but these mental-doctors can have you believing black's white.

'Well, Miss Wilson?'

I said, 'Somebody's been a naughty girl.'

He shakes his head, and then blow me if he doesn't start reading it out! '*I wouldn't lose any sleep over Albert Jenkins, not when you've heard the truth of it.*' He stops reading and looks at me. 'Shall I go on, Miss Wilson?'

I said, 'Why not? I like a nice story.'

He starts reading again. '*When I called to give him his ring back, I might have left it at giving him a couple of rounds with the poker. But while I was standing at his front door, I saw him, through the gap in his curtains, kissing his fancy piece.*'

I said, 'You certainly know how to tell a story, doctor.'

He raised his eyebrows and went on. '*Then I saw her shoot out the back door while he came to answer the front. I kept my cool. I thought, "Let's see how he plays it". All lovey-dovey, he was. "Oh, Ethel, I've been a fool," he starts. "Can you forgive me?" Next minute he's down on one knee. "Let's consummate our love tonight."*

'*Well, once he'd said that, I knew the die was cast. I said, "Albert, you're an old devil, but I'll give you your due: you know how to treat a lady." You should have seen the glint in his eye. He thought everything was sorted. That's a man for you. "I'll make us a cuppa," I said.*

'*He was a strong one, I'll give him that. He fought that poison for hours. I was in no hurry. I sat grinning like butter wouldn't melt, right up until I saw his light fading. Then I took that fool's gold off my finger and let him have it in the face.*'

The doctor stopped reading.

'I was just enjoying that,' I said.

'Is there anything you would like to add, Miss Wilson?'

'Yes, as a matter of fact.' I watched his eyes widen. I said, 'You don't have the first clue how to do voices.'

He gave me one of those smiley looks that's meant to confuse you, then took the note outside with him. Left me alone and thinking. They do that a lot. Anyway, I started to think that maybe he was right, that I had come 'out of retirement'. I felt all the old feelings starting to bubble up. All I ever wanted was a man I could trust and a child to pour my heart into. I might have asked for the Holy Grail. I tried turning a blind eye, keeping my mouth shut, putting it down to their nature. But the feelings always got too strong.

They want drowning at birth, the lot of them.

I heard footsteps coming back along the corridor. He came in, still holding his bit of paper. I could see he wasn't going to give up. I said, 'Some of it sounds a bit like the way

I take off when I'm upset.' I thought that might be an end to it. But then he turns the paper over and you've never seen anything like it. Things I'm supposed to have written, confessions that would turn the stomach of a butcher.

'What do you have to say about this little lot, Ethel?' he asks me.

I said, 'You sound more like a policeman than a doctor. And it's Miss Wilson to you.'

I looked at the page again. 'I'll be blessed,' I said. 'Something needs doing.'

'Any suggestions?' he asks, his face right in mine. But fancy aftershave can't hide the smell of deceit. *Out of retirement*, I thought to myself, and I felt the old shiver working down to my fingernails.

For a moment I pitied him. His ignorance was legion. All he could see was a withered old girl.

'I'm coming out of retirement,' I whispered.

'What was that?'

His face was close enough to kiss.

'Pay attention,' I said. 'This is my last performance.'

DON'T GO TO MARSH TOWN, JOHNNY RAY!

Charlie Flowers and Hannah Haq

'**S**hit.'

Johnny Ray Randell blinked once, blinked twice, and tried to sit up from his sofa. He sat right back down in the grip of an epic hangover and checked his watch. 9:25.

He grimaced and surveyed the wreckage of his flat. Neat stripped pine floors, immaculate posters on the walls... and several dozen cans and bottles, cored out and dead, littered about.

Johnny Ray sat up.

The television was still on and now showing Loose Women.

He hunted for the remote and after a minute, gave up. He looked around his flat, the most des res on Morris Avenue in Jaywick, the only one with locks on the doors, and he shrugged. Good enough.

And then his shrug stopped.

'Ella?'

No answer. No bark back.

Where the fuck was his dog?

He got up, and kicked over two empty cans of Nurishment, and wobbled, thinking about the day's schedule and his predicament. Dammit. The fog would lift soon. OK. First call was the post office to draw out the dole. Second was the landlord to hand out most of it. Third call was The Pelican, the estate pub which would be open, to ascertain what had happened over the last twenty-four hours and where the entire fuck his dog had gone.

***

Johnny Ray fixed up. He brushed his teeth, smoothed his hair, and changed his clothes. He then locked up his little house on Morris Avenue, and walked to the sea wall, leaning on his stick, and hopped up on it, cursing that bad leg, lit the first cigarette of the day.

'Where did it all go wrong, George Best,' he muttered; his own grim joke that he'd repeated like a mantra down the last decade of band success, band failure, publishing success, the coiled snake of hard drugs, and then a cut-snake of a fiancée he'd spent five years trying to escape.

And escape he had. To the coast.

He breathed in. Ah, the sea air. The ozone. Jaywick. To his right, the wind turbines turned lazily. They seemed to stir the sea.

He massaged his crocked leg. The pain was dull but it would be back with a vengeance. He had his medicine to hand, the old trusty bottle of Frosty Jack. A nice buzz on this late morning.

That buzz went as far back as the crash that had sent his life wonky. A van had gone into the back of his van at forty miles per hour on the A12; the driver had been uninsured and only held a provisional licence obtained under false pretences.

Johnny Ray had come out of the hospital two months later, alive but with smashed bones and multiple addictions. A month after that, his relationship had gone south when she realised he couldn't earn anymore. The job had gone two weeks after the smash. The flat had gone a week after she'd walked.

And the driver who had nearly killed him, and set his life on its glorious path, got a ban and a suspended sentence.

C'est la vie.

***

But then there had always been Ella, Johnny Ray's faithful Staffie.

She'd turned up one day and never left, schlepping along to every Johnny Ray gig going. He named her Ella after Ella Fitzgerald and she was the one thing the ex hadn't taken, the one link to his previous life and the one thing that saved him in this one.

Most evenings Johnny would sit on the old leather sofa that sat outside his trailer, drinking Frosty Jacks with Tex. Tex was a recovering alcoholic who had hit more bumps in the rehab road than a broken trailer trundling down Brooklands. He would store up his depressive episodes for weeks on end then have an abbreviated version of a complete breakdown on Johnny's sofa. When the drink ran out, the pills came in, and more often than not, Johnny would go there with him.

Ella had saved Johnny on more than one occasion, licking his face to bring him out of the drink-induced blackouts. That Devil Dog was Johnny Ray's very own personal Jesus. He smiled as he thought of her, her glossy brown hair and wide eyes. She reminded him of that bird out of the Pantene adverts.

Christ, he had to find her.

***

He looked out to sea.

The sea glittered, and the wind turbines turned, and far out on that sea, a ketch made a little sea trail of white foam.

There was a whoop of a siren and the town's one area car pulled up behind him. PC Danny Cole got out of the car and grinned at him.

'Oh hey, constable,' said Johnny Ray. 'Shouldn't you be out catching rapists and burglars?'

'Ain't no rapists in Jaywick, Johnny Ray. Plenty of burglars though. And I hear someone burgled your dog.'

Johnny Ray dropped down off the wall then cursed as the weight went onto his bad leg. 'Shit. Yeah. You heard right. You gonna help me?'

PC Cole checked his radio. 'Nah, not really.' He turned half away and his face became blank and professional, and he spoke codes into the radio.

After a while he turned back, and smiled at Johnny Ray. 'But I heard you might want to ask in the Pelican?'

***

Ping!

The front door went on the Costcutter next to the Post Office, and Johnny Ray limped in, in a killing mood. Mrs Malik was talking on WhatsApp or some other bollocks and Sunrise Radio was playing. Johnny Ray ignored that and manhandled a bottle of Frosty Jack to the counter, upon which Mrs Malik smiled indulgently and rattled up the cash register. 'Good morning. Johnny tiger, good morning. Tell me your problem.'

Johnny Ray smiled back. 'Good morning, auntieji. The problem is I've lost my dog.'

Mrs Malik gasped. 'Oh no, not Ella?'

'Yes. Ella.'

Johnny Ray looked out of the window, to where a crowd had formed around the pet shop. A man was handling a massive python to an appreciative crowd of local kids. Mrs Malik nodded at the kerfuffle. 'You could do worse than ask there.' She then grabbed his wrist. 'Then you go to that pub full of badmashes.'

He nodded. 'Absolutely, Mrs Malik.'

Mrs Malik shook her head. 'And keep me informed. I always had such hopes for you, Johnny Rayji.'

'I shall.'

***

Johnny Ray hit the door on The Pelican and all conversation stopped. Even the white ball on the pool table stopped and everyone turned.

'Right. Where's my dog?'

The Banana Boat song was playing and Rob, Johnny's

bandmate from years before, could be heard arguing with Tex. 'Nah bollocks it's HIGHLY deadly black tarantula!'

'It's HIDE de deadly black tarantula!'

Johnny Ray limped to the bar. It was 10:33am.

Julie looked at him. "Guinness? Extra cold?'

He nodded. 'Don't mind if I do. Thanks, Julie.'

Julie was The Pelican's matriarch. She had been there ever since Johnny Ray had moved to Jaywick, and he had come to think of her as family, a mother of sorts. She regarded him coolly, up and down, with the stare of the landlady who had seen every saint and sinner, and some you'd never heard of.

'You've lost weight.'

'Thanks. I've been losing weight since I was born.'

And with that, Johnny hobbled towards Tex and Rob. He sat, landing heavily on his smashed leg. Everyone waited a minute for the pain to subside.

Johnny took a sip on his pint and wondered how to start the preamble.

The investigation.

After a while, he knew and leant forward.

'You know our problem here in Jaywick? We love our dogs too much.'

Tex nodded.

'And we love our drama too much, and we love our mums and dads too much. Drama.'

'Hmm. Well, Johnny Ray, everyone in this town is here for a reason.'

A cigarette went round. Smoking was banned indoors but that didn't really impinge here.

Johnny Ray took a drag, held it in, exhaled, and spoke. 'The thing is, Rob, they tell you the drink and the drugs help you by blotting it out but that's not true. Oh no. Not true at all. They actually serve as some weird fucked-up magnifying glass. No hang on, what's the metaphor I'm looking for here?'

Rob squinted. 'You're looking for a moth?'

Johnny Ray looked back at him. 'Shut up, you silly bastard. OK, metaphor. Not a magnifying glass. Rob – imagine one of those echo chambers where they test sound. Seen one?'

'Yep.'

'OK, that's drink and drugs. An echo chamber, the one that gets you to ring your friends at two in the morning and Facebook message your exes.'

Rob nodded. 'I get that. By the way, how is your ex?'

Shit.

Johnny Ray still remembered the night he met Lisa. She had turned up to one of his gigs in London, dressed up like a tattooed dominatrix. He should have clocked on there and then that she wasn't going to be the submissive sort. As it transpired she had already been inside as a kid, mostly for theft and a tenuous case (according to her) of assault. Childhood in Jaywick didn't prepare you for anything constructive – you either drank yourself to death or hot-wired cars if you fancied a living. It was that sort of place. But Lisa didn't talk about home that much. She seemed keen to leave Marsh-laden idylls as soon as possible. That was part of the reason Johnny liked her so much. They were both trying to get away from themselves. And then when the accident happened, Lisa decided she couldn't wait to get away from Johnny either, managing to take all that they had worked for, aside from Ella.

And it was like a lightbulb had switched on in Johnny Ray's head. 'Holy Fucking Shit!'

Everyone around him jumped.

Johnny limped back to the bar and slammed down his pint glass.

'Julie. Lisa, my ex. You know she used to swear on her mother's life?'

'Yeah,' sighed Julie. 'All the time. But her mum died five years ago.'

The lightbulb was fit to burst at that point and Johnny Ray Randell could no longer contain his rage. 'Tell me everything.'

So Julie told him, and Johnny Ray gripped the bar until it seemed that it would splinter. Julie grabbed his hand. 'Johnny Ray. Please don't go to Marsh Town. No good will come of this.'

Johnny Ray gripped his walking stick, like the placebo or the talisman it was. 'Is this about my ex?'

Julie was crying and nodded. 'Yeah. And about all those people who died.' She looked up. 'Don't go, Johnny Ray! Please. You can't get past the ghosts, none of us can.'

But Johnny was off on the mission. He hit the pub door open and looked back. 'Julie, that's all very well, but I'm gonna get my dog.'

***

So Johnny Ray walked, and he walked, through the mist and under the moon, his bad leg giving out under him at every twelfth step, and his stick pulling up his shattered bones.

***

By 11:33, he was in Paradise Island residential park. He stopped and sat down to catch his breath. Around him the mobile homes were empty and sat looking at him like dead skull eye sockets.

He looked up. The pirate moon flew above with a cohort of white clouds.

Johnny Ray shook his head and took a nip from his hipflask. 'I will allow myself that,' he said.

He got to his feet and started to navigate against the moon.

At 1:55, he crested the rise and was in Marsh Town.

Marsh Town was an eerie dwelling, haunted by its past. They said it was where the ghosts from the floods had died, and where they'd put the spies who were going to fly in to fight the Cold War. All kinds of things, they'd said about Marsh Town. Some might even have been true.

Johnny Ray limped on.

A few yards or so down the rambling back road, prefab housing governed the landscape, exuding an air of a place long uninhabited. Yet it wasn't. Lights flickered behind the curtains and tumbled down shutters creaked against the only pub in town. Half-drunk whiskey shots remained abandoned against the broken glass of the old facade. And still the ghosts of this town remained invisible.

'Come on Johnny son,' he muttered. He lit up a cigarette and took a slow drag as he surveyed the dirt track and the strange balls of light ahead.

Johnny Ray Randell decided to walk towards them, knowing what he did, knowing what Julie had told him.

'The Hanged Man.'

'What?' Johnny Ray looked around once, looked around twice. 'What did you say?'

There was no one.

Fuck's sake. 'The Hanged Man. This shit is getting to you, Johnny Ray.'

He shrugged and halted on.

It was an unusually quiet night. The low howl of the wind murmured like a constant companion. Just standing in this decaying town made you feel like a ghost.

'Nothing good will come of this, choose the safe road,'

the voice continued. Johnny Ray looked down once more and there, outside a dilapidated old vardo wagon, sat a wizened gypsy woman shuffling a stack of dog-eared tarot cards. She looked up at him and smiled. She pointed to her left. He looked. Marsh Town, with its grim fairy lights, beckoned.

Johnny Ray was sure he had seen a ghost. Marsh Town was the kind of place where the living never died or perhaps the dead never lived. Or so he had heard.

He turned back round. Both the vardo and the woman had disappeared in what felt like an instant.

'Nope, definitely not there,' he muttered. *Got to get off the drink mate, probably need to get off the drugs too*, he thought, and with that, he turned back to the road ahead.

After limping onto the crest that separated Marsh Town from the real world, he was there. He stopped and got his bearings, then he made his way down the rise into a fug of dance music, caravans, and fairy lights. But the fairy lights were all wrong. The colours were all wrong.

And the crowd was waiting.

He stopped.

And the crowd parted.

Right in front of him was his ex. Lisa Sandgate. She turned and held out a dog collar. And beside her, whip-cowed, was Ella, looking at him with eyes that said 'I'd missed you' and 'Where have you been, you deadbeat human?'

'Missing Ella are we?' asked Lisa. 'And we've missed you too, Johnny Ray.'

The crowd laughed.

Johnny Ray leant on his stick and bowed his head, exchanging a look with Ella that said, 'I'll get you out of this.'

But Lisa was on a roll. 'Look everybody. Big bad Johnny Ray, the music guy. He did so many albums. And then he did drugs. And promised me he'd get me into the business, and lied! He's a deadbeat. So I took what is mine.'

A rumble went round the crowd.

'Swear on your dead mum on that would you?' asked Johnny Ray.

Lisa turned. 'Every time.'

Johnny Ray grinned and stood up, and addressed the crowd. 'That's funny, as Lisa's dead mum, Anna Maria, is seventy-four, still alive, and lives just up the road in St Osyth, so anyone who's been sworn on her might need their money back. Ain't that right, Lisa?'

The crowd shrank back from her.

And Johnny Ray spoke. 'Now give me back my dog.'

Dawn broke on Jaywick seafront, over a man leading his dog to the post office and the shops. Both looked happy. The man limped and spoke to the dog, and the dog leapt, charmed to be out and going to the post office and to see Mrs Malik. Behind them, the surf came in.

EVERYTHING COMES...

B.A. Steadman

There's nobody outside the gate. Not sure why I thought there would be, after all this time. I wait for the clank of the winding mechanism hauling open the wrought-iron gate. 'Calm down, girl,' I whisper, though I can't stop my feet doing a little shuffle on the gravel. A little 'one-two' leak of my desperation to get on the outside.

Blakey's watching me. She smiles and crosses her fingers. Must be hoping I don't come back. I look for Pauline, my link person. She's supposed to be here to meet me. I'm not supposed to just wander out on my own. Need to be 'acclimatised'. Need to know about Twitter and on-line shopping. As if I don't watch telly. Silly pillock.

The sun pops out and warms my face. It's going to be hot. It feels different. Sounds stupid but it feels different when it's free sun, and not sun that has to be paid for with twenty-three hours in a cell. My bag feels heavy but there's not much in it. Not much I wanted to save after fifteen years. And everything in it's all bleached out. Like me.

'Jay?'

I swing round and there she is in her grey trouser suit from M&S and her pink shirt and her strappy sandals and her straw bag.

'Shall we go? They won't keep the gate open forever, you know.' She tucks her hand in behind my elbow, like girls do when they go out together, and I have a fluttery feeling in my stomach, like when a boy looks at you properly for the first time. I realise it's excitement.

We walk over to her car. It's a yellow Fiat 500 with a black sunroof. 'Is that yours?'

She laughs. 'Yeah, had to have it. Gorgeous, isn't it?'

I'm speechless for a moment.

'D'you like it?'

'I love it.' And I do. I want it for my own. I love it,

and then I flounder under the weight of such longing. I feel my greyness, the black-and-white film plainness which has shrouded me for so long and kept me grey inside and out.

'Come on, girl,' she says, all cheery smile and neon lipstick, opening the car door with a little clicky thing. 'Let's go and see your flat. I bet you're dying to see where you're going to live, aren't you?'

I nod. But I'm not dying to see it at all. How will I cope on my own? Who will look in on me and check on me and tell me what to do? I haven't washed my own clothes or cooked a meal for fifteen years. It's scary.

And then I see him. I knew. I knew he wouldn't let me go. Checking up on me. Just standing on the corner staring. He's older, of course, greying hair cut short now. Pauline's too busy putting stuff in the car to notice. I want to wail, to scream. I want to run. I want to go back to prison. I want a knife. Every heartbeat pounds in my head. Old desire surprises me. How could I feel that for him? Old anger messes about with my heart and with my stomach. I yank open the door and slide into the seat, trying to pretend I haven't seen him, hand over my mouth.

'You alright?' she asks and follows my stricken gaze.

'Damn. Should have known he'd turn up. Keep your head down and we'll go straight past. He doesn't know where we're going.' She starts the car without an ignition key and I laugh. It's nerves, I know.

I don't keep my head down as we go past. I stare at him with greedy eyes, soaking him up. For years I've had this image in my head of him the last time I saw him, at the court, where he wouldn't look me in the eyes. Guilty. I thought I'd worked him out of my head, slashed him out in the scars on my arms, beaten him out on the punch bag in the gym. But he's still in here, in my head, festering.

'First time I've seen him since the trial,' I say, voice trembling. I risk a quick look at her face. She doesn't smile.

'You need to leave it, Jay. Move on. He put you in there in the first place. It's well over.'

But it isn't. It's not over at all. 'It was me that killed his wife, not him.'

Pauline shakes her head and growls at me. She shouts, 'You were eighteen years old, for God's sake! You were just a kid. He used you, love. Surely you can see that? He got you under his power and you did the deed for him.' She lets out a big sigh. 'You're different now, Jay. You're an adult who can make her own choices.' She slows down for the traffic lights. 'This is your chance to start again, love. You've paid the price. You're still young and gorgeous.'

She smiles so I know she's being nice. Gorgeous, I am not. I relax a bit and look out of the window. Andy shouldn't be watching me, but I knew he'd be there. Was counting on it.

It's hot in the little car. Sunny Manchester, who'd have thought? Pauline presses a button and the roof slides back. It's wonderful to feel the wind on my head, in my hair.

My new flat is near the city centre. Streets and people and noise and smells and colour pour in through the open roof. A fresh start, eh? Maybe I can do that. Christ knows I've paid for a fresh start. Maybe I can. Maybe.

We pull up in front of a huge, ugly tower block. Heat shimmers off the pavement and July sun beats on my head. The lift's broken. We slog up eight flights of stairs carrying bags and boxes, and I'm wheezing by the time we get there.

'Here you go,' Pauline says when we get our breath back, and she hands me a key. 'Let yourself in.'

The flat seems to have been furnished courtesy of a charity shop, but I don't complain. It doesn't take me long to explore. There's one room with a kitchen alcove, a sofa, a

TV and a single bed in the corner. The second door leads to a little bathroom. It's clean. I can see that Pauline has gone to loads of trouble to fix me up. She stands in the doorway smiling at me.

'Pauline, thanks. It's great.'

'Well,' she says, pleased that I am pleased. 'I'll leave you alone so you've got time to settle in and I'll be back tomorrow morning. There's food in the fridge, tea and coffee and milk. Do you need anything else? Is there anyone you want me to call?'

I think of my mum in Nantwich, and my sister in Worcester. No. 'No, I'll ring mum in a while, once I'm settled, and can work out how to use this new phone. Thanks again.'

She goes then, and I light a ciggie, turn and look at my little flat. White walls, beige cushions, cream bedding, no pictures. Yuk. There's no life in this flat at all. No colour. My few belongings disappear into the beigeness. I'd rather live in the little yellow car. Or, or back in my room in prison, with Kath and her terrible Oasis posters and Blakey having a go at me about smoking too much. Home.

I drift across to the window and look down. The people are specks; fleas on a white cat. Above, the sky looms. All of it, not just a barred square, two feet across. All of its bloody enormity over my head, pressing me down, forcing the rhythm of my heart into a stuttering lurch. I can't go out there. I can't. What a fool to think it would be as easy as walking out the door. Out there is not for me. I'm a different person, now. I know where I belong. If I can do it. If I just have the courage.

The phone squats silent on the work surface in the kitchenette. I should ring mum. But there is a pain, a longing, a scratch that must be itched. Better not to speak to her; she'll want to come and see me, and I'm not ready for her.

I murdered Andy's wife when I was eighteen years old and high on whatever Andy gave me. I took anything. No brains. Stupid with love. I followed her for three days. With a kitchen knife up my sleeve. When I got her alone, behind the gym, her in her pink Pineapple tracksuit with her bleached blonde hair and her 32DD implants, she laughed in my face and I lost it. I stabbed her. I kept trying to get her in the boob – to hear one of them burst and see all the fake gel slop out of her fake body.

Then, still stupid with love for him, I ran to Andy, thinking he'd be glad to see me. He turned me in to the police as I clung onto him, screaming. Denied any part in the plan. Said I was stalking him. Cried in front of them. I watched the disgust in his eyes, and I finally understood what he really thought, what he'd planned all along. He was free now, of both of us.

So I didn't fight. Didn't deny what I'd done. No point. I did my time.

I pick up the little phone and ring the number I have remembered for fifteen years. His voice sounds the same as the last time we spoke. The lies just as slick. I know what he wants. He wants to make sure I keep my mouth shut.

'Jay,' he says, *'great to hear from you. I can't believe you're out at last. I've really missed you, babe. We should meet up, go for a drink, for old times' sake, you know.'*

Opening the kitchen drawer, I run my hands over the cutlery, and test the edge of the bread knife. It will do.

'Where have they put you, then? Somewhere nice, I hope?'

I tell him.

BONUS STORY

#106

Jenna-Leigh Golding

an aspiring writer aged seventeen

It smells like wood, damp wood, and cobwebs. I sit, patiently waiting. A trace of a smile flickers across my face as I think of her copper hair blowing in the wind. Before today I've been waiting for a while, but plans like this take time and patience.

I hope the log cabin will stay up in this weather. It took me three weeks to cut the wood to build it. Three weeks during last summer. I have been back since to add an ice box, a metal table, and other bits.

When I walk through the door and look at the far right hand corner I see the large blue ice cooler sitting alone. In the middle of the room stands the metal table. When I lay across it my (now muscular) arms and legs flail off the sides. Then again I'm quite tall for a 28 year old man standing at 6"5. Aside from this there are piles of blankets all over the floor, hidden items underneath. A corkboard rests behind the door. The rest of the space is empty aside from the window on the right of the door, covered by bars, letting in lined sections of light. The emptiness is not helped with the breeze coming in from outside.

I am content with how the plan has come together. She runs past here every morning at ten a.m., like clockwork. It's currently nine-twenty. The sun has been in the sky for a while. I was here in time to see the sunrise. The blends of orange, pink, blue and yellow have now faded. The birds are squawking high up in the trees, the wind getting heavier, the drizzle of rain creating a rainbow in the sky as the sun shines down upon everything. Around me there are glistening spider webs and puddles reflecting the sun rays.

She gets up at seven, feeds her daughter, dresses her and takes her to school. I can see her angelic face in the glossy photos pinned to the corkboard behind the door. Amelia, aged six, around three foot ten, has blonde curly hair and light blue eyes like her mother. She likes wearing the colour green and hates wearing orange.

I met her in a coffee shop last May. Not Amelia but her mother. She hasn't seen me since but it has been forty-three hours since I last saw her. I don't know what it is about her but she's different to everyone else. She's alive.

It's now nine forty-five and I get ready for the sound of her faint panting and the heavy noise from her footsteps crunching on the already fallen autumn leaves. That flicker of a smile reappearing on my crinkled skin.

9:48. Paranoia is starting to set in.

9:50. She is a fine specimen. What if someone else got to her and chopped her up, feeding the pieces of her to dirty pigs?

9:57. Everything will be fine, nothing has gone wrong, so far.

My heartbeat starts to quicken. I may think it all comes easy, but it can go wrong. It just takes a small moment. The birds seem to chant a warning. The trees begin to move. Then silence.

9:59. Adrenaline bursts through my body as I step outside the cabin in time for her to stop and see me. Standing on the threshold is thrilling. Just behind me her fate awaits. Soon a little heart a few miles away will be broken, the innocence gone with the uttering of one sentence. In that moment Amelia's hope will flutter away like butterflies.

I rush at the start, like you do when you get nervous before performing a play, but all I can feel is the adrenaline, the excitement.

My charming smile draws her in and that old excuse that I am lost.

The muscles were a good idea. As a kid I was tiny, the smallest boy in my school, even in my last year. Yet now, people are intimidated by me. It helps that they stay away.

I pull her through the door, my right arm tight around her waist, my other hand clasped over her mouth. I'm about to shut the door but her thrashing legs slam it shut. Pulling up the blankets, rope, knives, and scraps of material, everything is going to plan so far. I catch myself humming a melody.

Step one. I tie the scraps of material tightly around her mouth, wrists, and ankles. If the skin where you've tied is turning red, you have tied them tight enough. If the skin isn't red, tie them again.

Step one complete. Redness visible.

Step two. I tie her body to the table with rope. One around the shoulders, one around the thighs and one around the waist.

Step two complete. Ropes tied securely.

Step three, the most thrilling, see how long it takes for her to bleed all her crimson blood out through small cuts.

Knives lined up, windows covered, door locked, participant #106 is ready.

Step three in progress.

A large cut every ten minutes, meaning a total of one hundred and forty-four cuts in 24 hours. She could bleed to death at any time. How amusing. Each time I must be extremely careful and that's all part of the fun.

When I was eight my grandfather gave me these leather gloves he had and I've found them to be very useful, especially for not leaving fingerprints.

I relish the planning of each demise. Each one undertaken in a different way. So far a large cut across the stomach has been the most thrilling. Blood and guts were everywhere, but there was still a slow enough passing to enjoy every drop of life that left his body. He was participant #52. The participant that spoiled the gloves my Grandfather out lived. I bought him some new ones for his birthday last year.

I subconsciously run my tongue over my lips as the largest of the knives glints in the light, more adrenaline fuelling me as I prepare for the first slash. A human body thrashing is harder to harm than a wriggling worm. You can't squish them, and pull out their innards as easily. *They* try to run away. *They* scream and fight. *They* can't tolerate pain.

As I raise my arm with the knife in my hand, I steadily and slowly bring it down, the humming growing louder drowning out her muffled screams. My methodical thoughts leaving in an instant, as at once I become savage.

All patience gone, one cut comes as soon as the blade is out, each slash puncturing her skin. The satisfying sound is like the heightened feeling of bursting a spot or pulling a daisy from the ground.

Blood spills over every surface, her body falls limp on the table. The blood keeps pouring, flowing out of her like a river. I wipe some spatters off my face and my heart fills with glee.

The next few slashes are created just for fun, the tip of the knife balancing under the bend of her right arm. I hold the top of the handle gently letting my fingers glide over the black plastic. With one swift tap a tiny hole is created, the burst rippling through the knife into my own body.

The satisfaction takes over and I sit for hours creating tiny holes and turning her body scaly until the blood stops pouring out.

Another name crossed off my list.

I look upon the scene, as if I am a camera panning across the room, and a wave of regret passes through me, because the moment is over.

Suddenly everything is quiet. The chatter in my mind now tamed to hushed tones of elation.

I sit on the blankets and pull a pencil and some paper out of my pocket. I draw for what feels like hours and hours. The texture of her hair, the thickness of her blood, her now paler skin depicted into one image of this moment.

As I turn the page of this drawing, I start to think of my next participant. The eagerness and impatience start peeking through. I take three deep breaths, tidy the cabin, and wrap her in three blankets. I throw her body over my left shoulder. There is a small thud heard as her bones hit my shoulder blade. Another thud echoes as I shut the door to the cabin.

Out here the birds are squawking high up in the trees, the wind getting louder while the drizzle of rain creates a rainbow in the sky. Out here the spider webs glisten and the puddles reflect the sun's rays that are beating down. Out here everything is calm.

Acknowledgments

This book would not exist without the hours of hard work put in by dozens of talented authors, who donated their time in order to raise money for charity. Please show your support by leaving a review for this book and discussing it with people you know. The sum donated to charity relies on readers helping to spread the word about this collection.

A special thank you goes out to Louise Ross who orchestrated the launch event and helped throughout the process.

Clare Law, thank you for the work you did on this book. Thanks also to Morgen Bailey and Heather Osborne for your editorial services. Thank you to Anita Waller for her proof reading.

Helen Claire and Alexina Golding, thank you both for the time you have invested helping put the book together.

A huge thanks has to go out to all the bloggers who have offered to spread the news about the book.

Thank you to Lin Barringer from Sophie's Appeal and Craig Duncan at Hospice UK who have had to bear the brunt of numerous emails.

Finally, thank you to all the people who have bought this book and helped to raise money for two very worthy causes.